The Highland Hawk

THE HIGHLAND HAWK

LESLIE TURNER WHITE

Crown Publishers, Inc.: *New York*

Affectionately dedicated to
HELEN
my collaborator in this as
in everything else

The Highland Hawk

Chapter One

Though it was the martial roll of the drum which jarred David from the depths of a deep sleep to the verge of consciousness, it was the shrill trumpet call that popped open his eyes. For a confused moment he did not know where he was, for instead of the familiar thatch of the stable roof being overhead, he was under a canopy of satin. Simultaneously, he grew aware of other paradoxes. His weary body lay not on the customary hard pallet, but seemed suspended on a downy cloud, and the air was heady with strange odors—perfumes and wine—rather than the usual smell of fresh hay and fresher manure. Perfume? Wine? The better to think, he closed his eyes. Who in the devil had he been drinking with . . . ?

A sudden stir on the pillow beside him caused him to turn his head, in the expectation of seeing the scarred muzzle of his faithful old wolfhound Gabriel. What he saw was no canine (although the appellative had been applied to her on all too numerous occasions), but the pale sensuous features of Lady Marguerite, wife of the Laird of Lochbogie!

The drum rattled again, but Davy needed no further summons. He bolted the bed like a scalded cat and made a dive for his clothes which, with practiced foresight, he had left in a convenient pile near the window. Already the whole castle was astir, preparing for the ceremony of departure about to take place; and with emotions so raw, Davy shuddered to think of the fate that would await a half-naked groom caught in the bedroom of the old laird's lady.

His precipitous exit from the nest brought her Ladyship to a sitting position. She, too, was slightly befuddled, and the sight of a groom frantically pulling on his shirt engendered a tardy streak of modesty. She drew the silk coverlet across her breasts and secured it with folded arms.

"Mother of God, Davy, what has happened?"

He yanked the garment over his head. "I overslept—that's what happened!"

She gasped, suddenly aware that it was daylight. "You cannot leave now, Davy!" she wailed. "*Bon Dieu*, someone will see you!" In moments of agitation, such as fear or passion, Lady Marguerite relapsed into the oaths of her nativity.

Davy paused to appraise her. Marguerite of Tuscany, as she styled herself in private, had been a very beautiful woman in her youth. She was still handsome at forty, though the bloom was fading. The impotence of her aged spouse had starved her avid sensuality, and even the uncounted offerings of potboys, lackeys and grooms, instead of appeasing had merely accentuated this carnal hunger to a point where it showed in her very glance and in the restless twitch of her lips. Everyone in the Castle of Lochbogie recognized it, save the old laird, her husband, and he, mercifully, could see nothing, for he was *blind*.

Davy snorted in impatience, feeling that, under the circumstances, he could dispense with feudal etiquette.

"Damn it, my lady, don't you realize what day this is? My Lord Ian is leaving with his company within the hour to join the King's army and, need I remind you, I am his groom!"

This was a two-edged thrust which made her wince, for Lady Marguerite loathed her dull-witted stepson with a virulence matched only by his hatred of her. Nor did she like to be reminded, so early and so baldly, that she had been adequately bedded by a common Scottish groom. To salve her pride, which served in lieu of a conscience, she had concocted a whimsical bit of fiction to the effect that David was *not* a lackey by birth, but the natural son of some great noble who, in visiting Lochbogie, had dallied with the serving-woman who had been David's undisputed mother. If this myth was founded without evidence, it was equally impossible of refutation, for his mother had long ago gone to her reward without revealing the identity of David's sire.

In support of her hypothesis, Lady Marguerite offered (to herself alone, to be sure) the beauty of his person. David Dugald—by custom all members of the clan bore the name of their laird—was no vulgar Scottish clod; in fact, to her eyes at least, he appeared a hundred times more noble than Ian, her despised stepson. He was tall, clean-limbed, and strong as a bull. (Marguerite used that metaphor advisedly.) She had no difficulty believing him a cross between peasant and noble, for though his features were sharp and finely chiseled there was an untamable earthiness about him that brought to mind the wild ferocity of the Highlands. He wore a regal crown of blue-black curls (perhaps, please God, his father was French!) yet his eyes were contrastingly fair, with a slight oblique cast, which could turn from sunlight to lightning with startling rapidity. His wide mouth was equally flexible, changing from tenderness to firmness with bewildering speed. There were times when Lady Marguerite was actually afraid of him, and this was such a moment.

"Davy, do not leave me, *ami!*" she beseeched. "We need you here to protect the castle!"

He smiled without speaking. His *filleadh,* or belted-plaid, was already carefully laid out on the floor. This Highland costume consisted of a plain piece of tartan about two yards in width and six in length, folded in pleats until the length was reduced to about five feet. Davy lay down on it so that the lower edge was level with his knees then, wrapping it around his half-naked body, he secured it about his waist with a leather belt. After that, he stood up, before draping the surplus plaid around his shoulders.

"*What* castle, my lady?" he said, with a mockery that made her blush.

Though her eyes shot fire, she kept her temper. Her heart began to pound unmercifully and she let the sheet fall from her breasts as if she could not bear the weight. In all her years of promiscuity, no man had ever affected her so. The mere sight of David sent her passions reeling out of control.

He was completely dressed now, his plaid fastened on the left shoulder with a great silver brooch, and a blue bonnet cocked jauntily over one eye. He looked like a laughing satyr. Her hunger grew reckless.

"David—listen to me!" she gasped. "He must not come back! He must not! Do you hear me?"

He cocked his head. "Aye, I hear you, but I don't ken you."

"You do!" she cried desperately. "You know I speak of Ian! He

11

hates me! If he brings back a wife, I . . . I'll be thrown out of my home!"

"You are the laird's lady," Davy reminded her.

She flushed again, disconcerted by the double entendre. *"Bon Dieu,* Davy, do not mock me! You know my lord is aging; he cannot live long. Then Ian will be the laird. He is insane, Davy! Insane!"

Davy shrugged and glanced restlessly toward the window. He could hear the pipers winding their instruments.

"There's naught I can do about it, my lady!" he told her.

"But there is, there *is!"* She started to climb toward him, but when she saw him draw back, she paused and remained on her knees, a naked supplicant.

"If he was to die, *you* could be the next laird, Davy!"

He burst into laughter. "Until I became impotent, my lady?" he jeered.

"That," she muttered grimly, "will never happen! Think of it, *ami!* It would be so easy . . . in a battle! You are so strong, so quick! No one would ever know he didn't die by the hand of an enemy!"

The pipes were wailing a wild pibroch. Davy's smile chilled and he stared at her with contempt.

"You are a slut!" he said brutally. "Come now, you'd better drag yourself down below before the laird sends for you."

She went pale at his tone. "You ill-bred whoreson . . . !" she began tearfully, but he did not remain for her tirade. Blowing her an airy kiss with his fingers, he threw his legs over the sill and vanished along the parapet.

It was too late for caution, so he ran boldly along the walkway until he came to the window to a little-used storeroom, which he had providently left open. The pipers' call had summoned all hands to the leavetaking ceremony in the main courtyard, so he ran little risk of encountering any of the domestics on his way to the ground. Long experience in *affaires d'amour* had taught him the value of advance preparations, and he knew that Cuddie, the feeble-minded stableboy and his devoted slave, would have his nag saddled and his gear in place.

Sure enough, when he eased out of the buttery, he saw his horse tethered behind the stable and faithful old Gabriel patiently waiting beside it. It was the work of an instant to release the reins and heave himself into the saddle.

When he trotted into the courtyard, he found the little company already assembled. The sight depressed him. Of the thirty-odd, two-thirds were frightened callow youths under twenty, while the remainder were ancients, mounted on nags that looked almost an age with them. The real flower of the clan lay sleeping among the bogs and lofty crags, victims of the eternal Highland feuds. Davy wondered, briefly, if peace would ever come to these hills. Then he brushed the sentiment aside and appraised the armament with a skeptical eye.

Only two—the fowler and the gamekeeper—carried matchlocks; the rest were armed with a miscellany of old swords, improvised scythes and a few cudgels. With the exception of the young laird, only one—old Gillie—wore armor of any kind: a pitted and battered back-and-breast.

The former, Lord (by courtesy) Ian, strutted impatiently up and down the flagstones, alternating his myopic glances between the now-rising sun and the great iron-studded door of the manor. A host of tenants and domestics formed a shadowy background.

Davy tried to sidle unseen into his place in the line, but as he neared the head of the company, Lord Ian chose that moment to turn.

"Damn your eyes, man—where have you been?" he burst out, slashing his jackboots with the whip in his hand.

"Your pardon, my lord," Davy murmured apologetically. "I o'erslept."

"With some serving-whore, I'll warrant!" stormed Ian, fast working himself into one of the insane rages for which he was notorious. "Name her, by God, and I'll have her whipped out of the castle!"

Davy repressed a smile with difficulty. From long association, he knew the lecherous young heir merely wished to learn the identity of any accommodating wench in the holding, since because of certain idiosyncrasies in his own physical nature, he was unable to find his own playmates in amours.

"Unfortunately, my lord," Davy replied, honestly enough, "my pallet was not shared by any . . ."

"You lie!" shouted the other. "I myself went to your quarters, seeking you before daylight. Your pallet was empty!"

"No doubt that was when I had stepped outside to relieve myself," Davy agreed, smiling.

13

Ian's sallow face blooded with temper. He lifted his whip and stalked across the flagging, his spurs clanking ominously.

"You insolent base-born liar!" he roared. "Name the whore! Name her, I say, before I cut that smirk off your foul face!"

Davy stopped smiling. He was accustomed to the outbursts of the pampered heir of Lochbogie, yet he had never seen him quite so berserk. It came to him abruptly that Ian was afraid of what they were marching into, and that this terror was momentarily affecting his mind. It was an explosive situation. Davy was fully aware of the fatal consequences which would swiftly follow if he lifted a hand against his vicious young master, whatever the provocation, yet he was equally certain he would be unable to sit quietly and let this cowardly bully whip him before the entire population of the castle.

"My lord!" he cautioned, in an undertone. "Remember yourself!"

The advice seemed only an aggravation. Ian caught the reins in his left hand and raised the whip in his right. Just as Davy had decided to hurl himself on the other and take his chances, an interruption came from an unexpected source.

Gabriel, the tawny old wolfhound, who had quietly followed, now moved into the open and set his huge bulk before the angry laird— hackles erect, yellow fangs bared. Just one low, rumbling growl escaped him.

Ian floundered backward in panic, tripped over a spur and almost sat down. Somewhere in the background, a peasant broke the awful silence with a titter. The last visage of the laird's restraint vanished.

"Kill him! Kill him!" he shrieked. "You, Donald—shoot!" This to the startled gamekeeper with the matchlock.

As the fellow automatically lifted his piece in obedience, Davy spoke to him.

"Touch so much as a hair on old Gabriel, Donald Gilcuddie, and as God is my witness, you'll never see another sunrise."

Although he spoke low, his voice cut into every remote crevice of the courtyard. The luckless gamekeeper glanced bewilderedly from one to the other, astutely weighing the alternate penalties, one of which he must necessarily suffer. His choice was not too difficult. The most the irate laird could do would be to have him whipped, whereas David was a man of his word. He lowered the weapon.

"Aweel, ye'll hae to dee y're ain killin', me laird," he groaned. "I dinna kin shoot the puir beastie!"

Nigh weeping with rage, Ian darted at him and jerked the matchlock from his hands. As he stood fumbling with the mechanism, anger making him even more clumsy than usual, he kept shrieking: "Ye mutinous dogs! I'll teach you discipline, by God! I'll have the whole company whipped! I'll make an example of this vulgar bastard who defies me!"

"Nobody is defying you, my lord!" Davy retorted firmly. "We are all your devoted servants, even to this dumb beast who would give his life to save yours, was it in jeopardy!"

But Ian was too far gone to be mollified. He got the matchlock readied, but instead of pointing it at the hound, he aimed it at Davy.

"Now, for the last time—will you name the whore you slept with last night?"

In that ominous instant, Davy had a sudden flash of insight: *Ian suspected the truth!* Certain heretofore scattered facts abruptly merged to form a terrifying picture. It was no secret at Lochbogie that Ian first resented, then grew to hate, the Frenchwoman who had replaced his own dead mother. This was not engendered by any filial devotion, but by a deep-rooted jealousy, which was ardently reciprocated by Lady Marguerite, and by a frustrated passion, which was not. In addition, Davy knew that Ian was fearful of going to the wars, and no doubt dreaded to leave his blind father to the machinations of his faithless spouse. This seemed the only possible explanation of the man's absurd conduct. No doubt the fool reasoned that if he could force David to betray the woman before the entire company, the proud old laird would deal with her as the adultress she was. Having scant affection for either of the sordid pair of schemers, Davy had no mind to be a tool—less to be a martyr.

Tensing himself to slide out of the saddle, he made one more attempt at peace.

"Will you not listen to reason, my lord?" he placated.

" 'Tis on your own head!" bellowed Ian, and closing one bulging eye, squinted along the barrel.

"*Ian!*"

At the sharp command, the young laird jerked up his head. It was too late to stop the fire, but the ball soared harmlessly into the air. Davy had already thrown himself sideways along the off-side of his horse, but now he righted himself to see the old laird standing on the threshold of the manor-house, his milky, sightless eyes staring frostily at the tableau in the courtyard.

Ian stood frozen, the smoking gun still pointed into the air. The one thing he feared above all else was his father, and not without reason. For blind and senile though John the Dugald might be, the grandeur of better days had not entirely eroded away. A deep sigh, partly of relief, partly of reverence, rose from the assemblage as the old patriarch limped into the courtyard, leaning on the arm of his dark-haired wife. With his tawny flowing mane, now silver streaked, his thick, wide jaw and toothless mouth, he resembled a majestic old lion. A tartan plaid was thrown shawlwise about his shoulders, and if his eyes were useless, his perception seemed that much sharper.

"Ian!" he repeated, in a terrible voice. "What goes on?"

Ian hastily pushed the weapon out of sight behind him, and when he spoke, the temper had wilted from his voice leaving it querulous and uncertain.

"My groom has mutinied, sir! I was about to correct him!"

"Ye mean *David*, and with a matchlock?" thundered the old man. "Why, ye churlish, ill-tempered clown! Would ye slay the only man in your company with the wit to keep you out of trouble?" He paused, with a rumbling growl, then in a more judicial tone, continued: "And what did David do?"

Ian marshaled his nerve and turned a brazen eye full on his stepmother for all to witness.

"The rogue bedded a woman of the castle last night!" he accused, and it was almost as if he had pointed a finger at Lady Marguerite. "He refused to name the slut!"

Lady Marguerite turned so deathly pale that Davy held his breath, dreading lest she faint and so betray them both. He saw her sway slightly, then the throaty roar of the old laird drew attention from her.

"God bless Davy then, I say!" he boomed, with a laugh. " 'Tis the mark of a true gallant! What ails ye, Ian, that ye should pry into the healthy dalliance o' a young buck? Fie on ye, lad! D'ye go to truckle with the Presbyterians, or to fight for your King?"

"But, Father . . ." began Ian, red to the ears.

"Whist, ye make a spectacle o' yourself!" growled the old man sternly. "Now enough of this disaffection! With the whole country

16

torn with quarrels and dissension, 'tis folly to have such in your ain company. Though he bears not your rank, perhaps, David has been raised like a brother to ye, Ian. It ill becomes ye to take advantage of your position. Shake hands now, and . . ."

"*Father!*" wailed Ian. "Consider what you ask! Would you debase me before . . ."

" 'Tis no debasement for a gentleman to concede a mistake, Ian! 'Tis the essence of nobility! Now shake his hand and beg his pardon, else by the great Jehovah, 'tis David who will ride as captain o' this company! I swear it!"

The ensuing silence was so profound that, as Davy afterwards described it, he could almost hear the fleas tramping up and down the spine of old Gabriel. Ian writhed like an eel on a spear, yet such was his awe of his father, he dared not refuse. He, as did everyone present, knew that when John the Dugald made a pronouncement, it was as final as any of the Ten Commandments, and the wrath that followed disobedience was not to be borne by mortal man.

In the pause, Davy came suddenly to understand the source of the laird's power over his clan. True, the very word clan, or *clanna,* was an ancient one meaning children, and all of these people were John the Dugald's *children.* His authority was nurtured in his paternalism, in his absolute fairness. If he was stern and terrible at times, it was the sternness of a father. Davy felt a sudden wave of shame that he should have "put horns," as the saying was, on such a splendid man, but he salved his conscience a trifle by arguing that, in his affair with Lady Marguerite, he had deprived the old laird of nothing he could use; as Davy reasoned, it was like borrowing a pipe from a man who has given up tobacco.

"Well, Ian . . . ?" exploded the laird impatiently.

As Ian moved toward him, Davy swung out of the saddle.

"My lord," he addressed the old man, "permit me to beg Ian's forgiveness instead! I fear it was my own insolence which provoked his . . . er . . . displeasure."

"Hold thy tongue, David!" barked the patriarch. " 'Tis the prerogative of rank to take the initiative in such a matter."

Ian extended a limp hand. "I was overhasty," he conceded grudgingly.

Davy grinned and pressed the damp paw in rough camaraderie. The clash had sharpened his recollection of happier days when he and Ian had romped together in the equality of childhood. Unconsciously, he sought to recapture the old mood.

"Let's forget it, Ian," he whispered, dropping into the old familiarity.

But Ian jerked his hand away and gave him a fish-stare which indicated plainly the issue would be reopened under more auspicious circumstances. Davy shrugged, and stepped back.

Then the aged laird began to speak: "Now, laddies, a word o' counsel before ye take your leave, for this be the first occasion in o'er three-score years the men o' Lochbogie hae marched off to battle without John the Dugald—Red Dugald, as my enemies called me— at their head. It is a sad moment for me, but God has willed it; He hath turned what was once red to silver and taken away my sight. No man can stand against time, for even Methuselah with all his hundreds of years was but a mushroom of night's growth in the eternal scheme of things. Thus, since I can no longer lead you, I send in my place my . . . son. Serve him faithfully, as thy fathers served me. And thou, Ian, remember thy heritage!"

"Bless you, Father! That I will!" Ian responded.

The old man paused, as if wearied from the exertion, yet when he spoke again, his voice was stronger than before.

"For generations to the number o' twelve, the men o' Lochbogie hae ne'er endured defeat. Oh, aye, they've been slaughtered to nigh the last man. No laird o' the clan Dugald hae e'er suffered the humiliation o' dying in his bed, and God grant my prayer I shall not be the first! Save for David and Gillie and three or four others, few o' ye who ride today hae faced death in battle. Yet fear it naught! As John Donne hath so well said: 'We hae a winding-sheet in our mother's womb, which groweth with us from our conception, and we come into this world wound up in that winding-sheet, for we come to seek a grave!' There be worse things than death, such as dishonor and cowardice; death we cannot avoid, the others we can. If ye find a coward in your midst, slay him as an enemy, for in truth an enemy he is!"

As he listened, Davy glanced sideways at his companions. On the faces of the ancients, he read resolution and admiration, but the youngsters had grown pale with fright, as if behind the sermon they heard already the rustle of death.

"Ye go to fight for the King," continued John the Dugald. "Whilest

18

I do not venerate Charles the First, and even less do I venerate the English, I still hold to the old ways. This is not to say I hold wi' Episcopacy or Papistry, for I take no orders from a churchman whether he be prelate or pope! For my ain part, I'd prefer the Kirk were it not dominated by bigotry and fanatical intolerance, and if it did not collect under its bloody standard such scum of hell, such misbegotten sons of Sodom as Robert Godolphin of Inventry and his clan MacKenna!" At this point, his voice thundered like the roar of an old lion, so that Gabriel, the wolfhound, commenced to growl.

Davy chuckled inwardly. Here, in a word, was the argument which had decided old Dugald—the *MacKennas!* In the scarlet haze of ancestral hatred, the merits of the warring factions were obscured. It was enough for John the Dugald to know that the Laird of Inventry had sided with the Kirk; the men of Lochbogie would throw in with the King.

"So I charge ye before God!" trumpeted the aged warrior. "Return not until ye hae fertilized the earth with every last drop of Mac-Kenna blood! Remember that ye hold in your hands the sword of vengeance, and that the bones of your forefathers, whitening in these beloved hills, are crying for retribution! The Lord of Hosts goes with you; he will strengthen your arm and harden your heart! Hunt these varmints into their lairs and slay without mercy! For let *one* survive and he will breed a new race to slaughter your children!"

He shook off the hand of his wife, who was attempting to quiet him, and throwing his arms above his head like an ancient prophet, concluded: "Go then, and be doing! Come back victorious, and though your garments be dyed with blood and your swords drip gore, I will clasp each of you to this proud old bosom of mine! Die on the field of honor, and I shalt erect a monument in your memory! *But*"—and the resonant old voice quivered with passion—"crawl back in defeat, and as the Lord Jehovah be my witness, I shall decorate these hoary walls wi' your craven carcasses!" His arms sagged to his side, and with a brief "Amen!" he turned toward the door.

The sudden switch from philosophic patriotism to angry passion left the audience stilled and shaken. Yet it was not entirely unexpected, for the lairds of Lochbogie had always been marked by a strain of unpredictable violence, and their quarrels and grudges seemed almost to descend through a hereditary bloodstream.

As the venerable laird passed into the manor house, Lord Ian barked a word of command and climbed shakily into the saddle. A quartet of pipers took their place at the head of the column, and to the doleful skirl of *Lochbogie's Lament,* the little contingent started into motion. In the absence of the austere old laird, the crowd found their voices, and as they trooped across the courtyard behind the horsemen, they set up a clamor of prayers, advisement and encouragement, copiously watered down with tears.

For his own part, David was eager to get away. During the past year, the growing tension between Ian and himself had reached the danger point, and his ill-advised affair with Lady Marguerite had long passed it, until his once beloved old Castle Lochbogie had now become more of a prison than a home. Too, he had recently turned three-and-twenty, and deep in the shadowy recesses of his consciousness was a restless, as yet undefined yearning. The war offered a welcome diversion, not that he cared a whit for either King or Kirk.

On reaching the ancient arch of the tower-gate, the troop paused to let the pipers turn back. Davy stood up in his stirrups for a backward glance. The old laird was gone, but his lady stood framed in the doorway. Seeing him, she lifted one hand in a tentative gesture of farewell. Davy did not return the salute, yet he felt a sudden surge of pity for her. He could escape the deadly boredom in travel and war; she was buried alive. Well, he thought with a bitter chuckle, he had done what he could for her. He turned away—to meet the malevolent stare of Ian.

Davy sighed. Perhaps, instead of escaping trouble, he was taking it along with him?

Then they were through the gate and heading for the pass at a trot.

Chapter Two

Without command, the little cavalcade drew rein at the summit of the pass. The action was instinctive, a genuflection of reverence, for the whole story of their heritage was clearly writ in the incomparable grandeur of the scene surrounding them. It was meet they should renew the impression and fix it indelibly on their minds.

Towering forbiddingly above them, seemingly carved out of the very rock on which it perched, was the old castle itself, a medieval stronghold that guarded and made impregnable the narrow defile called the *Raid na Gael,* or "Highlandman's Pass." Though long outmoded of design, the hoary fortress was by its situation almost irreducible by assault, while the pass served as a natural Barbican which a dozen stout men could hold against a host.

Behind and beneath the castle was the lake, now steaming with early mist, and beyond it the valley, sloping upward again to the lofty craigs. This was the Highlands; this was safety, and home.

All these things Davy knew and loved, yet he wanted to peer into the future. While the others looked back, he stared forward through the pass to where the panorama melted into infinity. He felt like a soaring hawk, eying the world from the sky. For the first few miles, the ground was rocky and irregular, spotted by jagged grooves and rude moors. Here, there was no habitation, save those of wild animals, for the Lowland husbandman did not care to risk his flocks and herds so close to the haunts of his wild Highland countrymen. But beyond this dreary buffer, the land grew gentler as it leveled off. Neat hedgerows marked the beginnings of cultivated fields, sparkling streams meandered through lush green pastures, and in the dim distance could be seen herds of black cattle.

This, then, was the rich Lowlands of Scotland, stretching south to the Border. Somewhere in the mists beyond that lay England.

At a signal from Ian, the journey was resumed. For reasons of security, the road had never been improved, thus the company had to descend in single file. Two of the more experienced men were sent ahead as scouts, while Lord Ian followed at the head of his straggling band.

Davy was well aware he should be riding beside his captain, but deemed it wiser to let time and the road diminish his temper, so he took up a position at the rear. Of all the younger men, he was the only one who had experienced clan warfare, and now as he surveyed the ill-equipped novices, he thanked God there was little likelihood of encountering any of the enemy before they joined the main body of the Royalist army at Westmoreland.

This choice of rendezvous had been considered by all the company as a shrewd diplomatic maneuver on the part of John the Dugald. Not only was it possible that Charles himself might be there—although there was no certainty about the movements of that unpredictable monarch—but it was the domicile of Bruce Sanderson, Earl of Westmoreland, with whom old Dugald had arranged for the marriage of their children. The doughty old laird had reasoned that when the earl had an opportunity to view the valor and person of his future son-in-law at close range, he might well increase the ample dowry already agreed upon.

To David, more familiar with the character of the young man in question than his father, this optimism proved merely that John the Dugald had indeed lost his vision in more ways than one, and that unless the Earl of Westmoreland had other axes to grind above the happiness of his only daughter, the presence of Ian might well give the contracted romance an unexpected denouement.

Like many betrothals of the age, this one had been settled when the principals were children. Davy well remembered the ceremonious visit of the Sandersons to Lochbogie back in 1634, when he was ten. He recalled Olivia Sanderson as a gawky, freckled tomboy of seven or eight, and the scene which had ensued when she refused to embrace her betrothed, shrieking that he looked "like a toad."

Now, jogging down the tortuous road, Davy chuckled aloud at the remembrance. Because the metaphor had been so apt, he had taunted Ian with it—until soundly whipped by their mutual tutor.

Yet the name had stuck through the years, and even Lady Marguerite, viewing with distaste the young laird's spindly legs, potbelly and protruding eyes, still referred to him by the same appellative.

By midday, the troop reached level ground where the road permitted riding in double files. After a brief stop for the noon meal, the journey was resumed. Ian had kept remote from the others during the pause, eating alone in a sullen, brooding silence, but when the company remounted, he summoned Davy to join him at the head of the column.

Davy spurred forward with misgivings. From long experience he knew that Ian's sulks ordinarily required a full turn of the clock to dissipate. However, when he rode up beside the other, he found him suspiciously affable. Ian smiled genially, but waited until they had forged ahead out of earshot of the others before speaking.

"I'm damned sorry I lost my head this morning, Davy. It was generous of you to try and take the blame before the pater."

Davy was a diplomat by instinct. "I spoke but the truth, my lord," he murmured, slightly puzzled by this unnatural change of mood.

"Whist, Davy! When we're alone like this, call me 'Ian' as you did when we were children." At the expression of genuine surprise on Davy's face, he added dolefully, "I get devilishly lonely at times. I think that is what's making me so touchy of late."

Davy could well have reminded him that his disposition had not altered appreciably through the years, but he merely bowed in acknowledgement.

"As you wish it, Ian."

Ian smirked. "Perhaps there's a mite o' jealousy in me; I may as well confess it. You've always had a way with the wenches that I seem to lack. Blast me, if I can fathom it! We're alike as two peas in a pod." He colored slightly at the imperceptible arching of Davy's brows.

" 'Tis the God's truth!" he insisted belligerently. "We're about the same in weight and height, although you have more of the peasant build and a ruder, more direct way of speaking. Why, then, should a serving-wench prefer you to *me?*"

Davy realized he was on dangerous ground and that Ian's temper had been merely repressed. He could sense a trap in the verbal distance without being quite able to see it yet.

"You are overmodest," he said, choosing each word with extreme caution. "I wasn't aware any wenches did prefer me to you."

"They do—take my word for it!"

"Then it is doubtless your rank, my lord, since it could not be your person."

Lord Ian fixed his eyes on the ruts ahead. "Aye, I've thought of that, and in the case of domestics, I grant it the only logical explanation. Obviously, it is safer to bed a groom than a noble." He paused, then suddenly swung his bulging eyes on his companion. "But in the case of a *gentlewoman*, Davy, the theory falls apart!"

Davy caught his breath. "I don't ken you!"

"I'll be more explicit," the other went on harshly, his voice rising with excitement. "I refer to that French bitch my father married, who has been fornicating with every lackey in Lochbogie, *including yourself!*"

Davy met his eyes unabashed. "Pardon me, my lord," he countered, "but as a lackey, even one so favored by your lordship, it would be criminal for me even to discuss the morals of so exalted a personage as the Mistress of Lochbogie."

Ian stiffened resentfully, then with a forced laugh leaned over and clapped Davy familiarly on the shoulder.

"By the Gods, Davy, you're a canny customer! I swear you'll go far! But come now"—his voice dropped to a conspiratorial whisper—"let's dispense with all this secrecy. We used to trust and confide in each other! Look—I'll be frank with you: I've tried to have a go at her myself, for she's in a perpetual heat. Doubtless I'd have made it if the moment had been right, but we were disturbed. You know she's nothing but a common whore!" He paused, but when Davy maintained a stony silence, he went on: "But her morals, or the lack of them, are not the point. What concerns me is her influence with my father. He won't hear anything against her!" He said this last plaintively, as if it were his chief grievance.

Davy nodded sympathetically. "The laird has always been loyal to his own," he agreed, with two-edged malice. "That's why he gets so much loyalty in return."

Ian's rising color indicated the thrust had not entirely missed its mark.

"I had hoped for some personal loyalty from you, David!" he retorted angrily.

24

"My entire life has been dedicated to serving you, my lord. You know that."

Realizing that Davy's verbal guard was impenetrable, Ian tried a new mode of attack.

"What would you say, Davy, if I secured you a King's commission?" he asked abruptly.

Davy laughed. "I'd say, my lord, you were a magician!"

"You mock me?"

"Nay, nay! I mock myself. I have not forgotten my station."

"Pshaw! Anything can happen during a war!"

"I understood one's station was fixed by birth!" Davy observed drily.

"Ordinarily it is," Ian said pointedly. "Yet powerful friends can work miracles." He avoided Davy's quizzical glance and stared ahead. "I could be that kind of a friend to you, David . . . if . . . !" He left the sentence dangling in mid-air.

Curiosity prodded Davy into putting one foot into the trap. "You were saying, my lord . . ."

"I was just thinking aloud," Ian went on, after a pause. "I was thinking, for instance, that a son has a right to protect a blind father, as well as his own birthright. Aye, more than a right; a bounden duty! As you know, I am soon to be married. I cannot bring a clean young bride to Lochbogie so long as that viperish French whore is alive to crawl around the castle!"

Davy began to sense the drift. "Ah, then you plan to postpone your wedding?" he asked, with feigned innocence.

Ian glared at him in impatience. "My God, you are stupid! Don't you understand there are some things a gentleman does not care to put into words? Let me phrase it this way: if anything should happen to remove—permanently, that is—a certain objectionable French female from Lochbogie, I should be very, *very* grateful!"

"Now I understand! You speak of assassination?"

The blood drained from the other's cheeks, leaving them a mottled bluish-white.

"I used no such word!" he barked sharply.

Davy heaved his shoulders. "Aye, I grant it has a harsh note," he conceded, with an audible sigh. "Yet . . ." He paused, then continued musingly, "I own to having wished at times my station was somewhat higher than it is."

25

Ian moistened his lips and leaned closer. "Ah-h! Then I can leave the matter in your hands, my friend?"

"We are departing Lochbogie, not approaching it!"

Ian made a gesture of impatience. "I shall send you back with a message from Westmoreland."

Davy sidestepped a direct promise. "It will require some thought," he temporized. "I have had no experience as a *Doomster.** Permit me a few days to consider."

"Aye, aye!" Ian agreed, chuckling. "Meanwhile, I shall make an initial payment on my indebtedness." He drew himself erect. "David, I herewith appoint you my aide and lieutenant of this company!"

Davy saw the trap closing. "But, my lord!" he protested. "This is premature! I haven't. . ."

Ian cut him off. "Fie! I know you, David, and I know your ambition! You'll always be on the winning side!"

Davy managed a smile, but under his breath he murmured, "God grant you speak the truth for once, Ian the Idiot!"

Obviously determined to involve Davy beyond escape, Lord Ian summoned the trumpeter, and without more ado, halted the company and formally announced the promotion, which was received with wild cheers and huzzas, for Davy was popular with all. Strangely enough, this enthusiasm did not please his lordship, and when the march was resumed, he spurred ahead of the column to brood alone.

That first evening they bivouacked in a small, secluded ravine within bow-shot of the road. Sentries were posted as a matter of policy, for though no Rebel troops had been reported this far north of the Tweed, many of the Lowland peasants and small farmers were rabid Covenanters. Bands of these ardent Presbyterians had, on several occasions, made night attacks on the King's own troops.

Wrapped in his tartan, Davy pondered the predicament into which his curiosity had enmeshed him. He cursed himself for his equivocation, for now Ian was determined to hold him to a promise he had neither made nor intended making. He knew he should have summarily refused the vicious request, yet it was dangerous to

* A professional Scottish executioner.

defy an unstable creature such as Ian of Dugald. There were times —and this was one of them—when Davy doubted his young master's sanity. He shuddered to think of Lochbogie when the full control passed into Ian's hands.

Yet the situation was not without a touch of ironical humor. He wondered what Ian would say if he knew that this very day his stepmother had solicited the same man to be *his* assassin? It made Davy's plight doubly dangerous.

While he did not even consider fulfilling either of the diabolical requests, in the background of his consciousness floated the prizes the precious pair of schemers had dangled before him: Lady Marguerite making him her consort—Lord only knew whether she would wait for old John the Dugald to die a natural death!—or, on the other hand, to be a King's officer, and so escape the eternal bondage of his present station! Ian's words echoed in his ears: *I know you, David, and I know your ambition! You'll always be on the winning side!*

Davy pondered that statement. Dreams he had had aplenty, yet he had never deemed them *ambition,* for they seemed utterly beyond hope of attainment. But now that Ian had plucked them out of the limbo, they became perilously plausible. Haunted by these visions, Davy drove them aside and drifted off to sleep.

It was Lord Ian's plan, as he explained to Davy, to make an early start and by dint of hard riding reach Castle Westmoreland in mid-afternoon. Thus with the first paleness of dawn, the trumpet awakened the band. Breakfast was hastily devoured, but as the men were saddling their mounts, two weary sentries marched into the glade, dragging an aged peasant between them.

Despite the ancient's years, he disputed every inch of the way with his captors, physically and vocally. In his rough coat and breeches of hoddin-gray, his clouted shoes and black leggings, and a shepherd's plaid about his stooped shoulders, he epitomized the Lowland farmer. Yet, at the same time, his flowing locks and long white beard and sunken, feverish eyes gave him the awesome look of an Old Testament prophet. This latter illusion was heightened by the scriptural language with which he anathematized his guards.

"Unhand me, ye wicked Philistines!" he roared, jerking this way and that. "Remove thy filthy talons, ye Bulls o' Bashan!"

"Hold yer tongue, ye feckless ol' loon!" growled one of the Highlanders. "Bulls nae hae talons anyway!"

"Ye'd deny the word o' Jehovah, Sodomites that ye be!" screamed the prisoner. "Release a true son o' God, ye crawlin' spawn o' prelates!"

Davy, with old Gabriel trotting at heel, walked to meet them. "What's the trouble, Gillie?" he asked the older guard.

Gillie wiped the perspiration from his forehead. "We encountered this auld fool down by the spring. Before he learned who we were, he mentioned that a company of Parliamentary dragoons passed this way yesterday."

Davy whistled softly. "How many were in their party, ancient?" he asked the squirming prisoner.

"Twelve!" trumpeted the old man. "The same number as the Lord's disciples, sent to punish ye malignant kine, ye worshippers o' the Golden Calf o' Popery, ye . . ."

"Windy ol' bastard, ain't 'e?" observed Gillie admiringly.

"Which way did they go, ancient?" Davy inquired.

"Verily they rode the winds o' Providence!" raged the shepherd. "Question me no more, for as Shadrach, Meshach and Abednego refused to bow down to the image set up by Nebuchadnezzar, so do I refuse to betray the servants o' the Almighty!"

Davy grinned. "Give him a tot o' ale, Gillie!" he told the guard. "Methinks it may quench the fire in his gullet. I'll report this to his lordship."

He left the furious captive denouncing ale and all kindred refreshments, and sought out Ian, whose valet was buckling him into his back-and-breast. He told him, laughingly, what had happened.

Ian turned pale. "*Dragoons?* God in Heaven, are we surrounded?"

Davy was taken aback by the other's terror.

"Hardly, my lord," he said drily, "since they number an even dozen."

But Ian was not so easily reassured. Seizing his sword, he hurried down the ravine to where a grinning audience stood gathered around the angry orator.

"Woe, woe, and thrice woe unto ye, spawn o' Babel! Flee whilest ye hae yet time before the wrath o' a righteous God! Crawl back into yer holes, ye foul serpents!"

Ian pushed through the press and faced the prisoner.

"Hold your peace, you old gowk!" he shouted. "Tell me how many of these dastardly Rebels . . ."

The shepherd viewed him with contempt. "I will nae heed the foul vaporings o' such a profane potsherd!" he roared defiantly. "Verily, the hosts o' the Lord are without number! They shall resist the arrows sharpened and the bows bent against them! They shall sweep ye vile Sodomites into the seas, even as . . ."

"Whist, mon, whist!" cautioned Gillie kindly. " 'Tis 'is Lordship his ain self 'oo questions ye. This be no time fer yer Whiggery!"

When even this warning failed to stem the torrent, Ian's face turned livid.

"Make him talk!" he snarled at the guards.

"Fiend hae me, sir!" protested the practical Gillie. " 'Tis to stop his senseless clackin' I been tryin', not encourage it!"

Ian shouldered him roughly aside and towered above the un-quenchable old rustic. He laid the point of his sword against the latter's breast.

"Enough of your treasonous utterances!" he raged. "Tell me ex-actly how many dragoons you saw and which way they traveled, or as God's my witness, I'll lay your guts open!"

"We have that information, my lord!" Davy interposed.

Ian ignored him. "Speak, I command you!" he warned the pris-oner. "Speak, or die!"

The old man eyed him as fiercely as a trapped hawk. "Truly, God hath delivered me into the hands of mine enemies! Yet I am no Judas—Him I will not betray!"

Ian poised his sword. "*Speak!*" His voice had risen to a hysterical scream.

Until that moment, Davy had not believed him serious, but now as he moved forward to interfere, the old shepherd suddenly spat in the face of his tormentor. Davy shouted: *My lord . . . !*" but he was too late.

With a strangled "The devil take you!" Ian plunged the sword into the prisoner's breast.

A look of vague surprise crossed the old man's face. As he sagged back into the arms of his startled captors, he glanced down at the blood spurting from his middle. A moment later, he raised blazing eyes to his murderer.

"If any man have ear, let him hear!" he gasped out. "Verily, the Lord hath said: 'He that leadest into captivity shall go into captivity and he that killeth by the sword must be killed by the sword!' "

Completely berserk, Ian stabbed him again and again, until the terrified guards leapt clear and the dying man fell flat on his back. Yet though his voice waned, as if fading into distance, his words came plainly to the shocked audience.

". . . and I heard a voice from heaven, as the voice of many waters, and as the voice of great thunder . . . !"

Ian stumbled back, trembling violently. "Gillie!" he screamed, as if trying to drown out the words of his victim. "Gillie! Finish him!"

Old Gillie, a hardened veteran of clan warfare, shrank from the assignment.

"He's ae but gone now, sir!"

". . . and I saw a beast rise up from the sea, having seven heads and . . ."

"Gillie! Obey me!" trumpeted Ian. "Else I'll have you flayed alive!"

The old clansman, seeing it was more of a kindness than not, drew his sword and made one clean thrust through the shepherd's heart. As the body ceased to quiver, Lord Ian glared around at the stricken company.

"Good God, what ails you all?" he demanded. "Are ye men, or gutless women, that you pale at a traitor's passing? Certes, I'll have no cowards in my company! Here—every man of you will draw his sword and plunge it into this carcass!" When they stared at him in mute disbelief, he cried, "Are ye afraid to stab an enemy of the King?"

"Forgive me, yer Honor!" protested a white-faced youth. "I ken the auld mon's an enemy nae longer!"

Ian lashed him with the flat of his blade. "Damn ye, obey me! A sword is useless until it is blooded! Have at it, and if any man shirks, so help me God, I'll leave him strung up by the thumbs above the body and left to the vengeance of other traitors!"

When the men moved reluctantly forward, Davy turned his back in disgust and strode toward a hummock which offered a view of the road. He had neared the summit when he heard the young commander call his name. He was about to retort, then changed his mind. The call was repeated, this time in fury, and when he still disdained to reply, he heard Ian running in pursuit. He paused to await him.

"God damn you, didn't you hear me call?" panted the latter.

30

Davy made no effort to conceal his contempt. Ian still carried his bloody sword and his eyes were wild and distended.

"Aye, I heard you, my lord," Davy said grimly. "Yet I thought I heard something even more urgent."

"How dare you! What is more urgent than my commands?"

"The presence of enemy dragoons, my lord!"

Ian gasped, then scrabbled hastily to the top of the knoll. "Where?" he choked. "Where are they?"

Davy scanned the landscape. The road wound through an open moor for a league before it was swallowed in forest.

"I could be mistaken," he temporized. "Yet when I put my ear to the ground a few moments ago, I thought I heard horses trotting."

Ian glared at the empty road, then swung on Davy. "Damn you!" he grated suspiciously. "If I thought you were defying me, I'd . . ."

"Defying? May I remind you, my lord, the dragoons are in the vicinity, whether I heard them or not!"

Ian wilted. "To be sure, Davy, to be sure! The old traitor confessed there were a vast host without number. . . ."

"Your pardon," Davy interposed drily, "he reported their number as exactly *twelve*. Since we have four-and-thirty, we need not be unduly concerned."

Ian shaded his eyes with his hand. "True, Davy. Unless they ambush us!"

Davy bit his lip to stifle his impatience, then pointed to the distant trees.

"If it please your Lordship, I could take a few men and scout the road ahead. I gathered from what the old man intimated, rather than said, that he expected the dragoons to return shortly. Possibly we could lay our own ambuscade."

The other grudgingly agreed. "But take two of the younger lads," he insisted, "for I want the experienced men about me. If you are surprised, be sure to give us warning. You'll do that, Davy?"

Davy sighed. "Aye, my lord."

As they walked back down the slope, Ian clapped him on the shoulder.

"You're a good lad, Davy! I know I can count on you to the death! But never cross me, Davy. I can't stand it! Something inside of me snaps when I'm defied! And I'd hate to hurt you, Davy! I swear I would!"

31

Davy tucked his tongue in cheek. "Your Lordship's safety is also my chief concern," he murmured.

Choosing two former stableboys, who if not soldiers were at least excellent horsemen, Davy rode out on his mission. There was scant conversation; the lads were still half sick from the atrocity they had been forced to share, and on his own part, Davy had enough to occupy his mind. The conviction that Ian was insane seemed inescapable and he realized it was only a question of time until he himself would run afoul of that maniacal temper. But as Davy was not given to soul-searching, he soon shrugged the matter aside, and touching spurs to his horse, put it into an easy gallop.

On reaching the woods, he slowed to a walk. Then, just as he traversed a minor ford in a brook that crossed the road, he discovered the tracks of horses in the soft mud. He dismounted and studied them with care. As closely as he could judge, there were about twelve horses in the group.

Satisfied now that the information they had gleaned from the old shepherd was correct, he ordered his companions to follow at a safe distance behind, then he mounted and continued deeper into the forest. Soon the ground became firmer and the trail wider until at last he reached a cloistered avenue which seemed designed by nature for the express purpose of an ambuscade.

For the distance of a bow-shot, the road was just wide enough for two horsemen to ride abreast, while the banks on either side were about chest-high and covered with a wild hedgerow tall enough to conceal a mounted trooper. The shadowy gloom would make discovery unlikely.

So perfect was the spot, Davy almost dreaded to enter it himself. On reaching the far end, he found himself at the foot of a long hill. He paused until Robin, the elder of the two stableboys, caught up with him.

The lad's face was pale. " 'Tis like a tunnel into Hell! I swear, Davy, I felt the fiends watchin' me!"

Davy laughed. "A likely spot, I own, and 'twill serve our purpose. You and Alan ride back and tell his Lordship that I have found the place to await these accursed Roundheads."

The boys were only too willing to return, and when they had galloped out of sight, Davy proceeded another half-league until he discovered a good spot from which a scout might survey the road ahead. Thoroughly satisfied, he retraced his steps.

· When the company came up, old Gillie was dispatched up the road to watch for the approach of the dragoons, while Lord Ian and Davy deployed the men.

Ian insisted that the half-dozen experienced fighters in the company be formed into a *life-guard* to protect his own person, which, excluding the scout, left five-and-twenty raw recruits to form the ambush. These were divided into two groups; one for either side of the trap. Half of each party was to remain mounted in the event any of the Roundheads survived the first assault and attempted escape.

At first, Lord Ian ordained that Davy should remain with him, but when the latter pointed out that, without an officer to control them, the inexperienced levies on the other side of the road could well be more of a menace than a help, Ian reversed himself. It was then agreed that Davy should command the smaller squad, but so station himself that he could watch Lord Ian, who would give the signal for the assault.

In such a diabolically perfect trap, the fate of the dragoons seemed a foregone conclusion. The Highlanders had barely taken their stations when the old scout returned.

"They come!" he panted. "I seen their armor glintin' in the sun!"

"How many?" Ian demanded shakily.

"Nae more than twelve, sir!" Gillie assured him.

"Praise God!" breathed his Lordship. Then, savagely: "Remember, lads—no quarter to the dogs!"

Chapter Three

During the ensuing wait, it seemed to Davy as if the very trees ceased their rustling, until the silence became empty and oppressive, as in the center of a storm. He felt a tendency to hold his breath. Then he saw the dragoons round a curve in the road and walk their horses down the gravelly slope toward their doom.

He had never before seen any Parliamentary soldiers, and he had been led to believe them a poorly equipped, rag-a-tag collection of jailbirds and tosspots, but these troopers were splendidly accoutred and mounted on excellent horseflesh. Each man wore a padded buff-coat, a steel helmet with a three-barred visor, and was armed with a pistol and saber. They rode two abreast in close formation, with the ease and cockiness of blooded veterans, and were led by the most evil-looking scoundrel Davy had ever laid eye to.

It was an ugliness so unique and outstanding that Davy was fascinated. The ruffian looked like the incarnation of the devil himself! He was squat, and proportionately as broad as a beetle, yet he sat his black courser as though he were another limb of it. Even at a distance, his rat-eyes seemed to glitter, and as he drew closer, the swarthiness of his skin was visible, pitted by pox. The protuberance that passed for a nose had long since been battered out of recognition. The lipless mouth was a wide scar with a slight sardonic twist on one side. Davy sensed that this was a face which had traveled far and had witnessed so much depravity as to be marked by it.

With an effort, he forced his eyes away from the dragoon sergeant and glanced across the roadway to where Lord Ian sat his horse in deep shadow. The young laird caught Davy's eye and made a patting gesture of caution. Davy passed the warning along to his men.

By this time, the dragoons had entered the trap and were fast drawing abreast the crucial center of the ambuscade. Davy sought to gauge them as a unit, but every time his eyes turned toward them, they lighted on the irresistible sergeant at the head. Then he saw Lord Ian raise his claymore, preparatory to sounding the attack. . . .

Suddenly the Rebel sergeant stood up in his stirrups and glared back the way they had come.

"Bugger me!" he roared angrily. "The 'ole bloody regiment be o'ertakin' us! Come, me 'earts, put spurs to yer nags, else the colonel'll 'ave us all a-riden' the wooden colt wi' a brace o' carbines tied to our shanks!" As one or two of the dragoons turned around in surprise, the sergeant cursed them.

"Eyes *front!* Damme, d'ye want the colonel to see ye peerin' back, wi' 'im so close, like calves eyin' their cows 'oo follow! *Forward at the double!*" He sank his spurs into the powerful charger under him and it lifted forward into a gallop.

Davy started up, expecting the signal, but when he looked askance at Ian, the latter, white-faced, shook his head. Cursing bitterly, Davy sank back and watched the dragoons disappear around the bend in a haze of dust.

When he again looked across the road, he saw old Gillie warily crawling from cover. Gesturing his own men to stay where they were, Davy eased out to meet him.

"In God's name, be careful!" Ian called hoarsely. "Don't let the regiment see you!"

The old scout peered in all directions, then glanced at Davy.

"De'il take me!" he growled. "I see no regiment!"

Davy exhaled wearily. "Did you expect to?"

Gillie met his eyes. "Nay, mon, I canna say that I did."

Seeing them standing openly in the center of the roadway, Ian finally joined them.

"What's the matter?" he demanded irritably. "Haven't they come in sight yet?"

"To whom does your Lordship refer?" inquired Davy.

"To *whom?* Why the Rebel regiment, you blockhead! Didn't you hear that ruffian say . . ."

"Aye," conceded Davy. "I heard what we were intended to hear. Yet the fact remains—*there is no regiment!*"

Ian's mouth popped open and his eyes bugged until they seemed to be resting on his high cheek-bones. He stared at Davy, then at Gillie. The old scout gave him a wry smile.

" 'Tis plain, sir, that black-hearted dastard gulled us. 'E must o' sensed we was there. I swear 'e looked the very deppity o' Satan. . . ."

Lord Ian almost wept with rage. "To horse!" he thundered. "To horse, and after them! They shan't escape us!"

As the Highlanders scrambled for their horses, Davy pointed out the futility of a chase. "They have had nigh a quarter-hour start and are better mounted. Doubtless they will expect such a move and may in turn lay an ambuscade for us. We have already wasted half a day, and if your Lordship desires to reach Westmoreland tonight . . . ?" He paused significantly.

Ian wilted. "Aye, I had forgotten my duty. We will continue." He glared sternly about him. "Let that be a lesson to you all, but, mark me well—I'll have the tongue cut out of the man who repeats what happened here today! Gillie, you and Andrew scout ahead! Davy, keep Robin and Alan with you and cover our rear. If those swine follow us, we'll give them a warm welcome, I promise you!" He sheathed his claymore with a flourish. "To horse, lads!"

Davy was only too well pleased with the order, for it served the dual purpose of removing him beyond the spiteful temper of his master and permitted him an opportunity to give way to the merriment he could no longer control. The quick wit of the Rebel sergeant had completely captivated him. Truly, as old Gillie had opined, the evil-looking scoundrel must have been the devil in disguise!

In this latter prognosis, Davy's young companions concurred, though they saw nothing humorous in the situation. To their inexperienced eyes, the well-disciplined dragoons had appeared indestructible monsters. Nor could they be convinced that the mythical regiment, so handily conceived by the indomitable sergeant, wasn't even now lurking somewhere in the forest to waylay them.

Thus, for hours the lonely trio jogged along, silent save for the soft drumming of hooves, the musical tinkle of bits and chains and the gentle retch of leather. Faithful old Gabriel padded beside his master. As the shadows lengthened, filling the dark green gloom with unfamiliar shadows, the youngsters edged their nags closer to Davy.

"Courage, my bairns!" he laughed. "We'll be at Westmoreland in a little while."

They had just crossed a desolate stretch of heath, when Davy noticed the old dog growling softly to himself.

"And what's the matter with you, Gabe?" Davy asked. "Surely you're not imagining things, too?"

The hound whined fretfully and turned his head. His hackles were erect and he moved with stiff-legged caution. Davy whistled thoughtfully, and swinging around in the saddle, scanned the road behind. He could see nothing. He cocked his head, listening, without result. Yet experience had taught him old Gabriel did not make mistakes.

Straightening, Davy tried to decide the best course of action. If he took his two companions and turned back, they might encounter the whole squad of dragoons. That would be fatal! Yet, to ignore the fact they were being followed was to court disaster if, as might well happen, Lord Ian should elect to camp before reaching the safety of the castle. No, he must find out what was behind them!

The sun had now set, but the darkness was relieved by a skittish full moon which played hide-and-seek with some gathering storm clouds. He pondered the wisdom of dispatching one of the lads to warn Ian, but eventually decided against it. There was no telling *how* his Lordship would react.

Fortunately, neither Robin nor Alan had noticed the dog's behavior, and Davy was loath to alarm them.

"We're not far from the castle, lads," he said casually, "so I think I'll tarry here alone awhile, just to make certain we haven't been followed. You two proceed as you are going. If I do not overtake you within the hour, gallop ahead and join the company."

Robin started to draw rein to discuss the matter, but Davy brusquely ordered him to maintain his pace, feeling that, if the enemy was within earshot, the cessation of hoof beats might create suspicion. So, with obvious reluctance, the two lads jogged ahead while Davy, with a touch of spur, guided his horse over a ditch and into a thick grove of trees that skirted the road. Warning the old hound to maintain absolute silence, he threaded his way back, paralleling the trail, until he found a place near a turn where the brush offered a screen. Patting the horse's arched neck to steady him, he waited.

For a seemingly interminable time, he could see nothing but the empty ribbon of silver which was the road coiling through the heath. Yet, just when he had decided the dog must have been concerned with a wild animal, his own ears caught the measured beat of hooves. Gabriel whined nervously.

Like a contrary woman, the moon chose this particular moment to flit behind a cloud. Davy cursed and drew his pistol, feeling for the prime with his fingers. The unseen rider drew closer. Davy stroked his horse's neck to reassure it.

Then, with terrifying abruptness, the moon reappeared—clear and cold—to reveal a solitary horseman bent over his saddle, manifestly following the tracks of the Highland contingent. The rider was almost abreast of Davy when he suddenly straightened. Davy felt the hair stiffen along his own nape.

It was the Rebel sergeant!

Now David Dugald was not unduly superstitious, and he feared no living man. Yet there was something so supernaturally evil in the pock-marked features of this Roundhead, Davy felt the sweat dampen his palms.

He would have preferred to have let the Rebel draw closer to his hiding place before accosting him, but he mistrusted the moon. So, at the first sign of wane, he spurred into the road.

"Hold, damn you!" he commanded, leveling his pistol. "Stand where you are!"

"*Leapin' Jesus!*" gasped the dragoon, taken completely by surprise. Yet an instant later he recovered himself, and with a defiant, "The 'ell ye s'y!" he ducked flat along the off-side of his horse and swerved into the trees.

Reviling himself for first speaking, Davy fired, and when the ball went wild, dug in his own spurs and careened in pursuit. The dragoon rode like a centaur, weaving through the thick stand of trees as easily as a hunted stag. Davy was hard put to keep him in sight, and twice, in quick succession, he was almost unseated as the wily chase led under low-hanging branches. Shortly thereafter, they broke cover into a small clearing.

As the gap widened, Davy realized he was outclassed. He was on the verge of reining in, when he saw old Gabriel streak past him. The sergeant's black courser was halfway across the clearing when

38

the gaunt wolfhound left the ground to seize his throat. The terrified beast missed his footing and crashed.

Even then the ugly rider demonstrated his masterly skill, for he freed himself from the saddle as the horse went down, somersaulted handily across the turf and landed on his feet. Before he could draw his saber, Davy was upon him.

Davy attempted to run him down, but the ruffian dodged nimbly aside, then snatched at Davy's leg and yanked him out of the saddle. Falling, Davy managed to snag the other's bull-neck in the crotch of his arm, and they hit the ground hard enough to wind them both.

Davy's hold was sufficient to restrain his quarry, but could not be bettered without risk. However, the dragoon had the strength of a bear and he battered the Scot about the middle with iron fists until the latter was nauseated. All the while, old Gabriel set up a frightful clamor, slashing at the dragoon between howls of fury.

Just when Davy was beginning to wonder how it was going to end, four horsemen thundered into the glade and hurled themselves from the saddle. In the half-light and confusion, Davy assumed it was the remainder of the dragoons until, to his incredible relief, he heard the rough burr of old Gillie begging him to release his hold so they could safely spit the rebel where he lay.

But the sergeant knew when to surrender. "Quarter, gents!" he panted. "I own 'tis time to gi' up! Quarter!"

As Davy rolled clear, he heard Gillie snarl, "Ye'll get quartered, nae quarter, ye heathen bastard!"

The old Highlander had already started a murderous thrust with his basket-hilted sword when Davy choked out a restraining order. "Hold, Gillie, *hold!* I . . . want . . . to . . . question . . . him!" He accepted Alan's proffered arm and hauled himself erect.

Meanwhile, Gillie and the stalwart Andrew had rough-housed the prisoner to his feet. Singularly enough, the sergeant seemed to regard the situation as humorous. His long slash of a mouth was bowed in a grin and his rat-eyes twinkled mischievously.

" 'Twas a right merry chyce, eh, yer Gryce?" he chortled. "Bugger me, I no counted on the bloody 'ound!"

In spite of himself, Davy felt a compulsion to laugh, but he held it down to a mere grimace.

"Aye, it was that, you rogue! What's your name?"

" 'Arf-'Anged Smyth, m'lud!"

The surly Andrew hit him a back-handed swipe across the mouth. "Jest, will ye?" he growled.

The prisoner glowered in indignation. "Jest, 'ell! 'E arsked me nyme, an' 'e got it! 'Tis 'Arf-'Anged Smyth—whether ye likes it or no, ye petticoated savage!"

"Let be, let be!" Davy barked at the belligerent Highlander, then frowned sternly at the sergeant. "Now, you self-styled Half-Hanged Smyth—we want the truth! Where are the rest of your men?"

"Gone back to their billets, sir."

Davy cocked his head. "Then why were you following us alone?"

The prisoner winked broadly. "So I wouldn't 'ave to divvy no reward wi' 'em. I ain't no fool, I ain't!"

"You lie! Who'd offer a reward for following us?"

The sergeant snorted disdainfully. "Certes, an' it ain't ye piddlin' Scots, to be sure! Yet I suspected ye was goin' to jine the King. Our colonel offered twenty pieces o' silver to the man 'oo found out w'ere Charles be stayin'!"

Davy whistled soundlessly. So Charles *was* in the north!

"Ye damned Judas!" Andrew swore at the captive. "Would ye betray your King for twenty pieces o' siller?"

Old Gillie leaned closer. "Whist, mon! Ye dinna say whether it be Scot's siller, or sterling!"

"Twenty pounds *sterling!*" insisted the sergeant.

Gillie sighed. "Aweel, tha's different. I ken 'tis a muckle temptin' sum!"

Davy burst out laughing. "Put the devil behind thee, ancient!" he warned the old Scot. "And as for you, Half-Hanged Smyth, you're a spy by your own admission. You know the penalty."

The sergeant jeered at him. "Fooled ye, by God! Ye can't execute me!"

"No?"

"No!" taunted Half-Hanged Smyth. "I already been executed an' *I'm dead now*—legally, that is!"

The four Highlanders looked profoundly shocked by this ambiguous declaration, but Davy merely shrugged and turned away. He was satisfied the wretch was mentally deranged, and while he knew the logical thing to do was saber him where he stood, somehow he couldn't quite bring himself to give the order.

"Bind him," he growled. "We'll take him to the castle. His Lordship may desire to question him."

"It'll bloody well cost 'im silver if 'e do!" snorted the irrepressible sergeant, adding, with a sly look at old Gillie, "An' in good English *sterlin'*, no worthless Scot's silver! I ain't in this damn war fer me *'ealth!*"

When they had mounted, Gillie fell in beside Davy. Davy asked, "How did you lads happen along at such an auspicious moment?"

"Aweel, 'twas this way," explained the ancient. "When we came wi'in sight o' the battlements, his Lordship orders Andy an' me to ride back. When we found Robin and Alan alone, we kenned some'at was brewin', so we set spurs to the nags 'til we heard the clackin' o' the hound."

"Bless you, man, it was a right good thing you did," Davy acknowledged grimly. "That scoundrel had the strength of ten fiends!"

Gillie shivered slightly. "I dinna ken what he meant by bein't dead, Davy! D'ye reckon he's the de'il himsel'?"

Davy laughed. "Why, I own he looks the part, Gillie, but I doubt the devil could be bought for a mere twenty pieces of silver."

The old Scot did not smile. "I would nae be too cairtain, laddie! 'Twas pounds *sterling*, he said, an' 'tis a muckle gude sum to tempt e'en auld Satan hissel'!"

Chapter Four

Within the hour, they sighted the turrets and battlements of old Westmoreland silhouetted against the swirling storm clouds, and to the weary little band, it seemed an enchanted fortress out of a fairy tale. Squatted atop a steep hill, with all the majesty of a venerable monarch on his throne, the history of Scotland was plainly writ in its ancient masonry. The great stone Keep was reputedly built by a vassal of William the Conqueror, and its chapel and curtain walls a century later. Princes of the blood had been born in its several towers; tyrant kings had languished in its dungeons. During childhood visits, Davy had played along its ramparts and had learned to swim in the inner moat. Of all the castles he knew, he loved Westmoreland best.

The drawbridge was raised, but when they rode up it slowly clanked down and they passed under the ancient gateway. Davy turned his prisoner over to the castellan, with instructions that he was to be held incommunicado for further questioning. Then he inquired about his master. He was informed that Lord Ian was in the upper chamber of the Keep.

Leaving his horse to Gillie, Davy strode in search of his young laird. He needed no directions, for the impressions of childhood were indelibly stamped on his mind. Crossing the historic tiltyard, he mounted a stairway in the Keep to a large hall on the upper story. There he found a lackey arranging faggots in a massive fireplace, so he requested the fellow to announce his arrival to Lord Ian. The servant vanished through a door, and a few moments later, Ian himself strode out.

His Lordship was gorgeously arrayed in a costume Davy had never before seen him wear—breeches and doublet of metallic cloth of brightest scarlet, surmounted at the throat by a wide collar of antique lace. His stubby-fingered hands were encased in gauntlets with embroidered cuffs, and his soft boots bore immense leather plaques over the instep. Yet even this grandeur failed to hide the toadlike figure, and his expression was, as always, an unpleasant blend of petulance, boorishness and irascibility.

"Damn it!" he greeted Davy ill-temperedly. "Why did you disturb me?"

"I crave your pardon, my lord," Davy murmured, with that faint tincture of disdain he managed to insinuate into his most humble speech. "But I thought you would want to know that we captured a spy—the dragoon sergeant who . . . ah . . . eluded us earlier."

Ian's dull eyes popped. "God's death! Did you slit his gullet?"

"No, sir! He had knowledge of something important."

"And that is . . . ?"

"That his Majesty is either here now, or is momentarily expected!"

"Charles? *Here?*" Ian snorted. "Ridiculous! I would have been informed on arrival!" He bit his lip, and as suspicion took root, the old familiar look of injured pride drew his brows together.

"Where is the scoundrel?"

"I turned him over to . . ." Davy paused as a young woman appeared in the doorway of the inner chamber.

He did not recognize her, though he thought her the loveliest creature he had ever seen. An oval face that was at once proud yet saucy was framed by auburn tresses the shade and glint of polished copper. She was gowned like a fairy princess in white satin with multicolored silk and metal embroidery. Her eyes, a laughing green, stared quizzically at Davy, then began to twinkle.

"Why, bless me—it's *Davy!*" She advanced with outstretched hands. "Glory be, have you forgotten me, Davy?"

Davy blinked in astonishment. There was absolutely nothing about this exquisite creature—Ah! Perhaps only in the eyes!—to remind him of the leggy, freckled-faced child he had romped with a decade before. Yet it had to be . . . !

Ian made a gagging noise, then hissed at him. "Make your obeisance, you blockhead!"

When Davy started to bend his knee, the girl caught his hands.

"La, how you've grown!" She laughed—a trifle too gaily, Davy thought. "Yet I declare I would have recognized you anywhere!"

Davy managed a bow. He was slightly uncomfortable, for he suspected her effusiveness was engendered not so much by him personally as by his interruption of what, on the surface at least, appeared to have been an awkward tête-à-tête with her betrothed. Howbeit, his own gallantry was irrepressible in the presence of a beautiful woman.

"And I, my lady, plead shock!" he replied gravely. "Your loveliness stunned me completely!"

Lord Ian gasped at this audacity. "Fellow! You forget yourself!"

Lady Olivia turned on him in astonishment. "How now, Ian? For giving me a pretty compliment?"

"My dear!" Ian muttered pompously. "Need I remind you this fellow is my groom?"

Davy felt a wave of cold rage sweep over him, but before he could speak, Olivia cut in tartly.

"Indeed? I seem to recall, my lord, that a few moments ago you boasted that David was your lieutenant!"

Ian went red to the ears. "This is unseeming!" he stammered.

"Fie, Ian, don't be boorish!" she snapped, then with mischievous contriteness, added: "Forgive me! I do hope I haven't embarrassed either of you, but as I often recall the pleasant days we spent as children, I am naturally delighted to see you both." She made a curtsy. "It is evident you have important affairs to discuss, so I beg to be excused. We will meet anon!" With a little flutter of her hand, she swished into the inner chamber.

Davy wasn't fool enough to think he understood women, but he was sufficiently sensitive and experienced to feel tension and to know that something had happened between Olivia and his master. And when the door closed and Ian turned his protruding eyes toward him, Davy saw the thunderheads.

He sought to dissemble. "Permit me to congratulate you, my lord!" he said suavely. "In her Ladyship you will have a wife worthy of the future Laird of Lochbogie!"

Unfortunately, this seemed to make Ian even angrier than ever. "You . . . you ought to be whipped, damn you!" he raged.

Davy chose to misunderstand. "I confess my lack of perception in disturbing you, my lord," he apologized soothingly. "Had I dreamt you were closeted with your betrothed, I would never have trespassed. Yet the rumor about the King seemed sufficiently urgent . . ."

"Doubtless a dastard's lie!" grumbled Ian. "Howbeit, now that you have ruined my pleasure, we'll question this knave. Woe betide him if he has gulled us!" Turning abruptly, he stalked toward the stairwell. As they started down, Davy caught the muttered plaint: "The slut showed more pleasure on seeing a common *groom* than she did *me!*"

And Davy, in his turn, chuckled softly to himself.

Before they interviewed the castellan, Lord Ian warned Davy to say nothing about the possible presence of King Charles.

"If his Majesty *is* here, then 'tis plain these people are trying to keep it from me—no doubt for reasons of jealousy!"

"No doubt," agreed Davy.

"On the other hand," Ian went on, with a sly smirk, "if Charles is en route, there is a possibility they do not know of it—a fact I may be able to turn to *my* advantage."

"You have a natural bent for diplomacy, my lord!" Davy admired.

Lord Ian shot him a quick look of suspicion, then turned away.

From the castellan, they learned that the redoubtable Half-Hanged Smyth had been conveniently lodged in one of the turrets, since the dungeons were so deep underground it made questioning difficult. The considerate castellan also volunteered the services of a professional torturer to facilitate the interrogation, but this courtesy Lord Ian hastily declined, vowing he could make a corpse talk.

After a shrewd glance, the castellan shrugged. "In that event, my lord, 'twould be well to hang the fellow tonight and question him tomorrow, for never in my day hath a blacker scoundrel darkened the portals of Westmoreland!"

"He'll be a lot whiter when I'm done with him!" boasted Ian. Then they headed for the tower.

Crossing the inner bailey where they had romped as children, Davy's mind drifted back over the years. The memory brought a sweet ache. In those carefree days there had been scant "lord and lackey" formality to interfere with fun. They strode across the ancient stone bridge over the spring which wound as a creek through the tiltyard on its way to fill the outer moat, and he was reminded

45

of the water games they used to play. Then they reached the tower and his dreams were dissipated.

This gloomy pile stood in the southeast corner. In the long ago there must have been a private chamber in the turret, for the remnants of a tiny gallery jutted out over the curtain walls. They first climbed an exposed staircase to the ramparts, where they dismissed the sentinel, after relieving him of the cell-key and a small hooded lanthorn. Then they entered the tower and proceeded up a winding stairwell to the room above.

When they entered the cuddy, they found the prisoner stretched full length upon a single plank which served in lieu of a pallet, his manacled wrists crossed on his middle. His sword, of course, had been taken from him, but his steel cap lay on the table in the center of the room. The only other piece of furniture was a heavy chair, which Lord Ian appropriated for himself and hauled closer to the door. Meanwhile, Davy hung the lanthorn on an iron sconce set high in the wall.

Half-Hanged Smyth placidly viewed these operations from a recumbent position, but when the visitors turned to stare at him, he swung his legs to the floor and sat up. His bright little button-eyes shifted from one stern face to the other, then he grinned.

"Yer servants, gents!" he offered jauntily, starting to rise.

Davy gestured him back. "Stay where you are, Smyth! Try any tricks and I'll break your neck!"

Smyth sank back with a chuckle. "Aye, ye be a big bastard!" he conceded, "but ye fancy-pants ain't no match fer 'Arf-'Anged Smyth, e'en wi' these ruddy bracelets. I be the bes' goddam bare'and fighter in Lunnon town!" He chortled deprecatingly. "Howbeit, gents, ye don't need to worry. I won't gi' ye no trouble."

Davy couldn't help smiling. "Thank you, Half-Hanged," he said drily. "Peradventure you give us the right answers, we won't give *you* any trouble."

"Don't patronize the dog!" Ian put in irritably. "He'll give the answers or I'll tear the tongue out of his filthy head!" He came to his feet, but moved no closer to the prisoner. "Now, you whoreson —tell the truth! Do you know where the King is?"

Smyth measured him with a practiced eye. "Mebbe I does, an' mebbe I doesn't."

"Do you mock me?" flared Ian, his voice rising. "We have ways of loosening your tongue!"

Half-Hanged leered at him. "Certes, an' methinks the passin' o' coins might 'elp, yer Gryce!"

"Bowels of God!" bleated his Lordship, aghast. "Dare you solicit a bribe from *me?*"

"Bugger me, w'y not? Ye looks like ye could pay yer own way, m'lud!"

Ian whipped out a thin-bladed *skean dhu** from the top of his boot and made as if to cross the room. But, apparently, he thought better of it, for he barked at Davy: "Lay your ain blade to his throat, Lieutenant!"

Davy reluctantly unsheathed his knife, but the prisoner was unabashed.

"Put up yer baubles, gents," he advised. "Steel be a bloody poor substitute fer silver, that I own, yet the choice ben't mine."

"You heard the question!" Davy prompted. "Answer it!"

Half-Hanged sighed. "Aye—the whereabout o' the King. Well, gents, as to that, I can't rightly s'y. 'E left the South, we know, an' our lieutenant general, 'e thinks . . ."

"You refer to that unspeakable traitor Oliver Cromwell?" Lord Ian interrupted.

"I refers to the bes' goddam soldier in three kingdoms!" snapped Smyth.

"Get on with your story!" urged Davy.

"Well, our troop was detailed to follow 'im," the prisoner went on, "but we lost 'is trail near Berwick, so Ol' Piety—that be our major, Ebenezer Priety, a gospel-'owler, damme if else!—divided us into squads to see if we could pick up the scent." The speaker spread his hands to indicate that was the extent of his information.

"What made you think the King was coming to Westmoreland?" probed Davy.

"Bugger me, 'e's got to be *somew'ere,*" reasoned Smyth. "An' w'en I got wind ye balmy 'Ighlanders was sneakin' 'ere to jine this papist-lovin' Earl o' Westmoreland, I smells a . . ."

"You lying English swine!" burst out Lord Ian. "I'll have your heart for that!"

* A Scottish dirk.

47

Half-Hanged looked him over with contempt. "Be ye so fierce on the battlefield, m'lud?" he sneered. "Damme, from the way I gulled ye w'en ye was lurkin' in ambush, I got a bloody poor picture o' yer valor!"

Davy caught his breath at this audacity, yet when he saw the mottled flush creep over his Lordship's face, he had difficulty in suppressing a smile. It took Ian a full minute to find his voice, but when it came it was loud with rage.

"Davy!" he shrilled. "Davy! Cut out his tongue! Cut it out of his head, I say!"

Davy turned away in disgust. "Come, my lord—leave the wretch!" he urged placatingly. "We've learned all he knows. Turn him over to the castle *Doomster.*"

But Lord Ian was beyond reason. "Do as I bid you, you ill-bred bastard!" he shrilled, thrashing his arms about. "Cut out his tongue, else, as God is my witness, I'll have you flayed!"

When Davy stood inactive, Ian reached forward and struck him a back-handed blow across the mouth.

"You coward! Obey me!"

Davy stiffened, and it required all his will to control himself. He felt the blood trickle over his lower lip, yet he contrived to keep his voice steady.

"It is because I am no coward I will not mutilate a helpless prisoner to no purpose. And, my lord, I warn you—*don't ever strike me again!*" Realizing his own temper was slipping fast, he jerked open the door.

Lord Ian moved to intercept him. "How dare you? I'll have your life if you refuse . . ."

Davy brushed him aside. "If you want his tongue so damn bad, cut it out yourself!" he grated. "That is—if you're man enough!" Sheathing his own dirk, he started down the circular stairwell.

He reached the level of the ramparts before he was aware that Ian had followed him, for the latter's soft soles made no sound on the solid stone. But just as he stepped through the archway onto the wall, a faint scuffling warned him. He had started to turn when the infuriated young laird sprang full on his back and plunged a dirk into his side.

The blade struck a rib and ricocheted a quarter of the way around his body. The pain was excruciating. Davy sank to one knee and

48

groped instinctively at the head thrust over his left shoulder. When the shifting moonlight gave him a glimpse of the uplifted blade, poised for another thrust, his own temper snapped. Hauling Ian over his shoulder, he slammed him against a merlon.

Ian bounced to his feet. "Guard!" he screamed. "What ho! Guard!" Completely berserk by this time, he threw himself on the wounded man.

Davy was too angry to bother with his own dirk. From the flow of blood down his side, he believed himself disemboweled, so with the recklessness of a doomed man, he parried the next stab with his arm, taking a cut from shoulder to elbow—and grasped the other around the waist. At the contact, all the pent-up resentments of the years burst loose. Cursing, he lifted the struggling man above his head and flung him over the rim of the wall into the cobbled courtyard. . . .

There followed one long wail, a sickening thud, then a brief moment of deadly silence!

But the silence did not last, for as Davy sagged wearily against the battlements, he heard a startled oath from the guard below, then the pounding of feet on the stairs.

Davy knew he was in for it! Danger sharpened his perception. He realized the utter futility of trying to explain the death of Lord Ian; the difference in their stations would nullify anything he might possibly say! Yet, as the footsteps of the guard neared the head of the stairs, he made his decision: if he had to die, it would not be on the gibbet!

He drew his dirk and pushed away from the merlon to meet the attack. But Ian's first murderous cut had all but severed the broad leather belt which held his plaid around him, and now, as Davy came erect, the belt parted. The blood-soaked plaid tumbled off his body, leaving him half naked, in only his shirt. Then he saw the guard come around the bend by the tower. . . .

He tried to kick aside the clinging cloth which hobbled him, but the smooth stones were slick with blood and he slipped to one knee. He glimpsed the bared sword in the guard's hand and sought to brace himself against the inevitable. . . .

And then Davy saw a vision. As the burly guard rushed past the dark mouth of the tower, a black fiend floated out of the deep shadow behind him and appeared to drop two hands over his shoulders, in a sort of hellish benediction! Davy heard the faint clank of chain. The guard emitted a weird, animal cry; his head stopped abruptly while his running feet continued, seemingly up into the air The fiend supported his head an instant longer, then the guard crashed heavily onto his back and lay still!

As Davy stared in open-mouthed awe, the shadowy "fiend" stepped out into the moonlight, and he saw that it was Half-Hanged Smyth. The latter wore his sardonic grin.

"Bugger me," he chuckled, "I swear these manacle chains makes as sweet a garrote as I e'er used! The bastard ne'er so much as bleated!"

Davy staggered to his feet. "My God . . . *you!*" He raised the dirk to protect himself, but the Rebel only wagged his head.

"At ease, laddie, at ease!" he urged good-naturedly. "I mean ye no 'arm! Damme, man—yer sliced from truck to keelson!"

Davy twisted around so the pale light illumined his wounds, and made a cursory examination. He soon discovered his injuries were far from mortal.

Half-Hanged Smyth reached the same conclusion, for he chuckled softly.

"Ye got off lucky, friend! Bugger me, 'twas a pretty bit o' man-handlin', I own! The crazy bastard got 'is comeuppance!"

Davy scowled. "You witnessed that?"

"Aye, an' w'y not? The idjit was in such an 'urry to git ye, 'e fair fergot to lock the door. 'Twas my intent to aid ye, lad, fer yer kindness. Then as I came down, I 'eard the guard runnin', so I waits to greet 'im."

"Certes, and I'm grateful for that," Davy acknowledged, "though, to speak true, I meant you no kindness."

Half-Hanged laughed. "Friend, o' the two small danglin' members o' me carcass, I prizes me tongue the best, fer in truth I gits the most use o' it in these sorry times. Hence, 'twas a kindness to 'elp me preserve it, an' one good turn deserves another, so they s'y!" He dismissed the matter with a wave of his stubby hand. "An' now, matey, since we're aboard the same craft—in a manner o' speakin'—w'at's our course?"

Davy was still partially confused. "*Our* course?"

Smyth guffawed. "Damme, I was warned the Scots was thick 'eaded!" He chortled without malice. "Well, let's look at it from another angle: 'ere's me, marked to 'ang, come sun-up, fer a spy; an'

50

'ere's ye, sharin' the same gibbet fer tossin' a bloody murderin' lud o'er the wall." He paused to let that sink in, then added: "That is— be we fools enough to wait fer the party!"

Davy set his jaw. " 'Tis not my thought to hang," he said grimly. "Yet you forget—you are a prisoner, a traitor and a Rebel!"

"No more'n you be a murderer—legally, that is!"

Davy chuckled without mirth. "True, Half-Hanged, and if you didn't actually save my life, you at least prolonged it. Hence, you deserve some consideration." He fumbled among his ruined garments and, producing a key, unlocked the shackles. Then, as Smyth stood rubbing his hairy wrists to renew the circulation, Davy stared at the defunct guard.

"I guess I'll have to borrow the poor devil's clothing," he mused reluctantly.

But Half-Hanged Smyth had another idea. "Hold, friend!" he suggested. "Gi' me a couple o' minutes!" He scooped up the tattered plaid, then, without further ado, disappeared down the stairs to the courtyard.

Davy shrugged. If the lout planned to escape, he was due for a disappointment, for the castle gates would all be closed and guarded. How Davy himself was to get out was a problem yet to be faced. Certainly the presence of the Rebel sergeant would make it tenfold more difficult. As the moments passed, he began to wish the villain would not return.

But the wish was not granted, for in a short time Half-Hanged bobbed onto the ramparts and flung a pile of clothing down beside Davy.

"Bugger me, Dyvy, we 'ad a bit o' pure luck!" he gloated. " 'Is ruddy Ludship landed squarely on 'is fyce, leavin' nary enough fer 'is own mither to recognize, yet ne'er so much as snagged 'is lyce collar!"

Davy stared aghast at the gorgeous scarlet doublet. "Good Lord, man! I can't wear *his* clothes!"

"An' w'y say ye nay?" demanded Half-Hanged. "Ye can't go flittin' o'er 'ill an' dale in yer birthday suit!" He shook his head aggrievedly. "Damme, an 'twas a messy chore dressin' 'is Ludship in yer rags!"

"My God! Why did you do that?"

Smyth clacked his teeth and gave Davy a sly dig with his elbow.

"Ye are a duffer, but I tolt ye ol' 'Arf-'Anged Smyth was a wily cove! Look 'ere—ain't 'is Ludship o' a build wi' ye? An' wi' 'is fyce mashed in an' in yer silly, wimminish petticoats, 'oo's to s'y it ain't poor Dyvy a-lyin' 'ere, cold an' dead?"

Davy shivered, and this time it was not from the wind. "You're a hellish ghoul, Half-Hanged Smyth!" he rasped. "Yet methinks it may open the gates for us!"

Using strips of the underclothing, Half-Hanged bound up Davy's wounds, then helped him dress in the purloined garments. True, they pinched a trifle at the shoulders and bagged at the waist, but otherwise the fit was adequate. Half-Hanged stood back and viewed the result after the manner of a critical costumer.

"Why, blast me eyes, matey!" he enthused. "I swear ye look more like a gen-yew-wine lud than 'is bloody bashed-up Ludship!"

Davy winced and surveyed himself as best he could. He had never worn such luxurious garments and the clinging sensuousness of silk and lace acted as a balm to his wounded body. As he took a few steps back and forth to test his strength, Half-Hanged knuckled his forelock and made an exaggerated obeisance.

"An' w'at be yer commands, m'lud?" he bumbled, with mock servility.

"We'll get the hell out of here," said Davy grimly, "for if we're caught, you'll be *All*-Hanged Smyth!"

"Ain't it the bloody truth? But 'ow, m'lud?"

Davy had been thinking about it. "Boldness is the only hope. Fortunately, barely a soul here knows either my late master or me, so if we can avoid the castellan, we may, we just *may*, bluff our way past the gate guards. I'll tell them I'm taking you out to show me something or other."

Half-Hanged scratched his close-cropped head. "Bugger me, Dyvy, it sounds like a rum go!"

"Very well—have you a better suggestion?"

Smyth shrugged. "Nay, I can't say that I 'ave, so if ye'll supply the brains, m'lud, I'll supply the brawn."

Davy grunted and, bending over, retrieved the two swords formerly carried by the guard and Lord Ian. He handed Smyth the guard's saber and retained the engraved claymore.

"These may serve if gall doesn't work," he said grimly.

The feel of a stout blade in his hand revived his confidence, and as he started down the long flight of stone steps with Half-Hanged close behind, he began to feel pretty cocky. Arrayed in such a lordly costume, it should be relatively easy to overawe the dull-witted sentries at the gate.

But his optimism was short-lived, for as he came to a bend in the stairway, he saw three armed soldiers examining the body of Ian by the light of a lanthorn!

There was no time to hiss a warning! Davy tied to dodge back out of sight, but Half-Hanged blundered against him, shoving him into the open. A soldier raised his head. . . .

"*Silence them!*" rasped Davy, and dashed down the remaining flight.

Chapter Five

The soldier who had seen them first drew a pistol and fired point-blank at Davy! Though the ball went wild, he was so close the powder stung his face. Off-balance for the moment, Davy tried a cut, but the soldier hurled the empty gun at his head, then, shrieking at the top of his voice, took to his heels. There was no time to pursue him, for the other pair had drawn their blades, and the fight was joined.

However, it was short-lived! Taken by surprise, the two troopers offered only token resistance. Davy spitted his man through the sword arm, and when the fellow begged for quarter, stunned him with a blow from the hilt. Then he turned to find Half-Hanged's opponent stretched on the ground.

But the cat was out of the bag, and even as they stared at each other, a trumpet peeled hysterically from the direction of the main gate, and then the drums began to roll.

Half-Hanged heaved a mighty sigh. "Damme, matey, that does it!"

Davy bit his lip and stared around, trying to orient himself. Already lights were bobbing along the ramparts and flickering across the inner ward.

"Hark man!" growled Davy. "Can you swim?"

"Aye, better'n a ruddy duck!" conceded Half-Hanged. "But w'ere kin we . . ."

"Come on then!" interrupted Davy. "Follow me close, for if we get separated . . ." There was scant need to enlarge upon the disaster.

"Closer'n a shadow!" agreed the other.

Davy broke into a run and cut diagonally across the quadrangle toward the old tiltyard under the shadow of the Keep. As he neared it, several men with lanthorns rounded the buttress. Davy had just time to hiss: "*Down!*" and throw himself full length on the ground.

The soldiers passed within ten paces of where they lay!

The narrowness of this escape set Davy's heart to pounding unmercifully, and when they were gone, he rose and proceeded with more caution. The castle ban-dogs had been loosed now, and he could hear them yelping enthusiastically not far away. He quickened his stride, and in a few minutes reached the edge of the stream that fed the outer moat.

"We'll follow this to the wall," he told Smyth. "If the dogs get your scent, take to the water."

"Be it deep?"

"About a fathom and a half," Davy admitted.

Running as fast as the pain in his side would permit, he followed the bank to the far side of the Keep and thence to the great wall. Then he sank down and explained his plan to Half-Hanged.

"There is a heavy iron water-gate here, but as I remember it, the lowest bars have rusted away. When I was a bairn, I could swim under it."

" 'Ow far down?"

"Nearly two fathoms!"

"Leapin' Jesus!" ejaculated the other. "That's an 'ell of a way, man!"

"Granted! But it's about the same distance they'll drop you from the gibbet if caught! However, if you'll pick up a heavy stone, it'll weight you to the bottom quick enough!" He put one foot tentatively in the water, and the cold made him gasp. " 'S'death! It's like ice! Well, there's naught else for it! Now mark you—I'll go first. You wait one full minute, then follow. But, heed me well—*go deep*, else you'll not make it! The break is near the center, as I recall."

"God grant yer memory's good!" Half-Hanged muttered dubiously. "I ain't no bloody 'errin'!"

Davy chuckled mirthlessly and stood up. He pushed his sword behind him, then chose a heavy stone from the many which lined the stream.

"Luck!" he said. Then, sucking in a deep breath, he dove into the water.

The shock knocked the wind out of him, and he might have turned back save for the stone which carried him downward at a sickening speed. His ears rang with the pressure until he was certain he could bear it no longer. Then he bumped against the silt.

Hanging onto the rock with his left hand, he groped about with his right. Unfortunately, he had misjudged the distance the gate was under the thick wall, and he lost priceless seconds clawing toward it. By the time he did locate the opening, his lungs ached insufferably. Only the knowledge that return meant certain death gave him the will to proceed.

He wriggled his head through the break, as he had done as a child, but the breadth of his mature shoulders was too much. In frantic desperation, he rolled onto his side, and thus managed to force himself between the lowest cross-bar and the silt. Before his hips were clear, he felt his senses slipping. He gave one mighty heave, then shot to the surface.

The first gulp of air seared his lungs like frozen fire. Too exhausted to swim, he floated on his back, gasping for breath. As the numbness left his limbs, he kicked feebly and made his way to the steep bank on the other side of the moat.

He made no effort to climb out, but clung wearily to a projecting root. Even now he assured himself that had he guessed the agony the dive was going to cost, he would never have made it.

With his back to the bank, he watched the black surface of the water, waiting for his companion. But waiting came hard, and as the seconds passed, he began to wonder if the fellow had lost his nerve. No, it couldn't be that, he reflected; this evil jinni who called himself "Half-Hanged Smyth" was devoid of nerves. The fellow had either been taken, had failed to find the opening, or, finding it, had drowned.

Time is comparative, and to Davy, clinging in the icy water to a rotting root, it seemed that hours had passed since he first entered the stream. All his instincts of self-preservation urged him to continue his flight, arguing that he owed nothing to a self-confessed criminal who was also an enemy and a spy. Yet when another minute had rolled away, some impulse stronger than reason impelled him to turn back.

Muttering something that was half-prayer, half-curse, he tossed his claymore away and ducked under the surface. This time he had no rock to hasten his descent, so he had to swim down. Once again his heart and lungs rebelled until, just as he was about to give up, his outstretched hands encountered the body of Half-Hanged wedged in the opening between the bars.

A hasty survey indicated the cause. The fellow had not removed his saber, and the blade had swung sideways, anchoring him firmly.

It seemed certain the man was dead. He did not respond to Davy's touch, but lay inert, like a sack of grain. Reason again insisted it was futile to tarry, yet that unnamed compulsion drove Davy on. He slipped the buckle of the sword-belt, then, wrapping his arm around Smyth's massive chest, he set his feet against the bars and tugged with the last of his strength. For seconds the body remained immovable, then suddenly gave way, and Davy fought with it to the surface.

On the very verge of unconsciousness, he struggled to the bank with his burden. He was quite satisfied it would be impossible for him to lift the heavy body onto the grass, yet in time he did that, too. He rolled the man onto his stomach, with his head hanging over the edge of the moat; then, straddling him, he kneaded the water out of his lungs.

After an interminable time, Half-Hanged Smyth began to choke and sputter. Too spent to continue the treatment, Davy rolled off him and collapsed on the grass. Smyth thrashed his arms about and groaned. Then he raised up on one elbow and began to swear.

" 'Ow the bloody 'ell did I get back 'ere?" he panted. "Couldn't ye myke it neither, y'r Gryce?"

Davy sucked air raspingly into his lungs. "You . . . are . . . not . . . back . . . there!" he managed. "We're . . . outside."

"We be?"

"Aye! Your saber . . . fouled on the . . . gate!"

Smyth sank back on the grass for a few moments. Listening, Davy could hear the shouts of the soldiers combing the castle grounds. It wouldn't be long before the search spread to the outside.

Half-Hanged reared up abruptly. "How'd ye know me saber'd fouled?" he demanded.

"It was obvious."

"Obvious, me arse! Ye came back down an' got me! Don't deny it!"

His seeming belligerence amused Davy. "You'll have to change your name to 'Half-Drowned' Smyth," he jested.

"Bugger me, it ben't no laughin' matter!" persisted Smyth. " 'Ere's ye an' 'ere's me; a ruddy 'Ighland savage an' an 'onest jailbird—enemies by rights. Oh, don't mistyke me, Dyvy; I don't cavil at ridin' wi' ye an' exchanging small favors, such as garrotin' a guard. But arter I try to kill a man, like I did ye, I don't want the ruddy bloke to risk 'is life to syve mine! 'Tain't fittin'."

"Would you prefer I had left you under water?"

Half-Hanged pondered that. "Damme, matey, I can't s'y rightly that I do," he admitted, chuckling. "To speak true, the question befuddles me. 'Tis only that I don't like obligations. They tie ye down, like bein' wedded!"

At that moment they heard the drawbridge rumble down, then a body of horsemen clattered over it, followed by a pack of dogs. Davy staggered to his feet.

"You can set your mind at ease on one score, Smyth—you and I are not wedded! And if you've breath enough for senseless argument, you can use it to better purpose. Let's get out of here!"

"Tyke the lead, Dyvy!" agreed Half-Hanged Smyth.

A brief dash across the open clearing before the walls brought them to a copse of woodland. They had barely scuttled in among the trees when, from the battlements, a trumpet sent out a thin golden summons, whereupon the dogs raised an excited clamor. For one ghastly moment Davy feared they had been sighted, but shortly thereafter, the baying of the hounds seemed to fade in the opposite direction.

Once again they paused. Their sodden clothes were like shrouds of ice and it was impossible to still the chattering of their teeth.

"B-b-bugger m-me, D-D-Dyvy, wi'out 'ors-s-ses . . ." Half-Hanged spread his hands in a gesture of hopelessness. "If w-w-we was on'y i-i-n L-Lunnon, I-I c-c-could steal . . ."

Davy laughed. "London hasn't a monopoly on thieves, Half-Hanged. Cut us a couple of stout cudgels with your dirk, then follow me. I'll show you a few Scottish tricks in that line."

Half-Hanged did as he was bid, then, armed in this primitive fashion, they struck off through the woods as rapidly as their conditions permitted.

However, they had progressed barely a hundred yards when Half-Hanged grabbed Davy's arm. *"Dogs . . . !"*

Davy stopped short, his heart pounding. He dreaded dogs far more than he did men, for a pack of savage ban-dogs could tear a fugitive to shreds before they could be restrained.

For a moment he could hear nothing, but just as he concluded that Half-Hanged had imagined it, his straining ears caught the excited yelp of a hound close by. The cry was peculiarly repressed, as if someone had cautioned the brute to be quiet. Davy almost hoped there was a man holding the dog in leash.

It was futile to attempt to outrun the brute, so Davy set his back against a stout tree and whispered a warning to Smyth to follow suit. They had hardly taken their stations when the huge dog broke cover and, with a triumphant cry, launched himself full at Davy.

Half-Hanged valiantly tried to save him. He stepped forward and started to swing his club—only to have his arm gripped from behind by Davy himself. Then the heavy brute crashed into Davy and carried him to the ground.

Once more Half-Hanged threw himself into the affray, then, to his utter consternation, he heard Davy's voice almost incoherent with laughter.

"Hold, man! It's all right!" More laughter. "Gabriel, you great buffoon! Get off me! Back, fellow, back!"

Watching, open-mouthed, Half-Hanged saw Davy struggle to his knees and wrap his good arm around the shaggy neck of the wolfhound who stood squirming in ecstasy and making little whimpering noises of delight.

A tardy gleam of comprehension flickered in the Rebel's head.

"Bugger me! Be 'at the brute 'oo brung down me 'orse?" he demanded.

At the sound of his voice, the dog whirled, apparently conscious of him for the first time. The sight of a man with a cudgel in his hand, towering above his beloved master, brought a savage snarl. Davy caught him by the ruff.

"Stop it, Gabriel!" he said sternly. "He is my friend!"

The tawny monster subsided grudgingly, his yellow eyes gleaming in the semidarkness.

Davy answered the other's query. "Aye, this is old Gabriel, my faithful bodyguard! Lord, am I glad to see him!"

"H'mmn! 'E 'pears to feel the syme, though I can't s'y as I does! Keep 'im off me throat, that's all I arsk."

Davy grinned. "You two had better make friends so we have no more misunderstandings. Come, Half-Hanged, pat him on the head!"

Half-Hanged took a jaundiced look at the drooling tongue and saber fangs, and grunted.

"Wi' me club, per'aps, but not me 'and!"

No argument could budge him, and on his part, old Gabriel seemed equally adamant against furthering the acquaintanceship. Finally, satisfied that an armed truce was the best he could hope for, Davy sternly admonished them both against any outbreak of hostilities, then, ordering the dog at heel, he continued through the forest.

Within the hour they came to the main high road over which they had traveled such a short time before. Pausing briefly to orient himself, Davy turned westward, and after an exchange of glares, Half-Hanged and Gabriel followed. They trudged another half-league to a place where the road wound through a grove of gnarled old trees. Here, Davy halted.

"This is it!" he announced.

Half-Hanged stared about him. "Damme if I sees any 'orses, or does ye expec' 'em to bob out of the woods like this damn 'ound?"

Davy ignored the gibe. He searched around until he found a tree with a heavy limb that stretched across the road. It was barely higher than the head of a tall rider and almost concealed in foliage.

"Perfect!" he breathed relievedly. Then he explained his plan to his companion.

Half-Hanged heard him out in amazement, then abruptly howled with glee.

"Certes, m'lud, 'tis genius! I'll swear ye're a man fit to ride the ford wi'!" Then, with less enthusiasm: "W'at o' the bloody 'ound?"

"Gabriel sits with me. He's better than another man."

Half-Hanged was dubious. "Bugger me, I on'y 'ope 'e remembers w'at side I'm on w'en the fightin' starts!"

Davy boosted the big hound onto the limb, and then got Half-Hanged to help him up. His wounded side had grown stiff and sore from the night's exertion. Half-Hanged climbed up, whereupon the three of them made themselves as comfortable as possible for the long vigil.

The perch seemed to have been designed for their express purpose: though concealed from the casual view of any unsuspecting traveler, by cautiously parting the branches with their hands, they were able to command an unrestricted view of both approaches.

Davy braced himself against a fork. "We'd better get some sleep," he suggested. "No one is likely to pass this way before dawn, and old Gabe will give us ample warning."

Half-Hanged nodded and closed his eyes, but though tired, Davy did not feel sleepy. He stared at the shadowy outline of his companion and thought of the colorful compliment the latter had given him. *You're a man fit to ride the ford with!* A pithy phrase which implied implicit trust. The narrow fords were the danger points in travel, for it was there a treacherous companion could jostle you to a quick death in the swirling currents. Truly, he thought, as some sage had put it, adversity makes strange bedfellows.

As if meditating the same truism, Half-Hanged opened one eye. "Dyvy, ye befuddle me!" he mused thoughtfully. "By the cut o' yer jib, I'd s'y ye was gentle-born, yet that frog-bellied bastard treated ye as a lackey."

"Which in truth I am, Half-Hanged. I was his groom."

"But, damme, ye be eddicated!"

"Aye. 'Tis the custom of lairds who have only one son to assign a young lackey to be tutored with the heir, as a sort of measuring stick for the tutor. Hence my lord Ian and I were raised almost as brothers when we were young."

"H'mmn! Lan'widges an' sech?"

"That's right. All the accomplishments supposedly necessary for a gentleman—mathematics, astronomy, the use of weapons, and so forth."

"Ah-ha! An' in each one ye bested 'im, didn't ye?"

"Why, I guess I did! Yet why did you say it with such emphasis?"

"Certes, it explains w'y 'e 'ated ye so!"

"Nonsense! We got along splendidly as children!" Davy paused, then amended: "Well, as good as most children, considering the difference in rank."

Half-Hanged chortled cynically. "An' wenches, Dyvy—ye bedded ten to 'is one, I wager?"

"Ian was ill-favored, I own," Davy conceded.

" 'E was betrothed to the earl's darter, I tyke it. Did ye by chanc't put 'orns on 'im 'ere?"

Davy scowled. "Certainly not, you damned scoundrel! I had not seen the lady since . . ."

Half-Hanged laughed. "Easy, lad, easy! Yer dander plainly shows the turn o' yer mind!"

"What in hell are you talking about?"

"Ye be daft about the maid! An' 'tis plain 'is bloody Ludship thought the syme, fer 'e came to the tower wi' murder in 'is eye!"

"Don't be a fool! Ian was enraged because I refused to obey his fiendish commands!"

Half-Hanged exhaled windily. "Dyvy, ye got a blind side! I'll wager last night wasn't the fust time ol' frog-belly sought yer life! Confess it?"

After a long pause, Davy acknowledged the truth of the statement. "Yet I cannot see by what wizardry you knew that!" he concluded.

"Wizardry, me arse!" snorted the other. " 'Tis the w'y o' men! Me, now, I ne'er trusted but one man in my life!"

"Who was that?"

The Rebel tapped his own chest. " 'Arf-'Anged Smyth!" he said emphatically.

Davy laughed in spite of his momentary irritation. Then, anxious to change the subject, he asked, "By the way, how did you ever get that weird name of *Half-Hanged?*"

Smyth chuckled. "S'elp me, Dyvy, 'tis legal—God'strufe! Ye see, 'twas one o' me rare mistykes, fer in my business there ain't room fer error. As it 'appened, I was relievin' an inebriated gent o' a small matter o' four guineas, an' carelessly o'erlooked 'is friends 'oo was close enough to grab me. The judge, 'e gi' me the rope. Yet w'en they come to 'ang me, the ruddy rope parted, an' I waked up in the morgue wi' a stiff neck!" He clucked happily at the memory.

"Damme, lad, 'em turnkeys was bug-eyed, but they couldn't 'ang me agin wi'out the judge say so, so I was carted back to Court. The judge 'e was madder'n a bullock wi' a bean in 'is ear! 'Ye damned scoundrels, I tolt ye to 'ang that knave!' he bawled so 'ard the bailiffs quaked in their boots.

" 'Certes, yer Worship, we did 'ang 'im fair an' square!' they w'ined. Then the judge s'ys, sarcasticlike: ' 'E's dead then, I tyke it?'

"Well, Dyvy, I seen me chanc't, so I spoke up. 'Yer Honor!' I s'ys. 'I been 'anged by the neck, like ye commanded, until the physick swore I was dead! M'y I remin' yer Worship, they on'y crucified the Lud onc't!'

"The judge 'e looked awful stern, then 'e bust out larfin'. 'E fair split a gut, 'e larfed so 'ard! 'Zounds, ye speak true!' 'e s'ys. 'An' 'oo's to s'y ye *ain't* dead, though ye myke a right lively corpse. To my w'y o' thinkin', yer on'y 'arf-'anged! But, damme, if ye tyke yer oath yer dead, 'Arf-'Anged Smyth, I'll accept yer word f'it! Release the corpse from custody!' 'e bellered at the bailiffs."

Half-Hanged spread his hands. "So, Dyvy, 'at's 'ow I got me nyme!"

Davy laughed heartily. "You were lucky, but I wonder what his Honor would have thought had he known you joined the Rebels?"

"Oh-ho, that was part o' the deal!" chortled Smyth. "I was turned over to a recruiter. Ye see, Parliament needed soldiers fer . . ." He stopped abruptly as the wolfhound gave a low growl.

Davy stiffened. "*Horses,* by God!" he whispered. He cautiously parted the foliage and peered eastward along the road.

Three horsemen came trotting toward them, silhouetted against the pale glow of dawn.

Chapter Six

The leading pair, riding stirrup to stirrup, wore the wide plumed hats and polished corselets of the Cavaliers. They were heavily armed and mounted on splendid chargers. Jogging painfully behind them on an ancient galloway was a thin wisp of a lad in the garb of a page. The party advanced at a trot.

Davy braced himself on the limb and flexed his wrist. "Strike true the first time!" he whispered to his companion. "There'll be no second chance!"

As the Cavalier he had marked for his prey drew closer, he let the branches merge together and raised his cudgel.

The last few seconds of waiting were sheer agony, for discovery would mean certain death. Less than a fathom distance away, one of the horses shied and reared on its haunches. Davy was sure the rider would suspect the trap, and he almost hurled himself into the road in his anxiety. But the cavalier only cursed impatiently and dug in his spurs. The big gelding sprang forward. . . .

Then Davy struck!

He felt the blow land, then he lost his own balance and toppled from his perch. As he was falling, he heard a startled oath from the other Cavalier, drowned out an instant later by a ferocious roar from Half-Hanged Smyth. Then he hit the ground so hard he was momentarily stunned.

The guttural snarls of fighting men prodded him to his senses. He raised up on his elbows and looked about him. One Cavalier lay spread-eagled inertly in the center of the road, while along the fringe, the other rolled in deadly combat with the Rebel sergeant. Davy twisted around to look for the page. The little fellow was clinging desperately to his terrified galloway which was being badgered by the wolfhound. Before Davy could call off the dog, the boy was precipitated into the thicket.

"Don't touch him, Gabriel!" Davy commanded, then, satisfied the lad was no menace, he recovered his cudgel and started up to assist Half-Hanged. But that worthy was already rising from his lifeless adversary. Without pausing to speak to Davy, he pounced upon the quaking page.

The boy screamed in terror. "Hout, mon, hout! Dinna take me life!" He appealed to Davy. "Oh, my lord, spare me!"

Davy jumped forward and caught Half-Hanged's dagger wrist. "Hold!" he ordered. "There's no call to kill the bairn!"

The sergeant glowered up at him. "Ye want 'im to tell . . ." he began, to pause at Davy's warning scowl.

Davy walked over and hauled the boy erect. "Do you know who I am, hinny?" he demanded gruffly.

"Aye, aye, sir! Ye be my Lord Ian!" the lad whimpered. "I saw ye when ye called on my mistress!"

Davy whistled softly and turned so that his features remained in the shadow.

"You know the Lady Olivia then?"

"Oh, aye, my lord!" sobbed the boy. "I'm her Ladyship's page!"

Half-Hanged glared at him like a hungry ogre. "If true, w'at in 'ell be ye doin' 'ere?" he thundered.

The youngster shook with terror and clung to Davy. "My mistress commanded that I accompany Sir Walter Cavendish and Sir Edward. I was to bring her news direct, so soon as I learned what had happened to your Lordship."

Davy felt an unexpected pang. "She asked about me by name, I presume?"

"To be sure, my lord! When the groom's body was found, she demanded to see it, but fainted at the gore. It was believed that the Reb . . ." He glanced fearfully at Half-Hanged, and caught himself. "That this *gentleman* carried you away by force, my lord! When she heard a search was to be made for you, she insisted I be taken along!" The boy sniffled. "Sir Walter didn't want me, sir! Be ye going to kill me truly?"

Davy shook his head. "Nay, hinny, we'll not hurt you. Now mount your palfrey and return. Tell your mistress that I left of my own free will and for personal reasons. Tell her, too, that . . . that I was not worthy of her. Can you remember all that, laddie?"

"Oh, aye! Every blessed word of it, my lord! Now—can I go?"

Half-Hanged swore through his teeth. "Not if I had me way, ye couldn't!"

Davy ignored him. Patting the boy reassuringly, he helped him catch his aged nag and remount.

"Go quickly, laddie, and don't look back!" he cautioned. Then he gave the ancient plug a cut across the rump that sent him jogging back along the road.

" 'Tis a mistyke, Dyvy, a bloody mistyke!" persisted Half-Hanged. " 'E'll report . . ."

"That *Lord Ian* is alive, you damned fool!" cut in Davy. "Haven't you the wit to see the advantage?"

Half-Hanged whistled softly. "Bugger me, I'd fergot! 'Twas me very own thought w'en . . ."

"Let's get out of here!" Davy interrupted, and turned away.

The horses had bolted down the road, but had stopped to graze. At an order from Davy, old Gabriel overtook them and herded them back. It was only the work of a moment to secure and tether them. That done, the two fugitives turned their attention to the men lying in the road.

Half-Hanged's victim was dead beyond a shadow of doubt, but the other—the one the page had identified as Sir Walter Cavendish —though unconscious, was alive. Half-Hanged whipped out his poniard, and was seeking a likely spot to insert it without damaging the exquisite tunic which he coveted, when Davy again interfered.

"For shame, you blackguard! Would you murder a helpless man in cold blood?"

Half-Hanged reared back in astonishment. " 'Ow the 'ell does I know w'ether 'is blood be 'ot er cold wi'out stickin' me knife in 'im?" Using his blade as a tutor uses a pointer, he indicated the features of the Cavalier.

"Mark 'at fyce, Dyvy! A snout like a fox, the cruel slant-eyes o' a Spaniard an' the mouth o' a rat! Ye arsk me to spare *that*?"

"I'm not asking, I'm *telling!*" Davy snapped.

Half-Hanged glared a moment, then rose with a shrug. "Blast me, I'll no quarrel wi' a frien' o'er a bloody Cavalier, fer many's the one I've kilt an' no doubt will anon. Yet, m'lud, I trust yer precious scruples will not object to relievin' 'im o' a few trifles from 'is person?"

Davy grinned. "Help yourself," he acquiesced. "I can use a corselet, sword, and a few odds and ends myself."

Thereupon they stripped the Cavaliers of what arms and armor they needed, then, dragging them out of the center of the roadway, propped them against two trees. But as they made ready to mount, Half-Hanged made one more plea to dispatch the surviving Cavalier.

"Dyvy, 'tis a weakness an' a crime to leave an enemy alive!"

Davy made a gesture of ridicule. "Nonsense! He's no enemy!"

" 'E's a goddam Cavalier, 'e is!"

"Aye, and so would I be—had the wind blown the other way."

Half-Hanged pursed his lips and climbed into the saddle. "Bugger me, I'd forgotten that!" He touched spurs to his mount. "Aye, I 'ad forgotten!" he muttered thoughtfully.

Davy paused for one last look at the man whose life he had spared. As Half-Hanged had observed, Cavendish's was a crafty, arrogant face. Davy couldn't be certain, but he thought he detected a perceptible movement of one eye, yet as the man was lying in shadow, he could not swear to it. He assured himself it made little difference, one way or another, so, with a shrug, he cantered after his companion.

They passed the next hour in a silence broken only by the rhythmic clatter of hoof and gear. The burly Rebel had volunteered no word since reminded that Davy was a Royalist, and what his thoughts were could not be read on the curious immobility of his ugly features.

On his part, Davy was too concerned with his own predicament to bother about his companion's cogitations. He had, unwittingly, burned his bridges behind him without giving thought to the future. Now it was imperative that he should. Yet it was difficult to concentrate on the problem, for, peculiarly enough, the vision of a laughing girl with hair of burnished copper kept flitting across his troubled mind. He found himself wondering how she would receive the news of Ian's death. The thought saddened him, though, as for killing the man, he felt no qualms. Ian had proven himself worse than a mad dog; much worse, for his murderous impulses had been prompted by human cunning. Viewed in retrospect, Davy realized what had happened had been inevitable. His concern lay only with the people who would be hurt by the tragedy—old John the Dugald and the Lady Olivia, and, he conceded ruefully, himself.

Half-Hanged asked suddenly, "W'at be ye goin't to do, Dyvy?"

Davy grunted. "I was just wondering that myself. One thing sure—I can't go back to Lochbogie."

"W'y don't ye jine up wi' Parliament?"

"Bah! A batch of rebels!"

Half-Hanged took no offense. "Bugger me, Dyvy, if ye ain't a *rebel* then I mark not the meanin' o' the word!"

"Well, I'm not against the King!"

"Mebbe ye ain't," retorted the other, "but 'tis a bloody certainty the King be against ye!"

Davy winced. "Aye, that I grant you. Yet I cannot agree with the principles of rebellion."

"*Principles*, me arse!" Half-Hanged snorted impatiently. " 'Oo jines an army fer principles, or, if so, 'oo's principles be the syme? Cromwell, 'e fights because 'e don't want to be taxed out o' 'is rights; Ol' Piety, 'e's in arms because 'e wants to cram 'is stiff-necked Presbyterianism down everybody's throat; me, I'm in it fer . . ." He hesitated, fumbling for the correct word.

Davy smiled. "Because, if I recall correctly, the judge gave you a choice of joining or hanging a second time."

"Certes, 'twould be easy to leave 'ad I a mind to! I st'y in because o' the possibilities."

"Of loot? I was told Cromwell was a tough disciplinarian who hanged any soldier caught stealing!"

Half-Hanged winked broadly. " 'Tis the God'strufe, Dyvy!" he declared solemnly. " 'E's a tartar, 'e is! Yet it be amazin' 'ow many *gifts* o' gold an' sterlin' come willin'ly from Royalists w'en certain truths be pointed out to 'em!"

Davy laughed. "Half-Hanged, you're a black-hearted rogue to profit from war!"

"Better a rogue 'an a fool! W'at's different wi' me gettin' a bit o' loot than Cromwell gettin' free taxes or Ol' Piety gettin' 'is w'y wi' the church? Or, fer 'at matter, wi' Charles seekin' 'is throne, or yer own laird graspin' fer honor? Ain't it all the syme—all *greed?*"

Davy stopped smiling and took a long, calculating look at his companion. He had known plenty of lawless, desperate characters in the Highlands, and he was accustomed to varying degrees of villainy, yet never had he encountered anyone comparable to this creature who called himself Half-Hanged Smyth. The fellow was a criminal by his own admission—nay, by his own boast, for he seemed inordinately proud of the dubious distinction of being a thief, murderer, traitor and the Lord only knew what else. Yet withal (or, peradventure because of it) the knave had a certain rough charm about him, and if Davy was repelled by the ugliness and the harsh London accent, he was also aware of the deep, underlying strain of humanness. And now, by a quirk of fate, this man was his only friend!

"Half-Hanged," Davy said slowly, "what you say is undeniably true. I'm in no position to be squeamish. And I'll confess that in the past I've had dreams of leaving the Highlands to seek my fortune where my lowly birth would not brand me a common groom. Sometimes I think it was no kindness for my laird to have given me a taste of life above my station. Yet to join your army as a lowly soldier would be to go back into a worse bondage than I have just left!"

Half-Hanged chuckled. "True, Dyvy, true! I been brownin' the question on both sides o' me mind fer the past hour. Ye seem to 'ave fergot the most important p'int—*ye ain't no common groom!* Y'r Ian o' Dugald, a Scottish laird, an' there's none to say ye nay—that be, if ye don't confide in no wench."

"I hadn't forgotten, but go on!"

"Well, Lieutenant General Cromwell is buildin' 'imself a fancy cavalry, an' 'e's lookin' fer well-born young gents 'oo can command a troop. Wi' me to adwise ye, ye kin become rich an' famous. 'Ow about it?"

"I'll think it over."

Half-Hanged snorted. "Then ye'd better think quick, fer 'ere's the fork in the road!"

Startled, Davy glanced ahead to where the road Y-ed in symbolic fashion. One fork led northward toward the lofty peaks of his beloved Highlands now thrusting their craggy heads into the eternal mists; the other turned toward the Border. In truth it was a time for decision.

He reined to a slow walk. One path led to the familiar, the other into the unknown. In the deep fastness of the Highlands, he could find safety of a kind; doubtless the clan MacKenna would welcome a deserter from the Dugalds. Yet the thought came to him that if he had to become a turncoat, why not play for bigger stakes? Moral squeamishness ill befitted a hunted man, and he might as well be slain for a wolf as a lamb. Then, too, he felt again those deep, half-resentful stirrings barely recognizable as ambition. Why shouldn't he play the laird? He had proved himself a better man than Ian of Dugald time without number! Suppose this ugly monster riding beside him *was* a tempter sent by the devil? What difference did it make now?

He swung sideways in the saddle. The swart, pock-marked face was as sinister as ever, yet behind all that, Davy thought he detected a certain lonely wistfulness.

"Who am I to question destiny?" He laughed. "We'll sink or swim together, Half-Hanged, and here's my hand on it!"

Smyth's dark face glowed. "An' 'ere's mine, matey!" he roared happily, leaning over to envelop Davy's hand in his own huge paw. "Now, methinks if we're to bivouac wi' Ol' Piety this night, we'd best put spurs to these nags!"

Chapter Seven

In the late afternoon a thunderhead began building in the northeast. Scudding clouds overrode the sun, while jagged shafts of lightning scarred the sky. The wind pursued them in howling gusts, one of which whipped Davy's cloak over his head and, at the peak of its fury, held it suspended straight in front of his face like a nun's cowl. Then the rain came. In a matter of minutes, the roadway was transformed into a bog. The riders went from a gallop to a trot, a trot to a walk, eventually to find themselves plodding and floundering through mud in places deep as the stirrups.

"By my troth!" sputtered Davy. "We can't keep this up much longer!"

" 'Tis an ill-favored route," grumbled Half-Hanged, in a voice that sounded as if his head were under water. "Yet if I don't disremember, there's an inn no more'n a league a'ead!"

"God grant your memory is accurate!" Davy said grimly.

With utter disregard for all normal astronomical calculations, an intense darkness closed around the two fugitives at least an hour before its time, and only the lightning served to illumine the treacherous trail. Hence it was nearly ten of the clock before a kindly flash showed them an old hostelry looming beside the road.

It was in truth a dingy hovel, more suitable for the housing of swine than humankind, yet under the present circumstances, it looked a veritable paradise to the sodden travelers. Thin slivers of light were visible behind closed shutters, and during a flare of lightning, they saw smoke swirling from a tottering chimney. The manifest promise of hot food and a warm bed buoyed their flagging spirits, so they spurred their exhausted steeds up to the stoop and bellowed for the ostler.

They bellowed and they bellowed, while the wind picked up their voices and carried them through the outbuildings and into the surrounding forest. Even old Gabriel contributed to the din. Yet though their clamor set the dogs in the kennels to barking and the nags in the stables to neighing, no one answered from the inn.

"Bugger me!" fumed Half-Hanged. "This is passing strange, for I'd swear I 'ear 'em stirrin' inside!"

"I'll make damn sure they hear me!" vowed Davy, flinging himself out of the saddle—only to drop into a mud-hole that poured water over the top of his jackboots.

This accident did not improve his temper, so he drew his sword and beat the hilt against the door.

Still it was not opened!

Davy stepped back to ponder. It was impossible that the inmate had failed to hear his thumps, for he had all but split the panel. It was equally improbable that the place was deserted, with the lanthorns burning and a fire blazing in the hearth. He bent his ear to the jamb, and this time he plainly heard someone moving just beyond the door.

His temper flared. Cupping his hand over his mouth, he bellowed, "Hallo, inside! We are two gentlemen seeking bed and board, and intend to have it! Unless this door is opened immediately, we'll blow it off its hinges!"

That did it! A hoarse male voice shouted sullenly through the panel.

"Gang awa' wi' ye! Dinna commit violence on the house o' an honest mon!"

"Then open this damned door!" Davy yelled back. "We require shelter!"

"Nae, nae! Ye'll no find shelter here!" came the reply, in a thick Lowland dialect which even Davy had difficulty understanding. "Better gang farther than faur waur! Ye canna set foot inside!"

"By the Gods, we'll see about *that!*" trumpeted Davy. "The carabine, comrade, and load it with a double charge!"

This time he was in earnest. But before Half-Hanged could comply, the bolt grated and the door opened a few inches, further swinging being prevented by a heavy guard-chain. The silhouette of a man's head appeared in the crack.

"Fer the love o' God, stranger, gang awa' in peace!" pleaded the terrified inmate. "Me puir house ha' been taken o'er by the de'il hissel', an' there's naught I can do aboot it!"

"I'd face the devil in his own hell rather than suffer longer in this purgatory!" raged Davy. "Open up!"

The host groaned as if he were on the rack. "Oh, the injustice o' it!" he wailed to no one in particular. "A foul fiend ha' taken the *inside* o' mae puir house an' turneth it into shambles, an' now cometh twa 'oo threaten to tear down the *outside!*"

"W'at the bloody 'ell be 'e cacklin' about?" demanded Half-Hanged. "Myke the cove spout decent English, Dyvy!"

"Come, come, host!" chided Davy. "What's all this nonsense about foul fiends and devils? We want naught but a place to lay our heads and victuals for our bellies. We mean you no harm, *unless* . . ." His voice grew stern again. ". . . unless you keep us standing longer in this accursed storm!"

"Woe is me!" whimpered the host, glancing furtively behind him. "If I thought ye could rid me o' this Bull o' Bashan w'at hae inflicted himsel' onto us like a plague, I'd gi' ye anything ye ask o' me!" Then a native frugality overcame his terror sufficiently to modify his generosity. "That be—anything wi'in reason!"

"Leapin' Jesus!" exclaimed Half-Hanged, who only comprehended an occasional word. "Did 'e s'y there be a *bull* loose inside? Lor' luv us, Dyvy, mebbe we'd best nest in the stables!"

Davy chuckled despite his discomfort. "Throw wide the door, honest landlord!" he shouted. "I'm a veritable Saint George when it comes to slaying dragons! Open it, I say, and if this Bull of Bashan gores me, then on my oath, I bequeath you my horse and gear!"

Upon that, the host unhooked the chain and bowed them inside.

"Yer a wilful mon, sir!" he said, in a dejected voice not untouched with hope. "May the Lord favor ye, though I pairsonally wash my hand o't! Leave yer 'orses there, an' I'll try to coax me bairn out o' hidin' long enough to take care o' 'em! The dog can go to the kennels." He eyed the dripping hound.

"The dog stays with me!" Davy said flatly. "As for the nags, see to it they are well fed and bedded. They've had a hard day and will have a harder one tomorrow."

"If ye live to see tomorrer," muttered the host. "Did I ken ye correctly that if ye both should di', I keep *both* horses?"

"Why, you blood-sucking ghoul!" flared Davy. "If you are contemplating murder . . ."

"Nae, nae, God perish the thought, sir!" protested the host. " 'Tis on'y the danger's so great, I deemed it but fair to consider the ee-ventualities! Now, 'tis mae understandin' o' the laws of inheritance . . ."

"A pox on your understanding!" Davy cut him off. "Go bring us food and a bottle of your best Burgundy!"

The host, who in the light turned out to be a wispy little gnome with a curious crabwise gait about him, wrung his hands distractedly.

"Lord save us, sir, there's nary a drap o' Burgundy, claret, nor other vintage o' the grape! E'en the ale an' mead be gone—all down the gullet o' this uncircumcised Philistine 'oo's debauched the premises o' honest Angus MacKiver, w'ich, gent'men, be mae!"

Davy grunted, and looked about him. The main chamber of this caravansary was a large, rectangular room with a fireplace at either end, each with a good-sized table and benches in front of it. But what struck Davy as most peculiar was the disorder in an otherwise orderly establishment. The larger of the two tables was cluttered with dirty dishes and overturned ale-mugs, while the floor was a litter of broken bottles and the bones of seemingly countless fowl and swine. It resembled the aftermath of a prolonged drunken banquet, but the remarkable point was—there was only a *single* place setting!

"Ah!" breathed Davy softly. "I see the bull has wined and dined!"

"Aye, aye, an' a black cast to 'is ill-faured face!" sobbed the host. "Now 'e sleeps it off like a sloth, on'y to begin o'er again in a few hours until he eats mae oot o' house an' hame!"

"If he sleeps, why in heaven's name don't you capture him, man! Surely a Lowland Scot doesn't fear one man more than ruin?"

"He's nae mon, but de'il!" protested the publican. "Furthermair, he's got mae auld wifey locked in a closet in his chamber, an' the outer door barricaded. He threatens to ki' her if disturbed!"

Davy laughed and spread his cloak before the fire. "Well, Angus, we'll not jeopardize your good spouse by disturbing this ogre until he awakens. Then, on my oath, we'll dispute the matter with him! Now rustle up some sustenance and what liquid refreshments still remain."

As the tearful host skipped out to the scullery, Davy dropped onto a bench, and pulling off his boots, emptied them of water. Half-Hanged shed his outer garments, then, placing his bared sword on the table close to hand, settled down to await the promised meal. Gabriel had already found a feast on the floor.

"W'at myke ye o' the loon, Dyvy?" chuckled Half-Hanged. "Damme, it sounds like the daft old tales o' giants an' dragons!"

Davy stretched his legs toward the blaze and wiggled his toes.

"Faugh! It is probably naught but some bully-boy who has terrified the old coot out of his wits," he said indifferently. "Doubtless when he awakens, he'll sneak out the back way without paying his reckoning."

Half-Hanged scratched his head. "W'ich reminds me, Dyvy—'oo's to p'y *our* reckonin'?"

Davy grinned. "Why, this Bull of Bashan, of course! You heard honest Angus swear he'd give us anything—within reason, of course—if we rid his house of this devil? Well . . . ?"

Half-Hanged looked at him with a new note of respect. "Bugger me, Dyvy lad, y'r a true-blue gem!"

"Which reminds *me*, Half-Hanged, from now on you better drop that 'Dyvy' stuff! Henceforth, my name is *Ian*—Ian of Dugald! And don't you forget it!" He swung his legs under the table. "Ah, here's our honest host with food!"

MacKiver pranced over to their table with a tray of warmed-over venison collops and other welcome remnants of food. Despite his previous pessimism, he had managed to locate a flagon of ale, upon which Half-Hanged fastened eagerly. Then, while they attacked the meal, he straddled the bench beside Davy and enumerated his troubles in great detail.

Stripped of all superstitious verbiage, his tale was simply that two nights previously, a desperado had galloped up to the inn on a massive cavalry charger and demanded bed and board. On being admitted, he had forced MacKiver to bar the doors and refuse entrance to all, either transients or locals. When MacKiver's son, a husky lad of twenty, had resisted the demand, he had been beaten insensible for his pains. After that, the terrified publican had submitted, praying at stolen moments that the Lord would remove the glutton before his stock was consumed and his trade ruined. It was Master MacKiver's considered opinion that the dastard was English, not only because of his accent, but because Angus was certain no Scotsman would be guilty of such barbarous cruelties—and such wanton waste.

"Aye," concluded the publican, "an' the Scant-o'-grace says to me: 'Host, if this dung-pit was close to London town, ye'd be braggin' o' entertainin' Michael Hogge!' "

"*Michael Hogge!*" gasped Half-Hanged Smyth, rising so abruptly he overturned his bench. "D'ye s'y—*Michael Hogge?*"

"Aye, so I kenned," said the Scot. "Though, de'il take it, the name meant naught . . ."

Half-Hanged leaned over the table. "Damn w'at ye thought!" he interrupted. "Tell me—be 'e a black-bearded ruffian above a fathom tall?"

MacKiver nodded vigorously. "Oh, aye, aye! A fathom an' a half, if an inch, I trow!"

"Wi' a burn-scar across 'is nose an' cheeks, drawn tight like a marsk?"

"Aye—a mask wi' holes fer his eyes what shoot fire!"

Half-Hanged righted his bench and sat down. "Bugger me, 'tis 'im!" he told Davy. "It be Michael Hogge, 'is ownsel'! I kin 'ardly believe it!"

"You seem impressed," Davy observed drily. "Apparently you know the knave."

"*Know* 'im? Certes, an' everybody wi'in fifty leagues o' Lunnon knows o' 'im!" Half-Hanged retorted soberly. "This Michael Hogge, 'oom we calls *Piggey*, be a col'-blooded killer w'at e'en the justices shy clear o'! Fer more'n ten years w'at I knows of, 'e's terrorized the night-life o' Lunnon an' the surroundin' towns! 'Tis said 'e exacts a private taxation on all the brothels an' gamin' 'ouses in Southwark un'er a secret agreement wi' the lord mayor!"

Davy sniffed. "If he's such a successful terror in London, what's he doing up here in the Lowlands? Doubtless this bully-boy has assumed the name."

Half-Hanged wagged his head. "The description, Dy . . . I mean, *Ian!* There's no mistakin' 'im wi' that marsk. 'Tis rumored 'e was borned full-grown, fer nobody can find out w'ere 'e come from; 'e just appeared. 'E's a fightin' fiend, 'e be, an' there's naught but *one* man in the south o' England 'oo'll stand up to 'im!"

Davy glanced across the table. "And that man is . . . ?"

" 'Arf-'Anged Smyth," conceded the sergeant modestly.

76

Davy laughed heartily, and was about to frame a suitable comment when from the floor above came a roar like a clap of thunder.

"Host! Where in the seven hells is the crawling varmint? *Host,* you spidery bastard! Answer me!"

MacKiver began to shake until he set the dishes on the table to rattling.

"Hout, stir, hout, stir!" he sobbed *sotto voce.* "Pairhaps ye'd best flee the wrath, good sirs . . ."

"I flee no potvaliant bully!" Davy announced flatly.

"*Host!* By the Mass, I'll flay the skin off your mangy hide!" bellowed the man above, clumping toward the head of the stairs.

"Aye, master, aye!" bleated MacKiver, skipping across the room. "Bide where ye be! I'm coming!"

"Don't tell *me* where to bide, you craven whelp!" stormed the unwelcome guest, tromping down the stairs. "Rouse up some wine, and, as you value your life, let it be better than that mare's urine you offered last time!"

The little host kept hopping from one foot to the other.

"God luv ye, sir! I hae no wine!"

"Ale, then! Damn you, there'd better be ale!"

Meanwhile, Half-Hanged had drawn his pistol and picked up his sword.

"Ye stan' aside an' let me 'andle this," he said grimly. "I be the on'y man in England w'at kin tyke 'im!"

Davy sternly ordered him to sit down. "You're not in England, Half-Hanged! This is my pleasure."

Before he could argue the point, the subject of their dissertation hove into view.

Davy leaned forward for a better look, and what he saw would have quickened the pulse of a much more seasoned brawler than Davy of Dugald.

It wasn't only that this Michael Hogge was a big man; he had a knack of seeming bigger than he was. Several factors, shrewdly utilized, combined to further this illusion, such as the slight stoop to the broad shoulders, as if in constant readiness to charge, the trick of impatiently rising up and down on heel and toe, and the aggressive jut of the shaggy black beard which, in turn, gave him the appearance of sighting along the bridge of his scarred nose as one would sight a harebusque. The only portion of his face visible between the top of the beard and the unkempt tangle of salt-and-pepper hair—worn over the forehead and trimmed even with his brows—was a swath of scar-tissue, manifestly from an old burn, which stretched like a taut parchment mask from ear to ear. As for the eyes, Davy could conceive of no more fitting metaphor than "burning ice," for contradictory as it sounds, they seemed to blaze while retaining the chilling quality of a shark's eyes.

So hard did he concentrate on this hideous visage, he barely noticed that the fellow's dirt-stained garments bore a vague resemblance to a military uniform, or that he had a long poniard thrust in his belt.

During this appraisal, the publican was chanting in a voice like the squeak of a stepped-on mouse: "Nae more ale! Nae more ale! Nae more ale!"

If Michael Hogge was aware of the two adventurers, he gave no sign. His attention seemed riveted on the huge flagon standing on the table between them. The silence grew portentous.

"What's that you said, host?" Hogge shouted, so suddenly little Angus almost swooned with fright. "*No more ale?* Why, damn my eyes, if I don't see a flagon on yon table!" He started across the room, flipping his arm to shake off the restraining hands of the terrified publican.

As he neared the table, Davy calmly reached for the flagon and raised it to his lips.

"Put that down!" Hogge roared at him. "All the ale in this swill-house belongs to me!"

Davy paused with the flagon in mid-air. "Why, you're welcome to it," he said mildly, "for in truth it is only fit for a hog!" And, with a backhand motion, he flung the contents in the other's face.

Hogge leapt backwards in a jump that carried him halfway across the room, where he stopped to wipe his smarting eyes. The only sound in the place was the patter of the host's feet as he danced from one foot to the other.

Michael Hogge looked at Davy, and smiled his terrible smile. "By the Mass, what a pretty little fribble!" he jeered. "And Half-Hanged Smyth, as well! Why, I thought you were some wench Smyth had picked up along the wayside! Methinks before I kill you, I'd best open your britches to make certain!"

"This will be your last opportunity," Davy told him. "Yet there's no

78

doubt what *you* are, though I swear it will be the first time I've ever butchered a swine with a sword!"

Hogge chortled delightedly. "Spunky little cockerel, by the powers!" He casually removed his tunic and flexed his arms. "Well, mine host, I'll carve up some tender meat for those half-starved mongrels howling in their kennels!"

Half-Hanged made one more attempt to intercede. "Fer the luv o' God, let me 'andle 'im! 'E's a perfessional fighter! Best put a pistol ball through 'is ruddy 'ead, I s'y!"

"For shame!" scoffed Davy. "A gentleman never resorts to a pistol when a sword can be used, though I confess a whip would be more fitting when dealing with a blackmailer of pimps and a scurvy whelp who shields himself behind old wives."

Hogge's smile vanished as a dark flush suffused his face. He drew his long poniard and hefted it as a sword.

"Now, pretty boy, we'll see what's inside you save wind! *En garde!*"

Davy was mildly surprised at the phrase, for it suggested the scoundrel had the effrontery to assume this was a duel rather than a common tap-room brawl.

"Carve away, bully-boy!" he taunted, and easily parried Hogge's first thrust.

Instead of killing him at once, Davy decided first to humiliate him thoroughly. But the disparity of the weapons made Davy careless, and before he quite realized what had happened, Hogge's point touched his shoulder. While it did no damage, it was much too close for comfort and proved that his opponent not only had an abnormally long reach, but was, in all truth, an accomplished swordsman.

Momentarily taking the defensive, Davy re-evaluated the other. He noted the man's hands, unusually long and expressive, and the unconscious grace of his motions, now that he was no longer posing. He recalled the incongruous softness of voice and, by a sort of delayed reaction, remembered that the loud blusterings had seemed affected. Adding up these factors, it came to Davy with something of a shock that Michael Hogge, despite Half-Hanged's lurid biographical sketch, must have been born and bred a gentleman!

This realization altered Davy's tactics, for if his assumption was correct, this character who called himself Michael Hogge could be doubly dangerous. He moved smoothly into the attack, but Hogge parried competently and snapped back a *riposte* that sent him leaping backwards.

Davy smiled. "Ah, I wasn't aware that hogs studied Saint-Didier!" he taunted, referring to the man considered to be the father of the French school of ducling.

Hogge glowered. "It is none of your damn business what I've studied!" he retorted savagely, forgetting his swaggering idiom. He lunged into a fresh assault.

Satisfied that his guess had been a good one, Davy decided to end the affair as soon as possible while he still had the advantage of blades. He forced the pace until he saw an opening, then drove a hard cut which, when parried, snapped Hogge's poniard at the hilt.

"Finish 'im!" Half-Hanged howled jubilantly. "Slice 'is bloody throat!"

Angus MacKiver was hopping up and down, clapping his hands. "Oh, that mae auld wooman could only see this!" he squealed.

That Michael Hogge expected the *coup de grâce* was patent. He hurled the useless hilt aside and stood his ground. But Davy only prodded him onto the bench.

"Now, landlord, some rope!" he ordered.

"Oh, aye, aye, sir!" shrilled MacKiver, hysterical with joy. "We'll hang him from the rafter dain by the ither fireplace so's nae to block yon door an' interfere wi' trade!" He hop-skipped on his mission and soon returned with three fathom's length of rope.

"Hout, stir, hout!" he cried. "Dinna hang 'im until I release mae auld wifey, fer I want she should see the muckle pretty sight!" He sidled around Davy and spat in Hogge's face.

Davy shoved him roughly away. "None of that!" he growled. "And you need not disturb your wife, for there'll be no hanging tonight."

MacKiver gaped in disbelief. "Nae hangin'? But the rope . . . ?"

"To bind him securely so I can have a good night's rest."

"God save us, sir!" protested the publican, with growing horror. "What then?"

"Why, then," laughed Davy, "after a hearty breakfast, we'll hold a drum-head court-martial and decide his fate."

MacKiver fell on his knees and clasped his hands in supplication.

"May the dear Lord bless ye, sir, dinna leave the foul fiend li' the nicht!" he wailed. "His master the de'il hissel' weel rend the ropes an' we'll a' be mairdured in our beds. Fer mae ain sel', I care na' a boddle, but think ye o' mae puir wifey . . ." He became so choked with emotion he could not continue.

Davy glanced at Hogge. "How about that? If we leave you live 'til morn, will you summon your master the devil to free you?"

Hogge made a grimace of disgust. "If you expect me to beg mercy, you are wasting your ill-timed humor," he said coldly. "Howbeit, as a mere statement of fact, now that I'm sober for the first time in days, the very sight of this caterwauling jackal and his filthy kennel nauseates me so I'd as leave hang as spend another night in this sty."

Davy chuckled. "Doubtless we can oblige you in the morning, Michael Hogge." He saw the publican working up to another torrent, so he headed him off. "No more, honest Angus; the trial is adjourned. Get you gone and prepare a suitable chamber for my companion and me. I'll be responsible for the prisoner."

While MacKiver flitted off to release his spouse, who was now clamoring loudly in a closet above, Davy bound his quarry hand and foot, then locked him in the wine-cellar, which, for economic reasons, was the stoutest chamber in the caravansary. Stationing old Gabriel on guard outside the door, Davy finished the ale and went to bed.

Half-Hanged, while vociferously elated by Davy's swordsmanship, insisted it was a mistake to leave the legendary Piggey alive. He swore he would be unable to sleep under the same roof with the desperado, rope and wolfhound notwithstanding. Yet ere the candle had been snuffed five minutes, he was snoring lustily. Stimulated by the brawl, Davy lay awake a few moments longer before he, too, drifted off.

Chapter Eight

Shortly after daybreak, Davy awoke to find his body stiff and sore and his wound throbbing from the exertion of the previous evening. He raised his head with a groan, wondering why Half-Hanged wasn't in the bed beside him, to discover his redoubtable comrade-in-arms sleeping in a chair set facing the door. He was holding a pistol in a limp hand which trailed on the floor and his sword lay across his lap.

Davy chuckled, braced himself up on his elbows, and yelled at the top of his voice, "*Look out, Sergeant!*"

Half-Hanged bellowed, set off the pistol—which blew a hole through the door large enough to take his head—and toppled backward, shouting: "I'll get 'im! I'll get 'im!"

Davy laughed so hard he forgot his aches and pains. The pistol shot had touched off a commotion downstairs, and soon the quivering voice of the host was asking what had happened. As Half-Hanged was still befuddled, Davy did the answering.

"A stout breakfast, mine host! And hurry it!"

Half-Hanged paused on his hands and knees to stare reproachfully at Davy.

"Bugger me, friend, 'at was a foul jest to play on a comrade! I might ha' shot ye!"

Davy whooped delightedly and finished his toilet, then, girding on his arms, marched downstairs. Angus MacKiver had two places set at the table, but Davy demanded a third.

"By my troth, honest Angus, we can't try a prisoner on an empty stomach!"

"Nae, mon, nae!" protested the host. "Dinna waste precious victuals on a mon aboot to hang! 'Tis muckle sinful, an' against the

Gospel, w'ich sayeth: *Waste nae, want nae!*" He cocked his head. "An' 'oo's to pay fer it, sir?"

Davy made a gesture of largess. "Faugh! Just add it onto our reckoning, if it please you, landlord!"

"Aye, aye!" piped Angus, and scuttled out of the room before Davy could change his mind.

"Bowels o' God, man!" groaned Half-Hanged. "Be ye balmy in the crumpet? Ha' ye figgered 'oo's to p'y our reckonin'?"

Davy grinned. "First things first, my stout comrade! Get you hence and bring up the prisoner."

Half-Hanged departed on his errand and soon returned with Michael Hogge, still tightly bound and flanked by the wolfhound. Then ensued another bitter argument with the publican when Davy insisted on removing the bonds. MacKiver compromised by squatting directly behind Hogge, all during the meal, with a huge musketoon aimed at the man's back.

Finally Davy pushed aside the empty dishes. "Now, I trow, 'tis time for Madame Justice to have her say! Gentlemen—what is your pleasure?"

"Ye promised to hang him!" yelped Angus MacKiver.

"Best slit 'is ruddy gullet," grunted the sergeant. "'Angin' doesn't allus tyke!"

Davy laughed. "You should know about that, Half-Hanged! What's your vote, Michael Hogge?"

Hogge appraised him sourly. "Just get me out of this sty, and I care not what happens."

Davy stroked his chin with mock judiciousness. "The opinions differ, gentlemen. Perhaps we'd best turn the case over to the local authorities. Honest landlord, have you decided precisely what crime has been committed?"

"W'*at* crime?" bleated the landlord. "Ye maunna jest! Dinna I tell ye he's eaten mae victuals an' swilled mae wine . . ."

"Hardly a crime, host!" Davy cut in. "Since you operate a public house."

"Hoot, hoot! He hae nae paid his reckonin'!"

"But he hasn't departed, host! It isn't customary to pay the reckoning until one is ready to leave!"

MacKiver's eyes stood out of his head. "Mairciful God, sir, dinna he abuse mae puir auld wifey an' lock her in a closet?"

83

Davy looked somberly at the prisoner. "H'mmn! *That* is serious! What say you to the charge, Michael Hogge?"

Deep in the sullen eyes of Hogge was a faint twinkle. "Aye, 'tis true I locked up the old termagant," he conceded, "but it was merely to escape her odious attentions. She wanted to bed me, so in order to sleep in peace, I was forced to lock her in the closet."

MacKiver howled in rage and would have discharged the musketoon had Half-Hanged not disarmed him

"A domnable lie, a domnable lie!" shrieked the distraught host "Mae good woman hae nae bedded e'en *mae* in seven years!"

Davy and Half-Hanged roared, and even Hogge's mouth twisted into a faint smile.

"Nevertheless, you'll be hard put to disprove my story before a justice," he told MacKiver

Davy agreed. "Look you, honest Angus, methinks that under the circumstances you'd best let this man settle his reckoning and call it quits."

MacKiver had tears of frustration coursing down his cheeks, yet his eyes squinted shrewdly.

"Woe threefold to me!" he moaned. " 'Tis ill-fittin' I should be bleezin' an' blastin' aboot mae puir spouse, an' i' he gie me proper monies, why I'll submit, fer there'll be sma' sorrow at our partin'!" He stopped his sniffling and began loudly adding up the account, charging off, in addition to food and drink, such items as damage to the premises, losses due to trade turned away—imaginary and real— with a sizable amount put on for loss of dignity.

He was still going strong when Hogge interrupted impatiently: "Oh, hold your tongue, you blathering jackanapes! I have no money, and if I had, I'd not pay you a farthing!"

"The law . . . !" wailed MacKiver, but Hogge silenced him.

"The law is explicit on that point! Since I am being ejected before the termination of my intended sojourn, and without due cause, I am obligated to pay nothing!"

Angus was stunned by this reasoning. Davy laughed again.

"As to the strict legality of this, mine host, I cannot say, but it looks like a long and *expensive* litigation. I think it would be cheaper for you if we just took him down the road and dropped him like a stray cat."

MacKiver objected shrilly, but when Davy threatened to wash his hands of the whole affair and leave Hogge in the place, he tearfully accepted. He sent an urchin to get their horses and meanwhile busied himself in an adjoining room. By the time the youngster brought the nags to the door, he pranced out with a lengthy reckoning which he presented to Davy.

Davy stared aghast. "'Pon my soul, what's *this?*" he thundered. "Did you not give your oath as an honest publican that should we rid your hovel of an unwelcome guest, you'd give us anything we wanted?"

The little host looked about to faint. "Mairciful God, 'oo's to pay fer all . . ." Emotion gagged him.

"You ungrateful leech!" growled Davy. "Only a soft heart prevents me from submitting *our* reckoning, for my comrade and I do not travel the countryside fighting other people's battles for naught! Now, if you wish to *exchange* accounts, 'tis all right with me, though you'll find ours the greater."

"Eneuch!" shrieked MacKiver. "Eneuch said! I hae been beset by rogues! Awa' wi' ye—an' the curse o' the MacKivers e'en unto your children's children!" He shooed them outside and slammed the door. And even as they mounted, they could hear him sobbing beyond the panel.

After the deluge of the previous night, the road was rutted and boggy, so they rode the center ridge in single file. Half-Hanged took the lead, followed by Michael Hogge, with Davy bring up the rear. For the first mile they traveled in silence, but when they reached a stretch firm enough to ride abreast, Davy spurred up close behind the bearded man and called softly, "My lord, if you please?"

The latter turned in his saddle and said, "Yes?" before he realized he had been trapped. Then an angry flush darkened the scar-tissue.

Davy rode up beside him. "Peace, man!" he said placatingly, glancing ahead to make certain Half-Hanged was beyond hearing. "Your secret is safe with me. I was just satisfying myself on a point I suspected last night."

"You will have to remain satisfied," growled the man who called himself Michael Hogge. He said nothing for several minutes, then, "Under the circumstances, I presume I'm in your debt, though the issue is as yet unresolved. May I inquire what you intend doing with me?"

85

Davy shrugged. "I hardly know, for to speak true, I have no definite plans of my own. I take it, from your garb, you are a Rebel deserter?"

Hogge gave him an oblique glance. "There's no harm in conceding that," he observed drily, "since, by the same token, you appear to be a Royalist renegade."

"*Touché!*" laughed Davy.

At this point the road had widened again, and Half-Hanged dropped back to join them. Conversation ceased, but as silence was intolerable to the loquacious sergeant, he commenced talking to the prisoner in a fashion that put Davy in mind of two strange dogs, for their figurative stiff-leggedness and tentative sniffings soon gave way to happy tail-wagging as they began discussing mutual acquaintances in London. Before long they were roaring and laughing over the manner in which they had gulled the Scottish landlord.

Though Davy took no part, he listened with increasing interest. Michael Hogge's observations about politicians and generals, about battles and campaigns, marked him for a man of shrewdness and wide experience. Whatever the mystery of his birth and unsavory record as a criminal, he manifestly knew his way around and saw things with eyes uncolored by illusions or idealism. It came to Davy that Hogge possessed certain characteristics which neither he nor Half-Hanged Smyth could hope to attain, and if these traits made him a desperado capable of any crime, they might by the same token be invaluable in the reckless course Davy was planning for himself. This Michael Hogge was just the type of unprincipled bravo Machiavelli had so strongly recommended to an ambitious prince.

"Look you," Davy said to him abruptly, "how would you like to throw in with me? I'm out to make my fortune, and in our mutual friend Half-Hanged Smyth, I have one loyal and amoral rogue. I might be able to use another."

A flash of surprise crossed Hogge's face, which he quickly covered with a mocking bow.

"You flatter me, sir! I understood you were on your way to join the army of Parliament. If you'll pardon a touch of cynicism, you'll find scant *fortune* there!"

Half-Hanged had been momentarily shocked into silence, but he soon found his voice.

"Bugger me, Piggey, Ian's a bleedin' lud, 'e is!"

Hogge arched his brows. "*Is* he now? Fascinating!"

Davy reddened in spite of himself. "I'm offering you your life, you scoundrel!"

"An object of small value," jeered Hogge. "However, your suggestion intrigues me if for only one thing."

"And that . . . ?"

"The opportunity of killing you!" When he saw the expression on their faces, Hogge laughed. "Oh, don't misunderstand me, my fine feathered friends! I speak naught of murder. But the *affaire d'honneur* of last night ended in a stalemate. I would like to resume it under more equitable circumstances and wipe out the stain on my honor!"

Davy smiled thinly. "You mean *pride*, not honor, you rascal!"

Hogge bowed. "I stand corrected," he admitted. "Yet I dislike being under obligation to a man. In the meantime, if I can serve you . . . ?" He spread his hands. "Consider me your most faithful servant, *my lord!*"

Davy winced. "Let's drop that *my lord* stuff!" he growled.

Hogge met his eyes. "On condition the agreement is mutual! Do we understand each other?"

Davy nodded shortly. "Aye, we do! Then you'll cast your lot with us?"

Michael Hogge patted his empty scabbard. "To the death!" He chuckled sardonically.

Chapter Nine

The trio maintained a stiff pace all day until, about sunset, they topped a small rise to see the hamlet of Doughadee nestled at the confluence of two swift streams. Half-Hanged signaled them to put their sweating horses into a walk.

"Yonder be the mill w'ere Ol' Piety's billeted," he explained, indicating an ancient structure balanced beside the smaller of the streams. "Ye gents 'ad better let me do the talkin'. Tyke yer cues from me."

Davy chuckled. "You think you're the better liar, Half-Hanged?"

Smyth took that as a compliment. "Aye! Any fool can tell the truth, but it tykes a smart man to tell a good lie! The on'y ones ye 'ave to be on guard wi' be Ol' Piety an' the miller."

"What's the miller got to do with the Roundheads?" demanded Davy.

Half-Hanged winced. "Don't use that word! 'Tis a capital crime in the Parliamentary army!"

"I'm sorry! I know naught of its significance."

" 'Tis a scurrilous epithet coined by the Royalists," Smyth explained, " 'oo clym our noble army be made up o' crop-'eaded felons from the Lunnon prisons! A dastardly lie!"

Davy winked at the grinning Hogge. "Aye, I'm sure it is!" he agreed with the sergeant. "Now, about this miller . . . ?"

"Aye, Colin Ramsay! 'E clyms to be a *Dissenter*, meanin' 'e don't believe in either Episcopacy, Popery nor Presbytry! 'E's a bloody atheist, if ye arsk me, but 'e's a frien' o' the lieutenant general."

"Cromwell? I thought he was a rabid covenanter."

Half-Hanged shook his head. "Rumor, lad, idle rumor! 'Is Excellency's a most tolerant man, w'ich be part o' 'is quarrel wi' Parliament,

'oo wants the army governed by bloody gospel-'owlin' preachers—
the mealy-mouthed bastards!"

"We'll watch the miller," Michael Hogge cut in. "What's the story
on this other menace—Old Piety?"

"Bugger me, I'd no call the major a *menace*," Half-Hanged went
on, "though 'tis true 'e's a strict, God-fearin' member o' the Kirk.
Jee-zus, 'e's strict! 'E don't stan' fer no lootin' nor swearin', an' he talks
like 'e swallowed the Bible, fer it keeps a-runnin' out o' 'is mouth
day an' night, like 'e 'ad the bloody flux. Hence, we calls 'im Ol'
Piety."

"An obvious pun," sniffed Hogge.

Davy laughed. "It's paradoxical, I trow, to hear you speak of such
a character with affection, Half-Hanged!"

Smyth shrugged. "Damme, lad, I measures a man like I does an
'en—'tain't the cacklin' but the eggs w'at counts! Ol' Piety vomits
enough scripture to gag ye, I own, but 'e's 'ooman fer all't!" He sighed
heavily. "Howbeit, if 'e found we'd gulled 'im, we'll all 'ang from the
nearest tree."

"An interesting prospect," Hogge observed cynically. "I'm surprised you're willing to chance it, Smyth!"

The sergeant chuckled. "Bugger me, lads, 'tis the fust step toward
fame an' fortune!"

"I hope you're as good a prophet as you are a liar!" Davy said,
smiling.

They had reached the narrow bridge crossing the larger stream by
this time and were challenged by the sentries—two mounted dragoons. These, on recognizing Smyth, greeted him with ribald camaraderie, to which Half-Hanged retorted in kind. After ascertaining
that Major Priety was at the mill, the three adventurers proceeded
in that direction.

As they walked their horses down the single, tree-shaded street,
Davy counted better than fourscore dragoons loafing in front of the
cottages where they were evidently billeted. And while most of them
were rough-looking fellows, doubtless a "company of pewterers and
poulterers," as the Royalists contemptuously termed them, Davy saw
many who showed indications of gentle birth. Certainly none looked
as fierce and villainous as Half-Hanged Smyth or as inhuman as
Michael Hogge.

A moment later, a turn in the road brought them to the mill.

Here a dozen or so horses were tethered to a hitching-rack, while an equal number of troopers, fully accoutred and ready to ride on an instant's notice, sat around listening with open amusement to the strident bellowings wafted through the open windows of the mill.

"Woe to ye, Colin Ramsay!" thundered a great voice. "Eternal damnation awaits he who doubts the Word! For the Lord sayeth: 'Surely your turning of things upside down shall be esteemed as the potter's clay!' Beware then the hail that shall sweep away your refuge of lies!"

"Hout tout, Major!" retorted an equally ominous voice. "Haud your claverin' tongue! I tell ye your prancin' an' neighin' aboot the wrath to come be drivelin' nonsense! 'Tis a perversion o' the intellect to argue that a Christian God, 'oo ye claim made mon an' wooman w'at they be, would then create a hell to roast 'em through eternity! Tut, tut! I suspect a mon would hae a deeficult time findin' some o' these scriptural quotations ye so blithely spout! But, coom now—fill thy glass!"

There followed a moment of silence.

Davy glanced at his companions. "Perhaps we'd best not blunder in with tempers so high?" he suggested.

Half-Hanged chortled. "Fie! They be the best o' friends!" he assured them, heaving himself out of the saddle. "Come on, me 'earts!"

Davy glanced at Hogge. The latter shrugged indifferently and dismounted. Davy followed suit, and after they had tied their nags, started in the wake of Half-Hanged Smyth.

As they reached the door, the major began again. "Do not harken to his evil vaporings, my little Jenny! Give thyself to the Lord! Lift up thine eyes to the glory! Lift up thy heart! Lift . . ."

Half-Hanged threw open the door. "Aye, an' lift up thy petticoat, Jenny!" he boomed good-naturedly, and stalked into the room.

The major roared like a clap of thunder, and Davy winced.

"Brother Smyth, ye ill-favored Judas! Where have ye been straggling?"

"Now if yer Honor be sober enough to hear me . . ." Half-Hanged began blandly.

"Sober?" bellowed the major, then stopped short as Davy and Hogge strode into the room.

Of them all, Davy was by far the most surprised, for the cannon-voiced major was comfortably ensconced on an upturned tub, a massive flagon of ale balanced on one knee and a buxom, giggling wench on the other. At sight of the two strangers, the major rose hastily, upsetting the girl onto the floor. Yet he took time to imbibe another drink before carefully placing the flagon on a near-by table.

" 'They be drunken, but not with wine!' " he quoted sententiously. " 'They stagger, but not with strong drink!' " He reeled slightly, as if to illustrate his text. " 'For the Lord hath poured upon them His spirit!' "

"Hout, hout, ye auld fraud!" jeered the bald-headed giant seated near the window. "Ye twist the words o' Isaiah into a lie o' yer ain servin'!"

Major Priety swayed around to denounce this profanation, but before he could frame a suitable retort, Half-Hanged cut in ahead of him.

"Beggin' yer pardon, sir—could we see ye private like? 'Tis important news we bring from yon Royalist stronghold at Westmoreland!"

The major appeared to sober so quickly the transformation was startling. Straightening to his full height, he fixed his jaundiced stare on Davy. Davy, in his turn, met the gaze coolly enough, though he had difficulty keeping his utter astonishment from being manifest. Heretofore, he had deemed Half-Hanged Smyth and Michael Hogge the oddest creatures he had ever seen, but now, in comparison with Major Priety, their uniqueness paled into the commonplace.

Thin to the point of emaciation, the major's body resembled an excessively tall clothes-tree, the sole purpose of which seemed to be to keep his head some six feet off the ground. This unforgettable object was shaped like a giant pear turned upside down. From three sides hung a curtain of lank black hair, while in front, the bulging forehead acted as a crag to shade pale but fiery eyes. Below that point, the visage became almost equine, for it consisted of a horsy muzzle, a wide, toothy mouth and a small chin.

"And who art *these?*" the major demanded, keeping his eyes on Davy.

Half-Hanged gave him an ingratiating leer. "If yer Honor will . . . ah . . . wait until . . ." he said provocatively.

The major nodded. "Verily, 'tis plain ye come in the Lord's work, so I shall sweep these false Ishmaelites from the temple, e'en as the Lord himself scourged . . ."

These false Ishmaelites consisted of the burly miller and two lasses. It took but one glance at the twinkling direct eyes, the shoulders as broad as an ox-yoke, and the powerful arms to realize that Colin Ramsay could be a dangerous man to quarrel with. He rose, laughing.

"The fates pairserve us fra' anither sermon!" he hooted, and slapped the girl nearest him playfully on the buttocks. "Whisht, Annie me darter, awa' wi' ye! Ye, too, Jenny, ye brazen huzzy! Shoo—afore Ol' Piety gets to win'ard o' ye agin!"

As the two girls moved into the light of the lanthorn near the door, Davy got a good look at them. Jenny, the wench the major had been dandling on his knee, had the pleasantly coarse face and figure of a serving girl, but the miller's daughter was something entirely different. Though pleasingly plump, she was small and dainty, and her simple housedress was immaculate. She had blue-black hair, drawn into an informal bun at the nape, and a creamy complexion a Court lady would have envied. Her eyes were veiled and sultry, her nose piquant, and a wide, full-lipped mouth hinted at ardor. Davy judged her to be about seventeen.

Though plainly irritated by her father's fondling, when she approached Davy she smiled and dropped him a curtsy.

"Good evening, sir!" she said softly. "Pay no heed to their coarse jesting and bellowing, for in truth they mean naught by it."

Davy bowed with all the gallantry he could muster. "Bless you, Annie!" he murmured.

There was no opportunity for further conversation, for the major was vociferously herding them out of the chamber. As he followed them outside, Priety barked at Smyth: "Remain here! I'll be back!"

Momentarily alone, the three comrades exchanged glances. "It's enough to make one believe in the *King's* cause," snorted Hogge disdainfully.

Davy grinned. "I understood you to say the major was a strict God-fearing Christian who would stand for no vices?" he challenged Half-Hanged.

" 'Tis the truth!" insisted the sergeant. "Though I said naught o' wenchin' or imbibin' o' the grape! Ol' Piety swears the Bible speaks kindly o' the cup, an' s'ys if the Lud 'Imsel' was gentle wi' the 'arlots, oo be 'e to do otherwise!"

"By my troth!" laughed Davy. "Methinks your major interprets the Good Book to his convenience!"

Further discussion was precluded by the return of Major Priety. "Now, Brother Smyth—thy report!" he snapped, seating himself.

Half-Hanged began, and listening, Davy marveled that so rough a shell could house such an agile mind, for the "report," so glibly delivered, was an incredible blend of fact and fancy, so cunningly interwoven as to be indistinguishable in its separate parts. Half-Hanged explained away his capture by claiming that he alone of his patrol had been sufficiently tireless to follow the Highland contingent, and that he had deliberately let himself be taken to learn the whereabouts of the King. Then, having adroitly penetrated Westmoreland Castle and ascertained that Charles was *not* there, he had utilized his extraordinary powers of persuasion, not only to escape but also to induce the "Famed Laird of Lochbogie" to accompany him. Barehanded, he and his "Ludship" had assaulted a company of armed Cavaliers and captured horses necessary for their journey. En route, they had rescued Michael Hogge from a desperate band of King's men—and here they were.

"An' I assured 'is Ludship ye'd grant 'im a commission befittin' 'is exalted rank, so's 'e could win o'er the 'Ighlands fer us!" Half-Hanged concluded brashly.

Davy hardly knew whether to laugh or blush at this transparent fabrication, yet through it all the major sat ramrod stiff, his pale eyes fixed frostily on the speaker. When the discourse was ended, he turned his attention to Davy.

"H'mmn!" he mused, after a lengthy inspection. "So thou art Ian of Dugald, eh? I seem to recall hearing of thee recently. The son of old Red Dugald, are thee not?"

"John the Dugald would have marched himself," Davy murmured warily, "save that he is now blind with age."

"Verily, the seasons take their toll, and as Moses sayeth, few of us now wandering in the Wilderness shall live to see the Promised Land!" The major exhaled wearily, as if speaking from experience, then demanded abruptly: "Thy conversion to our cause seemeth remarkably fortuitous, my lord!"

Davy saw the pitfall opening. "To speak true, Major, I have been dissatisfied with conditions for some time."

"In that event," shot back the major, "why did thee march into Westmoreland in the first place, only to fight your way out within the hour?"

Davy was caught with his guard down, and was about to withdraw behind the bulwark of dignity, when Half-Hanged blundered valiantly into the breech.

"Faith, sir, an' though 'is Ludship'll no want to mention it!" he chuckled with a knowing leer. "Yet 'twas the ol' earl's darter 'e went to see, to 'oom 'e's betrothed!" He clucked his teeth ecstatically. "Bugger me, Major, ye never seed a lusher wench, I swear!"

Old Piety hiccoughed, then gave Smyth a sidelong glance. "So, thou saw the lady, did thee, Sergeant? No doubt she favored thee with an audience for converting her future spouse?"

Half-Hanged sensed he had floundered beyond his depth. "Well, now, Major, she didn't exactly . . ." he began cautiously, but Priety pursued him relentlessly.

"In point of fact, Sergeant—thou never saw her at all, did thee?"

Davy attempted a rescue. "No doubt I spoke so feelingly about the lady, Major, that Half . . . I mean, Sergeant Smyth felt he had seen her."

Major Priety turned on him. "Young man, I need no interpretation of Sergeant Smyth; I know him much too well. The sergeant would rather climb a briar tree to tell a lie than sit comfortably on the ground and tell the truth!"

Davy drew himself erect. "Are you implying . . ." he began stiffly, but the major stopped him with a gesture.

"That thou art three scoundrels!" he rasped. "Smyth is a *liar*, this man Hogge is a *deserter*, and thou, Ian of Dugald, be a *spy!* Or so it appears at this time! Howbeit, further investigation may show . . ."

Davy thrust his jaw forward belligerently. "I'll save you that trouble!" he snapped acidly. "I withdraw my offer of service, and bid you good day!" He bowed, and was about to stalk out of the room, when the major stomped sharply on the floor.

Simultaneously, the door opened to admit a corporal and five troopers with drawn sabers.

"As I was saying," the major went on pontifically, "further investigation may prove me wrong, in which case the lieutenant general will doubtless welcome thee to the Lord's work! Meanwhile . . ." He paused to lend emphasis to his verdict, "I remit thee all to the custody of the guard!"

Davy was too surprised to speak, but Half-Hanged was under no such restraint.

"If yer Honor please!" he protested. "W'at ha' I done to . . . ?"

"Thou art charged with abandoning command, with perjury and with desertion!"

"Leapin' Jesus!" Half-Hanged groaned involuntarily.

"And twenty stripes, plus the jeopardizing of thy eternal welfare for thus profaning the Lord's name!" thundered Old Piety, rising. "Corporal, do thy Christian duty!"

Chapter Ten

They were duly lodged on the third story of the mill, in a windowless chamber which, in happier times, had served as a bin for the storage of grain. The only visible means of entrance or egress was by a single flight of stairs of ladder-steepness. Their one concession had been a small hurricane lanthorn, which accentuated rather than dispelled the gloom.

When the corporal's guard had left them, Hogge settled himself against the wall.

"So, Half-Hanged—you measure a man as you do a hen, eh?" he jeered. "What kind of an egg do you call *this?*"

"Damme, I didn't 'ear ye s'y nuthin', Piggey!" Half-Hanged retorted.

"Precisely! I know when to hold my tongue!"

Half-Hanged pressed his head between his hands. "Bugger me, I don't unnerstan' it! Ol' Piety seemed to doubt me word!"

Davy burst into laughter. "By my troth, it's plain your scripture-quoting major isn't as big a fool as he looks, for had he swallowed that unpalatable rubbish you offered, he'd not be fit to command a squad!"

Half-Hanged stared aghast. "*Rubbish?*" he exploded. "W'y, damme, every bloody word I spoke was the God'strufe! Didn't I foller ye? Didn't I talk ye into comin' 'ere? Didn't we o'erpower them desperate Cavaliers . . ."

"It was the *desperate* King's men from whom you rescued me," interrupted Michael Hogge.

Half-Hanged looked so tragic, Davy gave him a genial slap on the shoulder.

"Cheer up, comrade!" He chuckled. "You certainly made a good try. Had you not embellished it out of all plausibility, all might have been well."

Half-Hanged exhaled sorrowfully. "Mebbe I did exaggerate a mite," he conceded reluctantly. "But *twenty stripes!* Kee-rist!"

The conversation lagged, and soon each had retreated into the isolation of his own thoughts. For his part, Davy felt strangely saddened. Though a fugitive, the last two days had, paradoxically enough, given him a sense of freedom he had never known. It had all seemed so natural, too, as if he had been born to command. For the first time, he began seriously to wonder about his parentage. Could there have been any truth in the silly vaporings of Lady Marguerite, the old laird's French wife? Was it possible that his father *had* been a transient noble? It would be pleasant to know—not that it would make any difference now.

His wandering thoughts shifted to old Westmoreland Castle, and that last meeting with Olivia. Even as a child, he had revered her, but had never thought her beautiful. Now he was still astonished by the metamorphosis; from a freckled, leggy chrysalis, she had emerged into a creature of incredible beauty. And to think that she, *she,* had wept over the fate of the toadlike Ian!

His reverie was interrupted by the sudden opening of the door at the foot of the stairwell. Half-Hanged gave him a significant look, then crawled over and peered down the flight. Instantly, his clouded features cleared.

"Annie, me angel!" he yelped delightedly.

Anne Ramsay came stumbling up the stairs carrying a heavy hamper which she plumped down on the floor near Davy.

"I thought you might be hungry, my lord!" she said, with a breathless little laugh.

Half-Hanged crowed. " 'Ungrier than bloody vultures!" He ripped the covering off the hamper and hauled out a bottle of French wine.

"Why, damme, lookee 'ere, b'ys, gen-oo-ine . . ." he began, only to pause, open-mouthed, when the girl snatched the bottle out of his hand.

"That's not for the likes of you, Sergeant Smyth!" she snapped. "It's for his Lordship!" She wiped the bottle on her apron and proffered it to Davy. "There's ale for your lackeys, my lord," she murmured demurely. "Methought wine more suited to your rank."

"*Lackeys?*" sputtered Half-Hanged, while Hogge chuckled mirth-lessly.

Davy ignored them and accepted the gift with alacrity. "Why, bless you, Annie! It was uncommon thoughtful, I declare!"

"Oh, I know the prerogatives of nobility!" breathed the girl. "For though I appear naught but the daughter of an honest miller, my dear mother of august memory was gentle bred, my lord!"

Davy bowed. "On my oath, my lady, 'tis plain to any who have eyes!"

She clapped her hands with pleasure. "You truly think so, sir?"

"I swear it!" he assured her. "I trow your blood is as good as my own." He glanced at the enraged sergeant. "What say you, honest Smyth?"

"I s'y—a pox on blood!" fumed Half-Hanged. "It all looks the same w'en spilt on the ground!"

Annie tilted her piquant nose and appraised him with contempt. "You forget your station, Master Smyth!" she reproved him.

In a temper, Half-Hanged seized a chunk of meat out of the ham-per and savagely tore off a mouthful. Then, shaking the remainder in the girl's face, he muttered darkly, "Ye'd do well to drop yer 'igh-an'-mighty airs, Anne Ramsay! I knows w'at ye're up to, but ye'll wait many a lonely year a-waitin' fer some noble knight to carry ye off, like ye moon about! Ye'd better accept a stout, hones' man . . ."

"Such as yourself, no doubt?" sniffed the girl disdainfully.

Half-Hanged squared his bulldog jaw. "Ye could do worse!"

Anne laughed and turned to Davy. "What does your Lordship say to *that?*" she asked. "Would you advise a maid with gentle blood in her veins to throw herself away on a vulgar lout?"

Davy opened his mouth to jest, but when he saw the stricken look on the face of his friend, he temporized.

"Why, for myself, I have never considered my blood better than another's. And your own mother wedded an honest miller, Annie!"

She tossed her head. "Aye, and lived to regret it! Believe me, sir, I'll not make the same mistake! I pledge my word to that!" She was about to enlarge on her argument, when a strident bellow flooded the building.

"An-nee! *An-nee!*"

She was so startled, Half-Hanged grinned maliciously.

"Yer *vulgar* pater's callin' ye, Annie!" he taunted. "If 'e catches ye makin' eyes at 'is Ludship, 'e'll put a stick to them sacred aristocratic buttocks!"

"*An-nee!*" thundered the miller's voice, obviously angry.

The girl poised at the head of the stairs. "Farewell, my lord!" she whispered dramatically. "God protect you until we meet again!" Then she dropped swiftly out of sight.

Davy sank back against the wall and howled with laughter. "By my troth, 'twas better than a play!" he gasped. "What ails the wench, Half-Hanged! Is she tetched?"

Smyth bent over the hamper and rummaged for another delicacy. "Nay, she's bewitched!" he rumbled feelingly. " 'Tis the work o' 'er fool mither, w'at brung 'er up to sneer at honest yeomen."

"A slut, a dangerous slut!" grated Hogge, with so much bitterness that Davy stared at him askance. "I take it the bitch spurned your advances?"

"To that I'll naught say nay," Half-Hanged conceded. "She swears she'll not hoist 'er petticoats to none but a well-born knave!"

Hogge grunted. "You should congratulate yourself, man!"

Davy whooped with laughter. "I differ with you, Piggey! Zounds, 'twould be a bud worth the plucking! By Gad, now that I'm elevated to the nobility, I've a notion to dally in that Garden of Eden!"

Half-Hanged grinned in spite of himself. "Ah, 'ell, drop it!" he grumbled. "True, I laid siege to the fortress an' was beat off, but ye'll get no chance, fer a corpse makes a poor bedfellow, noble er no, an' I didn't like the glint in Ol' Piety's eye."

Davy sighed and uncorked the bottle. But as he raised it to his lips, a shrill scream filtered upward through the flooring. He paused, with the bottle in mid-air. Again, and yet again, the wail was repeated.

Half-Hanged chortled in malevolent glee. " 'Tis just the miller warmin' up yer Garden o' Eden!" he explained. " 'E watches o'er 'er like a gamekeeper! Them *noble* buttocks must be a permanent pink by this time, fer 'e's 'ad to switch 'em so often wi' all the young buck officers we've 'ad aroun' 'ere!"

The cries had ceased. Davy raised his wine and gestured to Half-Hanged and Hogge to hoist their ale.

"A toast, my stout comrades, to the aristocratic buttocks!"

Half-Hanged waved his bottle. "An' to the lucky Adam 'oo'll pluck the apple!"

"May he not get bitten by the serpent!" grunted Hogge.

Davy hadn't realized how hungry he was until they started to eat. By the time he had gorged himself and emptied the wine bottle, he felt drugged with weariness. Half-Hanged simply sprawled against the wall and started to snore. Michael Hogge had leaned back and was staring moodily into space. Davy wondered, idly, why the girl had incensed the man so, since it was obvious he had never seen her before. But he was too tired to wonder long. . . .

How long he slept, Davy had no way of knowing, but a faint rustling brought him starkly awake. Someone had drawn the hood of the lanthorn, and the chamber was dark. His hand went instinctively toward his belt, only to be reminded his dirk had been removed by the guards. He lay tense, listening to the sound approach. When something touched his leg, he was about to spring when a soft whisper gave him pause.

"Be not alarmed, my lord! 'Tis me—Anne!"

Davy exhaled relievedly. The measured breathing of his comrades told him they were still asleep. He reached down and guided the girl up beside him.

"Good Lord, child!" he reproved gently. "What brings you here?"

She placed an admonitory finger across his lips. "Quietly, sir, in heaven's name!" she cautioned. "My father would flay me alive if he should catch me here!"

Despite his surprise and reasonable apprehensions, Davy was not unaware of her femininity as she crept into his arms, ostensibly the better to whisper into his ear. But in so doing, she contrived to snuggle disconcertingly close until she lay full-length against him.

"My lord, they mean to hang you!" she whispered. "I heard the major say as much to my father. He does not believe the tale told by the sergeant!"

Davy swore softly. "You should not have put yourself in jeopardy to tell me this, Annie!" he chided. "There's naught I can do about it."

She brushed his cheek with hers. "There is, my lord! You do not have to hang—if you but grant my wish!" she breathed in his ear. "I will give you your life if you will give me mine!"

He felt the hackles rise on his neck. It seemed plain the girl was crazy. He hardly knew how to cope with the situation.

"I don't . . . I don't understand you, child!"

She gripped him convulsively. "I'm not a child; I'm seventeen! I can get you free if you—if you will marry me!"

He felt a surge of irritation. "*Marry you?* Why, that would be madness! If I could escape this hole, I'd be a marked man!"

"Oh, content you, my lord! 'Twould be better a thousand-fold for me to share your flight than remain in this hated prison to be coveted by every common curl that stops o'ernight!" She sobbed wretchedly and let her head sink against his breast. "Grant my plea, sir! My beloved mother made me promise to hold aloof from the vulgar until the day a gentleman should come and recognize my worth!"

Davy felt ridiculous. "Look you, Annie—you know naught about me! I may not even be . . ." He paused in caution.

"Oh, I do, I do!" she blurted. "When last the moon was full, I visited a white witch, and for two pieces of silver, she foretold your coming! Oh, just to see the life my mother talked so much about— the great castles, the bright ladies and their courtly gallants!" She clapped her hands ecstatically. "Would you not rather have me than hang, sir?"

He sighed wearily. "Anne, this is utter nonsense! Though I have small desire to hang, you might as well know the truth!" When she would have protested, he laid a firm hand across her mouth. "Hear me now—I am but a rogue with a price on my head! I have no castle . . ." He stopped short as the hood of the lanthorn was abruptly drawn aside to reveal Half-Hanged towering above them.

"W'at the bloody 'ell goes on?" he barked harshly.

Davy disengaged himself from the girl's arms and stood up. "Silence, you fool!" he growled. "Do you want to bring the guards up here?"

Hogge had awakened, and was glaring at the girl like a coiled snake. Half-Hanged scowled at her.

"If ye crawled up to warm 'is bed, ye might o' 'ad the gryce to ha' brought Jenny to warm mine!"

"You evil-minded lout!" cried Annie. "Major Priety means to hang you. I came to offer him . . . you all . . . *escape!*"

Half-Hanged squinted suspiciously, then seeing she was in earnest, broke into a broad smile.

"Bugger me, that's an 'orse o' a different breed! W'at be we waitin' fer?"

She looked meaningfully at Davy. " 'Tis for my lord to say!"

101

Davy snorted. "Bah! The child is bereft of her senses!"

She drew herself to her full height. "Think you so? Listen—there is a way out of this room known only to myself!" she said defiantly. "Less than a stone's throw from the exit, four cavalry horses are tethered and saddled. I stole them myself and with my own hands stuffed the saddlebags with food. I even tied your hound beside them! Now what say you?"

Half-Hanged gaped in wonder. "God luv ye, girl!" He eyed Davy. "W'at's wrong wi' ye?"

Davy wagged his head in exasperation. "You heard her say *four* horses, didn't you? *She wants to go with us!*"

"Bugger me, an' w'y not?" laughed the sergeant. "The more the merrier, s'y I! Eh, Piggey?"

Hogge maintained a stony silence that made the color mount Davy's face.

"Damn it, can't you understand!" he snarled at Half-Hanged. "She wants to go as . . . as . . ." He floundered over the word, but she supplied it candidly.

"As his wife!" she said determinedly. "Long have I dreamed of the life my precious mother . . ."

"You see what I mean?" Davy cut in. "I tried to tell her I'm not . . ."

Half-Hanged snorted him into silence. "An' 'oo can blyme 'er! Aye, Annie, 'tis a bonny life 'is Ludship leads, I swear, wi' more lackeys 'an a cur 'as fleas an' a great castle perched 'igh . . ."

"Smyth, you lying idiot!"

Half-Hanged looked him squarely in the eye. "M'lud, I know naught w'at passes in yer mind, but fer mesel', I 'ave no wish to 'ang, 'avin' tried it onc't! If Annie be content wi' ye, then I s'y ye're an ungrateful w'elp to spurn 'er. An' since me own neck be tangled up wi' yourn, I charge ye not to throw it aw'y!"

She put a hand on Davy's arm. "Do you not find me sufficiently attractive my lord?"

"Good God, yes! But I am not what you think!"

"Now 'oo's a lyin' idjit?" snarled Smyth.

"And I do not believe you, sir!" she said emphatically. "Yet the choice is yours—take me, or stay here and hang!"

"Vicious little bitch!" Hogge muttered *sotto voce,* but no one heeded him.

Davy spread his hands in surrender. "So be it," he acquiesced

"The plan is madness, and I fear you'll rue the day, Annie, when you learn the truth. Yet life is sweet, and will doubtless be sweeter still with you."

"Then you swear you will marry me, my lord?"

"Aye, I swear it, though I wish it were on different terms!"

She laughed delightedly and brushed his cheek with a kiss, then darted to the opposite end of the chamber and dropped to her hands and knees as if searching for something. The men followed, puzzled.

"Years agone, when times were good, this place was used as an extra storage bin," she explained excitedly. "The grain was hauled up here through an outer door, long since boarded up, but the old chute by which it was transported to the mill below is still here *somewhere*. When I was a little girl, I used to slide down it clear to the lower rooms, for the grain had worn the planks as smooth as glazing!"

Both Half-Hanged and Davy knelt to help her find the trap, but it was Annie who eventually located it beneath the fine coating of dust. Half-Hanged miraculously produced a dagger which he had concealed in his jackboot, and they pried it open, disclosing a black hole.

" 'Tis a breathless ride!" Annie warned. "Yet close to the end, the chute arcs upward to slow the sacks! But in heaven's name make no outcry, for you pass through the very room in which my father sleeps!"

Half-Hanged rubbed his jaw, then thrust his head down the hole, only to jerk it back in a hurry.

"Leapin' Jesus!" he said nervously. " 'Tis small fer a big man!"

"Peradventure you prefer to remain here!" jeered Annie.

"Peradventure ye prefer I would!" Half-Hanged retorted bitterly. "Well, methinks 'twill be no tighter'n the 'angman's noose! 'Ow about it, *Ian?*" The emphasis was a reminder.

"I'll try it first, if you wish," Davy volunteered.

Annie shook her head and dropped her legs into the hole. "Nay, I'll go first, so I will be at the bottom to guide you." She looked up at Davy. "Give me your oath you will follow, my lord?"

When Davy hesitated, Half-Hanged spoke for him. " 'E'll foller, that I promise ye, Annie, e'en if I 'ave to stuff 'im down the 'ole mesel'!"

Anne smiled, then, with a swish of petticoats, vanished into the black maw.

Half-Hanged turned savagely to Davy. "W'at ails ye, man?" he demanded. "Ben't ye man enough to bed the chit?"

"She's plain daft!" Davy grumbled. "What happens when she learns the truth?"

The other snorted impatiently. "Bah! W'at 'appens w'en any o' us learns the truth? We jes' mykes the best o' it! Yet, mark this, *m'lud*— ye'd best muzzle yer tongue an' confide naught to a wooman ye wouldn't pass to the town crier!"

Hogge grimaced. "The first trace of profundity you've exhibited these past two days," he observed sardonically. "Speaking strictly for myself, I'd rather burn at the stake than have anything to do with that treacherous hoyden!"

"Well, I wouldn't!" Smyth snarled belligerently. "Ye can st'y 'ere an' be damned to ye, but we're goin'!" He prodded Davy toward the opening. " 'Ere now—slide down this rat-'ole an' aw'y!"

Davy shook his head. "You're the broadest, Half-Hanged—you go first, so if you get stuck, we can help you. I suggest you try it head-on."

Half-Hanged winced, but concurred. Pulling his precious Cavalier hat around his ears, he went down on his knees, after the fashion of a Mohammedan at prayer, and thrust his head into the hole.

"Bugger me, lads, 'tis darker'n the bowels o' Satan!"

When he continued to hesitate, Michael Hogge put his foot on the upturned rump and shoved. Half-Hanged had time for just one strangled gasp before he, too, vanished into the depths of the ancient mill.

Hogge bowed to Davy. "After you, my lord!"

Davy studied him quizzically. "You'll come, Piggey?"

"Aye, to be sure! I'll go anywhere when someone else is paying the reckoning, though, to speak true, I think you a fool!"

Davy flushed, but this was not the time to debate the issue, so he made ready for his own descent. His wounded side had grown stiff and the necessary contortions sent little slivers of pain through his body. As he poised above the black square, he wondered, peevishly, why he was prone to tarry. Was it the girl? he wondered. Never heretofore had he been loath to tell a pretty wench anything she wanted to hear to gain her favors. Certainly he could see no reason for squeamishness in this affair, for if Anne Ramsay was a virgin it was due to ambition rather than virtue. Thus, dismissing the matter from his mind, he eased himself painfully into the chute.

Chapter Eleven

For Davy, it was truly a "descent into hell"! The planks, even though polished by a century of usage, gouged his wounds as if by a rasp. After a breathtaking eon of agony, he was shot, half fainting, into the waiting arms of the sergeant.

"Zounds!" breathed the big man, hauling him erect. "Methought ye'd snagged on one o' them accursed curves. Be ye 'urt, lad?"

Davy straightened with difficulty. He was relieved to see that Michael Hogge had followed him.

"No, no, I'm all right!" he managed, between clenched teeth. "Where is Annie?"

"Here, my lord!" the girl called softly from the darkness. "I just learned of your wounds from your lackey! By the way, sir, what *is* his exact position in your service?"

"Marster o' Conscience!" snorted Half-Hanged. "I keep the troublesome beast bridled an' out o' 'arm's w'y!"

"Your levity will be punished in season!" promised Anne. "As I was saying, my lord, I knew naught you were injured, but in my saddlebags I have secret unguents and balms which will cure you. Meanwhile, follow me closely and I will lead you to the horses." With that, she opened a small door in the wall and led them down another flight of stairs to a cellarlike hole that housed the gears and shaft of the giant water-wheel.

Padding along behind Davy, Half-Hanged chuckled. "The goose-brained ninny be already actin' the great lydy!"

"Well, it's a sauce of your own making," Davy reminded him. "You'll have to sup off it awhile."

"Aye, though bugger me, I'd rather 'ave the meat she's promised ye than the tart sauce drippin' from 'er tongue." The sergeant sighed. " 'Owbeit, I'll feed 'er conceit, though it galls me."

Anne led them through another opening, then across a hidden ford to the other side of the mill-stream where a narrow goat track wound drunkenly around the hill. By the time they reached the horses tethered near the summit, Davy felt himself again.

A brief examination proved that if Anne Ramsay's head was in the clouds, her feet were firmly on the ground. Even Michael Hogge was forced to concede he had never seen finer horse flesh than the four stout chargers awaiting them. In addition to adequate food for two or three days, the girl had thoughtfully provided weapons. And best of all—from Davy's point of view—there was old Gabriel, wriggling in ecstasy.

"I cry ye mercy, Annie me darlin'!" applauded Half-Hanged. "Ye ha' shown uncommon . . ."

"My good man!" she cut him off peremptorily. "Henceforth you will address me as *madame*, or *my lady*, as befits the difference in our stations!"

Half-Hanged was so taken aback he was momentarily speechless. Davy burst into laughter.

" 'Pon my honor, our lady speaks true!" he declared. "It behooves each of us to bear our proper positions in mind, as I have been justly reminded on occasion!"

Half-Hanged's rat-eyes began to twinkle. "Me lud, me lydy, I craves pardon! I lives on'y to serve yer bloody Gryces!" Then, with exaggerated servility, he bent his knee for the girl to mount.

Obviously missing the sarcasm, Anne accepted it as her due and mounted swiftly, after which she favored him with a carefully restrained smile.

"You are forgiven, fellow!" she assured him graciously. "Now mount yourself and lead the way. Follow this trail until the light is better, whereupon I will administer to his Lordship's wounds."

They rode in single file, and though the sergeant maintained a rapid pace, the trail was so tortuous the crow-fly distance covered was negligible. The moonlight, now on the wane, illumined the scene in a pale glow that gave Davy the eerie sensation of drifting through a dream. Occasionally through the trees he caught a glimpse of the hamlet below and realized they were working around it toward the main east-west highroad over which he and his companions had so hopefully traveled a few hours agone. Where they would go when they did reach the road was a problem yet to be faced.

The first gray streamers of dawn had come when they emerged into a little clearing on the hillside, well beyond the main bridge, that afforded a clear view of the road to the eastward. Here Anne called a halt, and despite Davy's fretful objections, insisted on dressing his wounds.

She forced him to lie full-length on the ground, and began to open his garments while the two others stood watching. Half-Hanged had edged around behind her, leering delightedly and making ribald gestures with his hands, until Davy savagely ordered him to betake himself—and Hogge as well—to the rim of the hill to stand guard.

As Anne went about her chore, Davy again had occasion to marvel at her duality, for if her chattering suggested a spoiled and wilful brat whose brain had been addled by romantic nonsense, her skill in practical matters astounded him. She bared the upper half of his body with adept impersonality and examined the wound. Instead of burbling with the maudlin sympathy he ruefully anticipated, she took his hat to a near-by brook and returned with it full of clear water. The manner with which she washed the injury and applied the unguents bespoke a sure hand and much practice. She then produced linen and strapped his torso in such a way it was both dressing and support. That done, she sat back on her heels.

"Now, my lord, you may dress yourself."

He did as she bid, then propped himself on one elbow. "By my troth!" he mused. "You are an incredible paradox!"

Her eyes widened. "How so, my lord?"

"Why, I know naught how to phrase it," he confessed.

She smiled enigmatically. "Because I have intelligence enough to outfit horses and dress a wound?"

"Not exactly, but . . ."

"Or, perhaps, because I forced myself on you? Tell me truly?"

He laughed softly. "That may be part of what I mean, Annie."

She nodded. "I have no doubt it is," she said soberly. " 'Tis the blind side of man, for you all deem woman naught but a bauble, a pretty painted piece of Eve's flesh, which, like a hare, should wait demurely until the hunter sees fit to offer chase. Unfortunately, my lord, when the hare is born outside the preserves of the lordly estates, it becomes game only for the yeoman and the peasant.

"What appalls you, sir, is to find ambition in a female! My conduct offends as if I had poached upon your prerogatives of the hunt. You forget that when a bud flowers, it is either plucked from its thorns in season, or falls amongst them to become less than dust!"

Davy stared in open-mouthed astonishment. "God's life, are you oracle or human?" he marveled.

She smiled her sly smile. "Exceedingly human—as you shall learn in due time! Nor will you find me a whit less pliable because the initiative was mine, rather than thine. My mother coached me well in the arts of pleasing my lord, believe me, and though her own life was ruined by an ill-considered moment of passion—of which, I blush to confess, I am the result—she taught me how to await the right man."

Davy winced. "And you thought I was that one?"

She laid a possessive hand on his arm. "Aye, I knew it! Could you not learn to care for me a little, *Ian?*"

Davy discovered that, despite the circumstances, he, too, was *exceedingly human*. He reached out and cupped her tiny chin in his hand, and the contact set his pulse to hammering.

"My God, Annie! I . . ." He drew her toward him and she came readily enough. But as his arms closed around her waist, a startled cry of warning from Half-Hanged brought them erect.

Half-Hanged desperately motioned them down.

"We're undone!" he groaned.

Davy's first thought was of pursuit, and so, apparently, was Anne's.

"My father . . . ?" she began, fearfully, but the sergeant wagged his head.

"Were to God 'twas on'y the miller!" He met Davy's eye. " 'Tis the 'ole bloody *Royalist army!* Look ye!"

Unbelieving, Davy wriggled over beside the two men and peered over the rim. Even then he found it difficult to credit his eyes, for the whole valley, which but a short time before had been empty, was now alive with troops streaming toward Doughadee!

Though Davy was a seasoned veteran of clan warfare, he had never before viewed a formal army, and for a few minutes he forgot his own plight in the dazzling magnificence of the scene. Leading the column, and almost directly below the startled watchers, pranced a gallant troop of horse, briskly followed by glittering files of English Foot-Guards. Behind these rumbled the artillery, then a brigade of loyal Highlanders. On either side of the road squadrons of alert dragoons combed the hillsides in search of rebel outposts.

It was these dragoons that brought Davy to a realization of their danger.

"By my troth!" he swore softly. "We'd better mount and away!"

Michael Hogge chuckled cynically. "Away *where?* We've the choice between Scylla and Charybdis."

"Damme, I sees no choice at all!" fumed Half-Hanged. " 'Tis the syme as stan'in' in the middle o' a bloody tiltyard—God 'elp us!"

Davy nodded. "True! Those damned dragoons are higher up the slope than we are!"

"Mebbe we could cut our w'y through 'em, lad?" offered Half-Hanged.

Davy glanced at the girl and shook his head. "There must be a better way out of this mess."

Anne caught his arm. "My lord, why not ride down to meet these Cavaliers? They are your kind; they'll welcome you back!"

Hogge emitted a hissing noise of disgust and Half-Hanged stared in disbelief.

"W'at o' yer father, Annie?"

She tossed her head. "He made his bed with the Rebels," she snapped. "He'll have to lie on it!"

Half-Hanged started a suitable retort, but Davy silenced them curtly.

"I've no reason to love the Rebels," he said, "but I think we can serve them and ourselves at the same time. It is obvious we cannot penetrate this Royalist screen, but we can run before it, rouse the Rebels, and slip out the other side of the village in the confusion."

Hogge touched his forehead. "Maestro, I salute thee! The idea is just crazy enough to work! Let us, therefore, mount . . . *ah . . . !*" He paused as a dragoon trotted out of the woods just above them.

Davy sprang to his feet and gave Anne a shove toward her horse. "Ride, girl, ride!" he urged. "We'll deal with . . ."

The roar of a pistol cut off his words. He spun around to see Half-Hanged lowering his smoking weapon. Following the direction of the gun, Davy saw the dragoon topple from the saddle.

"Bugger me!" exclaimed Half-Hanged, with a bitter laugh. "That'll put the fat into the ruddy fire, s'elp me!"

The observation was an understatement. The thunder of the pistol was a signal that sent even the birds in the trees screaming into action. It caused a tremor down the serpentine column below and brought it to a momentary halt. As Anne flung herself into the saddle and started down the slope at a mad gallop, more dragoons spurred out of the woods. From the village came the startled blast of a trumpet. The wolfhound whined fretfully.

It was quickly manifest the odds were too great to make a stand, so Davy and his comrades mounted hurriedly. Davy paused only long enough to shoot down the nearest horse, then spurred after the others.

Far ahead now, he could see Anne tearing down the steep slope. She was traveling a cowpath that offered good footing, so Davy signaled his friends to follow her. The pursuing dragoons had apparently not seen the trail, for they were stumbling and sliding through the underbrush. But, in the valley, the leading platoon of cavalry had spotted the fugitives and now turned up the hill to intercept them before they could reach the bridge.

This was a mistake that gave the fugitives the advantage of momentum, and when the cowpath emptied onto the road, the three adventurers were a good hundred yards ahead of their pursuers and a scant two furlongs from the bridgehead. For a few moments, Davy had lost sight of Anne among the trees, but now he saw her swerve onto the bridge and shout a warning to the startled sentries who, because of the bend in the road, had not yet seen the Royalist van.

Relief let in a flood of rage. Davy became tired of flight, and the impulse to turn and fight almost overwhelmed him. Perhaps, unconsciously, he sensed a golden opportunity for fame—even afterwards he was never certain exactly what had motivated his decision. But as he galloped toward the narrow bridge, a reckless notion came to him. He leaned out of the saddle and bellowed at Half-Hanged, "To hell with running away! Three stout horsemen can hold an army at bay in this bottleneck!"

Half-Hanged gaped. "Ye're daft! I ain't no bloody martyr w'at's buildin' up credits fer sainthood! Not 'Arf-'Anged Smyth!"

Davy glanced over his shoulder. The cavalry was gaining, yet would not overtake them before they reached the bridge. As Davy pounded onto the ancient stone structure, he shouted at the guards.

"Fire, damn you, fire! Try to stop their charge!" Then he spun his horse around on its hind legs.

The confused sentries did as he bade them, and a lucky shot brought down a leading horse. In the shricking tangle of man and beast on the narrow roadway, the pursuit lost its impetus. As Davy emptied his remaining pistol into the melee, he found Half-Hanged and Hogge ranging alongside him.

"I thought you meant to escape." He laughed.

"An' miss a good fight?" roared Half-Hanged. "Bah, save yer wind!"

Hogge flexed his saber. "Fight or flight—'tis all one with me!" he observed, and jockied his horse up even with Davy's.

One of the sentries was the corporal who had arrested the trio the previous night, and he now stared at them in consternation.

"See 'ere!" he bleated. "W'at the ruddy 'ell . . . ?"

"Silence, ye bitch-brained w'elp!" thundered Half-Hanged. "Rouse up yer drunken major an' tell 'im the devil ha' come to clym 'is own!"

"W'at d'ye aim to do?" muttered the corporal.

"Commit suicide, as any fool can plainly see!" snarled Half-Hanged, and sent him on his way with the flat of a saber.

The corporal and his companions were only too willing to leave the bridge, and in a trice the three adventurers were alone. Meanwhile, a Cavalier on a superb white courser had ridden up to see what had stopped his men.

"By the Mass!" he cried in anger. "Do you halt at the sight of three accursed Whigs!" He lifted his sword above his head. "Follow me, and kill! No quarter to Rebel dogs!" On that, he sank his spurs and the magnificent beast rose into the air like a rocket. Simultaneously, his troop followed.

"Stand firm, my hearts!" warned Davy. "If one gets through, we are undone! Leave this plumed braggard to me!" He pushed forward a pace to meet the officer.

With a shock that all but unseated him, the fight was joined. From that point, he was too hard pressed to know what was going on around him. It was cut and slash and parry, and though he felt no blows, he sensed that he was wounded. Yet this seemed merely to whet his wits, and he found himself screaming in sheer ecstasy of battle.

Suddenly the saddle of the white charger was empty! Dazed, Davy swung around for another antagonist. He had no difficulty finding one close to hand, for the Royalists seemed all about him.

Then, as a wave expends itself against a rock, there came a backwash, giving the defenders a brief respite. But pitifully brief it was, for barely had they dressed their line, when a second, and larger wave of cavalry surged forward to engulf them.

However, the narrowness of the bridge limited the number of possible opponents, and they never had to face more than four or five at a time. Yet, as fast as one Royalist was hacked out of his saddle, two more loomed up to take his place. Davy's sword arm began to ache. Through a lattice of flashing blades, he saw that some of the Parliamentary foot had come out to support them. It was no longer three against an army!

Nevertheless, the sheer weight of the oncoming force was irresistible, and inch by blood-slippery inch, they were driven back. In horror, Davy felt the horse under him begin to sink. He kicked his feet clear of the stirrups, and as the gallant beast rolled sideways, snatched the pommel of another empty saddle and made the transfer in mid-air. As he spurred his new mount around to get back in line, he caught a glimpse of Half-Hanged in the van. The latter was standing in his stirrups, bawling oaths and swinging his dripping blade as a reaper wields a scythe. Beside the sergeant, Michael Hogge was going about his slaughter with that cool detachment which characterized his every move. Then, out of the corner of his eye, Davy saw that a troop of Parliamentary horse had formed at the other end of the bridge.

He slashed a path up beside the sergeant. "Back!" he shouted. "Give ground slowly!"

"Hinder me naught!" thundered the redoubtable Half-Hanged. "I'll not flee these sons o' 'ores! Die, ye pimp o' tyrants!" he yelped happily, spitting a Cavalier out of the saddle.

Unable to draw them back, Davy fought beside them. But the momentum of the Royalists succeeded where he had not, and after a few moments of carnage, the trio were swept off the bridge. *Huzzaing* victoriously, the King's forces streamed into the clear.

In a trice the fight became general, and the flying wedge of Royalists cleaved the defenders in twain. Davy and his two comrades found themselves brushed aside with the smaller body of Rebel dragoons into a comparatively peaceful backwash. For a moment he was able to view the scene objectively.

It was plain that although the Royalist cavalry had cleared the bridge, they were merely an advance detachment, for the main body had not yet reached the other end of the span. If this van could be flanked, there just might still be time to stall the oncoming horde until Major Priety and his men could deal with them. True, to use Michael Hogge's expression, it was the choice betwixt Scylla and Charybdis, but in his fevered condition, Davy viewed it with the mathematical detachment of a chess master.

He appraised his support. He found himself in company of a score or so of bewildered and uncertain Rebel dragoons; there was no officer among them. Half-Hanged had lost his left ear and was now impatiently trying to stem the blood, but his chief sorrow was the loss of the plume on his beautiful hat. Hogge, though his clothes were spattered with blood, seemed unscathed.

Davy beckoned the pair close and outlined his plan. They both assented readily, and when Davy questioned whether the dragoons would follow his unauthorized leadership, Half-Hanged vowed profanely that he would see that they did. Yet even he was startled when Davy ordered them *away* from the bridge instead of toward it. Nevertheless, he bullied the little squad into following.

Davy led them about a hundred feet along the road, then, swinging his horse on its hind legs, ordered a charge at full gallop. Standing up in the stirrups, he gave the wild, spine-chilling battle cry of the clan of Dugald, and led the assault. Half-Hanged, knowing no clan call, trumpeted the notorious cry of the London thieves—"*Rescue! Rescue!*"

On they swept, bent low in the saddles, sabers extended like lances, gaining a momentum no standing horseman could resist! The elated Royalists, savagely decimating Priety's remaining force, were taken by a surprise from which there was no recovery. Davy's contingent severed both support and retreat. As Davy and Half-Hanged led half the band to sweep the bridge, the balance, under Hogge, fell upon the Royalist flank.

Yet though he cleared the span of all opposition, Davy had no illusions about the eventual outcome. True, the Royalist van was lost, but the main body was advancing rapidly, with the pikemen in the lead. Even if he held firm against them, the artillery would soon come up to blast a path. It came to him, with a touch of bitterness, that he had placed himself in precisely the same predicament as the trapped Royalist van behind him.

"Steady, lads, and follow me!" he urged the men over whom he had assumed command. "Never let it be said we fought less bravely than those swaggering minions of the tyrant Charles!"

Then, putting precept into action, he charged the glistening file of pikemen with a fury that routed the front ranks in confusion.

But even valor has its limitations, and Davy was like a man attempting to dam a swift-flowing river with his bare hands. Time and again he hurled his dwindling force against the human current, and each time he lost ground. Yet there was no retreat, for the fight on the other side of the bridge was still undecided.

The end came sooner than he anticipated. The Royalist commander, wisely deciding against further waste of men, had ordered up his artillery. This had been accomplished behind the screen of pikemen, and the first Davy knew of it was when their ranks parted suddenly to reveal the culverin placed squarely in the center of the road to clear the bridge. A gunner stood beside it with a poised linstock in his hand.

There was no time to issue an order, nor sensible order to issue Davy reacted by sinking his spurs and charging the gun head-on The artilleryman saw him coming and hastily touched off the gun as Davy crashed into it. Davy had a momentary sensation of being struck by lightning, then he knew no more. . . .

Chapter Twelve

Davy came drifting back to consciousness piecemeal, as it were. He found himself in a comfortable bed, and after his confused mind adjusted to that incredible fact, he became aware that the bed was in what appeared to be a chamber of a farmhouse. He tentatively tested his head, and was somewhat amazed to find it connected as firmly as ever to his body. Then he saw the trooper seated stiffly near the foot of the bed, staring at him.

The latter asked some question which Davy did not comprehend, as his whole attention was centered on the fragments of memory which lay scattered about his mind. A narrow stone bridge . . . dead men and dead horses in gruesome tiers . . . an artilleryman hovering over a culverin . . . his insane charge . . . the awful belch of the gun in his face . . .

Suddenly the fragments merged to form a whole, and he realized that in some miraculous fashion he must have survived the explosion. He looked at the trooper with freshened interest. In the trim, well-fitted tunic, polished corselet and crisp military bearing, he recognized the mark of a veteran soldier. It seemed obvious, therefore, that he must have been captured by the Royalists, for this trim trooper could be no rag-a-tag Rebel.

"What was it you said?" he asked dizzily.

"I wondered how you felt, sir?"

Davy grunted wryly. "To speak true—I hardly know. How came I here?"

The soldier stood up. "There are others better fitted to answer your questions," he said, saluting. "Be at peace a moment!" And with that he stalked out of the room.

Davy let his head sink back against the pillow. Now, he thought, it is coming; first the questioning, and then the verdict. In his present uncaring condition, he felt tempted to tell the whole truth, for if he had to die, he might as well be slain for a wolf as a sheep, as Half-Hanged Smyth had so colorfully phrased it.

And what of old Half-Hanged? The last Davy had seen of him, he had been charging the pikemen with happy disregard of consequences. Well, since he could not have escaped, the kindest thing Davy could wish was that the cheerful rogue had died swiftly in battle. And Michael Hogge—that strange creature who cared naught whether he lived or died—what of him? What tragic mystery was hidden behind that scarred mask? Davy sighed. He'd never know the answers now.

A ghastly crash brought him to a sitting position. The cottage seemed to quiver as from the impact of a cavalry charge. The door of the bedroom burst open, then with a roar like thunder—Half-Hanged Smyth stomped in, followed sedately by Michael Hogge.

"Bowels o' God, lad!" howled Half-Hanged. "So ye live, bugger me if else!"

And even more unbelievably, Hogge was smiling! "Greetings, my lord!" he chuckled. "How did you find things in hell?"

Davy grinned delightedly. "By my troth, I'm glad to see you, comrades! Though, as to your questions, I have not recovered sufficiently to know the answers!"

Half-Hanged threw himself into the chair lately vacated by the trooper, who had not returned. A swath of bandage concealed the stump of his late ear, but the remains of his Cavalier hat still sat on his cropped head.

"Damme, 'twas a miracle, laddie! I chanc't to look up jes' as ye charged that gun! Certes, 'twas a bloody sight! The ball took yer 'orse full in the chest and bust 'im wide from stem to stern! Fair blew 'im all to bits, leavin' ye sittin' in mid-air, in a manner o' speakin'!" He shuddered at the recollection. "On me oath, lad, that ball passed betwixt yer legs close enough to circumcise ye!"

Davy laughed heartily. "On *my* oath—it didn't, though it must have shaken me up!" He sobered. "How come you boys were taken, too?"

Half-Hanged looked puzzled. "*Taken?*"

"He thinks we're *prisoners!*" Hogge said, meeting the sergeant's glance.

"*Prisoners!*" roared Half-Hanged. "'Ell, lad, we're bloody 'eroes!"

"Oh, for God's sake, don't try to salve my feelings with more of your lies!" Davy snapped impatiently. "I know damn well Major Priety's few dragoons didn't rout that whole army!"

Half-Hanged's bewilderment turned to glee. He slapped his thigh boisterously.

"Bugger me, then ye don't know that the lieutenant general arrived?"

"*Cromwell?*"

"Aye, curse me if else! Ol' Noll 'imself, at the 'ead o' six 'undred o' 'is finest!" yelped the sergeant. "Damme, they swooped down like an 'ost o' avengin' angels, as Ol' Piety put it! God luv ye, laddie, 'twas a rare sight, I trow! 'Ere was me'n Piggey fightin' like fiends an' ye divin' into cannons, nary a one o' us expectin' another dawn, w'en out o' the south comes our blessed gineral! N'er a word 'e said, nor pause 'e myde, but brushin' us all aside, 'e swept o'er that bridge ye'd cleared like a furricano! Wi'in the hour 'twas all o'er!"

Davy looked at Michael Hogge in frank disbelief. The latter nodded.

"Fantastically enough, Half-Hanged speaks the truth—for once!"

Davy bumped his head with the heel of his hand to clear it. "It sounds too fortuitous!" he marveled.

"Fart-oo-tus 'ell!" shouted Half-Hanged aggrievedly. "Ol' Noll's scoutmaster* 'ad learned through 'is spies that the Royalists was advancin' on Doughadee to wipe it out afore 'e arrived. So 'e drove 'is cavalry all night to git 'ere a'ead o' 'em!"

Davy exhaled slowly. "Incredible! And Annie? What of her? Is she safe?"

Half-Hanged chortled. "Aye, syfe as a fledgin' in the nest, though she encountered 'eavy weather wi' the miller. Yet Ol' Piety said she was a blessed angel fer warnin' 'im, an' swore 'e'd 'ang the knave, miller or no, 'oo laid 'and on 'er!"

"I'm glad of that," sighed Davy. "Then Priety survived? I didn't see him during the battle, and thought him dead."

Both men howled. "You are not the only one who missed him during the fight," laughed Hogge. "He was back of the lines . . . *praying!* Some are churlish enough to suggest he was trying to save

* Chief intelligence officer.

his skin, but the major claims God gave us the victory through *his* intercession!"

"Every man to his last," Davy said, grinning. "Has our fate been decided?"

Half-Hanged hooted. "Damme, lad, didn't I tell ye we was 'eroes! W'y, I jes' come from the gineral, an' a long chat we 'ad! I tolt 'im all about ye, an' . . ."

"Oh, Lord!" groaned Davy.

Half-Hanged scowled. "Bugger me, ye can be an ungrateful w'elp! Didn't ye agree to leave the matter in me 'ands?"

"I did, foolishly," conceded Davy, "and came near hanging because of it!"

"Well, ye don't 'ang *this* time!" Half-Hanged continued. "An' if ye play yer cards proper, all will be well. I tolt the gineral naught but the truth, though I 'ad to fill up a few gaps, I own."

"Brace yourself, man!" laughed Hogge.

"Oh-oh! Let's have it, you rogue!"

Half-Hanged's little rat-eyes glistened. "Poof! 'Twas but a small matter o' no consequence! W'en 'is Excellency arsked about yer military experience, w'y I jes' casually mentioned ye'd served under the finest ginerals in the wars o' the Low Countries."

"You damned liar!" flared Davy. "You know bloody well I never even saw a regular army before yesterday!"

The sergeant shrugged deprecatingly. "Bah, w'at o' it? I 'ad to tell him something w'en he arsked me straight!"

"Obviously, the truth would have gagged you," put in Hogge slyly.

"As to that I cannot s'y, Piggey, fearin' to chance it," confessed the sergeant. "Howbeit, m'lud, I couldn't tell 'is Excellency ye'd never seen a regiment, then in the syme breath arsk 'im to gi' ye a commission—now could I?"

Davy jackknifed into a sitting position. "God in heaven! After what's happened, had *you* the temerity to ask General Cromwell for a commission for *me?*"

Half-Hanged looked surprised. "Bugger me, lad, I couldn't arsk it for mesel', since the gineral knows me record!" He snapped his fingers as a thought struck him, and stood up. "Damme, I fergot! Ol' Piety lef' word 'e was to be called the minute ye waked!"

Hogge rose languidly. "Don't worry about it," he advised Davy.

"I've long since learned that the conduct of men has little bearing on the course of destiny."

Leaving Davy in a welter of confused apprehension, they clanked out of the room.

Davy fumed and sputtered for a few minutes, but before long his sense of humor gained the ascendancy and he sank back against his pillow, chuckling. What a ridiculous situation. Damned one moment, praised the next! It seemed as if his destiny was turning handsprings!

When he came to contemplate the immediate future, however, he found it a trifle difficult to believe that the famed Oliver Cromwell was actually here in Doughadee. It was almost as if someone had informed him that God, or the devil (depending on who did the telling) had visited the hamlet! For, in the three years of the Civil War, the fabulous "Squire of Huntington" had sprung from obscurity to legendary fame.

From the pigeonholes of memory, Davy fished out all the fragments of information he had picked up over the years, and tried to fit them together. He soon discovered these odd pieces had been so stained with prejudice in the handling that the composite portrait they made was full of flaws. Cromwell was a back-biting mongrel peasant; a dull-witted country bumpkin, better suited to riding to hounds than sitting in Parliament. At the same time, there was no gainsaying that his dogged cross-bench intelligence and passionate sincerity had precipitated him to the heights of the new government. The Royalists stigmatized him as a harsh, stiff-necked, unsmiling Puritan, who cared only for piety and who chose for his officers only those who were godly or precious. By the same token, the Puritans charged him with having spent his early life in such dissolute pursuits as gaming and good-fellowship, and "kindred lusts of the flesh," and, currently, of preferring fighting men for officers rather than properly pious Christians. They even accused him of harboring Dissenters and—worst of all—Freethinkers, provided they were capable soldiers.

Yet, out of this tangle of contradictions, two irrefutable facts emerged, contradictory in themselves—that Oliver Cromwell had never seen military service until his forty-first year, and that three short years later he was the greatest military genius of the age!

Davy shook his head and gave up. It was all too much for his addled wits, and whether Cromwell was Satan or saint would have little bearing on the outcome of Davy's personal predicament—now further complicated by that lying fiend in half-armor, Half-Hanged Smyth. His only course now was to bluff it through.

He was toying with the notion of attempting to rise when the brisk stomp of marching feet pounded through the house and came to an abrupt halt just outside his room. He heard the rattle of sabers and the clank of spurs, then the door opened to admit a burly middle-aged man, closely heeled by Major Priety.

Davy automatically started up, but the stranger waved him back. Davy shot a quick glance at the major, whose somber arrogance appeared to have waned considerably. Davy suddenly realized he must be in the presence of the great Cromwell himself!

Old Piety tended to verify it. "Your Excellency, this is the young Scot who served the Lord at the bridge!"

"By fighting like a fiend incarnate," grunted the general, dropping into the chair the major pushed toward him. "Well, young man, I gather that when you first arrived in Doughadee, there were some doubts as to which side you were on." He looked up at the major, who squirmed in embarrassment. "Methinks your conduct this morning is sufficient answer. What say you, Priety?"

"Aye, your Excellency, aye!" the major acknowledged, rolling his eyes. " 'Twas a revelation! The Lord worketh His miracles in wondrous fashion!"

"H'mmph! Doesn't He though!" sniffed Cromwell, turning the full power of his blue-gray eyes on the young man before him.

Davy met the scrutiny as steadily as he could, for he was somewhat awed to find himself face to face with the most talked of man in the world. Eventually curiosity overcame his discretion, and he stared back.

In externals, Oliver Cromwell did not look the part assigned to him by fate. His garb was dusty and ill-fitting to a point of slovenliness on a body too long in the trunk and too short in the legs. His heavy ruddy features were drawn with fatigue and cares; the nose ponderous and the nether lip marred by a large mole—altogether an uncouth but unforgettable face. Yet as Davy stared into those deep troubled eyes, he thought he saw behind the murky chaos something of the greatness of the man.

"As I was saying," Cromwell went on abruptly, "there is no doubt you served Parliament well today, yet I understand your father is for the King."

Davy chose his reply with care. "Begging your pardon, sir, it would be more accurate to say the Laird of Lochbogie is against the Kirk."

Major Priety made a neighing noise. " 'Tis one and the same thing! Do not attempt to corrupt truth with evasions, young man!"

"Peace, man, peace!" rumbled the general impatiently. "The lad speaks true! It is *not* the same, and while it is a nice distinction, I grant you, some of the greatest contests of history have been fought on just such narrow margins."

"Your Excellency!" protested the major, raising his hands in pious horror. "No honeyed phrases can gainsay that he who is against the Kirk is against God! As St. Augustine hath stated: 'What can be more deadly to the soul than the liberty of error?' Whatever is against this is the soul-palsying narcotic of slothful . . ."

"*Silence!*" barked Cromwell. "Such quotations plucked from the Scriptures and other sacred writings, like the hairs in a horse's tail, concur in one root of strength, but, being plucked out one by one, serve only for springs and snares! So stay your tiresome canting until you trade back your armor for a cassock, and burden me no more!" Leaving the deflated major to swallow this heresy, he turned back to Davy.

"It is axiomatic that your Highland noble is always for the King when not against him," he observed drily, "for his hereditary foes have been either King or Church, he being the resolute champion of medieval privilege. Correct me if I am wrong, sir!"

Davy felt an irresistible impulse to smile, brought on not only by the general's weary skepticism but by the gloomy visage of Old Piety.

"It would be futile for me to deny what history affirms, your Excellency!"

"Well said! Now tell me why such lairds as your father are so opposed to the Kirk they will side with the King?"

Davy hesitated. The conversation had shifted on a tack he had not anticipated, and he wondered if a snare was being laid for him. His eyes strayed to the major. Cromwell caught the glance, and snorted.

"Be not dismayed by Brother Priety," he urged. "He would have

121

us believe he holds the keys to heaven and hell, but I know the sly dog too well to be gulled by his sanctimonious jargon. Speak plain, and no harm shall befall you because of it, either here or"—a ghost of a smile played on the corner of his mouth—"or in the *hereafter*."

Somewhat appalled at the extent of the question, Davy weighed his words.

"Your Excellency, I shall not speak specifically of John the Dugald, nor of any other individual laird, yet I own to having heard the matter debated in many a Highland castle. The collective reaction is that the Kirk, in its extreme zeal, has perverted the Gospel into an instrument of intolerable oppression which has cast a dark pall over Scotland. It has attempted to interfere not only with natural pleasures and innocent frolics but even with the most intimate affairs, demanding, by threats of eternal fire, that the individual surrender unto it his conscience and judgment as absolutely as any papist to his Pope." Davy spread his hands. "Such harsh despotism does not sit well with the independent old lairds, your Excellency, for they say they would rather be ruled by a King than a Divine, but intend to be tyrannized by neither!"

Cromwell did not smile. His stern mouth had grown grimmer and his eyes clouded until Davy thought he had gone too far. Yet, when the major began to bleat about blasphemy, the general turned on him savagely.

"Hold your puling tongue, Priety!" he commanded. "I'm in no mood for your psalm-singing!" He sighed heavily. "By the Powers, I sometimes fear the zealots cause me more trouble than the enemy, for they have neither a trace of instinct for government, nor so much as a grain of common sense!" As he continued to stare at Davy, his eyes narrowed in concentration.

"I take it, however, that in either instance, whether for the King or for the Kirk, the Highland nobles are at best lukewarm?"

"Yes, sir! They would prefer to stand aloof from the quarrel, but" —Davy permitted himself a smile—"neutrality is an unknown word in the Highlands of Scotland."

"Aye, I can believe that!" grunted the general. "Now—in your considered opinion, young man, would the presence of an army bolster the courage of the indecisive lairds?"

Davy flushed at having his opinion asked by a man whose military exploits were the talk of the civilized world. Yet when the question was repeated, he summoned his courage.

"Your Excellency, it would be a tragic mistake! The lairds would resent an army, whether sent by King or Parliament, marching into their domains!"

"A considerable number of them haven't resented the presence of the Marquis of Montrose!" snapped Cromwell.

"Montrose is a Scot, sir! And he did not come with an English army; he came with a small nucleus of horse which he expanded by enlistments from the clans."

"H'mmnph!" rumbled the general noncommittally. He sat with head bowed in thought a moment longer, then rose abruptly.

"Well, Dugald, I should indeed be ungrateful if I failed to find a suitable place for you in our service after your gallantry. I have been informed by one of your ardent disciples that you did valiant service in Holland. Under whom did you serve in that campaign?"

This was the question Davy dreaded. The truth would finish his career before it began, whereas a simple lie could hardly be challenged. He hesitated, then: "Your informant erred, sir," he confessed candidly. "While I have had some experience in clan warfare, I never saw a formal army until this morning!"

Cromwell leaned heavily on the back of the chair and stared hard at Davy.

"That's impossible!" he growled. "I myself saw your action as we topped the ridge behind Doughadee! Your precision indicated careful training and your tactics were those laid down by . . . by . . ."

"Gustavus of Sweden," Davy supplied ruefully. "Aye, sir, my tutor fought under that great Swedish strategist and also under Prince Maurice of Nassau, and he pounded their tactics into my head. Howbeit, the fact remains, your Excellency, I never saw an English army before."

"Upon my word!" gasped the general. "Here is a pretty pass! What make you of it, Priety?"

"Verily, 'tis the end of Demosthenes' search, your Excellency! An honest man!"

Cromwell sniffed. "Honest, but inexperienced. Obviously I cannot commission a lad who has never before seen a battle!"

"Your Excellency," bumbled the major. "With God's help, I could take the lad under my guidance and . . ."

Cromwell brushed him aside. "You and God again, Priety! Bah, I haven't time to discuss the matter further!" He shoved the chair away. "When you get on your feet, young man, I'll try to find a place for you."

He was about to leave, when Davy called to him: "Pardon me, sir! My comrades were under arrest . . ."

"No longer," snapped the general. "I marvel at your choice of companions, for I know them both, and two more disreputable scoundrels never infested a military camp! But as the devils served the Lord on this occasion, I have pardoned them. Howbeit, and mark this well—the next scrape they get into, I'll hang them both from the same limb! Good day to you, sir!" And he stomped outside.

Chapter Thirteen

For forgotten centuries, the hamlet of Doughadee had slumbered under the shadow of the Highlands; now it was the center of more activity than it had known in all its long history. Every cottage, every stable, was filled with soldiers. Couriers and dispatch riders on sweating horses pounded in and out at all hours of the day and night. It was like a hollow old tree suddenly possessed by a swarm of bees, although in this case the *queen* was represented in the person of his Excellency, Lieutenant General Cromwell. The very atmosphere was pregnant with suspense.

By the second day after Cromwell's visit, Davy, having recovered his strength, summoned his satellites to plot a course of action. And while he did not confide his true status to Michael Hogge, he deemed it only fair to tell them exactly what had happened between the general and himself. Half-Hanged was furious with him for conceding his inexperience, swearing they were undone, and he wailed even louder when Davy laughingly repeated Major Priety's offer to make Christians of them. It was Half-Hanged's considered opinion that the only thing left was flight, and, peculiarly enough, Hogge agreed with him.

"Old Noll is no fool!" he warned Davy. "He has uncanny sources of information, and if he learns the truth—whatever *that* may be—God help you!"

But Davy wouldn't agree. "We've seized the tiger by the tail," he argued. "We can't let go!"

"W'at 'appens w'en 'e shykes us off?" demanded Half-Hanged.

Davy laughed. "Why, man, we'll climb aboard his back and ride him!"

That same evening, Davy received a visitor who did nothing to alleviate his tension—Anne Ramsay! She slipped into his room about dusk, heavily muffled in a cloak, her eyes red from weeping.

"Oh, Ian, Ian!" she sobbed. "I'm in terrible trouble!"

Despite his gratitude toward her, Davy felt that strangled sense of entrapment the human male always suffers under such a condition.

"How so, Annie?" he asked warily.

"'Tis father! He called me a whore, and would have whipped me save only that the dear major interfered, vowing to see that you married me honestly, as you promised!"

Davy winced. "The *dear* major is stepping out of his territory, isn't he?"

She stared, aghast. "God in heaven!" she cried. "Did you mean to abandon me?"

In a sort of dazed mirage, there passed across Davy's mind a ghostly parade of all the women to whom he had made love. Many of these had sought to ensnare him into marriage, and now their wraithlike faces mocked him.

He sighed heavily. "It isn't a question of abandonment, Anne," he said. "We barely know each other."

"Father threatens to take the matter up with the general! He is terribly strict about such things!"

Davy hesitated, cursing himself for not having taken his comrades' advice about flight. But when the girl began to sob again, he surrendered.

"Don't cry, Annie!" he begged. "As soon as I . . . I recover my strength, I'll talk to your father."

This seemed to satisfy her, but when she was gone, Davy lay back and tried to shake off his depression by rationalizing. Why *not* marry the chit? Certainly she was comely enough, and with sufficient wit to make a good mate for an ambitious adventurer. She was going to be disappointed when she learned he was not well-born, but he believed she was resilient enough to recover. The more he dwelt on her capabilities, the better he liked the idea. Yet—deep in his consciousness was a reservation. When he probed it to the surface, he found himself face to face with a vision of another ghost—the memory of a saucy oval face framed with coppery tresses: *Olivia!*

He tried to cast the vision out of his mind. Olivia was forever beyond his reach, and it was rank heresy even to dream of *her!* Yet he knew that though he could never have her she had become his ideal, the measuring-stick by which he judged all others. He was a fool, he told himself savagely, and the best way to lay that ghost was to marry Anne Ramsay!

However, Anne did not return, and as time passed without his receiving word from the general, Davy began to think he had been forgotten. Half-Hanged, who had an acute ear for gossip, picked up various odd scraps of information which, with the assistance of Hogge's worldly wisdom, they pieced together. In this devious fashion, they learned that Cromwell had sent an ultimatum to the Earl of Westmoreland to surrender the castle or suffer siege—a bit of knowledge which revived memories Davy wanted to forget. In the meantime, Cromwell was identifying and burying the dead and arranging the exchange of prisoners.

It was on the fourth day that disaster overtook them. Davy was chatting with Hogge in their billet when Half-Hanged burst into the room, bug-eyed with apprehension

"Bowels o' God, we're undone!" he blurted "Ye recollec' that bastard, Sir Walter Cavendish—the Cavalier ye wouldn't let me silence on the road the d'y we escaped? Well, I jes' saw 'im!"

"*Here?*" gasped Davy.

"Right 'ere, damme if else! 'E's to do wi' the exchange o' prisoners, an' the like!"

"Did he see *you?*"

Half-Hanged's dark face purpled, and he began to sputter Hogge chuckled mirthlessly.

"It is plain he did—whoever he is!" observed Hogge. "But why the terror? Old Noll has pardoned you both for hopping so blithely from one side to the other!"

Half-Hanged looked askance at Davy, who reddened in turn " 'Tis a private matter, Piggey!"

Hogge rose to his feet, jeering. "In that event, I'll leave you two to worry about it. Adieu!" And he went out chuckling.

"Fer the luv o' God, hark to reason, Dyvy!" panted Half-Hanged. "Cavendish knows the truth, depend on't! We'd best get aw'y w'ilest the gettin' be possible, fer ye can't 'old *two* tigers by no tails! If Cavendish tells the gineral . . ." He shuddered at the mere thought.

Davy pondered the matter. He had become convinced Cromwell had forgotten them, but this would be a most unpleasant way of being called to his attention.

"Perhaps you are right," he conceded finally. "Tonight will be a good time . . ."

"The good time be right *now!*" Half-Hanged cut in. "Afore . . ." He paused as steps pounded up to the door. Without knocking, Major Priety stalked into the chamber.

"Peace be on thee, young man!" he announced sententiously, at the same time casting a bleak scowl at the open-mouthed sergeant. "I come to conduct thee into the august presence of his Excellency!"

"Oh, Jesus!" moaned Half-Hanged under his breath.

But it was not sufficiently *under* to escape the big ears of Old Piety.

"Seven days and thirty stripes for blasphemy!" he decreed sternly.

"Aye, an' gladly be I but alive in seven days!" sighed the sergeant. "W'at's 'is Excellency want to see us about?"

"He doesn't wish to see thy ugly face!" snapped the major, then turned back to Davy. "Art ready?"

Davy saw no escape, so with a shrug he reached for his hat. But as he prepared to accompany the major, Half-Hanged gave him a significant look.

"I'll saddle yer 'orse, m'lud, in case 'is Excellency . . . ah, er . . . gi's ye need o't!"

Davy grinned. "When we ride, we ride together, Sergeant!"

Priety glanced sourly over his shoulder. "Not for seven days, he don't, and then methinks he'll be too sore to ride far! Report to the corporal of the guard, Sergeant!"

As they strode along the crowded street, Davy tried to assure himself the summons had naught to do with Sir Walter. But whatever the motivation, Priety apparently knew nothing of it, for he renewed his offer to take Davy into his company as a common trooper—an offer which, under the circumstances, Davy was almost willing to accept.

On reaching the cottage where Cromwell had set up headquarters, they elbowed their way through a swarm of waiting officers and into an anteroom where they were stopped by an aide-de-camp.

"His Excellency will see you in just a moment," he told them. "He has a Royalist in with him now."

At the word "Royalist," Davy's knees quivered, and before he could recover his equilibrium, the intervening door opened and out stepped the last man in this world Davy wanted to see—*Sir Walter Cavendish!*

Too late, Davy recognized him! He tried, vainly, to slide behind the gaunt frame of Major Priety, but the Cavalier stopped short, his dark eyes lighting.

"By the Mass!" he exulted. "My old jousting comrade!"

Unfortunately, General Cromwell had come up behind him. "Ah, so you are acquainted with Ian of Dugald, Sir Walter?" he observed drily.

"Ian of Dugald?" roared Cavendish. "On my oath I am! Why, only a few days agone, I joined him in a toast to his fair Olivia!"

"Well, he has joined our ranks," grunted the general.

"*Ian* has?" laughed the Cavalier. "A miracle, no less!"

Davy, satisfied the game was up, had no desire to prolong the farce. He toyed with the thought of plunging his dirk into the jeering courtier, but had to be contented with damning himself for having restrained Half-Hanged when the latter had wanted to settle the matter permanently on the road.

"Have your say and be damned to you!" he snapped.

To his utter astonishment, Cavendish winked surreptitiously, then strode over with outstretched hand.

"Bless you, Ian!" he boomed jovially. "A truce on hard feelings! We can be on opposite sides without rancor, I trust!"

Bewildered, Davy felt his hand gripped, then Cavendish was talking to the general.

"By your leave, Excellency, I'd like a word with my old friend after you are through with him. I give you my oath as a gentleman I'll ask him no secrets, nor attempt to influence his decision. Howbeit, we have a private matter to discuss, which I beg you to permit."

Cromwell nodded impatiently. "Granted! You are under a flag of truce, so I shall accept your word that your conversation will confine itself to the personal." He beckoned Davy and turned back to his desk.

Davy shook off Sir Walter's hand and entered with all the enthusiasm of a man mounting the gallows. He heard Cavendish call: "I'll see you anon, Ian!" Then the door closed, and he found himself alone with Oliver Cromwell.

There was an austerity about the great man that made it a terrifying experience. The room was literally papered with maps and charts. They hung from the walls, they covered tables and chairs and lay like patchwork on the floor. Cromwell circled the big center table and seated himself to stare somberly at Davy. The silence grew unbearable.

"I have been considering what you said about the Marquis of Montrose," he announced abruptly. "He went into the Highlands virtually single-handedly, raised a horde of clansmen for the King, and taught us a bitter lesson. You claim that was possible because he was a Scot?"

Confused, and still concerned with the presence of Cavendish, Davy had difficulty concentrating on what the general was saying.

"That is the Scottish opinion, sir!" he admitted.

"Doubtless correct," growled Cromwell. He jerked to his feet and took a restless turn about the room, then stopped before Davy.

"Young man, you are aware of the situation here in Scotland!" he went on. "We control the Border and much of the Lowlands, and the entire line of the marches is dominated by the Covenanters. But the Highlands remain unconquered. Therein lies the crux of our problem, for though it is impracticable to march an army up in that wilderness to subdue them, the alternate, at the moment, is to maintain an army here in the event Montrose finally succeeds in raising all the clans against us! It is tying our hands in a futile war of attrition!"

Davy said nothing, so Cromwell continued: "Now the pivotal point of this stalemate lies in the hands of one man—Robert of Godolphin, the Marquis of Inventry and laird of the clan MacKenna. Do you know him personally by any chance?"

Davy stiffened, then shook his head. "No, sir, though of course I know of him."

"The old scoundrel has been well, if blasphemously nicknamed 'God-Awful,'" snorted Cromwell. "He has medieval concepts of his rights and privileges, and though he has admittedly no love for the Kirk, my information is that he has not yet thrown his influence to the side of the King. He's holding out to see which faction offers him the best deal, but we know that Montrose is working hard on him, for it is an axiom in the Highlands, as you are no doubt aware, that 'as Godolphin goes, so go the clans!'"

Davy felt his pulse quicken and for a moment he was able to forget the menace hanging over him.

"Old Godolphin has become something of a legend, sir!" he conceded ruefully.

Cromwell heaved himself into a chair again. "Aye, a bitter legend, but, unfortunately, no myth! When I was last in London, we debated the best method of handling him. Parliament is willing to make certain drastic concessions to win him to our side, but the difficulty of getting word to him through the Highlands was insurmountable until"—he leaned forward and impaled Davy with his eyes—"*until now!*"

Davy felt his scalp tingle. "I . . . I do not understand, sir!"

"Come, come—you are not that thick in the head!" snapped the general. "You are, in a sense, practically a nephew, for I am told he is the uncle of your betrothed, being the brother-in-law of the Earl of Westmoreland. You are the son of a laird, and you know the country and the clans. It would almost appear as if the Lord sent you to us for this express mission!"

"*Me*, your Excellency?" gasped Davy.

"I would not discuss the matter with you if I intended sending someone else, young man! You wanted a commission, and here is a heavensent opportunity tailored to your measurements! Oh, I grant you the risk is great! It is my thought to take a leaf from Montrose's book, and send Priety and a troop of, say, forty horse with you. This should be sufficient to deal with minor problems, yet not so large as to rouse the whole Highlands against you. Of course, you may encounter Montrose with his rabble, in which event I can only say— God have mercy on you!"

In panic Davy saw where his deception was leading him. "I care nothing for Montrose, sir!" he cried. "But Godolphin, sir—his clan MacKenna is the bitterest enemy of the Dugalds! Assuming I was fortunate enough to reach his lair, he would hardly listen to me!"

Cromwell shrugged. "Possibly not," he said indifferently. "But his personal feelings are not important. You will carry a message from *me*, which will be, in effect, an edict from Parliament. He may well tear it up and throw it in your face, in which event, you will have further orders." He paused, and his manner changed. He seemed to grow aged and weary in a matter of an instant.

"Lad," he went on grimly, "the great God who is the searcher of my heart knows with what reluctance I wage war against my countrymen and with what hatred I regard the taking of human life. Howbeit, this task has been placed upon my shoulders and I try to carry out the parts assigned me in the tragedy as expeditiously as possible, deeming it better to deal harshly with a few than prolong this struggle to the sorrow of the many. In this affair, you will offer Robert of Godolphin an opportunity to bring peace to his people, a peace with honor, for the terms are liberal in the extreme." His voice hardened abruptly, and with the straightening of his spine he again became the crisp commander.

"If he refuses, you will revert to the sword!" Cromwell said harshly. "You will place him under arrest and bring him in as a hostage, or, if he resists, take whatever action is necessary. You will be commissioned a colonel—in order to meet the marquis on an equal footing—and Priety will be your second-in-command. I shall include those disreputable henchmen of yours in the company."

Davy hesitated but a moment, for although a hundred dangers reared in his mind, they were mere shadows compared to the imminence of the disaster threatening in the person of Sir Walter Cavendish.

"Could I leave at once, sir?"

General Cromwell permitted himself a tolerant smile. "I'm glad to see you so enthused," he said. "But it will take some time to prepare my message to Godolphin and draw up your commission. I take it you accept?"

Davy bowed. "Aye, sir, though I am ill-fitted for the honor."

The general chuckled. "I presume you mean that in a different sense, yet I shall have Captain Vance, my aide, see to it you are suitably outfitted for the journey. Return here at eight of the clock tonight, and I shall have your orders prepared." He cocked his head and his eyes narrowed.

"For your sake, as well as mine, you must move with the greatest of secrecy. If the enemy got an inkling of your mission, you'd not get through the first pass into the Highlands! Remember *that* when you visit your Royalist friend, Cavendish. I trust him naught!"

"No less than I, sir!" Davy said grimly. "I'll tell him nothing!"

Cromwell waved him out. "If Priety is still waiting, send him in. He may as well get his orders now as later."

Like a man in a dream, Davy floated into the anteroom. When the major learned the general wished to see him, he peered closely into Davy's tense face, then patted him on the shoulder.

"Peace, lad, peace!" he said sonorously. "Our blessed general be a tern man, though just! I'll put in a word for thee!"

Davy grinned. "Thank you, Major! I hope you won't be as surprised by the results of your visit as I was by mine!" And leaving the major gawking in bewilderment, he passed outside.

When he returned to their billet, he found Hogge and Half-Hanged awaiting him with mixed emotions. The former was stretched lazily on the bed, his hands folded behind his head, and he glanced up with eyes mildly curious. Half-Hanged, however, was in a ferment of anxiety. Carefully refraining from any reference to Cavendish, Davy confided the details of his projected mission into the Highlands.

Half-Hanged danced around the room in jubilation. "Huzza! Didn't I tell ye to leave everythin' to 'Arf-'Anged Smyth? Damme, Ol' Noll did jes' w'at I tolt 'im! An' a full colonel, no less! Jesus, I'd gi' fifty guineas to see Ol' Piety's gloomy phiz w'en the gineral tells 'im 'e's to serve under us!"

"*Us?*" echoed Davy. "Why, man, you're supposed to be under seven days' confinement! I'll be at the other end of Scotland by that time!"

Half-Hanged was not to be denied. "'Ere now, lad, 'ere now! W'it ye a *colonel*, I ain't takin' guff from no major! An' don't be gettin' the big 'ead, fer ye'd no get far wi'out Ol' 'Arf-'Anged to advise ye!"

Davy grinned good-naturedly, but Hogge guffawed.

"By the powers, I do admire self-confidence in a man!" he jeered. So Half-Hanged Smyth, a small-fry Whitefriars thief, is setting himself up as a fairy godfather and king-maker!"

"I weren't no *small-fry!*" Half-Hanged snapped, his pride hurt. Howbeit, I own I on'y stole from the rich an' 'em as could afford it, an' not from the poor doxies o' Southwark—like *some* thieves I could mention!"

Michael Hogge took no offense. "True, but merely because you lacked the intellectual capacity for organization, Half-Hanged; a deficiency that keeps many another man honest!" He chuckled ironically, then turned back to Davy. "I take it you included honest Half-Hanged and me in this suicide pact?"

Davy shrugged. "You are at perfect liberty to refuse."

"God'sdeath! I wouldn't miss it for anything! It has possibilities a serious student of intrigue and double-dealings cannot afford to overlook. I particularly admire the essence of your instructions: *kill, kidnap or convince!* Succinct and euphonious!"

Davy frowned. "I received no such instructions!"

Hogge lifted one indolent eyebrow. "Didn't you? Then perhaps I misunderstood, or, possibly, you failed to see the priceless nugget screened by the general's masterly verbiage."

"Your skepticism has warped your judgment!" Davy said irritably. "All men are not as selfish and perverted as you either believe or pretend to believe! I grant you the journey is not without risk, but the mission itself is for the purpose of saving lives and bringing both countries closer to peace!"

"Bravo! Bravo!" applauded Hogge. "I stand corrected! And for this vital and diplomatic junket, the wise and godly Cromwell chooses as his dove of peace an inexperienced and youthful stranger whose salient qualifications are that he is a turncoat who has never seen an army and was utterly unknown to his Exalted Excellency until four days ago!" He laughed raucously. "Aye, my judgment must be warped!"

Davy felt the blood creep into his face. "Very well! Since you have set yourself up as an all-knowing oracle, suppose you entertain us with *your* version, my jaundiced friend!"

"Aye, damn ye!" snarled Half-Hanged. "Let's 'ear 'ow ye explain aw'y the fact 'at 'e's a gen-yew-wine colonel!"

Hogge doubled up the pillow under his head. "As to the *gen-yew-wine* colonel," he laughed, "even as amateur soldiers, you both should know that Cromwell has no authority to grant such a rank in the field, except as a temporary appointment in extreme emergencies, and then it has no validity until approved by Parliament. As to why Old Noll singled out our estimable comrade for this knight errand is less obvious, though no less devious, for as he candidly admitted, he could not send an army, hence it is a mission for one man, more or less.

"Howbeit, he failed to mention that he could not send a prominent Englishman on such a foolhardy venture because of the repercussions which would surely follow if he were slain, as in all probability he would be. Nor—if you'll pardon my saying so—would a reputable Englishman of noble blood accept such a frankly murderous commission." He paused and cocked one eye. "How am I doing?"

Davy bit his lip. "Continue, please!"

"Where was I? Ah, yes, we have Cromwell in a dilemma! Then, no doubt in answer to Old Piety's ardent prayers, the Lord sent a naïve angel, flanked by two somewhat lesser angels! And being a thorough, God-fearing Christian, the general accepts this bounty without asking embarrassing questions. Being no fool, he knows you cannot go back to the Royalist camp, therefore, in all probability, you will be reasonably loyal, and, being ambitious, will risk everything to succeed. Also, as a Scot—and again I beg forgiveness for my candor—you will have no nice scruples about using a dagger if, and when, diplomacy fails. Since your chances of returning alive are remote, he can afford to be lavish in his *promises*. If, on the crazy off-chance you succeed, you save Parliament millions; if you fail, the cost has been negligible. Have I made myself clear?"

Davy wagged his head. "I'm damned if I understand you! Believing all that rubbish, you are still willing to go? In God's name, *why?*"

"Ah! Now you raise a fine point!" Hogge chuckled. "Have I not explained that I am a student of human nature?"

"The worst side of human nature, it would seem!"

"Bah! There is only one side! Man is like a magician; he talks about one thing while his hands do something else. My friend, you confuse morals with intelligence. Look you—if virtue has any value, why did not Cromwell, a self-styled godly man, send the pious gospel-chanting Priety on this errand?"

" 'E is sendin' 'im!" rumbled Half-Hanged, only able to follow the high points of the discussion.

"Aye, for the purpose of spying on us to make sure we stick to the business at hand," jeered Hogge.

"You are wrong," Davy said as patiently as he could. "The general intimated that Major Priety lacked the necessary imagination."

Hogge hooted delightedly. "Damned with faint praise, by God! An imperishable evasion!"

Davy boiled over. "For two groats I'd leave you here!" he flared.

"Aye, an' I'll gi' ye the two groats, though damme 'tis all I 'ave!" Half-Hanged contributed.

Michael Hogge was unperturbed. "I doubt that, my lord," he said, grinning. "You haven't your conscience sufficiently muffled so that you can dispense with the services of a soulless and practiced cutthroat such as myself. For when you fail to *convince*, as you surely will, you'll need all the available support for the *kidnapping* or *killing* as required by that master of intrigue, his Excellency, Oliver Cromwell!"

Before Davy could reply, there came a soft rap on the door. Glad of the interruption, he jerked it open . . . to find himself face to face with Sir Walter Cavendish!

"Greetings, Ian!" said the Cavalier. "May I have a word with you . . . *in private?*"

Chapter Fourteen

For a moment or two, Davy was too nonplussed to reply, but he managed to step aside and permit the Cavalier to enter the room. The effect on the other two men was equally startling. Half-Hanged emitted a throaty growl and clapped a hand to his sword hilt. Michael Hogge, however, reacted even more strangely, for, on hearing the visitor's voice, he rolled over on the bed so that he came to his feet with his cloak wrapped around his face and darted out of the chamber like a cat with its tail on fire.

Cavendish stared in astonishment. "By the Mass!" he laughed. "Does the mere glimpse of a lone Royalist rout Roundheads in this unseeming fashion?"

Half-Hanged swaggered up to him. "Nay, by God, an' 'ere's one that knows 'ow to deal wi' an accursed lick-spittle!" he roared, and whipped out his blade.

Cavendish surveyed him from head to foot with studied contempt. "Get out of my sight, you ill-bred jailbird!" he grated. "You are no longer hiding in a tree limb, let me remind you! One word to your general, and you'll be hanging where you belong!"

Half-Hanged would doubtless have cut him down, but Davy had recovered sufficiently to motion his irate comrade away.

"Leave us!" he commanded. "I'll handle this!" He shoved the rebellious sergeant out the door and locked it behind him.

"Now," he said, turning to his unwelcome guest, "let us dispense with mockery. Why came you hence?"

Cavendish sprawled lazily in a chair and grinned up at Davy. "But let us not forget the amenities," he cautioned lightly. "Possibly I came to thank you for restraining that cut-purse when he wanted to slit my throat along the road."

"I hope I shall have no cause to regret my action!" Davy said pointedly. "You canceled out that debt by not revealing my identity to Cromwell."

Cavendish smiled. "I could hardly reveal what I do not know. All I know, and that definitely, is that you are *not* Ian of Dugald!"

"That doesn't account for your visit."

"On the contrary, it does!" laughed the other. "Knowledge, even limited knowledge, is not without a certain . . . ah . . . shall we say, monetary value—if you get my point?"

Davy paled slightly. "Your meaning is summed up in the word *blackmail*, isn't it?"

The Cavalier shrugged. "An ignoble word, sir, yet these are ignoble times, I own. Once I would have resented both the implication and the use of it, but we who follow the King have fallen upon evil days, and must profit by any means available, distasteful as they may appear." He sighed. "Be that as it may, I am not an unreasonable man. What is my . . . er . . . *forgetfulness* worth to you?"

"You contemptible dastard!"

The visitor held up a restraining hand. "Gently, sir, gently! Owing to the extreme delicacy of my business, I took certain precautions, such as having the general's aide guide me here to your lodgings with the promise of calling for me. Any delay would be regarded with suspicion. Now—shall we talk sensibly?"

Davy drew a quaking hand across his forehead. "In the first place," he said slowly, fighting to control his temper, "I haven't a solitary farthing, and being a complete stranger in camp, I have no means of raising any money."

Cavendish sighed again. "Ah, I feared as much! Yet be not disheartened; doubtless we can find some other means of exchange. While it is true I came here ostensibly to confer on the exchange of prisoners, I also came to keep my eyes open, which, may it please God, I have done."

"A *spy* as well as a *blackmailer!*"

"You have a most unfortunate vocabulary," clucked Sir Walter, "which leads me to suspect your breeding. No gentleman would apply such epithets to another. Howbeit, we'll not quibble over words. If *spy* creates a clearer image in your mind than *agent*, let it stand." He leaned forward and rested his forearms on his knees.

"Hark you—during my call on Cromwell, I took the liberty of

scanning certain papers on his desk. I saw a notation, *see young Dugald about Godolphin*." He smiled at the betraying flush which swept over Davy's features. "That note is pregnant with possibilities, is it not, my blithe impostor?"

"You're daft!" snapped Davy. "He merely asked me, as a Scot, whether I was acquainted with the Marquis of Inventry. I assured him I was not!"

The Cavalier laughed in his face. "By the Mass, either you're a fool, or you take me for one! Why even his Majesty, who is not noted for unwonted speed in such matters, is to, or has dispatched an emissary to Inventry! We have long wondered when the same notion would occur to your stolid squire from Huntington!"

"I know naught what you are talking about!" grated Davy. "Being a spy, you should have sense enough to realize I, a stranger, would not be in the confidence of the general! You are wasting time. Get out before I forget myself!"

Sir Walter rose with unhurried grace. "Diplomacy cannot be accomplished in heat nor haste," he drawled. "It is now about five of the clock. You have two hours in which to let reason and good sense gain the ascendancy over ill-bred temper, at which time I will return. Meanwhile, permit me to felicitate you on the ease with which you have assumed the role of a creature who, in all truth, was a beastly boor. In a government made up of jailbirds and country bumpkins, you should go far . . . *if you use your wits!* Good afternoon, *my lord!*" He bowed exaggeratedly and sauntered out of the room.

Davy was angrily pacing the room when Half-Hanged burst in a few moments later. The latter groaned when he heard what had happened.

"If ye'd on'y let me slit 'is bloody gullet like I begged ye, Dyvy!"

"God in Heaven, you can't slit every gullet you meet!" Davy retorted impatiently. "You wanted to cut mine not so long ago, then it was Hogge . . ."

Half-Hanged scowled. "Aye, an' mebbe I should ha' cut 'is! D'ye see the craven w'y 'e scuttled out o' the room w'en that bloody Royalist bastard strutted in?"

Davy *had* noticed Hogge's peculiar conduct, but had not had time to consider it.

"We have troubles enough without worrying about Piggey," he said. "You go out and keep an eye on Cavendish. I have a hunch he may be bluffing. If not, we'll have to make a break for it."

"An' ye, Dyvy . . . ?"

"I'd best stay right here. Cavendish may have a watch on *me*, and if I make a suspicious move, it might precipitate matters. But no violence, Half-Hanged!"

The sergeant agreed to the wisdom of this, and bustled out.

The next two hours were without parallel in Davy's experience. He felt like a man with one foot in heaven and the other caught in quicksand which must inevitably destroy him. In the narrow aisle formed by the bed and the wall, he paced literally for miles. About six of the clock, Captain Vance sent him some clothing and a new back-and-breast, so he fell to cleaning up his gear and re-dressing his wounds—half deciding it was a waste of time since he was almost certain to hang.

When seven o'clock arrived, with no word from either Half-Hanged or Hogge, his depression reached an all-time low. He was ready to believe the scoundrels had abandoned him after the fashion of rats leaving a sinking ship. That came from consorting with cutthroats and gallows-birds, he chastised himself, though on second thought he was forced to conclude that with a trifle more cutthroating on his own part, he might have avoided his present predicament.

The longer he pondered the situation, the angrier he became. If he had to die, by God, he'd silence the black heart of this sneering blackmailer! He'd toss the wretch's head into Cromwell's lap, either figuratively or literally! Suiting action to the thought, he whipped out his sword and made a few tentative passes through the air. No more talk, no more haggling! (A thrust to the heart!) Death to the spy! (A savage cut!) Give the dog no time to cry out! (A lunge to the throat!). . . .

Half-Hanged strode into the room so rapidly that only his shortness of stature saved his life. As Davy's blade *zinged* past his remaining ear, he gave a bleat of surprise and threw himself sideways onto the bed.

" 'Old, lad, 'old! 'Tis 'Arf-'Anged!"

Davy pulled himself up in angry embarrassment and kicked shut the door.

"Why in hell don't you announce yourself!"

The sergeant gaped, open-mouthed. "W'at be ye doin'?"

Davy flung the blade aside. "Never mind that! What did you learn?"

Half-Hanged wiped the sudden sweat from his swarthy face and prudently took his station on the opposite side of the bed.

"More'n enough, damme if else! Piggey be in cahoots wi' Cavendish!"

"Nonsense!"

"Say ye so? Hark then to this: I follered the blackmailer like ye tolt me. He sauntered down near the creek, w'en suddenly Piggey steps out from be'ind a tree an' accosts 'im! At first Cavendish acted like 'e'd seen a ghost, then they began a-chucklin' an' backslappin' like two thieves."

"Which they are," Davy grunted bitterly.

"Aye, but that's not all! I couldn't get close enough to 'ear much, yet I plainly 'eard yer name spoke amid gales o' merriment enough to myke me blood bile!" Half-Hanged fairly panted with indignation. "If y'd on'y let me finish that bastard Piggey w'en . . ."

"For God's sake, get on with your story!" raged Davy.

"Well, Piggey must o' tryded information fer 'is syftey, fer they waltzed across the bridge w'ich divides the line. Cavendish showed 'is pypers to the guards, an' Piggey passed o'er to the Royalist side an' disappeared."

Davy sank onto the edge of the bed and took his head in his hands.

"That does it!" he groaned. "No wonder Hogge called me naïve! I confided the whole plan to him and he betrayed me!"

Half-Hanged nodded sagely. "'Tis w'at comes o' 'ob-nobbin' wi' dishonest men, Dyvy!"

The sudden approach of footsteps brought Davy bounding to his feet.

"It's Cavendish, by God!" he hissed, snatching up his sword.

Half-Hanged drew his saber and tried to shoulder Davy aside.

"Stan' clear, lad, stan' clear!" he pleaded. "I've 'ad more experience . . ."

"Silence!" snarled Davy. "He's mine!" He crouched slightly and raised his voice.

"Come in!"

But it was Major Priety who stomped into the room. He stopped

141

short, staring at the bared swords and fierce scowls—now fast turning into red-faced embarrassment.

"Verily, this is passing strange!" he observed. When neither answered, he seemed suddenly to recall Davy's new eminence.

"Thy pardon, *Colonel!*" he went on, with a faint tinge of irony. "His Excellency's compliments, and would thou, and thy two *aides*"—this time the sarcasm was unmistakable—"kindly accompany me to headquarters immediately?"

Davy sheathed his blade, silently vowing never to draw it again until he had the proper recipient before him.

"Smyth is here," he said shortly, "but Trooper Hogge is not available."

The major inclined his head. "Unfortunate. Now if thou will be good enough to follow me . . . ?"

When they marched into the presence of his Excellency, they found him crisp and stern.

"Where is the other man?" he demanded.

Davy felt his mouth go dry. "I regret my inability to answer that, sir," he confessed. "I was not aware he was expected at this conference."

Cromwell dismissed the matter with a curt gesture. "It is not important; you can attend to it later. I am going to commission Sergeant Smyth and Trooper Hogge acting-lieutenants for the duration of your mission."

Half-Hanged welled over in enthusiasm. "Lieutenants! Leapin' . . ." He caught himself in the nick of time. "Oh, thankee, sir!"

Cromwell's eyes seemed to soften slightly, but his face remained harsh. He handed them each a parchment, had them lay their hands on a Bible, produced with incredible facility by the major, and solemnly swore them in as officers in the Army of Parliament. That accomplished, he brusquely congratulated them, then resumed his seat.

"Your orders are written out in complete detail," he told Davy, tossing a sheaf of papers toward him, "so it will not be necessary to go over them now. You will carry them on your person, for it would be disastrous if they fell into the hands of the enemy. If—and I pray God the contingency will not arise—but *if* misfortune should overtake you personally, then Major Priety will carry on. In the extremity that you should all face capture or worse, you are to destroy these papers. Any questions?"

"None, sir!"

Cromwell leaned back and eyed Davy calculatingly. "As to your route, I shall say nothing, since you are a native of the Highlands. However, you are to return via Lochbogie to see if you can induce your father to see the light. The Pass of Lochbogie is essential to our safety, and, to be perfectly candid with you, Colonel, I intend to secure it, either by diplomacy or . . . the alternative. You have my permission to report that to the laird if you see fit!"

Davy swallowed with difficulty. "Very well, your Excellency!"

"Now, you will have forty . . ." began Cromwell, only to pause at the sound of a commotion in the outer office. "What in heaven's name is the matter out there? Vance! *Vance!*"

Captain Vance thrust a red face in the doorway. "Your pardon, sir! A trooper just tried to force his way in here! We have him subdued now, sir!"

Through the half-open door, Davy caught a glimpse of Michael Hogge thrashing around in the grip of three or four stalwart sentries. He was beginning to congratulate himself on a narrow escape, when Priety burst out: "Your Excellency! That man is Trooper Hogge!"

"The devil you say!" grunted Cromwell. Vance had already closed the door, but the general ordered the prisoner brought in.

Michael Hogge was a mess! His tunic was torn and disheveled, and his clothes dripped mud and water. Only his bearded disfigured face remained as mocking and imperturbable as ever.

"How dare you create a disturbance outside my office?" thundered Cromwell.

"Because this lackey refused me entrance, sir," Hogge explained coolly. "My information was too vital for delay and too confidential for any ears save your Excellency's!"

Davy felt his heart begin to pound. He tried to read the expression on the prisoner's face, but failed.

Cromwell snorted. "It had better be vital!" he told Hogge grimly, then, to the others: "You men wait in the other room."

"Your pardon, sir!" Hogge interrupted. "Since my rather shocking story concerns these men, I beg you to permit them to remain!"

Half-Hanged gave Davy a wild here-it-comes look, and Davy

braced himself against the inevitable disclosure. Cromwell dismissed Vance and the guards, then nodded bleakly.

"Proceed!"

"Your Excellency will recall a certain recent visitor—Sir Walter Cavendish?"

Half-Hanged let a low groan escape him, which brought a sharp scowl from the general.

"I recall him," conceded the latter.

"Well, sir," Hogge went on calmly, "he accosted me on the road an hour or so ago and begged me to guide him to the line, claiming he had lost his way. Not suspecting treachery, I did so, but as we neared the sentries, he aimed a pistol at my side, under cover of his cloak, and forced me to accompany him into the neutral zone set up between the Royalist line and our own. Once there, he divulged a most astounding fact!" The speaker paused to heighten the suspense, then continued.

"You have been betrayed, sir! Cavendish was a spy! *He was informed about this mission!*"

The silence following this bombshell was numbing! Cromwell swung his icy eyes toward Davy who, for the life of him, could not restrain the blood from draining from his features.

Hogge gave a short grunt. "Nay, your Excellency! He did not learn it from Colonel Dugald! That I ascertained!" He turned his head and let his eyes rest briefly on the sergeant.

"Bugger me!" gasped Half-Hanged defensively. "'E got nothin' from *me!*"

"I made sure of that, also," Hogge said, with a faint sneer. "Howbeit, he seemed aware that I was assigned to the mission, for he attempted to bribe the details of the treaty to be offered Godolphin. That failing, he resorted to violence." Hogge spread his hands in resignation. "I was fortunate to escape with my life!"

Cromwell sprang to his feet in a lowering rage. "So they know the plan!" he stormed. "As God is my judge, I should have known better than to trust . . ."

"One moment, your Excellency!" Hogge cut in, but Cromwell was in no mood for temporizing.

"Silence! I've heard more than enough!"

Hogge shrugged. "As you please, sir," he murmured. "I presumed his dying . . . but, I beg pardon; you commanded silence."

Cromwell jerked around. *"Dying?"* he echoed. "What in hell are you talking about?"

"Of course, sir! Naturally I killed him," Hogge admitted, with an ironic smile. "It was with his last breath he cursed himself for not having confided his secret to another Royalist agent. From that intimation, I gathered he had meant to profit from his knowledge."

Cromwell stared in disbelief. "You mean—*they do not know?*"

"Not unless they had another source of information about which Cavendish was unaware!"

Cromwell threw himself into a chair. "Thanks be to God!" he said fervently. He brought himself under control at once and looked grimly at Hogge.

"Lieutenant . . ." he paused, and for the first time since their acquaintance began, Davy saw surprise on the scarred face of Michael Hogge.

"Nay!" went on Cromwell. "Not lieutenant—*captain!*" He seized a quill and drew a line through a word on the parchment before him, then scrawled in another. Sanding the document, he handed it to the astonished trooper.

"Here is your commission, Captain Hogge!" he said brusquely. "Colonel Dugald can take your oath at leisure. I commend your action, and though I have no time now, I want to hear more of this escapade on a later occasion!" He leaned back and included them all in his gaze.

"In the meantime, this incident points the need for speed. Be on your way before daylight!" He rose and herded them toward the door.

"Good fortune, and may God protect you all!"

Except for a rather stiff parting with Major Priety, nothing was said until the three reached the privacy of their quarters. Once there, Michael Hogge flopped wearily on the bed, and folding his arms angelically across his chest, stared dreamily at the beamed ceiling. Davy, not quite sure how to open the accusation, began to pace the room, while Half-Hanged Smyth took up a menacing position with his back against the door.

The stillness grew increasingly oppressive, and when the bearded man showed no sign of giving forth with the expected explanation, Davy finally halted above him.

145

"Out with it, you damned liar! I want the truth!"

Hogge rolled his eyes. "Bless you, my Colonel! Did you not hear my recitation to his Excellency?"

"Aye, I heard it!" grated Davy. "And a pretty yarn it was!"

Hogge chuckled. "Aye, I felt I did rather well—under the circumstances, that is! Naturally, as Half-Hanged did on another occasion, I had to gloss over certain unpleasant facts which did not pertain."

"Such as . . . ?"

"Mere gossip," taunted Hogge. "Yet interesting withal."

Davy bit his lip, but with customary directness, Half-Hanged blundered into the breech.

"Ye lied in yer black beard about Cavendish accostin' ye!" he challenged. "I seen ye—'twas *ye* 'oo stopped '*im*, then ye both went off a-laughin' an' twitterin' like a pair o' doxies, bugger me if else!"

Hogge turned his head and fixed the sergeant with a frosty eye.

"My thieving little compatriot, someone will do worse than bugger you if you don't stop following people, or at least not be so clumsy about it! I was afraid my erstwhile victim was going to see you floundering behind us during our walk to the bridge. I had difficulty distracting his attention."

Half-Hanged was so taken aback that Davy almost smiled. "That's beside the point!" he growled. "It is still true that you intercepted Cavendish of your own volition and that you are old acquaintances! How do you explain *that?*"

A faint flush purpled the scar-tissue on Hogge's cheeks. "I have no intention of explaining it!" he retorted coldly. "By a remarkable coincidence, the late lamented Sir Walter was perhaps the only man who held the secret of both *my* background and"—he paused to lend significance to his words—"to *yours!* I deemed it fitting the secret should pass with him!"

Davy caught his breath. "Am I to believe," he said slowly, "that you . . . ah . . . silenced him to preserve that?"

Hogge yawned. "My dear Colonel, you may believe what you damned please!" He stretched languidly. "And now, may I remind you that within a tragically few hours we again ride to join the legions of the damned. Let us enjoy the brief interim in the forgetfulness of slumber."

146

Chapter Fifteen

Shortly after three o'clock in the morning, the little cortege slipped out of Doughadee as quietly as their number and equipment permitted. As he rode stirrup to stirrup beside the dour and silent major, Davy could not help but recall that other morning, which now seemed so long ago, when he had ridden away from Lochbogie. Was it possible that had been less than two weeks ago? And what a miracle time had wrought! Then he had been a mere lackey; the captain's groom: now he was a colonel, and in command!

He chuckled without mirth. Had he actually bettered his position, he wondered? Was he anything more than an animated lie? The very name he bore was not his own; his exalted rank a mere sham for convenience' sake; even the clothes he wore had been stolen from a corpse, and the buff coat, the steel helmet and the shining half-armor naught but a loan from the general's aide. As for his brave command —though he rode at their head, he had never seen them save as vague shadows in the darkness. What a paradox his life had become!

They had covered nearly two leagues before the first rays of the rising sun smiled over the trees and revived Davy's innate gaiety. He glanced down at faithful old Gabriel padding along beside him. The hound had been of necessity locked up during their stay in the hamlet, and now he whimpered softly in the pleasure of freedom. Davy cautioned him to be silent, though he felt like yelping himself —especially when he thought of Anne Ramsay, baiting her trap in Doughadee. Annie was due for a surprise!

The sight of a stream ahead brought him back to the present, and he suggested to Priety that it might be a good time to refresh the horses. Thereupon, he pulled off the road and let his little company jangle past in review.

Michael Hogge, riding with Half-Hanged, whipped out his saber and presented it in a mocking salute. The non-coms down the line took the cue, orders were bawled, and the whole column trotted by at a crisp, well-disciplined attention.

Davy felt his spine tingle as he watched the rigid, hard-faced veterans passing before him. These were no half-frightened boys, or brawling gillies, but steely soldiers tempered in the crucible of war, and, by a trick of fate, they were his to command. The realization sobered him, and when the ride was resumed, he tried to reach an understanding with Old Piety.

"Look you, Major," he said, as they rode ahead together, "though I am responsible for this mission, I have no illusions about my rank. These men are accustomed to you, so I'd prefer to have you issue the necessary commands."

From Priety's oblique glance, Davy couldn't be sure whether the man resented him or not.

"Verily, sir, thou canst not separate responsibility from command!"

"I'm not trying to!" Davy snapped. "But this commission was not of my choosing."

"Truly, for thou art but an instrument of the Lord sent to carry the Word into the wilderness!" intoned Priety grandiosely. "It is not for me, therefore, who am but a humble toiler in the vineyard, to question Him who knoweth even the sparrow's fall!"

"A generous construction," Davy said drily.

"Thou profanest my intent, sir!" retorted the major. "I shall reframe my meaning in the carnal language of the world, which, peradventure, thou wilt more readily comprehend. The Lord maketh all things, even unto the jackal and the serpent. He likewise made thee, and by virtue of a heavenly reasoning, which I confess passeth my understanding, sent thee to his Excellency. Thou wert chosen for this task, which is further proof the Lord His miracles doth perform in strange ways. Therefore, I shall not risk divine wrath by shirking my duty in serving Him through thee."

"Well, at least we understand each other," Davy told him bluntly. "I intend to carry the cross, as you phrase it, but nevertheless I'll expect you to translate my wishes into such carnal jargon as these angels in half-armor can comprehend. Is that clear?"

"The Lord spake, and I heard His Voice!" mumbled the major.

They made excellent time, and at noon paused to eat in a little grove beside a stream. Davy withdrew by himself and spread out on the ground a rough map of the Highlands which Cromwell had included with his instructions. It was woefully sketchy; most of the smaller trails were omitted, and of those indicated many were inaccurate. Nonetheless, it refreshed Davy's memory and served to channel his thinking.

Above all else, he wanted to avoid Lochbogie, at least on the way into the Highlands, for the very thought of visiting his old home filled him with dismay. Whether or not he would stop there on his return, as the general had commanded, was a question he would deal with later—if he survived. At the moment, he felt much more like a tool of the wily Cromwell than an "instrument of God," as Old Piety had so unctuously proclaimed.

Studying the chart, he was reminded of another Pass into the Highlands about a day's journey further to the East. Having made up his mind, he summoned his "staff" and announced his plan.

Priety raised his eyebrows, but offered no comment, and Half-Hanged, knowing the reason, merely grinned. But Michael Hogge professed astonishment.

"Why pass up Lochbogie, Colonel?" he asked, in that sly way of his. "Not only is it the shorter passage, but you might pick up some gallant gillies to supplement our stolid English valiants!"

"Our force is adequate!" Davy retorted coldly.

"Aye!" chimed in Half-Hanged, "an' wi' all the winin' an' dinin' an' a-celebratin' we'd 'ave to do at me lud's castle, we'd wyste time!"

"Ah, to be sure!" laughed Hogge. "I had forgotten our colonel's identity for the nonce. Forgive me!"

However, when the others went for their horses, Davy drew Hogge aside.

"Heed me well," he said grimly. "I've had more than enough of your ill-considered wit! Priety may not be as big a fool as you assume, and I give you notice now—if any man attempts to jeopardize this mission, I'll slay him with my own hand!"

The other stopped smiling. "Precisely how do you mean that?" he challenged.

"*Precisely* as it sounds!" snapped Davy. "And I'll add this: I'm not satisfied with that facetious explanation you gave last night about your tête-à-tête with Cavendish! If I find we are betrayed, you'll not live to jeer!"

"Listen, my innocent!" growled Hogge, tapping him on the breastplate with a forefinger. "Without going into detail, let me assure you I have private reasons, quite as vital as yours, for not falling into the hands of the King's men! And as for being betrayed, I fear that is already a *fait accompli!*"

Davy stiffened. "Damn it, you said you killed Cavendish before he confided his information to another!"

"I did! But Cavendish was merely a self-appointed spy, hoping for profit. There were other Royalist agents in Doughadee."

"How do you know that?" ·

By this time, Michael Hogge had recovered his irritating *sang froid.*

"You will just have to take my word for it!" was the most Davy could wring out of him.

Yet the intimation haunted Davy, and when he was again in the saddle, his stomach knotted and he felt ill at ease. He had formerly planned to billet his men in a small hamlet along the road, but in view of what Hogge had told him, he changed his mind and decided to bivouac in the open. As the afternoon waned, his tension increased, until it was almost a relief when a trooper galloped up from the rear of the column to report they were being followed.

Davy had always preferred action to anxiety, so he wheeled his horse with the intention of riding back himself, when the realization came to him that command precluded such individual conduct. He reined in, and glanced at Priety, but the major showed evidence of a confusion akin to panic. Disgusted, Davy opened his mouth to summon Half-Hanged, then found himself calling for Michael Hogge. The action had been so unconscious, he was a trifle nonplussed when the bearded skeptic spurred up beside him.

Davy repeated the suspicions of the trooper. "Take the last ten men in the file and fall out of line," he concluded. "If you run into a vastly superior force, send me word at once."

Hogge grinned. "Very good, sir!" he said, and touching his helmet, pivoted his horse on its hind legs.

Half-Hanged came up in time to hear this, and as Hogge galloped back along the line, he looked aggrievedly at Davy.

"W'y didn't ye send me, Dyvy? Jesus, I ain't 'ad a brawl fer . . ."

"For exactly four days," Davy cut in, with a sour laugh. "You'll get a bellyful of fighting before we get out of the Highlands—that I promise you! Meanwhile, remember you're in the army now and stop haggling over every command that's issued!"

Half-Hanged blinked. "Well, bugger me . . . !" Then he saw Davy's face cloud, so he amended hastily, "Aye, aye, sir!" and backed away.

As they continued at a brisk trot, Davy fell to wondering why he had given the responsibility of a rear-guard action to the very man to whom, but a few moments before, he had bluntly stated his distrust. By all logic, Major Priety should have had the assignment, but that worthy's conduct seemed even more dubious than Hogge's. At the moment, the major was mumbling to himself and rolling his eyes. It was all very mysterious.

Davy shrugged the matter aside, but as time passed without word from Captain Hogge, he grew increasingly concerned. If the enemy had been close enough to have been heard by the rear of the column, why hadn't he had a report? Meanwhile, the sun sank in a splash of glory.

Soon the road wound down a steep slope to a small river swollen from the recent rains, and as Davy guided his horse across the precarious ford, he decided it would be a good place to make a stand. He confided his intention to Half-Hanged and the major.

Priety made a pious genuflection. "Whate'er befalls shall be the will of an all-knowing God!" he said.

"Nevertheless, you'll be good enough to help the Lord by deploying these men to the best advantage!" snorted Davy.

The twilight seemed pitifully brief. All too soon it was dark. Davy had just about decided he would retrace their route and risk an ambuscade rather than continue this uncertainty, when they caught the rhythmic beat of hooves. Priety barely had time to order his veterans to look to their primings before a group of horsemen topped the opposite rise and trotted down the slope toward the ford.

Fortunately, two of the riders in the van carried blazing flambeaus, so the major was enabled to recognize his own men. Nevertheless, Davy commanded them to halt.

"Where is Captain Hogge?" he bellowed across the river.

Out of the darkness came the familiar sardonic voice. "Right here, at your service, sir!"

Relief loosened Davy's temper. "What in hell delayed you?"

"Securing the prisoners, my Colonel!"

Davy whistled softly. So there *had* been action! "Well, hurry them over here!" he barked, and walked down to the water's edge to meet them.

In the darkness, he counted the shadowy forms as they floundered across the ford in single file. Thirteen! That meant there were only two prisoners, unless Hogge had lost some of his own men in the fracas. When the last man was over, he snapped, "Bring up those torches and let's have a look at the captives!"

Half-Hanged ranged on Davy's right, and Priety, openly quaking with nervousness, loomed at his left elbow, while the rest of the troop hastily formed a curious circle around the new arrivals. Hogge strode to the fore, propelling two figures shrouded in riding cloaks. He brought them to a halt before Davy, and as the torchbearers thrust the lights closer, Hogge jerked aside the cloaks in unison with the flourish of a magician uncovering a pair of rabbits.

There stood—*Anne Ramsay and Jenny!*

A spontaneous roar of merriment burst from the assembled soldiers, in which everyone joined save Davy and the Major. Even Jenny giggled.

When the laughter had subsided, Anne smiled.

"Are you not glad to see me, my lord?" she asked, unabashed.

Davy was mad enough to have killed her where she stood, but he was conscious of the troopers leering at him from the darkness, so he controlled himself as best he could.

"Lieutenant Smyth, take charge of the company!" he ordered grimly. "We'll bivouac here tonight!"

Then, as the reluctant Half-Hanged herded the equally reluctant troopers away about their business, Davy seized a flambeau from one of them, and commanding Hogge and the two girls to follow him, turned away to find a more private spot for the interview. When he saw Major Priety attempt to edge off into the darkness, he sharply ordered him to accompany them.

A few yards up the stream, he found a large boulder which offered a certain degree of seclusion. Here he halted, and once more faced the girls. From the major's self-conscious squirming, Davy was satisfied the affair was no surprise to him. Jenny lent support to this belief. She had been carrying a bundle in her arms, in the fashion of a mother holding an infant, and in the portentous pause that now ensued, she tenderly presented her burden to the red-faced Priety.

"I brung 'e a surprise, Major dear!" she giggled, forcing him to accept the carefully swaddled bundle. "Knowin' 'ow 'e love 'em!"

Despite his fury, Davy could not help but be intrigued by the tableau, so he held his peace while the major, in palsied confusion, peered into the bundle. What the man dreaded to find, Davy could only guess at, but it was with a whoop of relief that Old Piety drew from among the wrappings a large bottle of wine.

"Burgundy!" he gasped. "It be *Burgundy!*"

Michael Hogge howled with laughter. "Fooled you that time, by God!" he hooted.

Priety held up a restraining hand. "Take naught the Lord's name in vain, ye evil man!" he bawled. "Nor jeer at the grape, for the Good Book sayeth . . ."

Davy's temper snapped. "*Silence!*" he thundered. "Enough of this damned nonsense!" He glared sternly at Anne. "What means this? How dared you follow me?"

She met his frown with unruffled composure. Tossing her head to lay the ringlets about her shoulders, she gave him a knowing smile.

"*Dared*, my lord? Have you so quickly forgotten your solemn promise to marry me?" When he did not reply at once, she appealed to the smiling Hogge. "You witnessed his Lordship's vow, did you not, Captain?"

Hogge's laugh was rife with contempt. "I seem to have a hazy recollection of . . ." he began, but Davy cut him off.

"Conditions have altered since then!"

Anne set her jaw like the cocking of a pistol. "Not for me, they haven't!" she said tartly. "You cannot compromise a trusting maid and . . ."

"*Compromise?*"

"An ugly word, I own," conceded Anne, with a shrug. "It is cruel of you, my lord, to force me to confess my shame before these men!"

"*Anne!* Are you crazy?"

The major lifted his hand in pious horror. "Woe to the worshippers of Babylon who wallow in carnal sin!" he intoned. "As ye sow, so shall ye reap!"

Davy was too nonplussed to retort, for Anne's brazen implication

153

had taken him completely aback. But Old Piety was not to escape unscathed. Anne turned on him impatiently.

"Hold your peace, Major Priety!" she snapped meaningfully. "Let he who is without sin cast the first stone! Jenny has taken me into her confidence, and I'm shocked that a man of God, such as you profess to be, would so far violate the Commandments as to . . ." She paused and looked accusingly at the major, who stood rooted in embarrassment.

Hogge broke the stalemate with a raucous chuckle. "Since I am not in papist orders, I hardly feel qualified to hear these wholesale confessions," he drawled. "So with your permission, I shall retire." He saluted the men, bowed with mock courtesy to the women, then sauntered off into the darkness.

Davy offered no objection, being glad to see him go. The major, meanwhile, had found his voice.

"As Jehovah is my witness, I am as innocent of fleshly evil as our Savior was guiltless before Pontius Pilate!" he protested vehemently. "Jenny, lass, give the lie to these carnal imputations! Thou knowest I sought only to uplift thy immortal soul!"

Jenny giggled again. She was plainly a daft-headed wench, yet not without a crude native wit.

"As to a' tha', I canna say, Major darlin'!" she said ingenuously. "Ye speak such high-flown words as to pass the ken o' an ignorant lass such as maesel'! I know naught where mae puir soul be, preecisely, but wi' all yer fondlin' an' gropin' an' upliftin' o' petticoats, why to speak true, I believed ye arter some'at what goes by other names!"

The major seemed turned to stone.

"Jenny, you brazen hussy!" cried Anne, laughing in spite of herself.

"I on'y sought to answer 'im, ma'am!" Jenny murmured.

Anne looked sternly at the major, and sniffed. "That you did with a vengeance! He stands convicted in his own juice!"

Davy hardly knew whether to laugh or curse. It was manifest that, either directly or indirectly, the major was responsible for the presence of the girls. He began to have a new respect for Anne's intelligence. By bringing along the uninhibited serving girl, she had succeeded in compromising the major to such an extent as to make of him an ally; at least he dared not oppose her presence. Her diabolical shrewdness made Davy wary.

"Heed me well, Annie," he pleaded cautiously. "It was not my intention to break my word, but it is absolutely impossible to take you with us this time. We are on a dangerous mission which none of us may survive."

"All the more reason for my accompanying you, Ian! I accepted your promise on its face value, and have broken with my father."

He winced. "But *why?* You know there was . . . er . . . nothing between us!"

She cocked her pretty head. "That depends what you mean by *nothing,* my lord! Be that as it may, if I should attempt to return home now, my father would have me flayed for a common whore! He threatened as much the other time, but I assured him you promised to marry me as soon as you recovered from the battle." Her voice flattened. "You condemned me when you ran away without a word! There was naught I could do, save follow you!"

Davy pressed his temples between his hands. "I didn't *run away!*" he protested defensively. "I was ordered on this mission! God in Heaven, Anne, what am I going to do with you?"

"There's naught but one thing to do—*marry me!*" she said, with that characteristic air of finality which brooked no opposition. "It is quite customary for officers to take their wives along, as you are well aware, and even if we should run into a battle, no Scot would harm two defenseless women!" Then she turned aside to rake Old Piety once more to keep him thoroughly immobilized. "Doubtless the major will be happy to continue his conversion of Jenny!"

"The path to heavenly salvation is thorny!" muttered Priety gloomily.

Davy realized he had blundered into an emotional ambuscade from which there was no escape. He found it impossible to think clearly under the hammering impact of those large round eyes, so he thrust the torch into the ground, and walked slowly down the shore by himself. There he tried to marshal his routed objections, but found them woefully impotent.

Pondering the matter, it seemed that Anne's aggressiveness was the chief point of contention. Heretofore, he had always been the hunter, and to discover himself not only hunted but at bay, completely disconcerted him. Yet even this, Anne explained away with doubtful but unanswerable feminine logic.

Trapped, once more he began to rationalize. Why not surrender gracefully, since he had nothing to lose? Certainly he could not hope to find a more fitting mate! In shrewdness and wit, she had proven herself adept; in person she was comely and affectionate. Her ruthless, driving ambition was a match for his own, and if perchance he should claw his way to the heights, her mother's blood would add luster to his prestige. The question of "love" he shrugged aside. *Love*, he believed, was merely the antonym of *hate;* the synonym of *desire.* Obviously, Anne was desirable!

His decision made, he strode back to the others and dropped onto the ground beside Anne.

"Come, broach that Burgundy, Major!" he said, with a short laugh. "We'll toast our new comrades!"

The major happily seized upon a bottle and drew the cork with his dirk.

"Verily, 'tis the command of the Gospel, which sayeth: 'Wine maketh glad the heart of man!' " He passed the first bottle to Davy and reached for another.

Anne laughed and cupped one of Davy's big hands in her own. "Aye, drink, my dearest!" she urged.

When the second bottle was opened, Jenny grabbed it so avidly the major frowned.

"Easy, child, easy! Heed the warning of St. Peter: 'Be sober, be vigilant, because thy adversary, the devil, as a roaring lion, walketh about, seeking whom he may devour!' "

Jenny nearly gagged on her wine and snuggled closer to him. "Mon, mon, dinna speak o' de'ils an' roarin' lions stalkin' aboot!" she gasped nervously, "or I'll nae ha' courage to sleep alone!"

Old Piety looked as happy as a hound on a fresh spoor. He draped a bony arm about her shoulders.

"Fear naught, child!" he whooped cheerfully. "I shall light a candle of understanding in thine heart! Unto thee is paradise opened!"

Anne laid her head on Davy's shoulder. "The old hypocrite!" she whispered, laughing. "If I didn't know that Jenny is more than a match for him, I'd be concerned."

The Gospel proved to be correct, for under the mellowing influence of the wine, Davy's heart grew glad.

"It merely goes to show," he chuckled, "that Old Piety is a man first and a preacher second."

Anne raised her head slightly so that her lips were close to his. "And you, Ian . . . ?"

A collusive wind blew a strand of hair against his cheek and filled his nostrils with the provocative scent of her. Thus the last barrier of resistance was breached and he had the sensation of swaying toward his destiny in her arms.

Chapter Sixteen

By daylight, the column was on the move. The two girls rode at the rear, under a six-man escort commanded by Half-Hanged Smyth. Davy had decreed this for two reasons: it was safest in case of an ambuscade, and it removed the women from the hungry glances of the troopers.

As soon as Old Piety jogged up beside him, Davy spoke his mind. "You are an ordained clergyman, are you not?"

The major flushed guiltily. "Why, aye!" he stammered.

"Qualified to marry?"

The major looked surprised. "Under the ecclesiastic privileges . . ." he began sententiously, but Davy cut him short.

"Answer yes or no!"

"I am, by the grace of God!"

"Very well," snapped Davy. "Prepare yourself to perform a ceremony when we bivouac tonight!"

Old Piety gaped in consternation. "But, sir," he protested. "It is customary to post the banns and . . ."

"We'll dispense with that for lack of time."

"Consider what thou do," pleaded Priety. "Thou barely knowest this woman, nor she thee! I dislike to join those in the holy bonds of matrimony whom . . ."

Davy interrupted savagely. "Whether Anne and I know each other or not is none of your business, Major! You do the wedding and leave the bedding to me!"

Priety started to say something else, but apparently thought better of it. He squirmed restlessly a few moments longer, then flopping his bony elbows like a heavy vulture flapping his wings to rise, he turned his horse and began to busy himself with the troop, querulously inspecting equipment, until it was obvious he wanted to avoid further conversation with Davy. Thus, Davy found himself in the van paired off with Captain Hogge.

For over an hour they trotted along in silence. Unlike Half-Hanged, to whom silence was intolerable, Michael Hogge seemed to enjoy it, but in his current mood of relaxed content, Davy found it somewhat disconcerting.

"I suppose you heard my instructions to Old Piety?" he asked abruptly.

Hogge nodded. "One usually pays the asking price for a commodity."

Davy started to bristle, then realizing he had, in a sense, invited the remark, he chuckled drily.

"By my troth, you are a bitter skeptic! You must hate women!"

"You miss my meaning, Colonel. Skepticism augurs doubt, of which I have none, and hate implies an extreme aversion with active enmity, an emotional condition which in my case does not exist."

Davy grinned. "Then how do you explain it?"

"I don't!" the other retorted. "It is a matter of personal taste. He who is once poisoned on cabbage, avoids it in the future."

Davy wagged his head. "You are a complex character, Michael Hogge!"

"If you pardon my saying so, Colonel, you are prone to over-simplify people."

"But most of us are simple," argued Davy. "Take Half-Hanged and Old Piety, for instance . . ."

Hogge interrupted with a brittle laugh. "You take them; I've had a bellyful! Oh, I grant you Smyth is *simple* in one sense of the word: he has the intellect of a small child in the body of an adult, which results in a sort of hybrid monster."

"He's fearless and brave!" protested Davy.

"Aye, merely because he lacks mature imagination to be afraid."

Davy thought he saw an opening. "You are equally reckless!" he retorted.

Hogge chuckled. "Due not to bravery, but to a supreme indiffer-ence. Whether I die today, tomorrow, or ten years from now is of no moment." He deftly turned the subject away from himself. "Priety, on the other hand, might be deemed complex, for he is a peram-bulating battlefield of opposing forces everlastingly struggling with him. Given a Bible in his hand, the Lord—to use his phrasing—gains the ascendancy; but let him get a hold of a wench and a bottle of wine, and nature—or, if you prefer, the devil—makes him appear reasonably human."

"I take it, you have a penchant for the devil, Piggey?"

Hogge's pale eyes twinkled over the rim of his scar-tissue mask. "Aye, I confess a friendly reverence for his Satanic Majesty. He has been a valiant soldier, holding his own against overwhelming odds since the beginning of time. That in itself merits respect. He is the advocate of fun and frolic, in fact of most of the pleasures of this otherwise dreary life, yet he is meticulously honest about it. He holds out no bribes about a nebulous hereafter, nor sends a locust-swarm of priests and prelates to gain disciples through fear; you pay neither tax nor tithe to enjoy his bounties, nor suffer punishment if you choose to differ with him. He is a debonair sportsman; a true liberal. Why, according to your rabid Presbyterians, every child born of woman owes its very existence to the devil's kindly urgings, for he is held responsible for the original *sin*. Yet without this prompting, Adam and Eve would have died childless of sheer boredom."

Davy laughed heartily. "You realize you could be hanged for harboring such heresies?"

"I, and you, also, my brash young comrade, could be hanged for other things as well!" Hogge pointed out.

The marriage of Davy and Anne was solemnized that evening in a grassy loanin in a little copse of beech and oak, with the twin peaks of the mountain pass towering above them, like the steeples of a cathedral. It was an enchanted setting. The altar was composed of great boulders, presumably assembled by the Druids, and a tumbling brook filled the glade with music. Fir and pine had laid a lush carpet of bracken, which muted the harsh tread of martial boots and spurs, and as Old Piety took his place, the dying sun filled the vale with a roseate shaft of light no man-made temple could emulate.

Half-Hanged, nervous for the nonce, served Davy as best man; Jenny, looking unusually virginal, made a demure bridesmaid, and Michael Hogge, with a courtliness that belied his cynicism, gave the bride away. When Old Piety at long last droned to a welcome conclusion, Davy and his wife passed under a canopy of sabers to the seclusion of a wooded bower.

The morrow was forgotten—by all save Michael Hogge. He stationed sentries, and dispatched two troopers to scout the pass.

The company was astir at dawn, and breakfast was in the making, when the two scouts galloped into the camp with heartbreaking intelligence: just before daylight a little band of four well-mounted and armed Cavaliers had suddenly ridden out of the morning mists on their way to the Pass! The scouts had not deemed it feasible to dispute the passage, so they had remained out of sight, then, shortly thereafter, the haze had lifted sufficiently to disclose a large force of, perchance, a hundred Royalists, moving up the floor of the valley in the same direction.

This was appalling news!

Davy glanced at Hogge, and the latter gave him an I-told-you-so look that made him wince.

"You say the four got through the Pass?" he questioned the scout. At the man's nod of assent, he asked, "Can we reach it ahead of the main body?"

" 'Twould be nip an' tuck, sir!" the trooper conceded doubtfully. "At the nonce, they be about the same distance from it as us, but they're on the move!"

"But only at a trot, you said?"

"Aye, sir!"

"Then to horse, lads, to horse!" roared Davy. " 'Tis plain they mean to race us to Inventry, yet the force who first secures the Pass—wins! I know it well; twelve stout blades can hold it against an army! To horse, and we'll get there ahead of them, by God!"

As the troopers scattered to ready their mounts, Davy enlarged upon his plan to his officers. He'd leave Half-Hanged Smyth with a small escort to guard the girls, then, if they reached the Pass ahead of the Royalists, he'd assign enough men to hold it while the others rode on.

Anne, who had joined them, vetoed this flatly, and to Davy's disgust, Hogge sustained her.

"In the first place," he reasoned, "you cannot afford to spare an escort. Secondly, you would doom them, for no half-dozen soldiers could save them from the vengeance of the Cavaliers!"

The combination of logic and tearful lamentation was too much for Davy. He succumbed with ill grace, and ordering the girls to stay close beside him, he took his place at the head of the little cavalcade. Breakfastless, they struck off at a gallop.

Fortunately, a stiff wind was blowing from the east, which served the double purpose of cooling their lathered mounts and muffling the clatter of their breakneck progress. Thus, within a half hour, they topped a rise to discover the enemy toiling up the steep slope toward the Pass.

Warning his men to remain out of sight and cautioning them to absolute silence, Davy dismounted, and taking his officers with him, crept to a suitable vantage point.

At first glance, the situation appeared hopeless, for the enemy was already in possession of the only road to the Pass. But as Davy looked over the terrain, his mountain-trained eyes spotted a narrow ridge that went around behind the hump on which they stood in a sweeping curve which eventually bisected the road just under the rocky face of the Pass. If they had arrived just fifteen minutes earlier, they could have beaten the Cavaliers to the Pass, for this route was screened from the main road by a thick stand of spruce and fir. As it was—they were too late! Or so all the others agreed.

But Davy refused to accept that verdict. Failure at this juncture meant something worse than mere defeat. Then, as he scowled at the scene before him, a possibility dawned, a chance so desperate, he hesitated to suggest it. He browned it with both sides of his mind before beckoning the others closer and indicating the terrain.

"Aye, I saw the route," admitted Hogge. "Yet it's plain we cannot make it."

"We could if they halted!"

Hogge snorted. "An idle wish!"

Davy turned to peer into the ugly features of Half-Hanged Smyth. He noted the dogged cast, the childishly eager eye, and felt a quick surge of affection.

"Half-Hanged, this is no command," he said slowly. "I'll order no man to an almost certain death. Howbeit, you seem to bear a charmed life, and if you were to take a dozen men and create a diversion by falling on yon Royalist flank, I doubt not the rest of us could win through!"

Half-Hanged closed one eye and squinted thoughtfully at the winding column with the other. He was silent so long, Davy anticipated a flat refusal, but suddenly Half-Hanged laughed wickedly.

"W'y, bugger me, 'tis a pious suggestion, fer I swear I see a fancy back-an'-breast o'er yonder w'at'ud suit me better'n the dog 'oo's wearin' it! W'ere'll I meet ye arter we've looted the carcasses?"

Davy laughed relievedly. "You'd best fight your way back to Doughadee."

"An' miss the rest o' the fun?" objected Half-Hanged. "Damme, I'd rather 'ack me w'y to the Pass!"

Davy shrugged. "It's your show, my friend. Run it to suit yourself. But take only volunteers, for you'll want no man who may lose his nerve." He gripped the other's hand in parting.

"God go with you!" Old Piety called after him.

Michael Hogge chuckled sardonically. "This proves the point I made yesterday," he reminded Davy.

Davy scowled. "All I have to say is—I'm grateful for his simple loyalty. I wish I had more of it." Then he turned away to await results.

They were not long in coming. Half-Hanged had led his "forlorn hope" through the woods on the left, and soon they burst out of the covert at full gallop. Shrieking like drunken banshees, the valiant little band cut a swath through the tail of the Royalist column, then, wheeling, fell savagely upon the isolated remnant.

Fascinated, Davy was reminded of a sluggish serpent, for the long queue halted, wavered in bewilderment, then the head turned around and began to slither back toward the source of pain. This was the precious moment of confusion for which Davy had waited. He ran for his horse, threw himself into the saddle and spurred for the ridge. His troop thundered behind him.

It was a reckless gamble in which he had risked all on one throw of the dice, for if the trees hid his force from the enemy, it also hid the enemy from him. There were so painfully many "ifs": if Half-Hanged withdrew too soon, or were quickly repulsed, or if the Royalists suspected a ruse and galloped forward, Davy and his meager force would clash with them head-on. These possibilities haunted him during the mad plunge along the ridge.

But when they broke into the opening for the last two-hundred-yard dash to the road, he realized the diversion had succeeded beyond his most sanguine hopes. Of his heroic comrades, nothing could be seen, but the Cavaliers were still milling about, and when they discovered their mistake, it was too late.

163

Davy whooped in defiance when he hit the road, then spun his charger on its hind legs and waited until the last of his force had swept by on their way to the Pass. Meanwhile, the Royalists had reformed and came thundering forward in angry haste. Davy paused only long enough to give them a mocking salute before he spurred after his men.

According to legend, the Pass had been conceived by jealous gods to protect and isolate the Highlands from the hosts of evil. Two gigantic excrescences of solid rock jutted upward, like the breasts of a passionate woman, while the Pass itself, scarce wide enough for a wagon, squeezed between them. Nature—or the gods—had sculptured niches in the upper face of the rock on which bowmen or snipers could lie in comparative safety, and shoot down into an attacking horde. As Davy had foretold, a dozen seasoned warriors could hold an army at bay—so long as their endurance lasted.

Major Priety had preceded the company, and by the time Davy passed through, harbusquiers were already inching out onto the ledges to harass the oncoming Royalists. With the situation momentarily well in hand, it was time for a fateful decision: *who should remain?*

It was obvious Davy could not, for it was imperative he reach Inventry ahead of the four Cavaliers, and only he knew the Highlands. Yet the choice between Priety and Hogge was a bitter one, for he trusted neither. As he pondered the problem, a ball ricocheted off the smooth surface of the rock and droned past his head. It punctuated the need for haste.

He beckoned the major. "You will remain," he ordered crisply. "But do your fighting first and your praying later."

Without more ado, they divided the company. Priety was given sixteen of the older men—those more fitted to stand firm under pressure than for saber-fighting in the saddle—while Davy took the remainder. Even as they made the division, a sustained gunfire began to roar and echo through the hills.

Davy leaned down and offered his hand. "Good luck, Major! I hate to abandon you this way. Keep an eye out for old Half-Hanged."

"Aye! Yet fear for us naught, for as Solomon hath said: 'The souls of the righteous are in the hands of God, and there shall no torment touch them!'" Then, as an afterthought, he added: "Have a care for poor Jenny, lad; her soul be unshriven!" And with that, he scurried to his post.

Davy's detachment was ready and waiting. He viewed them with a sinking heart: Captain Hogge, a bearded satyr, Anne and Jenny, hungry and distraught, and twelve dragoons—a pitiful force with which to invade the savage Highlands!

Chapter Seventeen

Fourteen hours of marriage had wrought a singular change in Annie. Her former camaraderie and cheerful willingness to share the travail of the campaign seemed to have vanished with the nuptial night. They were barely out of earshot of the Pass before she began to complain bitterly about her lack of breakfast, and badgered Davy to call a halt. He sought to reason with her, for her noisy lamentations embarrassed him, explaining as gently as he could why it would be fatal to tarry until the Royalist agents had been overtaken. When logic failed, he made a flat refusal. At this, Anne swerved her horse off the road, threw herself out of the saddle, and when he tried to force her to remount, went into shrieking hysterics. Jenny flung her arms around the wailing Anne, and hissed at Davy that he was a "hateful beastie!"

Never having experienced such a situation, Davy was completely nonplussed. He stood staring helplessly at his wife, conscious that his men had formed a ring and were taking it all in from their saddles.

Finally, Michael Hogge dismounted and walked over to him. Davy dreaded to meet his gaze, but when he did, instead of the expected mockery, he found a kind of grim sympathy.

"Why don't you continue on," Hogge suggested quietly, "and let me handle this?"

"What can you do?" muttered Davy.

"I could slit her throat," the other grated between his teeth, "but I won't. Unfortunately, I am familiar with the type; she'll calm down as soon as you leave."

Davy was loath to comply, but as the situation was growing more desperate with each passing moment, he acquiesced. But as he turned away, Anne wailed tearfully: "Don't you dast leave me! Don't you dast!"

Davy hesitated. "If I do not, none of us will ever escape these hills alive, Anne! Can't you get that through your silly head?"

Annie only caterwauled the louder. Michael Hogge regarded her over the rim of his masklike scar, and flexed his long graceful fingers as if imagining a white throat already in his grip.

"For God's sake, tarry no longer!" he snarled, giving Davy a shove toward his horse.

Racked betwixt reason and emotion, Davy dragged himself into the saddle. He felt drained and exhausted, and only the pressure of the exigency supplied the will to continue. With bitter reluctance, he again cut into his meager force, this time assigning six troopers to remain with Captain Hogge. Assured the others would follow as rapidly as possible, he gestured his own men to follow and put their mounts into a gallop.

About ten of the clock, they clattered across a rickety bridge to discover a dingy little public-house planted at a fork in the road. Uncertain of the route and eager for information about their quarry, Davy called a halt. He cautioned his men to be vigilant, then dismounted and strode up to the door alone. It took several minutes of pounding and hallooing before it was opened by a stringy-looking slattern. A dirty brood of half-naked urchins hovered around her skirts.

She greeted him with such manifest hostility, Davy sensed she had been forewarned. Pretending not to notice her manner, he gave her a friendly salute.

"We travel on the King's business, good woman," he announced genially. "Four of our comrades rode this way whilest we here paused to deal with some Rebel dogs. Can you tell me how long since they passed?"

He watched her dull-witted face cloud with uncertainty, then narrow in animal cunning. In stammering dialect, she countered that her "gudeman was awa'" in the hills, though expected back within the glass; Davy would have to await his return, for she knew naught of worldly matters. From this tenuous position she refused to budge, parroting the same reply to every probe.

Defeated, Davy concealed his impatience as best he could, though he wanted to wring her neck. He dreaded the loss of precious time, yet reasoned that to take the wrong route would be more disastrous still. So he took out a purse of coins and jangled it temptingly while requesting food and drink for his men. The silvery music was irresistible. The woman threw open the door and bade them enter.

Leaving one trooper to guard the horses, Davy led the others into the hovel. There was no floor, only a woven mat of rushes laid on the bare ground. In the center of the room was an open fire of smoldering turf, the smoke from which struggled with only partial success to escape through a small hole in the roof. The troopers good-naturedly groped through this strangling fog to a rough table set near the wall. After a short wait, the woman, assisted by three of the older offspring, brought in some earthen mugs half filled with bitter ale. Then she withdrew to prepare the promised meal.

One of the dragoons took a deep swig, then, gasping and sputtering, spat the stuff onto the floor.

"God'sdeath!" he gagged. "This ain't ale! 'Tis horse urine, I vow!"

The men guffawed boisterously. " 'E ought to know!" hooted an old veteran. "I've suspicioned Charles o' milkin' that geldin' o' 'is!"

Smiling grimly, Davy warned them against offending their hostess, for while she herself was engaged in the scullery, a row of big-eyed youngsters ogled the troopers from the foggy shadows along the opposite wall. Davy's grin emboldened the oldest, a lad of about ten. This urchin sidled up to him and in Highland dialect asked if the finicky soldier addressed as "Charles" was *King* Charles.

Davy pretended embarrassment. "Why, that's a great secret, lad!" he conceded in a lowered tone. "How came you to guess it?"

"Your other comrades told my father the King was near by!" breathed the boy, adopting the same conspiratorial whisper.

"Did they so? And they let you hear it? By the Mass, 'tis plain they knew you a lad to be trusted!"

The little fellow expanded. "Aye, sir! They gave me a bawbee to water their beasties!"

"How long since?"

"No longer'n it would take to walk a half-league!" opined the boy. All the time he was talking to Davy, his eyes, wide with awe, kept swaying toward the ribald trooper named Charles.

Davy stooped down and whispered in his ear. "Look you, I'm not certain he will permit it, but if I arrange for his Majesty to shake your hand, will you tell me something truthfully?"

"Oh, aye, aye!"

"Then you wait right here!" Davy said, with a reassuring wink.

He went over to the table, whispered briefly to the soldier singled out for momentary fame—who blinked in incredulous astonishment —then beckoned the urchin to approach. As the lad squirmed closer, Davy asked, "What is your name, laddie?"

"Roland, sir, though Mamma ca's me Bonny!"

"I like that!" approved Davy. "We'll use it. Now bend your knee before his Majesty!"

"His Majesty" was enjoying his role. He now sat upon the table as if it were a throne—a scarred, saturnine-faced scoundrel obviously better acquainted with Whitefriars than Whitehall. The word had gone swiftly around the board, and the other troopers joined the farce.

"Your Most Gracious Highness!" Davy said solemnly. "This is Bonny, one of your loyal subjects. He begs the honor of kissing your royal hand!"

The "king" beamed jovially on his "subjects." "W'y, blarst me bleedin' buttocks!" he boomed. "A likely lad, I trow, an' a loyal subject these d'ys be some'at to cherish! Damme, 'e can kiss any part o' me royal arnatomy 'e chooses!"

"The hand will do, your Grace," Davy said, with a warning frown.

The jest began to lose its flavor when he saw the tearful respect with which the child bent over the trooper's grimy paw, and Davy almost regretted the business.

"W'at'll ye 'ave now, Colonel?" brayed the "king." "'Ow about m'ykin' 'im Knight o' the Royal Chamber Pot?"

"Charles could use a Royal Pimp, Colonel!" contributed a dragoon.

"So could we all!" echoed another.

"His Majesty," Davy snapped, "has already exceeded his bounty. With your Grace's permission, we will withdraw!"

Leaving the troopers to their bawdy merriment, he led the breathless youngster to a corner.

"Now, Bonny, I want the truth! Promise?"

"Aye, aye, sir! On me oath!"

"Which way did my friends travel?"

It was plain the boy had been cautioned against that very question. He hesitated.

"You'll nae tell mae father?"

"I swear it!"

"They took the left fork, sir, thence o'er a secret trail known only to mae father!" faltered the boy. "He pulled a drag behind his nag so that no one could follow their tracks!" The little fellow's lips began to tremble. "Whist, sir, he'd skin me alive if he knew I'd tattled!"

Davy pressed a coin into the grubby hand. "On my oath, Bonny, he'll never learn it from me! Now run along before your mother catches you talking with me."

The youngster had barely scuttled into the murk before his mother and sisters brought in the food, which consisted of a large vessel of haggis, supplemented with broiled moor-game, ewe-milk cheese and rough oaten bread. Though the English soldiers balked at the unfamiliar haggis, they wolfishly attacked the rest of the meal.

But Davy had no appetite for food. He knew now that he could never hope to overtake the Cavaliers before they reached the safety of Inventry, for without skilled local knowledge, those secret Highland trails would be impossible to follow. Yet, if it was folly to continue, it was almost impossible to withdraw. Alone, he might survive, but with his handful of English troopers—too many to hide, too few to fight—the chances were slim. His predicament was unenviable.

The troopers, happily unconcerned, were halfway through the meal when a warning bellow from the guard outside brought them to their feet. Davy ran out in time to see a large body of horsemen, almost enveloped in a cloud of dust, come swirling down the slope toward the bridge. He ordered his men into the saddle for instant flight, but on taking a last look before mounting himself, to his intense relief he recognized Major Priety in the van! When they clattered onto the bridge, he could distinguish Michael Hogge, with Anne and Jenny cantering behind him, and—incredibly—Half-Hanged Smyth!

Soon the explanation of his seeming miracle came in curious blending of scriptural quotations and Billingsgate profanity. Old Piety burst forth in raucous prayers, insisting that their salvation was entirely the work of the Lord, but since Half-Hanged was a mass of blood and gore, this seemed to Davy hardly the whole story. Yet even Half-Hanged was scarcely more coherent, for he had suffered the loss of his remaining ear, and wanted to talk of nothing else. Nevertheless, Davy learned eventually what had happened at the Battle of the Pass.

Early in the fight, a lucky ball had downed the Royalist commander, and in the resulting confusion, Half-Hanged and the survivors in his suicidal sortie had won through to the Pass. In high dudgeon over the loss of his ear, Half-Hanged had prevailed upon Priety to furnish him sufficient men for a sally. This had been so devastatingly successful, the Cavaliers had picked up their dead and withdrawn.

"Verily, the Lord hath blessed His servants!" intoned the major. "It augurs well for our success!"

"On the contrary," grunted Davy, "it augurs ill! The very fact the Royalists withdrew so easily . . ."

"*Easily?*" yelped Half-Hanged bitterly. "W'y, bugger me . . ."

Davy had to smile. "Bless you, old comrade, you did a terrific job, I own!" he interrupted. "Yet the point I make is this: if the Royalists had not gained their major objective, which was obviously to secure a passage for their four agents, I seriously doubt they would have withdrawn. Having gained that, however, there was small advantage in losing men at the Pass."

Hogge concurred in this. "In apparent victory, we have been defeated," he conceded.

"But, damme, we can o'ertake them four agents!" argued Half-Hanged.

Davy moved them out of hearing of the company, and told them what he had learned from the boy. "So you see," he concluded, "there's no possible chance of reaching Inventry ahead of them!"

The major spread his hands in resignation. "The Lord hath punished our sins! There is naught for it save to return to Doughadee!"

Hogge grimaced. "Though it pains me to agree, we'd better have at it before the Royalists recover the Pass, else we'll be literally caught betwixt the devil and the sea."

Davy pointed toward the road over which they had just arrived. "If that's your pleasure, gentlemen—there's your route!" he snapped. "As for me, I've an insatiable curiosity about this *devil* who waits in Inventry. I'm going on!"

171

Half-Hanged chortled delightedly. "W'y, bugger me, lad, w'at're we waitin' fer?" He flipped the reins over his horse's head.

Major Priety looked startled, but Michael Hogge burst into laughter. "I thought that prod would bring a decision! The major can . . ."

"The *major*," barked Old Piety, "can speak for himself! We will carry the Word even unto the very den of Satan!" He cast a nervous glance over his shoulder. "Methinks, Colonel, thy wife . . ."

Davy swore softly. In the excitement, he had momentarily forgotten about the girls.

"Have the men dismount, Priety," he ordered. "We'll refresh ourselves here before continuing." Then, leaving Half-Hanged to care for his horse, he strode over to where Anne still waited in the saddle.

She welcomed him with a contrite little smile, and as he lifted her down, she threw her arms around his neck and kissed him ardently.

"Can you forgive me, darling?" she whispered. "I was overwrought!"

Davy was only too willing to forgive, and led her into the hostelry. Even when she refused to sit at the same board with the common soldiers, he took no umbrage, but bribed the hostess to set a place for her at a small table on the far side of the room. However, when she begged him to remain with her, he explained that he had already eaten and must see to his men.

He went outside again to find Michael Hogge tightening his saddle.

"I'm eternally grateful to you," Davy said. "Did you have any difficulty with her?"

Hogge straightened and combed his beard with his fingers. "We're here, aren't we?" he grunted.

Davy grinned ruefully. "A miracle in itself! Yet I would fain know your methods in the event a similar occasion arises."

"You can be assured it will arise as long as she has a breath in her vicious little body!" Hogge said. "Howbeit, my methods are of no use to you, for, as the ancients had it, a physician doth not work cures upon them that know him!" He cocked his head. "How long do you calculate it will take us to reach 'God-Awful's' lair?"

Davy bit his lip. "Three days of hard riding—with luck!"

Captain Hogge gave him a mocking salute. "My dear Colonel,"

he sneered. "You are the first man I ever met who seemed to thrive on trouble!"

Davy was saved the necessity of replying by the troopers' coming out of the inn.

Chapter Eighteen

In mid-morning of the fourth day, they plodded to the summit of a rocky saddle to see Loch Inventry, dun-colored under a cloudy sky, spread out before them. An island of granite thrust itself out of the lake some two hundred yards offshore, reached only by a tenuous natural causeway. On the island was a castle.

It was not without justification that the natives spoke in awed tones of Castle Inventry as the "old eagle's eyrie," for skulking on its lonely eminence, it did resemble the nest of a bird of prey. With none of the symmetry and architectural graces of Westmoreland, nor even the simple indigenous charm of Lochbogie, it crouched bleak and forbidding on its barren, wind-swept rock. There was an alien mood about the harsh black towers and thick jagged walls as if, perchance, it had been thrown together by a foreign invader as a retreat for his ravishing hordes. It seemed significant, too, that no roads went beyond it; like a gloomy sepulcher, Castle Inventry was in itself a journey's end.

Davy reined in and tried to repress an involuntary shudder. More awesome than the haunted pile was the fact that he could see no living creature on or about it. No sentry paced its ramparts, no cattle grazed among its heather; not even a flag fluttered from its staff. As far as eye could detect, it was a place of death.

"Methinks the Laird of Inventry drew his nickname from his castle, rather than any travesty on his family name," commented Michael Hogge.

Half-Hanged shivered. "Bugger me, it do look the abode o' the devil 'imself!"

Davy, having recovered from his initial shock, laughed drily. "Well, it's naught but the home of a mortal man, and for him I have

174

a message which I mean to deliver in person. However, it would be foolhardy to attempt an entrance with our whole force, hence I shall go alone."

Hogge snorted. "My dear Colonel, have you forgotten that what you carry is less a message than an ultimatum? In effect, your orders are to kill, kidnap or convince. Obviously, you cannot accomplish either of the first two alone, so having no particular desire to reach old age, I beg leave to accompany you."

"An' me," put in Half-Hanged Smyth, " 'oo 'ave been closer to 'ell than either o' ye, will keep ye company!"

Major Priety rolled his eyes heavenward. "The Lord is my refuge and my fortress! Hence it is meet that I, who serve God, should assist in the delivery of His message!"

Davy laughed heartily. "By my troth—three would-be suicides! Howbeit, much as I appreciate your courage, someone must stay with the . . . er . . . troop."

"Let Piggey st'y!" Half-Hanged suggested. " 'E's a w'y wi' the wimmen, an' fer mesel', I'd rather fight me w'y out o' purgatory than 'andle them wenches!"

"I can remember the time when you were only too eager to *handle* either of them!" Davy shot back.

"Aye, you simple-headed cut-purse!" sneered Captain Hogge. "What our esteemed colonel needs with him is brains, not brawn! But let the parson remain. His prayers will have as much weight on the outside as on the in."

Old Piety stared down the rim of his nose. "Godless knaves! Thou knowest I can't control these females!"

Davy chuckled. "It would appear you all prefer the terrors of the unknown to the known terrors of our fair companions! Nevertheless, I think Piggey's suggestion the best. Major, you will remain with the company."

Though he tried to look disappointed, it was plain the major was relieved.

"As a man of God, I like it naught," he murmured. "Yet as a soldier, I must obey."

Davy suppressed a smile. "Keep the girls and half a dozen men with you, and distribute the rest in a thin line along the hills. Have them build a series of small fires to create the illusion of a large force.

You might let little groups of them be seen here and there. Do you ken my meaning?"

The major nodded somberly. "Aye, for all the good it will do once those portals have devoured thee!"

"It may have a salutary effect," Davy grunted. "Howbeit, let no one enter or leave the castle, *nor under any pretext go you into it!* If we are seized as hostages, so let it be. Return to Cromwell and say to him that we have failed."

"How long doth I await thee?"

Davy scanned the overcast. "It lacks about an hour of noon. What say you, Captain?"

Hogge's scar had grown taut as it always did under excitement, yet his smile remained coolly skeptical.

"Certes, I doubt a lifetime sufficient to convince my Lord Godolphin," he replied. "Yet the killing will not take long. I should say we shall either be dead or out of there before the night falls."

Davy nodded. "My very thought. So, Major, if we have not returned by sunset, you will have nothing to wait for, so utilize the twilight to put as much distance between the castle and yourselves as horseflesh will stand!" He glanced over his shoulder to where Anne sat unhappily beneath a tree. "Make my excuses to my lady, Major," he added in an undertone. "I lack the courage to face tears at this juncture. And be good to Gabriel!"

Priety nodded dourly. "God keep thee, sir! And . . ." With noticeably less enthusiasm, "thy two pagans as well!"

Riding down the stony incline with Hogge on his right and Half-Hanged on his left, Davy appraised the castle closely. The utter lack of life began to assail his nerves. The silence created an atmosphere of almost unbearable suspense. Even the veteran war-horses sensed it and grew increasingly restless.

The ancient Barbican, or outer defense tower set on the shore-end of the causeway, was in ruins, yet as they rode under its crumbling arches, a gust of wind whimpered like a startled ghost. Davy felt the hair rise along his nape.

The three adventurers cantered boldly across the narrow causeway to be halted by a massive door of oaken planks heavily studded with iron which gave entrance to a blocked-up gatehouse, long since converted into a Keep. Motioning the others back, Davy turned his horse sideways and pounded on the door with a gloved fist. But the planks were so thick, he might as well have pounded solid rock. After an exchange of grim glances with his comrades, he drew his saber and beat the hilt against the panel.

"Damme!" Half-Hanged muttered, *sotto voce*. "Me skin crawls!"

"Be grateful!" sniffed Michael Hogge. "It won't crawl long, methinks!"

Davy frowned them silent, and once again rapped his summons on the door. This failing, he backed his horse away from it, and shouted, "Halloo, the watch! Halloo!"

Little echoes picked up his cry and carried it along the walls like mocking heralds. *Halloo, the watch! Halloo!* Chagrined, Davy was about to fire his pistol, when at last a querulous voice answered through a cross-bow slot just above the door.

"Who comes, and why?"

The question, seeming to emanate from solid rock, took Davy unawares. He drew a deep breath to steady his voice, then replied boldly, "An officer of the Army of Parliament with a message for my Lord Godolphin from Lieutenant General Cromwell!"

"Go ye back the way ye came!" retorted the voice. "The laird wants no dealings with Rebels!"

"Then let his Lordship tell me so in person!" barked Davy. "Open this door!"

"I hae me orders! Get ye gone!"

"Why, damn your eyes!" roared Davy angrily. "Has the Master of Inventry grown so cowardly he dares not face a lone *Dugald!*"

The gasp this engendered was plainly audible. "*Who?*"

"*Dugald!*" thundered Davy. "Dugald of Lochbogie, now Colonel in the Army of Parliament! Tell your master *that!*"

"Aye, aye, I will, I will!" chortled the voice.

They could hear him withdrawing, muttering to himself. "Dugald! A *Dugald*, by the Mass!"

"Well, that did it!" Davy commented grimly to his companions.

Hogge stroked his beard. "Aye, it also removed the element of chance."

"W'at d'ye mean?" growled Half-Hanged. "'Twill get us in, I wager!"

Hogge laughed nastily. "No doubt. It will guarantee our *staying in*, too."

177

The gatekeeper returned in a remarkably short space of time. "His Lordship welcomes ye!" crowed the voice, and then the door began to clank slowly open, apparently operated manually by chains. The trio found themselves staring down a long, arched passageway—half-hall, half-tunnel.

Suddenly, out of the shadows formed by the open doors, popped an aged hunchback, his deformity made more grotesque by his skirted Highland costume. For a moment he blocked their way as he stood leaning with both hands on a gnarled walking stick, staring at Davy with myopic eyes.

"A *Dugald!*" he marveled, then broke into a spine-chilling cackle. "Follow me!" He spun around and started sidling along the corridor.

Hogge winked. " 'Abandon hope all ye who enter here!' " he quoted, prodding his horse forward.

Davy took the lead, and as they drew away from the entrance, the massive doors groaned shut, plunging the passage into a darkness relieved only by the opening at the further end. This turned out to be a small circular courtyard, where, at order of their guide, they tied their horses to rings fastened into the walls, after which they were conducted into the great hall of another building which seemed to be the central section of the castle itself.

The march down that hall was the most trying experience of Davy's life. He endured a sensation of pure unadulterated terror; an instinctual reaction over and above physical fear. Doubtless the setting was in part responsible. It reminded him of a charnel house, or the den of a wild beast. The dark, soot-stained walls were covered with ancient arms and armor, not hung as in decoration, but seemingly tossed there, like the bones of carcasses from which the meat had been plucked. He had the feeling that before the day was over, his own weapons might well be added to the collection.

But if Davy's nerves were raw, his demeanor was calm. He strode along behind the cripple, erect and martial in his bearing, to the jingle of spurs and the occasional clank of his scabbard on the flagging. When the ancient castellan veered abruptly and passed through another arch, Davy shot a quick glance at his companions.

Half-Hanged's ugly face might have been chiseled out of granite for all the expression it reflected, and only an exaggerated hard-heeled swagger belied his utter indifference. Michael Hogge glided with the confident grace of a leopard. If there was perceptible pallor to his scar, his eyes were like slate. Davy risked a wink, then turned after their guide.

He found himself in a vaulted throne room, such as one would expect to find only in the castle of a monarch. Pale shafts of light slanted down from slotted windows high up on the walls. The great chamber was utterly devoid of any furnishings, save at the farther end, where, upon a dais, stood a gilded throne chair. In the chair, the Laird of Inventry awaited them.

There could be no mistaking him. All that rumor and legend whispered about him seemed epitomized in his person. Truly, this was the "old eagle" nesting in his eyrie!

It came to Davy that the wily old laird sought deliberately to dramatize his reputation, for his appearance made the metaphor seem all too apt. His stooped and angular frame was encased in a black velvet suit of yesteryear and his bald head seemed to glow in the wan light. His eyes, too, had an unnatural brilliance, yet without any human warmth. But it was his great arched beak, accentuated by the puckering of shrunken jaws, which added the crowning touch to the illusion of a gigantic bird of prey. He was bent forward, one elbow (one is tempted to say *one wing*) resting on a bony knee, watching the unwelcome visitors approach. A huge, though shabby tapestry covered the wall behind him like the backdrop of a stage.

Davy stared with unabashed curiosity. So *this* was the terrible chieftain of the clan MacKenna! This the monster against whom the widows of Lochbogie directed their wailing curses! Davy had been taught to hate this man before he had been taught to hate the devil!

And now they were face to face!

Peculiarly enough, Godolphin was unattended as far as Davy could see, for there was no one else in the chamber save the venerable hunchback. Yet Davy had the uncomfortable feeling of being watched by unseen eyes.

Thus far they had moved in utter silence except for the measured clatter of their own progress. But halfway down the long room, the old seneschal motioned them to halt, whereupon he slithered closer to the throne and made his obeisance.

"My lord, now comes Colonel *Dugald* of the Army of Parliament, late of *Lochbogie!*" The identifying names were delivered in the triumphant snarl of a jackal turning a kill over to a lion.

Lord Godolphin exhibited no surprise at this announcement. "We will consider matters in that order," he said. "If the colonel has a message, let him draw hence and deliver it."

The hunchback groveled, then turning, beckoned Davy to advance.

Davy was about to comply when he had a sudden inspiration. Just so long as he continued the role of a soldier, he was subject to the limitations of rank. He decided to elevate his status to that of ambassador. So with a lordly gesture, he jerked off his steel helmet and thrust it into the hands of the startled Half-Hanged; then, shaking out his curls, he strode confidently up to the foot of the dais. There, instead of a soldier's salute, he made the restrained bow of a gentleman.

The old laird gave him a haughty stare. "Hand over your message and have done with this posturing!"

Davy met the stare boldly. "I cry pardon, my lord!" he retorted. "I presumed your age if not your position entitled you to the customary courtesies!"

The ominous silence was broken by an astounded gasp from the hunchback. Godolphin's eyes pin-pointed until Davy half expected him to fly out of his chair.

"Bowels of God!" he trumpeted. "Is this the manners of an accursed Roundhead?"

Davy held his ground, though his heart thumped against the inner surface of his breast-plate.

"On the contrary, my lord, my manners were taught me by *John the Dugald,* who has been administering lessons of varying kinds in the Highlands for over half a century!"

For a moment Lord Godolphin's hands turned blue as they gripped the arms of his chair, then abruptly he laughed.

"By the Mass!" he cackled. "The old lion spawns cubs in his own image! You are a *Dugald* beyond a peradventure of doubt! Has hell not yet claimed Red Dugald?"

Davy smiled. "He was in excellent fettle when last I saw him, several weeks ago, my lord."

The old man arched one brow. "Weeks ago? You did not visit Lochbogie on your way into the Highlands?"

Davy sensed the mockery in the query, since the Royalist agents had doubtless informed Godolphin of his route. He was also oppressed by the sensation of invisible watchers. He shook off the distraction and tried to cope with the present situation.

"Unfortunately, my lord, the urgency of my mission would not permit personal considerations," he said firmly. "I am here not as a Dugald but as an emissary of Lieutenant General Cromwell!" Then, in an effort to forestall further interrogation, he proffered the letter Cromwell had given him.

Godolphin accepted the missive with indifference, and was about to lay it aside, when Davy added grimly: "My lord, this letter is self-explanatory. It necessitates an immediate reply!"

His Lordship looked faintly amused. " 'Pon my soul, I admire your gall!" he observed. He broke the seal, then twisted sideways in his chair so that the slanting light illumined the document. He read slowly, soundlessly forming the words with bloodless lips. When he began to read through the message a second time, Davy risked a backward glance at his companions.

The ancient castellan was crouched among the shadows along the wall, his gaze riveted on his master, as if waiting a prearranged signal. Half-Hanged Smyth stood with his legs apart, Davy's helmet cradled in the crotch of one arm, his other hand resting on the hilt of his saber. Michael Hogge balanced lightly on the balls of his feet, ready to spring in any direction. His eyes, hard as flint, were eloquent. *It must be now or never,* they said plainly.

Davy nodded imperceptibly, then turned back to the Laird of Inventry. Somewhat to his embarrassment, he found the latter staring at him. Meeting Davy's eye, Godolphin rustled the papers in his hand.

"This astounding communication indicates you are more of an agent than a courier!" he observed.

Davy bowed. "I am empowered to mediate any slight differences which may arise between the wishes of my general and yourself, my lord."

The old man settled deeper in his chair after the fashion of a bird rustling its feathers.

"*Slight* differences?" he jeered. "He demands I turn against the King!"

"You pardon, my lord! He asks that you support the constituted government of Scotland."

The other smiled sardonically. "And behind this so-called request is a threat of conquest which you, Colonel *Dugald*"—the taunt was plain—"are only too well aware cannot be enforced."

Davy chose his phrasing with care. "My lord, I mislike the word *threat*. Permit me to substitute *plea,* for his Excellency is loath to carry the war into the Highlands."

"And if I refuse?" challenged the laird, inching forward to the edge of his chair.

Davy hesitated. "May God forbid it, sir!" he said slowly.

Lord Godolphin wore the look of a cat with a bird. He stood up abruptly, as if determined to prolong his sport.

"A decision of this kind requires reflection," he said lazily. "I will weigh it carefully." He made a little motion of dismissal.

This was the moment Davy dreaded, for he read treachery in the evasion. He took a quick step forward to block the other's descent from the dais. It was time for plain talking.

"My lord!" he said sharply. "I must have your answer at once!"

There was a portentous pause, then Lord Godolphin straightened haughtily.

"*Must?*" he echoed. "How dare a miserable Dugald adopt that tone with *me?* And remove your hand from that poniard instanter, else, by the Mass, I'll have my *Doomster* take your measurement on the rack!"

Davy held his ground. Almost as if he had eyes in the back of his head, he was aware that Half-Hanged and Hogge had closed in behind him. His Lordship saw it, too, for he took a couple of backward steps which brought him against the tapestry. But if his sharp features betrayed any expression, it was contempt, not fear.

"Softly! Softly!" he admonished. "Remember where you are! You shall have your reply in due time . . . but at *my* convenience. Meanwhile, gentlemen, my home is at your disposal!" And with that, he backed through a slit in the tapestry and disappeared.

Momentarily nonplussed, Davy gaped open-mouthed, then recovering his wits, sprang across the dais and jerked aside the hanging. A small door, by this time securely locked, barred his progress. It was several minutes before he could accept the devastating truth that his quarry had not only escaped, but had so neatly turned the tables that the trappers were now the trapped!

He turned slowly. Half-Hanged, saber in hand, was glowering at the tapestry.

"W'y, bugger me!" he boiled over. "The tricky bastard didn't trust us!"

Captain Hogge chuckled softly. "A masterpiece of understatement! Yet I confess admiration for his Lordship, for on my oath, I never witnessed a more artful display of chicanery in my not uneventful life!"

"This is hardly the time for admiration," Davy retorted sourly. "Don't you realize the implications?"

"Perfectly!" Hogge acknowledged, smiling. "Having proven us would-be assassins, he has made us prisoners."

"Prisoners, 'ell!" roared Half-Hanged belligerently. "We'll myke ol' knobby-knees open the . . ." He looked wildly about him. "Hey, w'ere's 'at damned spider w'at baited us into this trap?"

Thus they made their second disconcerting discovery: the hunchback had also vanished.

"That was to be expected," Hogge observed philosophically. "The lion would hardly leave his jackal at our mercy!"

Davy turned on him savagely. "By God, there are times when your perverted sense of humor gets on my nerves!" he snapped. "If you're willing to have him play cat-and-mouse with you, I'm not!"

Hogge gave him a sweeping bow. "My dear Colonel, if you know a way out of this tangle, I am only too happy to follow you!"

Having no ready answer to that, Davy could only stalk angrily back to the great hall. The others followed, but when they reached the other end of the hall, their progress was blocked by massive doors. Cursing bitterly, Davy retraced his steps, and as his eyes adjusted to the gloom, he discovered several arches which led into other chambers. However, these had no other exit, and showed little evidence of recent usage.

With his apprehension increasing with the passage of time, he wandered despairingly from room to room. Paradoxically, though he neither saw nor heard any evidence of human life, he had the feeling of being under constant surveillance.

"If I may be permitted an observation," Hogge commented, as they ended their tour of inspection. "I know now how a pebble feels bouncing about the inside of a rattle."

Davy grinned bitterly. "That's apt enough. Still, I don't understand this place!"

"It is ridiculously simple, my Colonel," sniffed Hogge. "His Lord-

183

ship merely had us steered into an unused wing of the castle, and here we'll stay until . . ." He spread his hands.

Davy shuddered. He had been nursed on the spine-chilling leg ends of these ancient Highland strongholds where skeletons were found in forgotten chambers or sealed in secret passageways. The thought that he and his two companions might be thus buried to wander idly from room to room until starvation ended their misery was almost unbearable.

An excited bleat from Half-Hanged momentarily revived his hopes.

"Bowels o' God! Look-ee 'ere!

Davy, close heeled by Captain Hogge, ran down the hall to where Half-Hanged stood staring incredulously into one of the smaller chambers. To their astonishment, they saw a table laden with food and drink and lighted by a candelabrum!

"S'elp me, I was in this room but an instant ago!" swore Half-Hanged. " 'Twas emptier than a chamber pot at bedtime!"

What made it doubly eerie was the fact that no other entrance to the chamber was visible, save the one in which they stood, and it was obvious the food had not been brought in that way. But Hogge, after a minute search, discovered traces of a concealed panel in the wall. Davy immediately tried to force it with his poniard, but without success.

As Hogge reached for a great wooden trencher of ale, Half-Hanged warned: " 'Old, Piggey! Belike 'tis poisoned!"

Captain Hogge shrugged and dropped onto a bench. "Belike it is. Yet in a choice betwixt a quick death or a slow one, I prefer the former." He lifted the trencher. "Your good health, gentlemen!" He quaffed deeply.

Half-Hanged stared as if expecting him to keel over, then abruptly flung his saber onto the table and straddled the bench beside him.

"Bugger me, an' w'y not!" he roared, seizing a large leg of venison. "I die better on a full belly! 'Ow about goin' to 'ell wi' us, Ian?"

Davy joined them at the board and seized a mug.

"Your *continued* health, comrades!" he toasted.

They ate heartily, on the theory that food sustained courage, yet on his own part, Davy found that much of what he took congealed in the region of his diaphragm. He tried to match the casualness and banter of his friends, but failed miserably. He had neither the stolid, animal-like stoicism of the ill-bred Half-Hanged Smyth, nor the ingrained *sang froid* of the noble he knew only by the pseudonym of Michael Hogge. And he was tortured by a sense of responsibility and guilt. In his brash egotism, he had sought to match his poor wits against the wiliest old chieftain in the Highlands. He had not only made a complete fool of himself, he had led his friends into disaster.

Overwhelmed at last by his emotions, he rose abruptly from the table. Half-Hanged started to rise, but Hogge restrained him. Davy strode out of the room alone.

For the better part of an hour he paced the ancient hall, tormenting himself with recollections . . . of old John the Dugald, the only man he had ever revered . . . that last agonized scream of Ian as he plunged from the turret, the thud of his body striking stone below . . . his serio-comic encounter with the mysterious Michael Hogge . . . and then the uncontrolled spinning of his mind slowed, to stop finally on the lovely features of Olivia Sanderson.

The vision startled him, for, in a sense, it seemed like heresy. If he had to conjure up the image of a woman at a time like this, he chided himself, it should be that of Anne, his wife. He winced involuntarily. Poor little Annie, with her insatiable longing for nobility and rank! Well, it was obvious he would trouble her no longer and she could continue her futile search for the unattainable.

Then Olivia's apparition firmly blotted out the called-up picture of Anne. He no longer resisted her presence, but let his mind wander unrestrainedly down the corridor of yesteryears. He realized now that he had always worshipped her, and that, like Annie, he, too, had been striving and groping for the unattainable. In a sudden flash of insight, he understood that his first pangs of dissatisfaction with his station and the genesis of his disastrous ambition had been born of their childhood association. Even in those long-gone days, he had begun to compare himself with Ian, and the determination to alter the unalterable had been conceived.

Yet, if this revelation somewhat abashed him, it did clear away much of the cloudiness which had long confused him. He saw himself with clarity for the first time in his life. For that, at least, he was grateful. Pulling himself together, he rejoined his companions.

"What! Still alive?" he jested. "By my troth, 'God-Awful's' poison must be impotent!"

Half-Hanged grimaced. "Ha' ye figgered a way out?"

After a quick, shrewd glance at Davy, Hogge turned to Half-Hanged. "Do you refer to the physical or the spiritual, my good fellow?"

"In my case," snapped Smyth, " 'tis one an' the syme!"

"I can well believe that!" Hogge retorted.

Davy dropped onto a bench. "Let's give Old Piety's prayers a chance to work," he suggested.

"Aye!" chuckled Half-Hanged. "If them ruddy femyles gi' 'im any time to pray!" He peered into the trenchers on the off-chance of finding a few more drops of ale. "W'en I remembers them wimmen, I think mebbe we ain't so bad off arter all!"

Suddenly the stillness was shattered by a sepulchral voice that seemed to come from the very stones in the wall.

"Gentlemen!"

Half-Hanged dropped his half-raised mug with a crash and reached for his saber, but Davy laid a restraining hand on his arm. With frankly thumping hearts, they waited for the unseen speaker to continue.

"Gentlemen!" repeated the voice. "His Lordship is ready to receive Colonel Dugald in a private audience. Colonel, if you will lay your saber and poniard on the board before you, and step out into the hall, you will find a door opened for you at the north end. Your comrades must remain seated where they are, as hostages to your good conduct. Do you comply?"

The acoustics of the vaultlike chamber were such that Davy could not determine the direction whence came the voice. He found it difficult to reply.

"How now!" he roared indignantly. "What manner of treatment is this for accredited emissaries?"

The invisible speaker laughed without mirth. "That is a question you can discuss with his Lordship! I await your decision!"

Davy was about to refuse, when Hogge intercepted him. "By all means go, Colonel. Smyth and I are very comfortable here."

"Aye," growled Half-Hanged. "Concern yourself naught o'er us!"

Davy pondered a moment longer. He felt no fear, yet he reasoned that if he had to die, he would prefer it in the company of his friends, not led out singly like a sheep to slaughter. Yet a flat refusal would be tantamount to suicide, and if the flames of his confidence had been somewhat dampened by recent events, the coals still burned. There just *might* be a chance, a slim chance!

He rose with a calmness he was far from feeling, and unbuckling his sword, placed it on the table. He turned toward the door when the voice chided: "The poniard, too, if you please, Colonel!"

Davy was loath to part with this last weapon, but there was no help for it, so with feigned indifference, he tossed it alongside his sword. As he started away, Michael Hogge stood up and proffered his hand.

"God go with you, sir!" he said formally. "In the performance of your duty!"

The gesture was so utterly alien to the irreverent rogue that Davy did not comprehend—until he clasped the outstretched hand and felt the firm hilt of a small *skean dhu* press against his palm. *In the performance of your duty!* The implication was so clear, Davy felt the hair tingle on his scalp as he surreptitiously slid the little dagger up his sleeve.

"Bless you, my friend!" he murmured gratefully, then stalked out of the chamber.

Chapter Nineteen

Davy traversed that great hall in the company of ghosts. Some few were of his own conjuration, but the rest had haunted this ancient place through the ages, relics which bespoke the long and bloody history of the violence of the Highland nobility. He wondered how soon his own shade would walk amongst them. If the dagger cached up his sleeve did not offer hope, at least it gave him purpose. Of that, he swore a silent oath: let him get within striking distance, then if Godolphin refused his terms, his Lordship would make his journey to hell in Davy's company!

As the unseen messenger had promised, a door—heretofore closed —stood ajar at the end of the hall. Davy hesitated but an instant on the threshold, to test the slide of his blade and to compose his nerves, then strode inside.

He found himself in a small chamber, furnished only by a long refectory table, with a chair on either side of it. The chair nearest the entrance was empty, but in the other, with his back to a tapestry-covered wall, sat Lord Godolphin . . . alone.

The old bastard has a penchant for tapestries, thought Davy grimly, *but this time he shall not elude me!*

"Sit you down!" barked the old laird, savagely gesturing toward the vacant chair.

Davy bowed. Yet, as he moved to obey, he got the feeling that Godolphin's ill-humor was not caused by his visit. He shrugged the reaction aside and sat down. His sharp eyes caught a faint, almost imperceptible movement in the draperies that might have been caused by a current of air. Satisfied it was more than that, he dropped his hands into his lap and, under cover of the table, let the dagger slide into his palm.

"Have you reached a decision, my lord?" he asked bluntly.

Lord Godolphin leaned back, resting his elbows on the ornate arms of his chair, and tapped the tips of his long fingers together. His eyes, shaded by craggy brows, were difficult to read.

"Since we are alone," he grated, obviously holding a violent temper in check, "let us dispense with rhetoric. To be candid, I hold no brief for either King or Kirk; both are nuisances. The Marquis of Montrose has solicited our arms for Charles, so it was only to be expected Cromwell would do likewise. But"—the restless hands clenched spasmodically—"what baffled me was that a Dugald, a *Dugald,* would have the temerity to come here to Inventry!" His voice became a rasp.

"My lord, I came hence, not as a Dugald, but as a representative of Cromwell. His Excellency knows nothing of clan disputes! I had, and have, a duty to perform."

"So it would seem!" snapped the old man caustically. "Be that as it may, there was an important factor you neglected to mention at our earlier meeting."

When he paused, curiosity baited Davy to ask, "And that is, my lord . . . ?"

"That you are betrothed to my niece, you scoundrel!"

Davy felt as if he had been hit over the head. Taken completely aback, he could not immediately adjust himself. He must have appeared the fool, for the old laird leaned forward on the table.

"How now? Do you deny it?" he demanded.

As Davy struggled with his amazement, he found time to offer up a grateful prayer that he had not brought Anne, his wife, into this mess.

"Deny it?" he countered, with as much dignity as he could muster on short notice. "By my troth, sir, 'tis a treasure too sacred to be used for barter! My lord, I came here as an emissary of the Army of Parliament, not as a private supplicant! Yet were I waging this war single-handed, with every laird and gillie of the Highlands against me, I would not use my love for the Lady Olivia as a shield!"

"Bah!" sneered the other. "How the silly chit would relish that effusion! But you misinterpret my meaning! I'd almost as soon see her dead as wedded to an accursed Dugald!"

"Then leave her name out of this discussion!" snapped Davy.

Godolphin sank back slowly. "Am I to take it you did not come to seek advantage due to a possible future relationship?"

Davy colored angrily. "I did *not!* Personalities are not involved, my lord; the issues speak for themselves! By this time, nearly all the Lowlands are in the hands of the government, and it . . ."

"*All* the Lowlands?" interrupted Godolphin. In the deep cavernous eyes, Davy could see the red lights of danger.

"Castle Westmoreland is under siege," Davy went on grimly. "It must inevitably succumb!"

"Not if I choose to march!

Davy realized that the four Royalist agents had done their work well. He played his trump card.

"My lord, have you looked from your ramparts within the last few hours?" he challenged coolly. "No one marches from Inventry!"

Godolphin staggered to his feet, his peaked face livid. "You dare threaten me! By the Mass, I'll dangle three corpses from three ramparts for your rebel horde to shoot at!"

"Certes, and you'll never see it yourself!" grated Davy, and raising his dagger, sprang onto the table.

Quick as he was, the other was quicker. With a back-hand jerk, the laird swept the tapestry aside, revealing two stalwart gillies armed with target and claymore

"Cut him down!"

Unable now to reach the old man, Davy jumped back to the floor. The door behind him was closed. Disgusted, he kicked the table against the advancing bravos, and though it tripped one, the other hurdled it. Davy tossed aside the inadequate little dagger and scooped up a chair. But as he momentarily drove one gillie back, he glimpsed the other charging from the opposite angle.

"Bowels of God!" raged Godolphin. "Must I summon more than two MacKennas to deal with an upstart Dugald? Hack him in twain!"

Strangely enough, through Davy's fevered brain flashed a question: *how would a gentleman like Michael Hogge meet this sort of death?* He recalled the scene in the roadside inn, when he had had Hogge at his mercy. Resistance now was futile; there was little point in brawling to the last like a cornered rat.

He hurled the chair aside and folded his arms. "Come on, Mac-Kennas!" he taunted.

Enraged, the gillies converged with upraised claymores, yet before a blow could fall, an imperious voice cried: *"Hold! In the name of God, what means this?"*

Davy couldn't credit his senses! It took all his will power to turn his eyes from the infuriated Highlanders to the slim, haughty figure in the wall's opening. Even when his eyes verified his hearing, his mind was slow to adjust to reality.

"How could you, Uncle?" she demanded of the angry laird. "Know you naught who this man is?"

Davy flinched. He began to wish the blow had fallen, for he dreaded her reproaches more than death. He braced himself for the inevitable exposure.

"Aye, I ken him well!" stormed Goldophin. "Get you gone, lass. You have no business here!"

The Lady Olivia held her ground. "I will *not* leave!" she snapped, meeting his scowl with one equally as threatening.

"Mistress . . . !" thundered the old man, but she interrupted.

"My father's very life is involved in this!" she cried him down. "If you failed to deal with him, I claim the right myself! This is no time for your hateful feuds! Go now—leave me to handle this matter!"

The two gillies stared open-mouthed at this defiance; it was plain that they had never before witnessed such a spectacle. On his part, Davy was even more astounded. This was not the dainty little beauty he had known, but a woman of steel and fury.

"Go!" she reiterated, in a voice that bit like a knout.

Godolphin hesitated, incredibly enough. Then the black thunderhead of rage that darkened his peaked face gave way to an even more dangerous hint of cunning. Finally, he shrugged his shoulders and squinted at Davy.

"Faith, and the young cub appears more terrified of you than he did of my blundering gillies!" he sneered. "Have your way, child, but if he attempts to leave this room, he'll nae cross the threshold alive!" With a jerk of his head, he dismissed the two retainers. As he was about to follow them, his eyes spotted the *skean dhu* on the floor. He retrieved it.

"You'll have no more need of this bauble!" he cackled, then, chuckling as if at a private joke, he passed out of the chamber.

Olivia stood staring at the closed door a long time after he was gone.

"That was too easy," she muttered to herself. "Much too easy!"

Davy held his breath, dreading the moment she would turn to face him. His mind was still a total blank, for he had not recovered from the shock of her unexpected presence. After what seemed an interminable time, she crossed the room and pulled the tapestry over the door. Then she turned.

"*Davy!*" she said tautly, and her face paled. "Then it was Ian . . . ?" She put a hand behind to steady herself against the table.

He did not reply immediately, for he was still awed by this new facet she had exhibited. Somehow, she did not even look the same, then it came to him suddenly that this, in part, resulted from her costume, which she must have borrowed from a crofter's wife. It was fashioned of rough linsey-woolsey, with a rose-colored bodice and bright blue skirt, over which was draped a belted plaid of the Mac-Kenna sett, held at the throat by a huge silver buckle. Yet the very coarseness of the material accentuated her loveliness. She had plaited her coppery hair into twin braids, and around the crown she wore a green ribbon which matched her eyes.

She colored slightly under his stare.

"Answer me, Davy!"

He was loath to relate the facts, but when she insisted, he told her the sordid truth, nor spared himself in the telling.

"My Lord Ian always had a temper," he concluded, "but up to that time, I had always managed to quiet him. That night he seemed to have lost his reason. He went berserk!"

To his surprise, she did not appear to disbelieve him. "I think I understand," she murmured, so softly he could barely catch the words. "I'm afraid the fault was mine."

"*Yours?*" Davy gasped incredulously. "Good Lord, my lady, you had nothing to . . ."

She stopped him with a little gesture. "Ah, but I had! Just a few moments before you arrived at Westmoreland that awful night, I had told Ian I would not"—a blush suffused her features—"that I wished to cancel our betrothal! He took it ill, poor bairn!"

"I can imagine he would!" Davy blurted, then reddened in confusion.

She stiffened her spine. "While all that may explain Ian's lack of control," she went on austerely, "it does nothing to clarify *your* subsequent conduct! How could you assume the identity of the man you had slain? Why came you here, of all places, masquerading in his name?"

Painfully, falteringly, he summarized his experiences, taking the full responsibility onto his own shoulders. And all the while he talked, her green eyes held rigidly on his face.

"I had no idea you were here, my lady," he ended lamely.

"*No?*" she mocked. "Even though you hounded me clear across the Highlands?"

His mouth sagged open. "God's death, my lady! Were *you* one of the four . . ."

"I most certainly was! And a right merry chase you gave us, you knave!"

"I cry you mercy! Had I so much as dreamed you were in the party, I . . ." He paused, trying to control his nerves. "Believe me, my lady, I would never have come had I known you were here!"

She waved a little hand impatiently. "Fie! I can well believe *that!* You know how quickly my uncle would have hung you for an impostor!" Try as he would, he could not read her mood. "I presume you thought to trade upon my alleged relationship to the man you pretended to be?"

He straightened his shoulders and met her stare. "Mistress, as God's my witness, I plead guilty to all the crimes you have listed, save *that!*"

Under his hard scrutiny, she lowered her eyes and stood tapping her tiny foot on the flagging.

"What *am* I to do with you, sir?"

He shrugged. "You have no alternative but to call back your uncle. As a small measure of retribution for the hurt I have caused you, I shall tell him the truth!"

"After which, he'll hang you!"

"He'll hang me in any event."

"No doubt you deserve it!" she said grimly. "Yet my father's safety is involved in this!"

When he stared bewilderedly, she continued: "Apparently you are not aware that Cromwell sent an ultimatum to my father which was, in brief, that if Inventry declared for Parliament, he would not reduce Westmoreland. Father has been growing weary of the broken

193

promises and vacillations of Charles, and knowing that I have more influence than anyone with his temperamental brother-in-law, he permitted me to come here to plead with him."

It took some time for Davy to digest this. So the wily Cromwell had put *two* strings to his bow? What a shrewd move, and how Michael Hogge would enjoy it!

"But . . . but what has my fate to do with this?" he stammered.

"Are you so stupid!" she cried angrily. "If Godolphin hangs the emissary of Cromwell, can he then become an ally?"

"I am a confessed impostor!"

She stamped her foot in temper. "You are an impostor, aye, but you are still a representative of your general! Haven't you the wit to comprehend that?" She threw up her hands in disgust. "Oh, dear Lord! I was having enough troubles with my uncle without having to concern myself with *your* safety!"

Davy chuckled in spite of himself. "By my troth, mistress, I cannot in good faith beg you to urge my hanging! Yet if there is any way in which I can serve you, pray command me! I throw myself at your feet!"

"I wish you had thrown yourself in a river!" she retorted sharply, then abruptly burst into laughter. "Merciful heavens, what a perfectly ridiculous situation! We are both here on the same mission, more or less, yet have irretrievably complicated it, like two people trying to sit in the same chair."

Davy could not resist the opening. "Even that has been done successfully, my lady! One merely sits on the other's lap!"

Olivia tried to look stern, but her eyes twinkled. "This is an ill time for jesting, sir!" she said acidly. "I assure you I have no desire to have a big clod like you on *my* lap, nor intention to sit on yours! Kindly restrain your vulgarity! You have caused me sufficient embarrassment!"

"*Embarrassment*, my lady?"

She avoided his stare. "Aye! Prior to your untimely intrusion, I had told my uncle that I had broken off our betrothal. This pleased him mightily, for he hates a Dugald above the devil! Now"—color once more flooded her cheeks—"now—for my father's sake, of course —I shall have to pretend I have again changed my mind! And I hate to lie!"

Davy bowed. "My lady, I, far more than you, regret the . . . the *lie!*"

Olivia chose to ignore the *double-entendre.* "Don't raise your hopes too high," she warned. "Uncle will not readily forgive your attempt on his life, so he may hang you despite anything I can say. However, due to certain family involvements, I have considerable influence with him, and I hardly think he would slay my betrothed if I can convince him you are truly such. So, sir, sit you down while I try to pacify him. And stop trying to murder everyone who crosses you!"

Davy's face clouded. "That gibe was unnecessarily unkind, my lady!"

"Is there any particular reason why I should be kind to you?" she burst out heatedly. Then, without waiting for an answer, she jerked aside the tapestry and passed out the same exit taken by Godolphin.

Left alone, Davy idly straightened the furnishings, then dropped heavily into a chair. His mind was still befuddled, having been unable to absorb the multifold complications which had pyramided so confusingly. Most of all, he was puzzled by Olivia's sudden shifts of emotion. Why had she turned on him so savagely at the end? Heretofore, he had believed he knew women; now, he realized that though he had *known* them, he had never understood them. The difference was obvious.

A little later, he heard the door open behind the hanging, and assuming Olivia had returned, he sprang to his feet. With a stab of disappointment, he saw that it was only one of the gillies. Yet, in the short interval the door was ajar, he caught the angry buzz of voices in the background. Then the closing door shut them off.

This was the same man whom Davy had knocked down with the chair; a brawny savage wrapped in a *filleadh mór*, with a rakish blue bonnet on his lank, dun-colored hair. He still carried his claymore unsheathed in one hand and his target in the other. Davy stood motionless, satisfied that his sands had run out, but after staring hard for a few moments, the gillie nodded toward the door behind Davy.

"Ye can go back to your comrades for the nonce," he growled in guttural dialect. "His Lordship will summon ye at his pleasure."

Davy thought it unwise to appear too compliant. "Very well, but you can notify his Lordship I must have my answer before the sun sets this night!"

The big Highlander chuckled, muttered something about a *daft gowk,* which in his language meant a *silly blockhead,* and opened the door into the hall. He stood aside for Davy to pass, then shut the door behind him. An instant later, the bolt slammed home.

His two comrades were still seated around the table when Davy returned to the chamber. Half-Hanged was frankly astonished to see him, but if Michael Hogge felt any such reaction, his masklike features failed to reveal it.

"By ye alive, lad?" yelped Half-Hanged delightedly. "Or be ye another ghost? I swear *they* been clankin' up an' down the 'all 'ere since ye left us!"

Hogge grinned. "Aye, Half-Hanged's been alternately praying and cursing for the past hour!"

Davy threw himself wearily onto a bench. "No doubt he's trying to cover all eventualities by soliciting favor with both the Lord and the devil."

"No doubt," Hogge agreed, chuckling. "Yet methinks he'd be wiser to concentrate on the devil, whom he's served so faithfully these many years."

"Ye go to 'ell, Piggey!" growled Smyth.

"I expect to," retorted Hogge. "The only question is—how soon? Can you enlighten us on that point, Colonel?"

Davy opened his mouth to reply, then suddenly remembered the secret passage behind the walls. Doubtless old Godolphin would have stationed someone there to spy on them. He looked Hogge in the eye.

"I know little more than I did before," he said. "Yet this hole makes me restless. I would fain take some exercise in the hall." He rose with deliberate casualness.

Hogge evinced his comprehension. "Aye, 'tis stuffy. I'll join you in your walk." As he came to his feet, Half-Hanged did likewise.

Strolling up and down the great hall, with Hogge on one side and Half-Hanged on the other, Davy, in guarded tones, told them what had happened. But when he mentioned Olivia, they both gasped in unison: "Lady Olivia . . . *here?*"

"Certes, and she could hardly have interceded from Westmoreland, you clods! She was one of those so-called 'Cavaliers' we were so intent on killing!"

Half-Hanged thumped his head with a burly fist. "One o' the few people w'at knows 'oo ye are," he groaned, "an' the last ye'd want to meet up wi'! That done it! W'at did ol' eagle-fyce s'y w'en she tolt 'im?"

"Therein lay the miracle!" sighed Davy. "She did not tell him!" Then he detailed the rest of the happenings.

Half-Hanged was incensed about what he regarded as Cromwell's double-dealing, but Captain Hogge viewed it objectively.

"My respect for his Excellency increases," he commented. "I thought him rather naïve to entrust three strangers with such a vital mission. Now it develops we were in effect only carrying a duplicate message. Diabolically ingenious, I swear!"

"Granted! Nevertheless, it has irrevocably complicated our problem," grumbled Davy.

"My very thought!" echoed Half-Hanged. "W'at's to be done?"

"There's nothing we can do, save wait," Hogge pointed out. "Howbeit, if the situation is no better, I cannot see it is much worse. Very likely the damsel will prevail." His scar paled perceptibly. "Women usually get their way," he muttered, in an undertone.

"If we could on'y get word to Ol' Piety!" mused Half-Hanged.

Hogge jeered. "That would be delightful! Perchance you would like to invite the colonel's lady into the castle? A tableau with potentialities, I own: the *wife* meeting the *betrothed!*"

Davy felt the blood creep up around his ears. "Watch your tongue!" he barked sharply. "The Lady Olivia is not betrothed to *me!*"

"As to that, I'll naught say nay," drawled Michael Hogge. "Howbeit, you will do well to keep that secret from her even more carefully than you must conceal it from Godolphin! Take the advice of one who has had experience in such matters!"

Recalling Olivia's inexplicable shifts of temper, Davy glumly held his peace. On one point they were all agreed: there was naught to do save wait!

Chapter Twenty

It was late afternoon before the summons came. Davy hurried along the trophy-lined hall, too impatient this time to concern himself with ghosts. When he entered the small audience chamber, he found Lord Godolphin seated as before, but this time Olivia sat beside him. Pausing briefly on the threshold, Davy tried to glean some hint of his fate from their expressions—without success. He bowed low, in part to cover his disappointment, then, at a crook of the old man's finger, approached the table. He was not invited to sit down, although a chair stood beside him.

"Your Lordship sent for me?" he said.

Godolphin gave the girl a sidelong glance that set her face aflame before swinging his hard gaze to Davy.

"Aye, though on my oath, I should have sent my *Doomster* to deal with you!" he rasped. "'Tis a sorry day when women meddle in the diplomacy of men! Unfortunately, it has come, and Inventry is momentarily a matriarchy—though God grant not for long!"

"*My lord . . .* !" protested Olivia, pale with embarrassment.

"Silence!" thundered the old man. "By the Mass, if I can't have my way, I'll have my say!"

In the ensuing pause, Davy caught his breath. Dare he begin to hope, he asked himself? He held his eyes as steady as he could.

"I repeat," fumed his Lordship, "I'd prefer to hang you and consign your red-faced squire to hell! Howbeit, tears and wiles have had their way." He angrily tossed two documents across the table. "Here is my reply in duplicate, my compromise, for your precious Cromwell! In brief, though I will *not* send my bonny gillies out of the Highlands as he requests, Inventry will declare for Parliament against the King!"

Davy exhaled a long sigh, but before he could speak, the laird waved him silent.

"There are conditions, sir, which must be rigidly adhered to!" Godolphin continued. "The siege of Westmoreland, if begun, must be raised instantly without reparations or retaliation. Furthermore, the earl is to be permitted to depart freely with his officers and journey in safety to join his Majesty, if he so elects, or else to remain in his castle and declare for Parliament should he desire. It is agreed Cromwell may garrison the castle, but his soldiers shall be restrained from sacking or looting, and shall be fed at government expense." He paused expectantly.

Davy bowed again, this time to conceal his elation. These terms were far more generous than he had dared anticipate.

"I am authorized to agree to such stipulations, my lord!"

Godolphin snorted, then clapped his hands. At once the door behind him opened to admit a lackey bearing a tray on which were a quill, ink and sand, and a candle for melting sealing wax. This was placed on the table, and the manservant withdrew.

"Having been browbeaten by petticoats into this concession," went on the old noble, "I intend to make certain at least one of these documents reaches Cromwell promptly. You will sign both copies, accepting the conditions for your general. I have already affixed my signature. One, you will keep with you to deliver in person when you return; the other, you will dispatch *tonight* by one of your fiendish companions." He dipped a quill in the ink, and proffered it to Davy.

Davy smelled treachery. "But, my lord!" he protested. "My officer cannot return more swiftly than I will myself!"

Lord Godolphin glared across the board. "You will do as I say, or I shall destroy these treaties!" Then, less heatedly: "These are perilous times, and I cannot be responsible for what may happen to brash young fools wandering about in these Highlands. 'Tis my thought your man can journey by an alternate route, thus assuring at least one copy reaching your bull-headed squire! Do you refuse?" He made as if to reach for the documents.

Davy hastily pulled them toward him. He read them over, and since they were substantially as agreed, he signed both copies. Godolphin carefully sealed them with wax and affixed his signet. As

Davy picked them up, expecting to be dismissed, the old man leaned back.

"There is one further condition," he added archly. "Since I was fool enough to capitulate to this daft chit, the least I can do is protect her interests. Now, at our last meeting, you made some maudlin . . ."

"Uncle, *please!*" cried Olivia. "Don't spoil everything!"

"Hold your tongue!" stormed Godolphin. "By the blood of God, if you interfere again, young woman, I'll hang this knave and cast in with Montrose!" As she sank back limply, he thundered on: "Why this senseless child wants you, is more than I can comprehend! Howbeit, I most sternly warn you to make her happy, and while I have not incorporated *that* in my formal writing, my conditions are predicated upon it. Any defection on your part will nullify the agreement. Is that plain?"

Here was ice too thin for maneuvering. Davy handled his words like hot coals.

"My lord," he said cautiously, "I pledge my life I shall never again cause my lady any unhappiness!"

The old man sneered. "You hear him, child?"

Olivia's face was scarlet. "I believe him!" she murmured weakly. Then fell the blow!

"At daybreak tomorrow," intoned the laird, "*Olivia and her attendants will accompany you back to the Lowlands!*"

Davy felt as if he had been hit on the head. He could visualize the ghastly scene Anne would make and the resultant embarrassment to Olivia. His pledge would be broken before they were out of sight of Inventry!

Olivia, too, seemed taken completely by surprise. "Uncle!" she gasped. "I couldn't!"

He swung on her impatiently. "By the Mass, and why not?" he exploded. "Are not you two betrothed? You'll be suitably chaperoned with your cawing maidservant and those stiff-necked English Cavaliers, and if you could ride here in their company, you can certainly leave in it! I want this place cleared of interfering females. By God, you'll do as I bid or suffer the consequences!"

Davy sucked in a deep breath and glanced at Olivia. She seemed to have lost control of herself. Out of sheer desperation, he thought he glimpsed a tiny loophole.

"My lord," he said, as calmly as he could, "under other circumstances, your thoughtful suggestion would overwhelm me with pleasure. However, as you pointed out so aptly, these are perilous times, and her Ladyship might be safer out of the company of Parliamentary troops. Furthermore, my orders make it imperative that I return by a more tedious route, by way of Lochbogie. Hence, it would be advisable for her Ladyship to journey direct . . ."

Godolphin cut him short. "How now? Why this stilted formality?" he sneered. "Are you ashamed to take your betrothed to Lochbogie?"

"God forbid!" Davy muttered.

"Then say no more about it!" roared the old man. "I want the whole kit-and-boodle of you out of here by sun-up!" He snapped his fingers as if an idea had just come to him. "By God, I will ride with you the first three leagues to make sure you do not disobey my commands!" He stood up to signify the audience was ended.

Worse and worse! Stunned, Davy could only stand mute as the old man pulled the tapestry aside. But as Godolphin opened the door, Davy found his voice.

"My lord! You mentioned my dispatching an officer tonight! Permit me to arrange it, else there may be an unseeming delay in the morning!"

The laird shrugged. "I shall have a gillie escort him within the hour." He beckoned the girl. "Come, my child!"

Olivia stood gripping the edge of the table. "I'd like a few words with . . . with Ian!" she whispered falteringly.

"Nonsense! I forbid it!" snapped Godolphin. "You'll have a week of chatter with him! Let him alone now; he's got his own business to attend to!"

She had no choice save to obey. She gave Davy one long, agonized look, then turned abruptly and passed out of the chamber.

With his heart in his boots, Davy went out by the opposite door.

This time his friends awaited him in the great hall, where there was less risk of being overheard. On viewing his dejected appearance, they exchanged significant glances. Then Half-Hanged clouted him affectionately on the shoulder.

"Chin up, lad!" he urged jovially. "Ye made a good try, e'en though 'twas to fail in the end!"

"That's the hell of it!" moaned Davy. "I succeeded only too well!"

"Ho-ho!" said Hogge, with a chuckle. "I trow I see the hand of a woman in this gloom!"

Davy gave him a sour glance. "You'll see more than a *hand*, my witty friend! We are to escort the Lady Olivia to Lochbogie! And as if *that* wasn't disastrous enough—'God-Awful' rides the first three leagues to make certain all is well!"

Hogge exhaled in a long, slow whistle. Half-Hanged cackled mirthlessly.

"Bugger me, I reckon I'll just st'y 'ere cozylike in the castle, w'ere it's comparatively syfe!" he observed.

Davy sniffed. "On the contrary, *you* are leaving here within the hour! So heed carefully my words! In the presence of Anne, announce that our mission has succeeded; that you have been delegated to carry the news to Cromwell and that she and Jenny are to accompany you!"

"Oh, Jesus, *no!*" wailed Half-Hanged. "Not them, too, lad!"

"Yes, *them!*" snarled Davy. "Why do you think I'm sending you on this wild-goose chase? If Godolphin found I already had a wife, we'd all hang—Anne included. So hold your tongue, and mark what I tell you!

"Anne may object—in fact, I'm sure she will. Howbeit, you are to insist. Tell her I may be detained here for weeks, and that Godolphin won't allow her or any of the others in this castle. Tell her anything! You boasted of being an accomplished liar, so here's a golden opportunity to prove it! Then, after you arrange that, get Priety aside and explain the true situation. Quote him the Bible—anything to make him understand!"

Half-Hanged whimpered dismally. "Ol' Piety'll no tell an untruth to syve 'is soul, that I know!"

"He doesn't have to; just warn him to keep his mouth shut! You're to take half the troop, in addition to the girls, and go back the way we came. Most imperative of all—*you must leave tonight!*"

"Laddie, laddie, I see trouble!"

"Not half the trouble you'll see if you don't carry out my instructions to the letter!" warned Davy bitterly.

"But, bugger me, man, I don't know these bloody 'Ighlands, nor e'en understan' their savage lingo!"

"Anne kens the dialect," Davy assured him. "She'll help you get local knowledge of the trail." He saw Half-Hanged marshaling further argument, so he forestalled him. "Damn it, Smyth, obey my orders! Ride hard the first day, but after that, take it easy. We have to visit Lochbogie, and I want to reach Cromwell ahead of you!"

Half-Hanged rubbed the back of his neck. "If ye visit Lochbogie, you'll ne'er live to see Cromwell!" he muttered darkly.

"Perchance, that's so," Davy conceded. "In that event, give this copy of the Treaty to his Excellency!" And with that, he handed the disgruntled Half-Hanged one of the documents.

He had barely passed it over, when the humpbacked castellan appeared in a doorway.

"Who's the lucky lad who's getting out alive?" he chortled.

Half-Hanged opened his mouth to retort, but at a warning scowl from Davy, subsided. He clapped his helmet on his head, nodded curtly to his two companions, then clanked after the vanishing cripple.

Chapter Twenty-One

By daybreak, Davy and Hogge had breakfasted and seen to their mounts, and soon the circular courtyard was aswarm with sturdy Highlanders preparing to escort their laird. Even to Davy, a clansman himself, they looked unusually savage, but to the Englishman, who had never before seen a Scots gillie at close range, they had the appearance of untamed barbarians. All wore the great belted-plaid, of the distinctive MacKenna sett, and rough shoes of untreated hide. On their shaggy, unkempt heads they wore blue bonnets, each decorated with an eagle's feather. Brandishing claymores and round targets, they were as villainous a horde of scoundrels as either Davy or Michael Hogge had ever seen before.

Their survey was suddenly interrupted by a tumultuous shouting as Godolphin and his retinue entered the courtyard. His lordship was arrayed in a *filleadh mór*, but in addition he wore a gorgeous leather jerkin, dyed bright blue, and fur-trimmed gauntlets of the same material. The eagle's feather on his bonnet was secured by a large silver brooch of the Inventry crest embedded with precious stones.

Also in his private party were two obviously English Cavaliers and a middle-aged woman, but Davy had eyes only for Olivia, who walked beside the old laird. A phrase he had once heard about Queen Elizabeth came to mind—*daughter of a hundred kings!* How aptly it fitted the Lady Olivia! For, despite the fact that her costume was entirely concealed beneath a long linen riding cloak with a starched nunlike cowl, she looked every inch a queen!

He saw her eyes anxiously search the crowd, yet when their gazes met, she did not nod. Somehow, it was unnecessary, for telepathically she contrived to convey a message that was at once a plea for understanding and a warning to move warily. He bowed his understanding, then watched her mount a stately palfrey held for her by a groom. She sat astride the splendid beast with all the grace and dignity befitting the *daughter of a hundred kings.*

Lord Godolphin was assisted into the saddle of a heavy charger, whereon, with his peculiar stoop, he more than ever resembled an eagle poised for flight. When he raised his gauntleted hand in signal, the whole castle seemed to explode in sound. Ancient guns thundered along the ramparts, the assembled gillies fired a salvo of small arms, all the while shrieking like demented fiends, then to the skirl of bagpipes and blare of trumpets, the great gates clanked open.

Davy had mounted, meanwhile, but when he looked around for Michael Hogge, he saw him skulking on the opposite side of the courtyard. There was no time to summon him, so Davy took his place behind the laird and Olivia. Since cavalry, as such, was virtually unknown in the remoter Highlands, the gillies marched on foot. In this wise, the procession wound out of the castle and moved onto the long causeway.

Once they cleared the ancient Barbican, Davy stared apprehensively ahead. Far off, at the foot of the rocky incline, he could make out a little troop of horse awaiting them, but as the rising sun was in his eyes, he was unable to distinguish one from another. His mind began to play tricks on him: one moment he was certain that he could recognize the squat, beetle-shaped outline of Half-Hanged Smyth; the next, that he could see Anne standing eagerly in her stirrups.

The realization that he hoped he was mistaken jolted him a trifle. By God, he had taken Anne to wife, for better or for worse, and if, perchance, she *was* there, he swore he would not disown her, even though avowal would cost his life! Nevertheless, he glumly conceded it would be much better for all concerned if he was mistaken.

Yet looking for Anne, literally over the shoulder of Olivia, brought the issue of the two women into sharp focus. True, Anne was his wife, and as such was entitled to his faithfulness, yet, he rationalized, there was nothing disloyal to her in his reverence for the Lady Olivia, for, he assured himself, *reverence* was what it amounted to. There was no question of comparison; one did not compare an earthly light, no matter how dazzling, with the shining stars of the heavens! The former was desirable, but the latter was above desire, being unattainable.

Soon this phase of his torture was resolved, and he could see Major Priety, gaunt and cadaverous, sitting stiffly astride his big nag, with twelve troopers drawn up behind him. That was all—thanks be to God! There was no sign either of Half-Hanged or Anne!

Then the two groups met, and Davy spurred forward to present Priety to the laird.

Godolphin acknowledged the introduction with a curt nod, then glared at Davy.

"Mother of God! Is this the niggardly handful you dared threaten me with?" he snarled.

Recalling Olivia's unspoken warning to move warily, Davy framed his words with care.

"My lord, nothing was further from my intention!"

His Lordship was in a querulous mood and seemed determined to make an issue of the matter. But when he began to curse, it was Old Piety who, for once, stepped into the breech.

"Sir, it was the colonel's order that I dispatch the bulk of our force to accompany Lieutenant Smyth. This was done last night!"

Davy could have shouted with relief, for without tampering with truth, Priety had managed to convey the impression that their force had been considerable. But Godolphin was not assuaged.

"By the Mass!" he stormed. "I've a mind to go with you to Lochbogie myself!"

If a bolt of lightning had struck Davy of Dugald, the effect could hardly have been more paralyzing. It came to him, abruptly, that Godolphin was deliberately seeking a quarrel. So *this* was what Olivia had tried to convey? In the awful pause, he weighed the chances his own pitifully meager force would have against the MacKenna horde—and found them nil. Only wit could save him now!

"Why don't you, my lord?" he drawled, in a mocking tone that skirted the very fringe of insolence. "We could accommodate our pace to your foot, and I ween John the Dugald would accord you a most fitting reception!"

The old laird seemed to swell in the saddle, and his shrunken face turned livid. Reading the signs, Davy decided his hour had come, and he dropped his hand to his saber. Then, miraculously, Lord Godolphin sank back with a curse.

"May God strike me dead if I proceed another furlong in such ill-favored company!" he roared. He turned toward his niece. "Come, child, we turn back to the castle!"

Olivia sat very straight. "Nay, Uncle, I will not!" she said with a coolness that astounded Davy. "Your conduct is unseemly! Colonel Dugald merely carried out your own unreasonable demands when he divided his force, though why you insisted upon it is beyond me. Howbeit, much as it distresses me to anger you, I am determined to proceed. If it saves one life at Westmoreland, it will be worth it!"

There was a long moment of pregnant silence. Davy was torn between two conflicting hopes: that she would comply with the laird's demand, and that she would stick by her refusal.

Then the laird spoke with a deadly calmness. "Mistress, heed well what I am about to say, for the responsibility for what may happen shall be on your own head! It is too late to revoke my treaty, else I most surely would, but I call upon all assembled here to witness that I both beseech and command you to return with me to the safety of Inventry!"

Olivia paled, but her voice held steady. "I thank you for your concern, my lord, and I accept the responsibility for what may befall me. Be that as it may, I will go on!"

Godolphin burst into a mirthless cackle. "Well, I have done my duty. But, by heaven, child, you are cut from the same cloth as your mother—a woman who always got her way! Sobeit, for in God's truth, in your going I shall have revenge on this assassin-minded young hawk, for if you browbeat him as you have browbeaten both your father and me, Lord pity him!"

Before either Davy or Olivia could recover from their embarrassment, he turned a jaundiced eye on the serving woman. "As for you, Dame Reynolds," he bellowed sternly, "I charge you to see to it that her Ladyship doesn't have too much time alone with this rogue, for, on my oath, I want her naught again on my hands! Now—God speed, all of you! I've taken my vow, and vows must be adhered to, so I return to Inventry!" Without more ado, he pivoted his mount and cantered through an avenue formed by his gillies.

Nothing was said until the old chieftain and his following had passed out of hearing, then Davy turned slowly to face Olivia. For an instant, he thought he detected a look of pure terror in her eyes, but if so, it was gone in a trice and she managed a wan smile.

"Colonel Dugald," she said clearly, obviously for the benefit of their little company, "I trust you accept my uncle's libel as the dour wit it was meant to be?"

Davy bowed. "Doubly so, my lady, since most of his slander was directed against myself!"

She forced a laugh, then introduced him to her retinue. There were two Cavaliers: a Sir Thomas Dudley, a tall, austere man in his middle thirties, and a Captain Ashby, young, burly and soldierly. Both acknowledged Davy with the cold courtesy of one treating with an enemy. Dame Reynolds had the martyred look of a poor relation. She was a sharp-featured shrew of some fifty-odd summers, who had disapproved of things so long she had a permanent ripple in her nose from elevating it.

Davy ignored their manifest hostility and greeted each as graciously as he could, after which he presented Major Priety. But when he looked around for Michael Hogge, the man was not in evidence. A trooper reported he had seen Hogge ride off over the saddle-hump.

Olivia shrugged the matter aside. "We have a long journey, sir," she said formally. "Do you not think we should have at it?"

Davy agreed. "Too true, my lady. If you would deign to ride with me . . ." he began, but she firmly cut him off.

"Thank you, sir, but I shall remain with my friends. Doubtless you have military matters to discuss with your officers."

Davy took the hint and rode to the head of the column where Priety awaited him. Riding knee to knee well in advance of the others, Davy asked the questions which had haunted him.

"Aye, Half-Hanged departed at thy orders," sighed the major, "God pity him! The Bible mentions the fury of an angry female— though memory fails me in what connection. He went away like a slave going to the lions!"

Davy grimaced. "Poor devil! Perhaps I should have sent Hogge in his stead. By the way, I wonder why Hogge took himself off?"

"Thou wilt have to question Satan on that score," grunted Priety. "That knave is his faithful disciple!"

Davy chuckled. "Oh, come now, Major, it is not necessary we all see eye to eye. There's an old Scots saying to the effect that if we all worked as consistently as the devil to attain our ends, there'd be few failures."

"I'll not argue such heresies!" snapped the major. "As to Hogge, I saw him slinking around the fringe of the crowd, as if to avoid the lady and her companions." When Davy made no reply, he changed the subject. "Smyth reported thou intended to take the route to Lochbogie?"

"Aye," grunted Davy. "Well, hold this pace. I'll try to overtake Captain Hogge." So saying, he put spurs to his nag.

Within a quarter hour, he passed through a cleft in the summit where the impact of the view halted him. The valley, stretching far off to the dim cliffs beyond which seemed to shoulder the very clouds aside, was a dreary succession of heather, swamp, tussock marsh and desolate moorland. It had about it a quality of hopelessness and deadliness that repelled him, and he imagined that hell might look something like this if the fires were burned out and it was abandoned.

A nebulous trail wound tortuously between the rocky debris and skirted the bogs, yet in all that frigid inferno, Davy could see neither horse nor rider. Depressed, and somewhat reluctant to trespass alone into the awesome silence, he sat still and waited for the others to overtake him.

By midday, they had traversed the valley, whereupon they paused to eat beside a lonely little loch. An hour's tedious climb carried them into the mists which swirled about them in shifting layers.

Davy had again taken the lead. The coolness of Olivia, the penetrating stare of Sir Thomas, and the tight-lipped gloom of Major Priety had begun to merge into a pall which all but suffocated him. He thought he understood why Michael Hogge had preferred to lose himself in this wilderness rather than face it. He cursed himself for having sent Half-Hanged on the mission instead of Hogge. There was a roguishness about old Half-Hanged which Davy found irresistible; his parodoxical philosophy, his fretting over trifles while facing major crises with fatalistic calm, his earthly humor—all these Davy missed more than he cared to admit even to himself.

Yet these were surface disturbances, and deep inside of him he was oppressed by an unidentifiable foreboding, a sense of misgiving which set his nerves on edge. It had naught to do with the insoluble situation awaiting him at Lochbogie, of that he was sure; there was a quality of immediacy about his apprehension which placed it in the here and now.

He felt the evil shadow of Lord Godolphin hovering darkly above him. Reviewing the seemingly contradictory actions of the wily old laird, they seemed to fall into a sort of rhythm or pattern, like the gambits of a master chess-player. What they portended, Davy could not foresee, yet he had the feeling of being maneuvered into disaster. And in some peculiar fashion, the supicion persisted that Michael Hogge fitted into the scheme.

With his nerves raw, he was startled when Olivia suddenly cantered out of the mists and drew up beside him. She peered closely into his face, then burst into laughter.

"Why, David!" she cried. "You have the air of a gravedigger! Have I intruded upon some strictly masculine brooding that you should stare at me so reproachfully? I'll go back if I'm not wanted!"

"Not wanted? God forbid, my lady! It's just that . . . that I wasn't expecting such a pleasant surprise. How did you escape the clutches of that old vulture?"

"Reynolds?" Olivia laughed softly. "Why, to speak true, I left her quarreling with her poor palfrey. She accuses him of trying to crack her spine with every step."

"I was referring to Sir What-ever-his-name-is," Davy said. "He glowers at me as if he suspected I wasn't . . ." He stopped short. That was a subject he did not want to reopen.

Olivia passed it lightly. "Sir Thomas is really a gem, Davy, but having the reputation of being one of the best swordsmen in England, I think he tries to look the part. Father assigned him to guard me, and he takes it seriously. He acts more like a jailer."

Davy grunted. "You can assure him he has nothing to fear from me—I mean, in regard to you, my lady."

She seemed in a jesting mood. "How unflattering and unkind! Am I so repulsive that I am safe even around such a notorious rake?" She giggled as the color spread over his features. "Ah, you see, young man, I've been forewarned about you!"

"I cry you mercy, my lady! There's naught I can say."

"Oh, yes there is! You can pay me pretty compliments. I promise not to take them seriously. I just want to be amused."

"Alas, my lady, I am no courtier," he said grimly. "Anything I could say to you would stem from the heart."

She sobered instantly. "Then *don't* say it, Davy!" she pleaded. "I was being silly, *intentionally*. These last few days have been ghastly, and when we entered this fog, I felt an intense desire to lose myself in it forever. Look—we are on top of the clouds! Why, it's like heaven!"

They had reached the peak of a mountain which thrust itself above the clouds. Here the sunlight was intense, and as far as the eye could encompass was a vast sea of billowing clouds. The rest of their party were still somewhere below, and for a little while they drifted through a world of unreality.

"Dear Lord, it's beautiful!" Olivia breathed prayerfully. "I've often heard the expression 'having one's head in the clouds!' but never until this moment did I understand it. Isn't it wonderful, Davy? There is no earth with its wars and tribulations. No soldiers . . ."

"I'm a soldier, my lady," he interrupted gently.

She laughed gaily. "Oh, no you're not! This is heaven, Davy, and you are just a fellow angel flying beside me with wings on your heels!"

"That contradicts what you said about me a moment ago," he chuckled, trying to match her mood.

"Oh, but you've been purified! Well, perhaps what I took to be wings are only spurs, but you are riding Pegasus, the winged steed! I hope we never come down!" Her laugh grew reckless. "La me! I must be getting dizzy from the altitude!"

But come down they did. The descent plunged them swiftly into the enveloping mists, and in a perverse fashion, Davy was almost grateful. He, too, had become light-headed from the vista, and he dreaded lest his tongue lead him into disaster. The clammy fog served as an immediate stage and cushioned their crash back to reality.

"I'll never forget that," he told her sincerely. "My one, and doubtless only, glimpse of heaven! Thank you for pointing it out, my lady, for, I own, I'd not have recognized it by myself. 'Twas *you* who made it real."

She was subdued. "Forgive me, Davy! My humor was unseemly. What I really came to ask you was—why are you going to Lochbogie?"

He stared a long while at his horse's mane before answering. "My general ordered it, my lady."

"Is that the *real* reason?"

He shook his head. "Not entirely. I must tell the laird the truth."

"In heaven's name—*why?* He will certainly hang you!"

"I've considered that," he admitted. "It is difficult to put the thing in words, but he raised me like a son, and somehow I just cannot allow him to go on waiting and hoping for Ian to return."

It was her turn to pause, and when she spoke, there was a catch in her voice. "I did not know you were like that," she said quietly. "It is fine and idealistic. Yet, I wonder: is not hope, even futile hope, preferable to bitter disillusionment? Believe me, I love John the Dugald very deeply; he has been a second father to me, and I think it was my affection for him that made it so difficult to break off my betrothal to his son. But he is a very old man who cannot live much longer. In his hope, he is happy and content. If you rob him of that —what is there left?"

"Nothing!" Davy conceded. "Nothing at all! That's why I feel so hellish about it! Yet there are others to consider—all the tenants and dependents at Lochbogie. With Ian dead, the clan Dugald has no hereditary successor to the chieftaincy, and unless the laird appoints one, bloodshed and chaos are inevitable."

She stared at him in astonishment. "You would sacrifice your life because of that?"

He winced. "You make me sound like a martyr," he retorted. "I am not. I haven't the slightest intention of hanging if I can avoid it. Anyway, there's more to it than that. Cromwell will lay siege to Lochbogie unless I can induce my laird to come to terms."

"Cromwell, Cromwell, Cromwell!" flared Olivia. "Dear God, how I hate that name! What manner of monster is he who can bring such horror and desolation to his country?"

"Tarry, my lady, you do him wrong!" Davy protested. "Cromwell is merely a general. As such, he is no more responsible for the war than Prince Rupert, on your side."

"Rupert serves his King!"

"Aye, but Cromwell serves England!"

She shrugged the matter aside. "We shan't quarrel over politics, Davy; not now, at least. Nevertheless, I am very sorry you deem it necessary we should go to Lochbogie. I had hoped to dissuade you."

"*We?*" he echoed, startled. "God's death, my lady, *you* will not go? That would be doubly embarrassing to everyone. No, I have a logical plan. A league or so this side of Lochbogie is a road that cuts over to the other Pass by which you entered the Highlands. When we reach that point, I shall have Major Priety escort you and your party . . ."

She raised a small gloved hand imperiously. "*I will not!*" she declared, in the same definite manner with which she had defied her uncle. "No argument, please! If you go to Lochbogie, so go I!"

He set his jaw. "That would be rank folly, my lady! You would only intensify my lord's hurt!"

"You are wasting words, young man! You will find that I am just as welcome at Lochbogie as you are!"

Davy felt his face redden. "A thousand times more welcome, I grant you!" He swung sideways to face her. "Howbeit, I presume you realize your presence there would seal my fate?"

Her eyes were cool and impersonal. "That remains to be seen!" she snapped. Then before he could reply, she wheeled her mount and trotted back to her party.

Their quarrel, if quarrel it could be called, seemed to mark the turning tide of Davy's fortune; from that point on, his luck ebbed swiftly. Olivia rode with him no more. The weather worsened, and for the rest of the day they floundered through a relentless drizzle which dampened the spirit as thoroughly as the body. It required all Davy's skill and experience in mountain lore to cling to the trail. Tempers grew edgy, and Davy had to admonish his troopers sternly against baiting Sir Thomas, whose frigid hauteur had begun to rankle everyone.

At eventide, Davy called a halt at the foot of the snow-capped Ben Eilrig, in the lee of a rocky barrier known as Shelter Stone. Here they were protected from the worst of wind and weather, and here they made camp. When all had eaten, Davy sought out Olivia in the hope of reasoning with her so as to settle his torment.

He found her deep in the shadows—carefully screened by Sir Thomas on one hand and her angry *duenna* on the other. Whether or not she guessed his purpose, he could not be certain, but she pointedly refused to leave her companions to talk with him privately. Snubbed and irritated, Davy stalked away. After stationing his sentries, he moved off by himself and rolled up in his plaid. Faithful old Gabriel, almost forgotten of late, snuggled gratefully against him.

But long after the fires had burned out and the others had found peace in slumber, Davy tossed about in a welter of anxiety. Twice he heard the guards change, and knew it must be after midnight, but sleep would not come. The poignant sense of foreboding came back to him, stronger even than before. He found himself listening expectantly.

Suddenly, the old hound growled. Davy caught him by the ruff, and raised up on one elbow. Once again he thought his imagination was playing him tricks, then his eyes caught a movement near the rock. He tightened his grip on the dog and, sitting up, reached for his saber with his free hand.

After a pause, the silhouette of a man detached itself from the mass of stone and moved surreptitiously toward him. Tense, Davy drew his legs up under him for a spring.

"*Colonel!*" the figure called softly. "*For God's sake, make no outcry!*"

Davy caught his breath. It was the voice of Michael Hogge!

Chapter Twenty-Two

Paradoxically, though Michael Hogge was the one man in his company whom Davy did not entirely trust, he was the only one whom Gabriel did. The old hound whined softly on recognizing the voice, so Davy released him and rose to his feet. Though he dropped his saber, he kept a hand on the hilt of his poniard.

Hogge seemed able to see in the dark. "Fear me naught!" he said, with a bitter chuckle. "But come where we can talk unheard, for I bear bad news." Giving Davy no chance to question him further, he glided between the sleeping troopers like a prowling panther.

Intrigued, Davy followed him around to the far side of Shelter Stone. The rain had stopped, and the stars shone with brilliant austerity in the cold night air. Davy wrapped his plaid over his head, and waited grimly for the other to speak.

"Though I mislike adding to your troubles," Hogge said bluntly, "you have ridden into a trap. By this time, the Marquis of Montrose will have flying squadrons both ahead and behind you!"

Davy felt his blood run cold. "How do you know this?"

The bearded man laughed his mocking laugh. "A gift of my poniard! Once again that faithful little instrument has extracted information as well as blood."

"Damn you—stop talking in riddles!" raged Davy. "Out with it!"

"It is a long story which I shall make as brief as possible," chuckled Hogge. "Suffice to say, if you were satisfied with the remarkable antics of the Laird of Inventry, I was not. His acquiescence was much too pat and his offer to accompany you out of the castle, illogical. Yet I own I could not read the handwriting upon the wall until he perpetrated that farce about 'ordering' his niece back to Inventry. Then I knew."

"Knew *what?*"

"I knew that he meant to see that neither you nor the Lady Olivia ever reached Lochbogie!"

Davy snorted. "You're daft!"

"Am I?" laughed Michael Hogge. "Then hear me further! It dawned on me, knowing that Montrose was somewhere near by in these accursed hills, that Godolphin had ridden out with all that barbaric horde solely to offer a screen behind which messengers could be dispatched to the marquis. Acting upon this hunch, I slipped away to watch. Sure enough, at the height of his touching farewells, two of his savages ducked out of sight and headed east. I attempted to intercept them." He laughed and, with his left hand, raised his right arm, which Davy now saw was limp and useless.

"Unfortunately, Colonel, they were better swordsmen than I expected," he went on. "One escaped me. The other, on his way to hell, confessed their purpose."

Davy rubbed the back of his hand over his eyes. "This is incredible!" he muttered. "I can't believe even a MacKenna would jeopardize the safety of his sister's daughter! And why would he turn to Montrose after declaring against the King? At his own insistence the treaty was signed in duplicate!"

Hogge snorted. "You are naïve, my dear Colonel!" he sneered. "There is no question of *jeopardy;* her Ladyship is to meet the same fate as you. What influence she holds over Godolphin, I know naught, but whatever it is, he means to terminate it. As for 'turning to Montrose,' you should have seen that his so-called 'declaring against the King' was mere lip service, since he candidly told you he would take no active part in the struggle. But Smyth, at least, is assured a safe passage, for you can be certain our wily Godolphin wants at least one copy of his precious treaty to reach Cromwell, and thus lull any suspicion of his duplicity. Whate'er befalls you and her Ladyship will appear a normal casualty of war. To further clear his skirts, he *forbade* his niece to accompany you. Remember?"

Davy resisted as long as he could. "But Montrose is a gentleman!" he protested. "He'd not lend himself to *murder!*"

The other chuckled. "Be realistic! Naturally, Godolphin did not confide his nefarious design to your esteemed marquis. His message was delightfully simple: a small Parliamentary force, including some female spies, are escaping to the south; all must be liquidated. Need

I remind you that Montrose's reputation is not founded on gentle-ness?"

Davy felt his temper soar, but he brought it firmly under control. This was no time for futile rage. It would require all his wit and coolness to extricate himself from this trap.

"Are you certain the courier reached Montrose?"

Hogge shrugged. "His fellow seemed sure of it. The marquis was resting between jousts at a place called Black Loch."

"H'mmn! I know of it. Have you any suggestions?"

The bearded man laughed drily. "I'm afraid not. By this time, you have a numerically superior enemy both ahead and behind you, hence you can neither advance nor withdraw. You haven't sufficient supplies to hide in the hills, even if that were possible, and if you surrender you will inevitably be slaughtered. No, my Colonel, I have no suggestions. The unenviable responsibility is yours alone."

Davy spread his plaid on the ground, rolled himself in it, then, rising, belted it in place.

"Sobeit!" he said briskly. "I'm eternally grateful to you. Come, let me tend that wounded arm, then we'll rouse the company."

Hogge shook his head. "Though the arm is useless for the nonce, there's nothing wrong with it that time won't heal. As for waking the company . . ." He paused momentarily before continuing. "For purely personal reasons, I feel myself overwhelmed with shyness, so with your permission, I'll . . . er . . . remain out of sight."

"Sir Thomas?"

Hogge grinned. "*Quién sabe!*"

Davy turned away, and after ordering a sentry to awaken the troopers, he himself prodded Old Piety to his feet. After a moment's reflection, he summoned the two Cavaliers. Taking them out of hear-ing of the others, he explained what he had learned. Major Priety and Captain Ashby listened in a grim silence, but Sir Thomas interrupted haughtily.

"Preposterous! If you think to trick me into turning my sword against a loyal servant of his Majesty, you underestimate me!"

Davy looked him coldly in the eye. "You can keep your sword in its scabbard, and be damned!" he snapped. "But if you attempt to turn it against any of *my* men, as God's my witness, I'll kill you with my own hands!" Then he went on with his story.

By the time he had finished, even Sir Thomas began to waver. "Where is this mysterious informant?" he demanded.

Davy parried that. "Tending his wounds, no doubt. But we waste time. Do you ride with us, or not?"

Dudley heaved his shoulders. "Certes, there's no alternative! And while it galls me to accept this fantastic tale, I own I, too, was somewhat suspicious of my Lord Godolphin's peculiar shifts. May I inquire what you plan to do?"

Davy spread his hands. "Push ahead immediately."

All three protested. "At night? In these strange mountains?"

"The night can be our friend," Davy said, then added something he himself did not believe: "Perchance we can outrun them."

Sir Thomas tried to argue the point, but Davy squelched him curtly.

"Be good enough to get your party mounted! We leave here in ten minutes!"

After cautioning the company to absolute silence, Davy rode on ahead, alone save for the canny wolfhound. He would cheerfully have exchanged half his troop for old Andrew, or any other good Dugald gillie, for it was painfully difficult to hold the trail in the darkness. However, he was grateful for the assistance of the wise old dog. Gabriel, at least, was a Highland Scot, and for him the mountains held no mysteries.

Davy had never endured such a sensation of aloneness. He wondered what had become of Michael Hogge. He was alternately troubled by the thought of him lying wounded and helpless, and irritated by his inexplicable conduct.

Despite the darkness they made good time, and at the first glint of morning light, he halted the company. While they breakfasted, he withdrew to a sheltered glade and studied his maps. If they could be trusted, the only trail from the Black Loch bisected their present route about eight leagues further on, in a wooded valley which afforded natural screening for an ambuscade. Unfortunately, there was no way of avoiding this place.

While he was pondering the matter, Hogge slipped out of the thicket. In the raw daylight he looked haggard and ill, his right arm swollen and stiff. He walked over without speaking and bent over the maps.

"Have you solved the insoluble?" he asked.

Davy shrugged. "We'll race them."

Hogge made a mocking salute with his left hand. "As the ancients phrased it: *audentes fortuna juvat!*" he observed. "Fortune favors the bold!"

He mounted quietly and rode ahead, and after a brief interim, Davy followed with his company. They pushed hard until in the late afternoon they reached the foot of another range. Just on the other side of this hump was the fateful meeting of the trails, and Davy was loath to stop. Yet common sense decreed it, so he ordered camp to be made, though forbidding any fires. By this time, the company was too weary to care, and after the horses had been staked out, all but Davy stretched on the hard ground. Hogge, meanwhile, had melted into the shadows.

Davy was too keyed up for rest, and about an hour after darkness had closed in, he quietly saddled his horse and with Gabriel's help guided him up the trail. A gnawing apprehensiveness angered him, and he tried to cry it down. He argued that by his forced march he had gained a full day's normal travel; a factor Montrose's renegades could not have anticipated. Therefore, if he broke camp by daylight, by midmorning he should be safely past the dangerous intersection before the enemy arrived. It was a comforting speculation.

But this illusion was short-lived, for as he neared the summit, he was met by Michael Hogge returning from a voluntary scout. Hogge bore the worst possible news: a Royalist force, estimated at sixty or seventy horse, had ridden into the woods below about dusk and straddled the trail.

The trap had closed!

"I fear I used the wrong proverb a little while ago," Hogge concluded drily. "I should have said: *l'homme propose, et Dieu dispose.*"

Though bitterly disappointed, contradictorily enough, Davy felt a lessening of tension. Fears disturbed him; facts he could deal with.

"Let's have a look," he suggested, and dismounted.

They tethered their horses and trudged to the summit on foot. There was no moon, but the stars had a cold brilliance that illumined the salient characteristics of the terrain.

The little basin was much smaller than Davy had expected from his study of the map: a sort of unroofed corridor with sheer rock walls on either side. Their route veered close to the eastern wall, following the bank of a turbulent stream which was fed by a noisy waterfall cascading in a hundred-foot drop from the westward. The floor of the valley was heavily wooded, and the small cooking fires of the enemy laid a pattern among the trees.

Davy's quick wit alighted on that phenomenon. "I doubt if the marquis himself is down there," he mused. "He'd not have allowed those fires."

Hogge sniffed. "True! I saw them arrive, and Montrose was not with them. But build no hopes on that score, my friend, for they are commanded by Alastair MacDonald, the Irish wild-man, who is even more savage than your barbarous Highlanders! The fires merely indicate they do not expect you before the morrow."

"My own thought," grunted Davy. "You seem to know this *Irishman?*"

"Careful, Colonel," Hogge chided. "Your emphasis suggests an hereditary dislike for the Irish. Don't underestimate the rogue! I know naught of Alastair but the common gossip. He's no soldier in the formal sense, for he's incapable of any complex strategy and is inordinately vain, but he's a born leader of men and a valiant fighter. Your plight is delicate to say the least."

Davy made no comment. He was busy sketching the visible details of the basin on his mind. Finally he turned to the other.

"Keep a sharp watch for any unusual activity," he said. "I'll be back." Then, giving the other no opportunity to question him, he hurried down to his horse.

Less than two hours later, he rode into camp and awakened the company. This time he did not single out the officers, but assembled the whole contingent, for his plan required perfect timing and the cooperation of each individual in the party.

When they had gathered, numbed by sleep, he explained their predicament. When they were shocked into complete wakefulness, he explained his plan.

"We have just one slim chance of survival," he told them bluntly. "To cut our way through in the darkness!"

This brought a general gasp of protest which found a voice in Sir Thomas.

"God in Heaven, man, that would be certain death! The odds are nearly five to one against us! And we have the ladies to consider!"

"The ladies are my chief consideration," snapped Davy. "Yet rather than have them ravished by Irish Royalists, I would prefer to see them dead! As to the odds, Sir Thomas, I might remind you that in most of the battles your marquis has fought and won, the odds against him have been nearly *ten* to one!"

"You are not the Marquis of Montrose, my precocious Highland hawk!" the noble retorted scornfully.

Davy grinned. "To that I'll naught say nay, my cautious Cavalier, yet I'm willing to match my *stoop* against his!"

It was Olivia who ended the argument. She stepped forward, silencing the belligerent Dudley with a gesture.

"I appreciate your concern, Sir Thomas," she said, in a clear vibrant voice that rang through the night like a trumpet call. "Yet I deem Colonel Dugald's not merely the best, but the *only* course. For my own part, I gladly place myself at his side. If any man amongst you chooses naught to accompany us, I beg leave to borrow his sword that I may try to fill his place!"

This brought such a spontaneous cheer, Davy had to plead for silence. Once again, it was Sir Thomas who acted as spokesman for them all.

"My adored lady," he said humbly, "I cry your pardon! Your courage has multiplied our ranks by the number of ten. I ask nothing more than to die in your service."

She blessed him with a smile. "If you all *live* in it, I'll be better pleased." She turned back to Davy.

"Your commands, Colonel?"

"To horse," Davy said gruffly, not trusting his voice.

Shortly after midnight, they toiled to within a stone's throw of the summit. Here, Davy halted them, and while the troopers tightened the saddle cinches and muffled their accouterments, he took Priety and proceeded to the summit on foot.

To his disappointment, Michael Hogge had deserted his post. Davy pointed out to the major the general lay of the basin. Most of the fires had burned out, but here and there a heap of coals smoldered redly against the black background.

The major was not enthused. "Verily, 'twill be a passage through hell!" he muttered doubtfully. "In yon woods, we'll not see our hands in front of our faces!"

"So much the better," Davy told him. "For by the same token, the enemy will not see them."

At this juncture, Michael Hogge came toiling up from the valley. Davy had a bad moment, for the one thing he feared now was betrayal, but the bearded man's cynical chuckle was reassuring.

"Certes, and I'm becoming an accomplished assassin," he chortled. " 'Tis the first time I've ever killed a man with my left hand!"

"What man?"

Hogge feigned surprise. "Why, the sentry, of course! You didn't think a wily Irishman would sleep without a watch, did you?"

Davy flushed at his own carelessness. "You took a desperate chance, in your condition!" he growled.

Hogge laughed softly. "You speak of desperate chances? *You*, my Colonel?" His voice ended in a whisper as Sir Thomas and Captain Ashby loomed out of the darkness. An instant later, he had vanished.

"We place our swords at your disposal," Sir Thomas said stiffly. "Command us!"

"See to the ladies," Davy told him. "Ride through, and leave the fighting to us. Keep to this road, and within fourteen leagues or so, you'll reach the Red Stag, an hostelry operated by Inness Swan. If we do not overtake you, tell Inness I sent you and ask him the route to Westmoreland. Do not attempt to pass Lockbogie, e'en though her Ladyship may insist. Bear right at the Red Stag, and it will lead you to the road by which you entered the Highlands."

"And you . . . ?"

Davy squared his jaw. "The major and I will delay pursuit as long as possible." He nodded back the way they had come.

"Let us get mounted!"

The others were already waiting. Davy heaved himself into the saddle and led them to the crest. As he paused there while Priety gave last instructions to the troopers, Olivia rode up beside him.

"Davy," she whispered, "I just want to say—God bless you!"

"Thank you, my lady," he said softly, "yet I'd rather hear you say that you forgive me."

"I thought that was understood, Davy! And had I not perfect confidence that we will all get through to Lochbogie, I . . . well, I'd be tempted to tell you something else." Leaving him to mull over that, she drew away.

He stared after her uncomprehendingly, yet her ambiguous words swept away all weariness and gave him new strength. If he was not unduly optimistic, at least he felt no fear. What was it Dudley had called him—a precocious Highland hawk? He smiled grimly: the metaphor was apt. Poised on this rocky crag, staring down into the darkness, he felt precisely like a hawk—a Highland hawk—ready for the stoop!

Major Priety rode up.

"All is ready, sir!"

Davy squared his boots in the stirrups, raised his hand in signal . . .

The bolt was loosed!

Chapter Twenty-Three

Down they plunged, down into the valley of shadow! Once clear of the starlit summit, they had to trust their mounts to find the trail. They made no further effort at concealment, yet the thunder of the waterfall served them well. They reached the haugh before a startled scream touched off the explosion. In the space of a heartbeat, pandemonium roared through the grove.

Someone kicked a campfire ablaze, and by the sudden flare, Davy glimpsed a swarm of men running toward their horses, like figures in a dream. A pistol crashed, and he heard the ball *zing* past him.

He hesitated for an instant. Perchance he could get through without a fight, for the surprise had been complete, but the thought of Olivia swept the impulse from his mind. He shouted to Sir Thomas to ride on, then turned his horse toward the enemy. He heard Old Piety's sonorous bellow behind him. Then the fight was joined.

In the darkness, it was truly hell! The slashing hooves churned up dying ashes which gave off spasmodic flashes of light. It was impossible to tell friend from enemy; any man on foot was presumed to be a Royalist.

Davy hacked his way toward the tethered horses. Once a giant of a man loomed before him with upraised claymore, as if rising from the very earth. Davy rode him down and felt the jar as his veteran warhorse crushed the breast-plate with his hooves. The man's last shriek was lost in the general tumult.

It was dangerous work cutting loose the maddened horses, for they were screaming and plunging in terror. Yet those he did not cut loose, broke their own halters and careened away.

Soon it was done! Davy turned back to the bedlam behind. The startled screaming had settled into a businesslike cursing in three languages. He paused a moment, trying to orient himself. Then he heard a familiar voice bellow: "Ye shall fall down before the wrath of God, ye wicked Philistines!"

Grinning without mirth, Davy cut a path toward the major, and when he drew within range, shouted, "Carry on with the next phase!"

If Old Piety was reluctant to get into battle, he seemed equally reluctant to withdraw. Davy had to repeat his command before the doughty major could bring himself to abandon his labors. Then his harsh order alerted the surviving raiders, and with a last shout of derision, they spun their horses and dashed into the darkness.

They did not draw rein until they had reached the crest of hill at the other side of the valley. There, by the light of the stars, Davy counted his little force. Seven! Five, including the Charles who had been "king" for an hour, had fallen; two others were sorely wounded. Miraculously enough, Davy had escaped unscathed, but Major Priety had a bone-deep gash along his thigh. They had paid dearly for their survival.

Davy said nothing, but leaving them to tend to each other's wounds, walked to a vantage point where he could again survey the valley. The campfires had been rebuilded, and though the water-fall drowned any human sounds, he could imagine the confusion reigning below. He offered up a little prayer for those of his men who had fallen; he hoped they were dead, for the vengeance of Montrose's Highlanders would be fiendish.

He was surprised that he felt no elation. His *coup de main* had succeeded; he had a right to be proud of his masterly stroke. Instead, however, he felt only a consuming weariness, an exhaustion of the spirit. For the others, the worst was over; for Davy, his real troubles were yet to come.

Dispiritedly, he trudged back to his mount.

The horses were tired, and as pursuit was unlikely, they proceeded at a walk. There was no conversation. Davy would have given a good deal to know that Olivia was safe, yet he hoped that she would not tarry at the Red Stag. For some reason which he refused to examine, he was afraid to see her again.

By daylight they had reached the moorland plateau and the road stretched clear and uninterrupted to the crossroads. They increased their pace to a trot, hoping to reach the hostelry in time for the evening meal. Davy tried to shrug his depression aside. He told himself sternly that he would cross his bridges when he reached them, and until they reached the inn, he had nothing to worry about.

Once again he was proved wrong!

Shortly before midday, they came upon a crofter's wife resting by the roadside. From her they learned that Cromwell had moved his army up to the foot of the *Highlandman's Pass* for an assault on Lochbogie.

Davy was appalled! Among the Highland Scots, Castle Lochbogie was deemed impregnable, and perchance it was—against a *direct* assault. But having listened to the Parliamentary veterans, Davy had no illusions as to how long the ancient fortress could stand against Cromwell's miners.

Questioned closely, the old crone admitted the siege had not actually commenced. Local rumor had it that negotiations were to take place between General Cromwell and the old Laird of Lochbogie.

But Davy took no heart from that. He could well imagine a picture of such a meeting when the flint of old Dugald's Scottish insularism struck the steel of Cromwell's long view. The inevitable sparks would, in effect, touch off the mines the Rebel sappers would sink beneath the castle walls. It would take only one such explosion to topple the outer defenses over the rim of the cliffs, and, thereafter, lovely Lochbogie would become just another lonely ruin, peopled by ghosts and bats.

The shock was followed by a suffocating sense of failure. Almost unconsciously Davy had come to regard himself as bearing the total responsibility for the peace of the Highlands. He saw now that he had been a fool; he might have known a genius like Cromwell would not have entrusted such a charge to an untried tyro. Nevertheless, it was a bitter awakening to realize he had been naught but a very minor pawn in the master chess-game of politics.

Still, he couldn't quit now! Perhaps the old gossip was wrong; perhaps Cromwell and Red Dugald had not yet met, and clashed. If only he could reach either of them before the meeting, he might, he just *might*, stave off the otherwise certain explosion.

But first, he had to make certain Olivia was safe. On this score, he got some assurance from the crone. She reported that an hour earlier, a man and two women had passed this same way, and had asked directions to the Red Stag Inn. From the description of the Cavalier,

Davy knew it was Sir Thomas. That meant young Ashby had fallen.

Tossing the old woman a silver piece, Davy bellowed for his men to follow, and touched spurs to his mount.

Though they pressed on until the horses stumbled from exhaustion, it was not until late afternoon, on topping a rise, they sighted three riders galloping toward the inn which lay beyond. With a little prayer of thanks, Davy urged his weary nag to one last burst of speed.

Measured by English standards, the Red Stag was a very humble establishment, but in the lonely Highlands it had an excellent reputation for adequate comforts, edible food, a satisfactory wine-cellar, and, best of all, modest reckonings. The host, Goodman Inness Swan, was a jovial if canny Scot who belonged to the Dugald clan and was —by Davy's lights—a man to be trusted.

When Davy pounded into the courtyard, Olivia and her party had just gone into the inn. He bellowed at the top of his lungs for Inness Swan, and as he flung himself out of the saddle, he heard a door slam and footsteps hurry toward him. He turned to greet the publican, then his eyes widened and his mouth sagged open.

For instead of the genial landlord, he met the guilty eyes of . . . Half-Hanged Smyth!

"*You . . . ?*" he breathed.

Half-Hanged came squirming toward him in the manner of a delinquent puppy.

"Wayo, Dyvy! Ye didn't expec' to see me 'ere, I wager!"

Davy clamped his jaws. "By God, I didn't, you treacherous bastard!" he grated. "Where's Anne?"

The other wore the look of a thoroughly beaten man. "Upstairs, in 'er room! 'Ear me, lad, afore ye bust wide open!"

"Damn you, there's nothing to hear! You had your orders and you disobeyed them! I ought to pistol you where you stand, but, by God, you'll die with more ceremony!"

Half-Hanged exhaled wearily. "Bugger me, then I wish't ye'd done yer pistolin' afore ye shipped me off wi' them she-Satans, fer I swear there can't be no 'ell below earth like them two can myke above it! I tolt ye I didn't unnerstan' the 'Ighland gibberish, but, says ye, 'Oh, Annie'll 'elp find the w'y!' Aye, she bloody well 'elped to find it, orl right! She brung me right 'ere w'ilest I was h'expectin' to see Doughadee most any minute!"

Infuriated as he was, Davy could see the fault was not Smyth's, but his own.

"But why here?" he fumed. "Why in hell should Anne come *here?*"

Half-Hanged's expression turned from guilt to sympathy. "Lor' lumme, lad, the bitch—beggin' yer pardon, sir—can't wait to get to yer *ancestral* 'ome, as she calls it, to tyke 'er plyce as a gryte lydy! She suspects ye're tryin' to styve 'er off, an' she ain't a-goin' to be styved!"

Major Priety interrupted grimly. "Verily, thou better do a mite of staving thyself, man! Those four females be already under the same roof, and if they meet"—he shuddered slightly—"truly it will be another Armageddon, with the Day of Judgment thrown in!"

Davy nodded and tossed his reins to a near-by trooper. "I'll deal with you later!" he told Smyth. "Meanwhile, get you upstairs and keep Anne and Jenny out of sight! Lock them in, truss them up—anything short of murder. *But do not let them come downstairs, at your peril!* Now away with you!"

Half-Hanged did not move, but stood nervously shifting his weight from one foot to the other.

"God damn you, jump when you get an order!" raged Davy.

Half-Hanged groaned. "Bugger me, Dyvy, ye ain't 'eard it all! *Piggey's 'ere, too!* An' 'e's thrown a shoe again! Plarstered, 'e be! Drunker'n 'e was the night ye met 'im!"

Davy closed his eyes. He had momentarily forgotten about Michael Hogge. "Oh, Jesus!" he moaned.

"So s'y I! 'E's gone cryzier 'an a 'ootowl! 'E bust out larfin' w'en 'e saw Annie an' swore we was a-goin' to witness the bloodiest battle in all 'istory right 'ere in the Red Stag! Myle an' femyle, 'e s'ys! Some'at about a Cavalier w'at 'e use't know 'oos lookin' fer 'im an' . . ." He stopped short with bugging eyes as a shout of rage emanated from the inn.

"May the Lord be merciful!" said Old Piety. "I greatly fear the Battle of Armageddon be joined!"

But Davy was even then halfway to the door.

The sight that met Davy's eyes when he burst into the common-room was dramatic enough to give him pause. Spotlighted under a smoky oil lamp, Michael Hogge and Sir Thomas faced each other with drawn swords, while the astounded company formed a ring around them. On the fringe, Dame Reynolds was visible, trying to restrain Olivia from interfering.

". . . your blade!" Sir Thomas was challenging in a voice as cold as steel. "*En garde,* I tell you, or, by the Mass, I'll run you through as you stand, you despicable cur!"

To one blinded by passion, or who did not know the man, Hogge might have appeared perfectly sober as he stood erect, staring steadily at his tormentor. But Davy, forewarned, saw the imperceptible swaying, and realized that even a casual shove would topple the man like a felled tree. Michael Hogge was blind drunk!

"*Hold!*" Davy roared from the doorway, then charged through the circle to face the irate knight. "What means this, Sir Thomas? How dare you threaten my officer? Have you forgotten you are . . ."

"I have forgotten nothing!" cut in the Cavalier. "This is a private affair, and, as such, is no business of yours! Stand aside while I deal with this traitor!"

Davy held his ground. "Traitor? By God, watch your tongue! This is an ill time and place for mouthing Royalist sentiments, I warn you! Captain Hogge is . . ."

"Captain *Hogge?*" Dudley hooted scornfully. "Zounds, 'tis a fitting alias for the swine! Yet, the world once knew him as *Lord Robert Lowry,* who escaped his deserts by presumably getting killed in Flanders! He'll not escape my steel this time, I warrant you! Now be good enough to remove yourself!"

Davy glanced at the man he knew as Michael Hogge, who gave him a fuzzy smile. "Shtan' ashide, my dear Colonel! Shtan' ashide!" He attempted to take a stance and almost fell over his own feet.

Disgusted, Davy pushed him into the waiting arms of Major Priety, who started to haul him away. Sir Thomas moved to follow, but Davy stepped in front of him.

"Enough of this!" snapped Davy. "Sheathe your sword, sir, or, on my oath, you'll cross blades with me in his stead!" He dropped his hand to his own hilt.

Then came the low blow!

Sir Thomas stepped back to look him over from head to foot with studied insolence.

"God'sdeath!" He spat out each word as if cleansing his mouth of a bad taste. "Think you I'd degrade myself by crossing swords with a churlish, base-born *groom!*"

The shocked silence was broken by a sharp feminine cry. Pale of face, Davy swung around to meet the horrified stare of Anne, now crouched at the head of the stairs. He turned back grimly to the business at hand.

"Major Priety! Have this man placed under arrest! He is to be confined under guard in a room until I order his release!" Then he spun on his heel to look for Olivia. She was gone! An instant later, Anne was clutching his arm.

"Ian! Ian! What did he mean by calling you a base-born groom? Why did you permit it?"

Davy looked about frantically. He spotted Half-Hanged lurking in a doorway, but before he could summon him, the knave had vanished.

"Not here, Annie!" Davy pleaded. "For the love of God, don't make a scene here!"

"You haven't answered me! Why didn't you kill him for that deadly insult of calling you a *groom?*" Her voice had risen until everyone in the room was staring at her.

"Come up to your room and I'll explain!" Davy rasped grimly. He took her firmly by the arm and piloted her through the crowd toward the stairs. At the first landing, he paused for a backward glance. Sir Thomas had haughtily surrendered his sword to Old Piety. There was no sign of Olivia.

With a heartfelt prayer of thanks for that one small blessing, Davy followed Anne to her room.

Once inside, he shoved her onto the bed and turned the bolt in the door. He wanted desperately to avoid one of those shrieking tantrums for which Anne had become notorious. He cursed his folly in not having confided to Olivia the truth about his marriage. It would have been infinitely kinder than to have her learn of it in this brawling fashion.

Only too well aware that offense is the best defense, he decided to take the initiative and, if possible, bluster through until he returned from Lochbogie—if he ever should return—before telling Anne the truth. So, the door locked, he turned angrily.

"By my troth, is this how you obey your master?" he roared into the assault. "I told you to go . . ."

But Anne was no mere Royalist troop that could be crushed by a *coup de main.* She reared from the bed and hurled into an overwhelming counterattack.

"I demand an answer!" she screamed him down. "Why did he call you a base-born groom?"

Her voice was a weapon against which Davy knew no defense. Treed, he decided the truth might as well come out now as later. He had delayed too long as it was.

"Because that is precisely what I was!" he conceded bluntly. "*A common groom!*"

She slumped back onto the bed as if he had knocked her down. "Ian! You jest?"

He glared at her savagely. "Do I look as if I jest?"

She covered her face with her hands. "Oh, God have mercy on me!" she bleated. "A *groom!* I wedded a filthy base-born *groom!*"

Her agony was so intense, he felt a sudden surge of pity. "Damn it, Annie, I tried to tell you the truth, but you wouldn't heed me! All you wanted was a title, so you listened to the others! It was a mistake, and I'm sorry!"

She dropped her hands and stared up at him from the bed. Never in his hectic life had Davy seen such venom in a pair of eyes.

"*You're* sorry?" she cried, her voice gathering momentum. "*You?* Mother of Christ! I thought I was giving myself to a genuine nobleman and he turns out to be naught but a vulgar, manure-wallowing *groom!* Dear God, why didn't that gentleman kill you so I could be free!"

In spite of himself, Davy was profoundly shocked. "You'd prefer *that*, Anne?"

"Prefer it?" she screamed. "I'd love it! Oh, Christ, how I hate you! Hate you! *Hate you!* Oo-oo-ooo! I wish to God you were dead!"

"Well, just be patient," he said drily. "Unless I miss my guess, you'll have your wish before another sunset. Then you can continue your whorish pursuit of a title! Meanwhile, do not attempt to leave this room!"

But Anne was not listening. She had flounced around until she lay face down upon the pillow, sobbing hysterically. As he let himself out of the room, the last words he heard were:

". . . hate you! Lord, I wish you were dead!"

It was a very chastened and subdued trio that Davy encountered on entering Hogge's room at the other end of the corridor. As he stood staring at them in silence, Old Piety blurted forth a biblical quotation for once so apt it broke the tension.

" 'He that is without sin, let him cast the first stone!'

"By God, Major, you sank your point that time!" Davy said ruefully, and sank into a vacant chair. "You might have added that the way of the transgressor is hard."

Priety's funereal features lengthened. "I did not speak in jest, sir! Only fools make a mock of sin!"

"Aye, yet methinks we're a parcel of fools!" Davy grunted. "We've piled blunder on blunder until we'll be damned lucky to get out of this with a whole skin."

Half-Hanged agreed. "Bugger me, there's naught but one w'y— take four good nags an' ride like all ol' 'ell for Lunnon town!"

"A man cannot flee his conscience!" warned the major.

"I can 'andle me conscience!" snorted Half-Hanged. " 'Tis me 'ide I'm worried about! Look ye, Dyvy—the gyme's up! Let's get out o' 'ere! W'at s'y ye, Piggey?"

Hogge had been sitting with his head buried in his hand. He raised it slowly, and the mask of scar-tissue was gray. Miraculously enough, he seemed cold sober.

"I have a rendezvous with hell!" he said bitterly.

The statement was so atypical of the man, it irritated Davy. "It you're referring to Dudley—forget it!"

Hogge shook his head. "I cannot! He carries my secret!"

"Aye, and he carries mine!" Davy rejoined. "Yet as the protector of my lady, he must remain inviolate."

Hogge's ashen features cracked into a cynical smile. "Oh-ho! So *that's* how the wind bloweth?"

Davy half rose, then sank back. "Enough! By my troth, her name is not to be bandied about by rogues!"

"Aye!" echoed Half-Hanged, trying to make peace. "The colonel's a wedded man, damme if else!"

Old Piety winced. "God forgive us our sins!" he muttered to no one in particular.

Davy snorted. "It was worse than a sin, Major; it was a mistake! Anne just informed me she wished I was dead."

Priety, not yet comprehending the truth of Davy's imposture, stared aghast.

"If you feel that way, sir—why did you two insist on marriage?"

232

" 'E done it to syve our necks!" Half-Hanged put in angrily. "She 'eard ye meant to 'ang us back at the mill an' bartered wi' Dyvy to get us out if 'e'd marry up wi' 'er."

The major frowned. "What nonsense is this? There was never any thought of hanging any of you! If Annie said differently—she lied!"

Hogge burst into laughter. "Is that surprising, Major?"

Priety wagged his head. "The Proverbs sayeth: 'As a jewel in a swine's snout, so is a fair woman without discretion.' "

"She's in Dyvy's snout!" Half-Hanged interposed seriously. "Not no swine's!"

Even Old Piety grinned at that. "Nor a Hogge's either," appended Davy, "else he'd not find it so humorous. But enough of this. As you all know, Cromwell has moved up to the foot of the Pass. I've got to see my laird before he does."

"What good will that do?" inquired Hogge.

Davy shrugged. "To speak true—I don't know. But he is old and out of touch, and he believes Lochbogie impregnable. He's got to know the truth!"

"*Which* truth?" persisted the bearded man. "About Lochbogie, or about *you?* Certes, and he can hardly learn one without the other!"

"I'm quite aware of that!"

"H'mmn! Well, passing over your personal fate—what happens if he chooses to resist? I mean, what do *you* do?"

"I stay with him!"

Old Piety was aghast. "Against Cromwell and the Covenant?"

"If it comes to that—aye!"

Half-Hanged let go a long-drawn sigh. "Bugger me, ye'r determined to commit suicide! Well, sobe't! W'en do we start?"

"*We* don't!" said Davy. "This is strictly personal. You lads take Anne . . ."

All three joined in such a clamor of protest, he held up his hands, laughing.

"All right! All right!" he quieted them. "You can all do as you damn please!"

"In w'ich cyse, I goes wi' ye!" Half-Hanged said firmly.

Hogge chuckled. "If Half-Hanged goes, then 'tis meet that I go also to keep you out of trouble. Which leaves the major . . ."

"Nay, nay, ten thousand times *nay!*" thundered Old Piety. "Ver-

233

ily, having cast my lot with sinners, 'tis too late to turn back. I, too, go with thee!"

Davy groaned. "This has a familiar ring; we've been over it all before. All I can say is—God bless you, comrades!"

"W'en do we ride?"

Davy hesitated. "We'd never get them to open the castle gates at this hour," he reasoned. "So we'll leave here at daybreak. Major, double the guard on Sir Thomas' door. We don't want another outburst from that source."

"What of thy wife, sir?"

Davy shrugged again. "She's through with me, now that she knows I'm not a nobleman. A title was all she wanted."

"The bitch!" cursed Half-Hanged between his teeth.

"Easy, man, easy!" cautioned Davy. " 'Twas her mother's fault, not hers. I'm chiefly guilty, for I should never have agreed to marry her, knowing how she felt."

Michael Hogge regarded him quizzically. "Have you someone *else* in mind now, Colonel?"

Davy felt the color drain from his cheeks. "On your peril, never touch that subject again!" he snarled.

Hogge bowed. "I understand," he said softly.

Davy shoved to his feet. "At dawn, then!" he reminded them, and went out.

Chapter Twenty-Four

Davy was rudely awakened by Major Priety shaking his shoulder. He pushed up on his elbows, hating to abandon the forgetfulness of sleep.

"In the name of heaven, wake up, sir!" pleaded the major. "Her Ladyship hath gone!"·

That acted as a prod which brought Davy to his feet, eyes wide, senses alert.

"Gone! Gone *where?*"

"I know naught, save only that she and that murderous Cavalier slipped through the windows during the night, saddled their own horses and galloped away!"

Davy swore bitterly and reached for his jackboots. "Don't you even know what direction they took? There must be tracks!"

"Aye! On my soul, I hate to report this, sir, but the tracks led . . ." He paused.

Davy filled in for him. "Toward Lochbogie, eh? Well, that guarantees us a reception, to say the least!"

"Thou won't go there, of course?"

"On the contrary, it is now more imperative then ever. How much of a start do they have?"

Old Piety's horse-face looked gloomier than ever. "Possibly an hour!" he confessed.

Davy groped for his buff coat. "It's better than three leagues. Perchance we can overtake them. Have the mounts saddled . . ."

"Smyth's saddling them now, sir!"

"Let's be on our way then!" snapped Davy, and ran for the stairs.

It was still dark when they pounded out of the courtyard, yet even then the first steely fingers of dawn were reaching tentatively over the horizon. For the first mile, Davy rode bent far out of the saddle, his eyes on the fresh tracks. It was plain from the placement of the hooves that Olivia and her escort were riding hard. It was equally plain their destination was Lochbogie.

Convinced of that, Davy straightened and let Gabriel worry about the actual spoor. The wise old hound knew they were close to home, and he loped along, yelping with delight at every familiar scent. But if Davy could share the dog's eagerness, he could not share his pleasure. Memory, he discovered, was a hydra-headed ghost that could be unbelievably cruel. As they galloped into the lower ground, the bog mists silently enveloped them in a mysterious obscurity which reminded him of that wonderful day he and Olivia had ridden side by side with their heads in the clouds. He ruthlessly brushed the remembrance aside: that was a glimpse of heaven, never to be repeated.

Strangely enough, now that they were so close to Lochbogie, many of his earlier apprehensions vanished; all he felt now was a desperate anxiety that he might arrive too late to prevent old John the Dugald from hurling a suicidal defiance at Cromwell. He was conscious, of course, of the multifold complications awaiting him: if Olivia and Sir Thomas branded him a murderer before he arrived, his intercession would never be heard. Then there was Lady Marguerite—how would she react to his unexpected appearance? He had almost forgotten her.

He made no plans. He had a vague sensation of carrying out a predestined course of action somehow above and beyond his own control. He would play the cards as fate dealt them.

Then almost before he realized it, they swept around a bend, and Castle Lochbogie lay before them!

The old wolfhound dashed on ahead, and by the time Davy and his companions rode up, he was already baying and clamoring at the gates. In a matter of minutes they were admitted, and Davy found himself ardently embraced by old Humphrey, the one-eyed castellan. To his dismay, he learned that he was expected, for word had just come from the laird that he was to be brought into the audience chamber the instant he arrived. In answer to his anxious query, he was informed that about an hour earlier a man and a woman, riding hard from the north, had come up and been admitted.

Davy and his friends exchanged significant glances. Hogge canted one brow.

"We shall accompany you, Colonel," he drawled, and the other two echoed assent.

But this time Davy was adamant, and so, with grim faces, they stood and watched him march off with the castellan.

"Hegh, laddie," babbled the ancient, as he and Davy crossed the old tiltyard, with Gabriel bouncing deliriously beside them. "I be muckle happy to see ye. In troth, we haird ye was daid!"

A ghastly thought struck Davy. He stopped short.

"Humphrey! Did the laird ask for me by *name?*"

The aged man paused and scratched his thinning locks. "De'il take it, lad, I canna say truly he did," he confessed hazily. " 'Twas mae thought to see the young maister ride up, but . . ." He broke into a toothy cackle. "Aweel, I ken 'tis mooch the same thing."

"I'm afraid it isn't," Davy murmured, continuing his walk. "Tell me the truth, old friend—the laird is expecting *Ian*, is he not?"

The castellan dismissed the matter with a shrug. "E'en sae," he babbled cheerfully. "Yet pairsonally, wi' all the comings an' goings, wi' accursed redcoats bivouacked under the walls, an' ranting ginerals demonding we tairn our backs on the King, an' naught but a handful of puir silly fallows, a few daft auld wimmen an' sae worn-out ancients sich as mae ain sel', why, de'il take it, Davy lad, I'd a muckle raither see ye than a brace o' Ians—God pardon me f'it!"

They had entered the building by this time, and once more Davy halted their progress. It was evident that whether or not old Dugald knew of his son's death, the news had not got about to the people. Davy shuddered. It was enough to be branded a killer without having to be his own betrayer as well.

"Who is with my laird, Humphrey?" he asked grimly.

"Why, the Lady Olivia—God bless her!"

Davy winced. "And who else? Is Lady Marguerite . . . ?" he hesitated.

Old Humphrey winked broadly and gave him a dig with an elbow. "Whisht, mon, ye're a sly dog!" he chortled. "Dinna ye hear what happened to her Ladyship? When word reached us that young Ian had killed ye in a brawl and left Westmoreland, her Ladyship lit out fer France as if someone had built a fire under her. She ain't come back, nor will she. Hoot, lad, ye'll hear more o' that later, but here we are at the chamber, an' the maister be impatient to see ye."

Davy understood what must have passed through Marguerite's mind; doubtless her own guilty conscience made her think Ian was returning to seek revenge. Davy brushed the incident aside; he was grateful only that she wasn't here to add to his troubles.

But the thought of meeting his degradation in the presence of Olivia was unbearable, so Davy made one last effort to evade it.

"Do you think you could draw my laird away from her Ladyship?" he pleaded. "I prefer to speak privily with him."

Old Humphrey wagged his head. "Troth, lad, I'd be blythe to oblige ye if I could. Yet I canna ree-sist his ain commond, which was to usher ye in at once!"

Davy saw the futility of argument. "Sobeit! I'll ask just one favor which will not compromise you: just announce me as 'Colonel Dugald'—nothing else. Do you ken me?"

"I dinna say that I do," grumbled the old man. "But it will been e'en as ye ree-quest!" And with that, he threw open the doors of the audience chamber, and in his high-pitched voice, croaked: "Mae laird! Now comes . . . Colonel Dugald!"

His heart in his throat, Davy strode into the chamber.

A long red carpet, unrolled only on occasions of vast import, stretched from the doorway to a circular conference table at the opposite end of the room. Facing the entrance crouched the aged patriarch, his flowing beard touching the polished surface of the table, his unseeing eyes fixed straight ahead, like watch beacons which had been extinguished.

On his right, holding one of his massive paws between her own slim hands, sat Olivia. Her drawn face was bleached to the pallor of death.

No one spoke, and in a silence broken only by the clank of saber and jingle of spur, Davy strode slowly but firmly to his destiny. Never had he endured such a march, and never had he so fully appreciated the appalling results of his deception. He heard the castellan close the doors behind him, as if cutting off escape. But there was no turning, and, like the run of sand through the glass, his footsteps all too soon brought him to the rim of the table. Squaring his shoulders, he looked into the sightless eyes.

"My lord . . ." he began.

With a deep-throated roar, the old man jerked his hand away from the girl and slapped both palms flat on the table.

"*David!*" he trumpeted. "By the gods, what means this? Where is your master, and what is this madness about *Colonel* Dugald? Has his Majesty sank to such a sorry plight he makes *colonels* out of grooms?" When Olivia tried to interrupt, he turned his wrath on her.

"Silence, child! I need no help from chits!" As she sank back, crushed, he glowered at Davy. "Speak, you scoundrel!"

The sight of Olivia's humiliation stiffened Davy's resolution. "If your Lordship will stop bellowing for a moment, I shall!" he retorted grimly. "Sire, it pains me to be the one to tell you this, but . . . *my Lord Ian is dead!*"

John the Dugald started out of his chair, then sank slowly back. "*Dead?*" he echoed. "In battle . . . ?"

Davy braced himself. "No, my lord. I killed him!"

The silence was a clamorous thing which seemed to flood the room. The old man appeared to wilt in his chair, and he waited, as if anticipating an explanation, but Davy said no more. After a long, agonizing pause, the laird said slowly, "I'll not ask how Ian died— or why. I do ask why you come here. You must know I will have retribution!"

Davy bowed. The old man's controlled calmness was more awesome than his thundering.

"I know that, sir! Yet I also know that General Cromwell is determined to secure this Pass . . ."

The laird interrupted with a snort of impatience. "That Rebel upstart! Bah, he'll blunt his claws scratching at these stout walls! But what has that to do with your visit here? Did Charles, perchance, send you with a force to aid our defense?"

Davy sighed. It almost seemed as if the aged laird was seeking deliberately to ensnare him. He dreaded to look at Olivia.

"I was sent, not by Charles," he said slowly, "but by Cromwell. I hold a temporary commission in the Army of Parliament!"

This brought the old man to his feet. "A traitor, as well as a murderer!" he thundered. "By heaven, your commission will be *temporary* indeed! Had I a sword in hand, I'd sever it at once!"

"That is your privilege, my lord!" snapped Davy, stung to anger. "But, in the meantime, if you will listen to what I have to say, you may prevent these walls from being tumbled around your ears!"

Dugald sank back in astonishment. "Go on!" he growled.

Davy took the bit in his teeth. "My lord, times have changed since you last marched to war! Lochbogie is no longer impregnable, believe me! Cromwell has reduced fortresses far stouter than this."

"You ask me to surrender to this English rebel?" John the Dugald cut in harshly.

"It is not necessary to *surrender*," argued Davy. "I ask only that you deal with him. Cromwell will give you generous terms if you barter wisely." He saw the old man's jaw begin to jut. "Consider, sire, I beseech you! You have nothing with which to fight save only courage. The men of Lochbogie who marched from here are bottled impotently in Westmoreland. As her Ladyship can tell you—even the earl, her father, has seen the futility of a lost cause."

"Let *me* ask a question," put in the old man. "If we are assaulted, do you turn your sword against me?"

"No, sir! I pray to God you will not offer battle, but if you do— and withhold your punishment of me until later—my sword, as always, is at your service."

The laird slumped back in his chair and stared at Davy with eyes that saw nothing—or perhaps too much. Then he turned to the girl.

"My child, tell me—have my ears gone the way of my sight? Is this David the groom who stands before me, lecturing like an oracle, or is it some rival chieftain in disguise? Forsooth, he speaks as if he had authority!"

"That is because he speaks with the authority of truth, my lord!" cried Olivia. "Nor is it fair for you to cry him down because he was a groom! He has proven himself the equal of any man in the Highlands!"

The old man grunted noncommittally. "H'mmn! I take it you agree with the scoundrel!" He leaned forward and balled his great hands. "Hear me, both of you, for on this I take my vow—*I, John the Dugald, will make no terms of any kind with your Oliver Cromwell!*"

Davy exhaled wearily and shrugged his shoulders, but Olivia sprang to her feet.

"Sir! It is just such stubborn vanity that has brought continuous bloodshed to the Highlands and impoverished them of men as well as wealth! Haven't you the wit to see . . ."

At that moment the doors crashed open and old Humphrey's voice, rattling with awe, croaked: "Mae laird! Now comes his Excellency— *General Cromwell!*"

Chapter Twenty-Five

If he lived to be twice the reputed age of Methuselah, Davy would never forget that awesome moment when he watched the sturdy bulk of Oliver Cromwell stride up the red carpet. His mind keened by apprehension, he absorbed every detail of the general's appearance: the brightly polished breast-plate with its nicks of battle, the prim white turned-down linen collar, the ruddy, wind-bitten features, the mole on the harsh underlip, the frame of gray-streaked hair. He forced himself to meet the pale cold eyes, but the characteristic murkiness obscured whatever thoughts brooded behind them.

Olivia had lurched to her feet, more from horror than respect, but the old laird remained hunched in his great chair. If Cromwell sensed the tension, he gave no sign of it. He clanked to a stop at the edge of the table beside Davy, and bowed to John the Dugald.

"Your servant, my lord!" he said, in a voice that reminded Davy of the snap of a drover's whip.

The old chieftain omitted the customary welcome, but with a growl of acknowledgement, called for a chair for the visitor. Since Humphrey had withdrawn, Davy did the office. As Cromwell lowered himself sedately in the chair, his eyes asked a question.

Davy shrugged. "I but lately arrived, sir!" he explained.

Cromwell frowned slightly, and turned to the laird. "My lord, doubtless your son has already told . . ." he began, but old Dugald cut him short.

"My *son?*" he rumbled. "What about my son?"

Taken aback, Cromwell looked at Davy in surprise. Davy braced himself against the inevitable.

"Your Excellency," he said heavily. "You have been . . ."

"Hold your tongue!" thundered John the Dugald. "By the gods,

I'm still master of Lochbogie, and no one speaks without my permission. Keep your mouth shut until you are spoken to, young man!" He leaned toward the Englishman.

"So—*that's* how the wind bloweth, eh?" he continued grimly. "Believing this young cub to be my son, you decorate him with a commission as a Rebel colonel to gain an advantage over me? Is that it, sir?"

Cromwell stiffened belligerently, then relaxed slightly.

"My lord," he said slowly, obviously choosing his words with care. "If ever a father had reason to be proud of a son, it is you, sir! And as for his commission, he won that on his own merits, by a display of leadership and valor such as I have rarely witnessed."

Old Dugald leaned back and stroked his beard. "Interesting," he growled. "Most interesting!" It was difficult to know whether he was mocking or serious.

A trace of impatience clouded Cromwell's stern features.

"Sir, I did not come here to discuss personal matters," he said brusquely. "You received my communication relative to your position in this unfortunate struggle. Have you reached a decision?"

This was the fateful moment Davy had been dreading. He waited for the explosion. There was a long period of pained silence during which John the Dugald held his sightless eyes fixedly on Davy. Then at long last he spoke.

"I will make no such decision," he said bluntly. "I am an old man and blind, and my days are numbered. As was recently pointed out to me, times have changed and my ways are not the ways of today. Therefore, it is meet that he who must bear the burden should have the deciding of so vital a question. So, with that in mind, I herewith abdicate my authority in favor of my son and empower him to negotiate with you, sir!"

Davy came as close to fainting as he ever did in his life. As he stood staring stupidly at the trio, he was vaguely aware of the tears welling in Olivia's eyes. Finally old Dugald barked at him: "Come, lad, have you lost your voice! By the gods, you were giving tongue lustily enough a few minutes ago on how I should conduct my affairs! Let's hear *you* handle it!"

Cromwell moved forward to the edge of his chair. "My lord, are you serious? Colonel Dugald is my officer, and I seek no unfair advantage because of it!"

Old John snorted. "I know naught of the *colonel* part, but he's a *Dugald!* Hence, you have no advantage, sir!"

Olivia leaned across the table. "Davy," she whispered. "God has given you this opportunity! Use it!"

Still dazed, Davy rested the tips of his fingers on the board. "Thank you, my lord!" he said to the old man, then turned slowly to Cromwell. "Your Excellency, as you bear witness, this comes as a surprise to me."

"Do you wish time to confer with your father, Colonel?" Cromwell offered.

"He needs no time!" growled the laird. "Have at it, lad!"

Davy bit his lip. "Permit me to resign my commission, Excellency, that I may be free to act."

"Granted!" said Cromwell. "It is hereby revoked."

Davy took from his pocket the treaty he had secured from Godolphin, and tossed it on the table, just out of Cromwell's reach.

"Your Excellency, I have here the conditions by which the Marquis of Inventry has agreed to peace, which, if Lochbogie sides with Parliament, can assure you a peaceful Highlands."

Cromwell arched his brows. "*If . . . ?*" he snapped.

"*If!*" Davy reiterated firmly. "Oh, I have no illusions that these ancient walls could offer much resistance, but know this, Excellency —the true spirit of the clan Dugald is not a tangible thing to be conquered by siege or sapper. You have no counterpart of the clan in England, but I give you my oath that if you reduce Lochbogie, that spirit will live on in these hills to harass your every move."

"Is that a challenge, sir?"

"Quite the contrary! I merely want to prove that a friendly Lochbogie, sitting astride this Pass, can be of immeasurably greater service to the Cause than a heap of rubble which will leave the Pass defenseless!"

Cromwell stroked his chin. "Continue, please," he urged, with more restraint.

"Since my lord has seen fit to honor me with the responsibility of decision, I deem it wisest to cast our lot with Parliament," said Davy. "But *only* on the same terms you granted Inventry."

Cromwell frowned. "You have taken advantage of me there!" he said sharply. "Those conditions were tailored by Parliament to fit a certain peculiar situation."

Davy smiled thinly. "Your Excellency, any Highland Scot will tell you the Dugalds are more dangerous enemies than the MacKennas —e'en though you do not have to march so far to fight them! And if the Dugalds threw in with Montrose, you'd be forced to cross the Highlands to Godolphin's defense, or make an enemy of him as well!"

Cromwell drummed impatient fingers on the table a moment, then burst into laughter.

"Heaven help me!" he chuckled drily, and turned to old Dugald, "My lord, you've coached this young cub well, upon my oath! He has interlarded his argument with enough threats to make it irresistible, and 'tis more to keep him personally on our side than to secure Loch-bogie itself that—I agree to his conditions!" He swung back to Davy. "I ask just one thing more, sir—will you accept a permanent commission, with command of a regiment?"

Davy hesitated, and glanced at the old laird. What he saw, told him nothing. He faced Cromwell again.

"Excellency, nothing would please me better. But I . . . er . . . have some unfinished business to discuss with my laird."

Cromwell rose to his feet and reached for Godolphin's treaty. "My offer remains open," he said. "Meanwhile, I will have my secretary draw up the agreement along the lines you request. Thank you, my lord, my lady, and . . ." He bowed to Davy. "Would that the Highlands send us more hawks of your stripe sir!"

When Davy returned from seeing the general out, he found the old laird alone. The latter beckoned him close.

"Davy," he growled wearily. "Tell me *why* you slew Ian?"

So Davy told the whole sordid story as simply as he could. At times he faltered, hating to damn the dead, yet seeking to bring out the truth as he knew it. However, when the time came, he couldn't bring himself to betray the confidence of Olivia about her broken betrothal, so he attempted to explain away Ian's homicidal madness as extreme tiredness. The old man prompted him no more, and the pauses were more terrifying than the tale itself. And when he reached the end, the silence was unbearable.

For a seemingly interminable time, the venerable patriarch sat staring into space, his bearded chin resting on his chest. Then at long last he exhaled in a sound that was half-sigh, half-sob.

"Aye, 'tis much as the wee lass told it," he muttered, "save only the

244

true reason why the poor bairn went berserk. Nor do I blame her for rejecting him; the lad was not good enough for her. 'Twas a tragic deed, Davy, yet I own you could do naught but defend yourself."

Davy sank to his knees and put a tentative hand on the old man's knee.

"Sir! Dare I hope you can forgive me?"

The laird groped out and ran his gnarled fingers through Davy's curls. "My boy, my boy!" he said brokenly. " 'Tis I who beg forgiveness!"

"*You*, my lord?"

"Aye, Davy, *me*—for no man is so base as he who will not acknowledge the get of his loins!" He stifled a sob, and went on. "You are my first-born, David, the natural son of the only true love of my life!"

Davy could not speak, so, after a moment, John the Dugald continued. It was an old familiar story; of passionate young lovers and a stern unyielding parent who had forced another marriage for political expediency, with the inevitable unhappy result. John the Dugald had not dared own Davy as a son while Ian's mother lived, so he had tried to ease his tortured conscience by giving him equality in everything save station. He confessed that it was he who had advised Olivia privily not to permit anyone to force her into a marriage against her will.

"It goes without saying," he concluded, "that I am saddened by Ian's death, yet I have had time to adjust to it. Word reached me that *you* were dead and that *Ian* had gone over to the Rebels, but when I heard that he was accompanied by a wolfhound, I knew it had to be you, David. Poor Ian could not win even the loyalty of a dog."

Davy looked up, astounded. "Then when I entered here today, my lord, you knew, even though you . . ." He stopped.

"Aye, Davy, I baited you to see if all the lass said about you was true. I'm proud of you, my son, and, thank God, it is not too late to rectify my mistake in part." He gestured toward a door leading into an anteroom.

"Be good enough to summon Olivia. The poor chit's on tenterhooks."

Bewildered, Davy stumbled to his feet and opened the door. The girl was waiting, her face pale and tense. When Davy beckoned, she ran into the room and went over to the old lion.

"My lord, my lord!" was all she could whisper.

John the Dugald took one of her hands, then reached for one of Davy's.

"Olivia kens the truth, David," he said, and this time his voice was clear and unfaltering. "I wonder if you do?"

"You explained everything, sir!"

"Not everything, son, not everything! I did not tell you she has *consented to be my daughter.*"

Completely confused by the impact of what had gone before, Davy did not comprehend until the old laird had placed Olivia's hand in his own. Then he was too horror-stricken to speak.

"Aye, I saw it coming when you were bairns playing together," Dugald said, with a chuckle. "I dreaded it then, but the Lord in His infinite mercy hath arranged it. It is evidence of His forgiveness for my past sins and will at least brighten my last few years."

Davy stared blankly at the girl. A wave of color suffused her cheeks, but she met his eyes.

"As Father says, Davy, I guess it was always," she whispered. "Yet I didn't know for certain until that day we glimpsed heaven above the clouds!"

A cry wrenched itself from Davy's throat. "No, oh dear God, *no!* I'm not worthy to touch . . ."

"Silence, you young gowk!" roared the old man good-naturedly. "If you can face a regiment of English regulars, you can face a lovely lass! *Worthy,* is it? Did you not hear me abdicate in your favor? I meant it! By the Laws of Tanistry, which govern the succession of Highland chiefships, I have the power to nominate my successor— which I have done! As Laird of Lochbogie, you have the station to marry e'en a daughter of the Earl of Westmoreland—if she'll have ye! And since she has agreed, 'tis blessed ye are!"

This was the nadir of Davy's life. Here was everything he had ever dreamed of—fame, fortune, rank, and, most incredibly priceless of all, Olivia! All within his grasp—yet he could not have it. He stood mute.

Olivia was the first to break the portentous silence.

"Davy!" she cried. "Don't you care . . . ?" She hesitated, her eyes growing large.

"My darling, as God's my judge, I've worshipped you since we first met!" he blurted. "Only I can't . . ." He choked off, hanging his head in shame.

"Lord in Heaven, what nonsense is this?" thundered John the Dugald. "Why *can't* you marry her?"

Davy squared his shoulders. "Because," he said, "because I am already married!"

Chapter Twenty-Six

In after years Davy was never able to recall clearly the scene which followed his shocking revelation. He was vaguely aware that Olivia had fled the chamber and that the stricken old man had furiously ordered him out of his presence. Davy had been only too willing to escape.

After that, there was a period of several hours for which he could not account. His next conscious remembrance was when, about dusk, his friends found him wandering blindly through a deserted section of the castle and led him to their quarters in the guard tower.

There, his features hidden in the friendly darkness, he recounted everything that had happened during his interviews. His comrades heard him out in understanding silence. After a long and painful pause, Half-Hanged was the first to speak.

"Bugger me, friend, 'tis sorry I am!" he said from the heart. "I own the fault be mine fer bringin' ye an' Annie together! Yet, 'ad I known 'ow much ye stood to lose by't, damme if I wouldn't a-wrung 'er bloody neck!" He snapped his fingers as a happy thought came to him. "By God, I can *still* wring it!"

Davy's confessional had served as an emotional catharsis, and though he felt drained, his head was clear.

"Nay, man," he said wearily, "Anne is my wife, though I may never see her again."

Michael Hogge grunted. "You'll see her again, worse luck! You may as well be forewarned, lad—she followed us, and is here in the castle!"

Davy flinched. "Here? Oh, Lord, *no!*"

Half-Hanged snorted in disgust. " 'Tis the truth, Dyvy! The bitch wouldn't speak wi' me, but she fawned o'er Piggey 'ere, 'avin' 'eard

248

'e was a gen-yew-wine lud!" He scowled at the bearded man resentfully. "Gwan—tell Dyvy w'at the slut said!"

Though his face was masked by shadow, it was plain Hogge was
embarrassed.

"She's pieced the whole story together, lad, and is determined to
betray you to Cromwell. I managed to keep her occupied until his
Excellency got out of the castle, but she vows she'll see him on the
morrow. I don't know how to prevent it."

"B'Jesus, *I* knows 'ow!" grated Half-Hanged.

"No!" snapped Davy.

"W'y the 'ell not?" argued Half-Hanged. "She's no damn good!
Wi' 'er out o' the w'y, ye'll 'ave a clear road to fame an' fortune, an'
the lass ye *really* wanted!"

He was so pathetically earnest, Davy couldn't be angry with him.
"You just don't understand, old friend," Davy said quietly. "The mistake is done. Think you the Lady Olivia would have me with my
hands stained by the blood of my wife?"

"If she wouldn't, more fool 'er!" Smyth growled.

Old Piety had sat through the ordeal with his head buried in his
hands. When he looked up, his eyes seemed to glow in the darkness.

"May the Lord Jehovah pardon our sins!" he groaned.

Hogge said angrily, "A pox on your platitudes! It was just such
driveling sanctimony that forced our friend into his damnable marriage! To hell with a pardon; what we want is a *solution!*"

Half-Hanged Smyth rose determinedly. "Well, bugger me, I knows
the best solution—we'll all get gloriously drunk an' ferget it! Tomorrow's another day, we got our 'ealth, our blades, an' our nags, an' the
world be big! W'at s'y ye, mates?"

Though Davy had no enthusiasm for the suggestion, Michael
Hogge agreed.

"The most sensible thing you ever said, Smyth! Have at it!"

Half-Hanged hastily departed to procure the wherewithal.

By this time, the little tower room had grown very dark, and in the
absence of the exuberant Half-Hanged Smyth, the stillness was even
more depressing. Peculiarly enough, the major seemed the most up-
set, and after a few minutes, he slid to his knees and began to pray
aloud. Michael Hogge, as if unable to bear it, stomped across the
chamber to stare moodily out the window.

"There must be a way out!" Davy heard him mutter to himself. "There *must* be!"

Soon Half-Hanged returned with two demijohns and a lanthorn. It seemed to Davy that Old Piety was almost too anxious to drown himself in forgetfulness, for he drank steadily. After a few passes of the jug, Half-Hanged and Hogge became merry, but the liquor served only to clarify Davy's thinking and intensify his hurt. When Half-Hanged and Hogge put their heads together and began singing: *"Ho, 'er mither was a lydy . . ."* Davy rose to his feet and slipped unnoticed from the room.

With old Gabriel padding behind him, like an understanding shadow, Davy crossed to the wing of the castle where he knew Olivia would be quartered, yet when he asked to speak with her, he was told she had left word that under no circumstances would she see him. From a kindly guard, however, he learned she had made arrangements to leave for Westmoreland at daybreak.

Defeated there, he thought of trying to reason with Anne, but the futility being at once apparent, he stifled the impulse. In her insane desire for prestige, the girl was beyond reason. Yet even now he could feel no malice toward her, only a sort of consuming pity. In a broad sense, she and he were much alike; they had aimed at the stars, and their bolts had collided in mid-air.

His undirected footsteps led him onto the now deserted ramparts where, through the embrasures of the battlements, he could see the campfires of the Parliamentary army bivouacked in the valley far below. He raised his eyes to where the riddle of all life was hidden in the fiery firmament of the stars. The vastness of the infinity dwarfed his troubles, yet he could not resist thinking of the what-might-have-been. If only the God of all this immensity would give His creatures a second chance! Yet, even while he wondered, he realized that must have been the eternal cry of man since the dawn of creation.

In an instinctive urge to go back to the beginning of things, he wandered to his old quarters above the stables. Here the pungent aroma of the horse stalls was a welcome reminder of happier days. He brushed aside the webs which had guarded the place in his absence and crawled gratefully onto the dusty pallet. Despite all his grasping ambitions, he was naught but a lowly groom, and here he belonged. He had the poignant sensation of coming home.

Whimpering softly, Gabriel wriggled up beside him. Davy put an arm affectionately around the old hound. He slept, and in his dreams captured the bliss denied him by reality.

L'Envoi

Pounding and angry shouts precipitated him awake. His first thought was of an attack, but as he sat up, Half-Hanged burst noisily into the room.

"W'at the ruddy 'ell be ye doin' 'ere?" Smyth roared excitedly. "I been searchin' arf the mornin' fer ye!"

Davy thumped his head with the heel of his palm to jolt his wits together.

"What's wrong now?" he groaned.

"Plenty, damme! 'Tis that no-good bastard Piggey! I tolt ye not to trust 'im, but ye wouldn't lissen. Now, by God, 'e's done it!"

Davy crawled erect. Sunlight streamed through the chinks in the walls, but the loft itself was cold and damp. He felt chilled to the marrow. A fire had been laid before he went away, so now he went down on his knees before it. As he fiddled with flint and steel, he asked, "Well, out with it—what's he done?"

"W'at? W'y, bugger me, Dyvy, the treacherous son-o'-a-bitch 'as *run off wi' yer wife!*"

A spark caught, and as the flames licked up the dry faggots, Davy sat back on his haunches and laughed bitterly.

"W'at's funny about it?" raged Half-Hanged. "Ain't ye got no pride?"

Davy shook his head. "Not a whit, old comrade!" he admitted. He stopped smiling when he saw the pain on the other's ugly face, for he remembered that Half-Hanged had first wanted Anne for himself.

"Are you certain he went away with her?" he insisted.

"Yer bloody well right I'm certain! 'E got the castellan to let 'em out afore daylight. E'en a'ead o' the Lady Olivia an' 'er party!"

The mention of Olivia plunged Davy back into gloom, yet having

252

suffered so many disappointments, he had scant emotion left. He turned to the fire—the only cheerful thing in the room—and warmed his hands by it. Half-Hanged continued to assail the man they both knew as Michael Hogge, but Davy scarcely heard him. So poor deluded little Annie had at last found her "noble gentleman"! What irony!

Yet, despite Half-Hanged's assurance, Davy found it difficult to accept the facts. Hogge was an avowed misogynist and had never shown anything but contempt for Anne. Too, it seemed incredible he would have betrayed Davy's friendship; that was atypical of him.

Davy sprang to his feet as a terrible thought crossed his mind. Was it possible that Hogge, in one of his drunken rages, meant to destroy her?

At that moment, Major Priety stumbled into the room.

More than ever, Old Piety resembled a perambulating cadaver, but thought he showed evidence of a debauched and sleepless night, he was cold sober now. He stopped short, obviously disconcerted to discover Half-Hanged in the room, and made no secret of his displeasure. Yet when he heard what Michael Hogge had done, he dropped to his knees and loudly thanked God for it.

Davy and Half-Hanged were flabbergasted, and they stared at each other in amazement.

"Bugger me!" exclaimed Half-Hanged. " 'E's still drunk!"

Priety stopped his blatant prayers and stood up. "Nay, nay, man, I was never soberer!" he insisted. "But the Lord God in His infinite mercy hath again demonstrated His powers of forgiveness for our sins!"

"Bah!" sniffed Half-Hanged impatiently. "Ain't we got troubles enough wi'out listenin' to ye whine o'er a bit o' carousel! That damn Piggey 'as betrayed . . ."

"Peace, fool!" thundered Priety. "Thou know naught whereof thou speak! If anyone is a *betrayer* it is I. I come now in humility to confess!"

Half-Hanged slapped his cheek. "Lor' lumme!" he groaned. "*Another!*"

Old Piety fished a crumpled paper out of his pocket and fingered it distractedly. Davy noted with surprise that it was his marriage contract.

"My boy," intoned the major in a sepulchral voice, "I fear I have done thee a ghastly wrong! I also betrayed my Church and my God! Last night in a vision, the Lord revealed to me that in my ignorance I . . ." He paused and fixed Davy with his great feverish eyes. "I . . . may God forgive me . . . never legally married thee at all!"

Davy was too stupefied to grasp his meaning, but Half-Hanged seized upon the last sentence.

"W'at's that?" he shouted. "W'at was *that? Dyvy ain't wedded?*"

Old Piety nodded sagely. "So Pig . . . I mean, so the Lord hath revealed," he said somberly. "Last night a voice sayeth to me: 'Brother, did thou not join in holy wedlock a woman named Anne Ramsay to a man named Ian Dugald? Yet the man now afflicted by her is named David! Hence, in truth, you married her in proxy, for her actual spouse be Ian!' So spake the voice!"

"W'y, bugger me, so ye did!" marveled Half-Hanged. "This Ian 'e be dead!"

Priety bobbed his head. "Which, God willing, makes her a widow!"

Davy stared hard at the major. "Did this 'revealing voice from heaven' have something of the tone of Michael Hogge?" he demanded drily.

Old Piety rolled his eyes. "Now that thou mention it—there was a striking resemblance," he conceded. As he talked, his long hands shredded the document and tossed the pieces into the fire. "To speak true, when the fruits of my sin were laid bare and my tongue loosed by spirits, I sought his advice, for he hath had more experience with sin than I."

"Go on," Davy prompted grimly. He began to suspect that the major was enjoying his confession.

"Hogge pointed out that it was only fair I immediately tell Annie of her unwedded condition," Old Piety went on. "Woe unto me that I should thus have betrayed an innocent maiden!"

"I don't imagine she busted 'er stays weepin'!" sneered Half-Hanged.

"Thou art a godless jackanapes!" snapped Priety. "Only the fact that I had the foresight to take Michael Hogge along to comfort her saved her from grief. I left him with her while I returned to the tower to pray God for guidance. Later, Hogge joined me there and assured me the devil had given him a solution. More than that, he would not say, save only that he made me promise to tell thee the whole truth, but not until midmorning, which is now. He gave me this letter to hand you *after* I had made my confession." The major fumbled in his tunic and offered Davy a sealed packet. "He did not tell me he planned to run away with her."

Davy accepted it with shaking hands and wrenched it open.

To the ryght worchypfull David of Dugald, Laird of Lochbogie, yn haste, it began. *My Lord David, I pray that it may plese yew to forgive my taking leave without speaking. From our reverend comrade I have learned that Anne is not truly married to yew, hence is free to do as she chuses. Therefore to remove tew people who could cause yew naught but embarrassment, I have offered to wed her since that is her grete desire. Yr secret will therefore not be bruited about. Fear ye naught for the maid. In gratitude to yew for the first true friendship I have ever known, I hereby take oath I will be good to her.*

So my lord, do yew now good servyce and tayke yr rightful station. Do naught cast aside yr birthright as I have done. God sende yew good fortunes.

Written yn haste, by yr lovying comrade-in-arms . . .

He had first signed it "Lowry," then scratched that name out to write "Piggey."

Davy had to read it twice before he grasped the full implications, then he handed it to Priety. Though the major perused it carefully before passing it along to Half-Hanged, he showed no surprise.

"May God cherish him!" he murmured unctuously. "Greater love hath no man! He hath set thee on thy true path, my son!"

Davy groaned. By this time, Olivia would be well on her way to Westmoreland, and it would be too late to overtake her. Once safely behind the walls of that castle, he knew she would never afford him an opportunity to explain.

"Why in hell didn't you tell me this sooner, you damned old fraud!" he roared at the major. "You must have known . . ."

"I knew *nothing!*" Priety cut in firmly. "Although I had my suspicions from the first, and therefore did not wish to perform the ceremony, when thou insisted, I tried to protect the lass by marrying her to the name thou had assumed, not to thee. It wasn't until last night, when Smyth told who thou really wert that the truth was revealed."

255

"Revealed too late to do . . ." Davy began, only to be interrupted by a yelp from Half-Hanged.

"Dyvy! 'Ere's a line scribbled on the back o' this pyper! Fer the luv o' God—look!" Smyth thrust the letter back into his hands.

Davy read these words aloud: *I have loosed a shoe on the Lady Olivia's nag, so if yew ride hard, yew can overtake her. M.H.*

Half-Hanged Smyth and Old Piety were halfway out of the loft before he had finished.

"W'at the bloody 'ell be we waitin' fer?" bellowed Half-Hanged over his shoulder. "To 'orse, me 'earts! To 'orse!"